PROMISES KEPT

Cindy Bradford

ISBN: 1450575633
ISBN-13: 9781450575638

To You
Who Have Made Promises and Kept Them

Acknowledgements

My heartfelt thanks to all of you who have supported me by responding to my blogs and buying my first book. Your comments have buoyed my spirits and given me reason to continue my writing. I promised myself I would write a novel. I kept that promise. And Chris, my agent, here's to the second time around—another journey that we travel together, and another promise fulfilled.

The true character of a person
is reflected not by the promises he makes,
but those he makes... and keeps.

Chapter I

Patrick was in his study when the phone rang. She barely gave him time to say hello.

"Let's go after the perverted son of a bitch."

Patrick laughed and said, "Congratulations Faith, you must have passed the bar."

"Yep, both Texas and Massachusetts. I got Texas scores yesterday, but I wanted to have both before I called. Now I'm ready to squeeze his ..." she stopped. "Well, you get the picture."

Laughing again, Patrick said, "Yes, quite vividly."

He knew that several years earlier she might have finished her sentence and gone a step further, but during the last few years, she had become more refined, softer around the edges. In law school she had learned cases, canons and codes, and she had acquired sophistication as well. Both made her more confident, determined, and firmer in her resolve. The refinement made her delivery poised and articulate, although she could still be brash and blunt with a comment. Undoubtedly, she was tough, but sensitive, a fighter with a heart. She cut no slack, yet she was generous in her compassion. *It is the total package of complexity and contrasts that makes her a good lawyer already, before her first case,* Patrick thought.

"When can you come to Maine?" Patrick asked.

"As soon as I get a ticket and pack. Where should I fly into?"

"Why don't you see if you can get a ticket to Bangor? If not, then Portland. We'll probably want a couple of days here to talk and plan."

"Okay. I'll call you back as soon as I know times and which airport."

"Faith, hang on. How's your mother?"

"Good," she said. "She wants to come as soon as things begin."

"Really? She really wants to do that?"

"Yes, she has a lot of vacation coming and she can stay with me."

"Tell her that would be good and that I asked about her, will you?"

"Sure, Dad, but you could tell her yourself, you know."

"Yes, maybe I will. We'll see."

But Faith knew he wouldn't call Sue nor could she figure out why. She had asked him several times why he wouldn't make the first move to mend the scars of their past, but he never had an answer. She wasn't sure he knew. He appeared afraid to become involved once more; maybe he was fearful he might hurt her again or maybe he just felt guilty for having a life without her for so many years. None of her sociology and psychology classes helped solve this puzzle so she put it out of her mind and called the airlines.

When Patrick picked her up in Portland, he thought how different she looked than just six months earlier when he had last seen her. He couldn't put his finger on it, but something had changed, maybe it was her hair. She was wearing it curly now, not tight curls, but a wispier, light, bouncy look. Dark, almost black, with a twinge of auburn highlighting it naturally, the color was a combination of her mother's black and his red, and Faith had often indicated she was proud of the connection to both. Today she wore jeans and a light blue sweater that accentuated her sparkling, gentle blue eyes and she wore only a hint of make-up. Mother Nature had given her a smooth olive complexion and high cheekbones. *She is beautiful,* Patrick mused. *So fresh and young and eager.*

Patrick smiled when she looked his way and thought how everyone said their eyes were so alike. Though the color was the same, Patrick knew his were more serious and constrained, never giving him away. Faith's, on the other hand were a window to her soul, reflecting her wit, enthusiasm and mischievous nature, and when she was nervous, sad or pensive, they didn't hide the emotion. She had worried about this in law school until one of her trial professors worked with her, encouraging her to use it to her advantage, "Confuse the hell out of everybody! Use those emotional eyes of yours, but always be in control of them, aware that they are as important to you as they are to a high stakes poker player."

Thinking back to the first time he saw her, Patrick remembered that she was in many ways then a typical eighteen year old, but immediately he knew she was head strong, independent and questioning. She had the spirit of a survivor, the instincts of someone much older, yet the hint of a childish nature belied her strong demeanor. Maybe that was what was different today; it was the child that was missing. When she smiled and waved to him, he realized he was seeing a mature young woman, one determined to help him do the one thing he couldn't do by himself.

"You look good." he said, kissing her on the cheek.

"Oh, Dad, you say that every time."

"Well, you look good every time. I like your hair."

"Do you really? Do you think it is too wild?"

He laughed. "Since when have you worried about that?"

She smiled at him. "I want them – those people in Boston to take me seriously. I want to look smart, mature, in control.

They'll know I'm inexperienced, so I need anything I can get in my favor."

"You mean, like brains, looks, personality and charm!"

"Thanks, Dad. I want this guy to suffer for what he's done. I truly hope yours was an isolated case, but if it wasn't I have to be good enough to convince others they must come forward. I have to be tough enough to give this guy no mercy. But, if I'm not, we still win because you will have come forward and cast off this demon, come out from under this shadow. In a strange way, you'll be a new person, ready maybe to start over and find happiness."

"What do we need to do first?" Patrick asked, ignoring her assessment of his future.

"First, we have to go to the authorities, either the police or the Cardinal. We can go straight to the police and skip the church completely and let it hit them in the media, or we can tell them first, to try to determine if they know something, not that they will admit it, but we might be able to sense it. Our chances of getting past the ten year statute of limitations is likely impossible so we must get the story out in the newspaper one way or the other."

"I need to call my brothers and sisters so the news won't catch them off guard."

"How do you think they'll react?"

"It's hard to say. I think the guys will be fine, but I'm worried about Margaret and Rose, who remain committed to the Catholic Church and to Father Michael. I guess I'll know when I call them all tomorrow."

Riding along, they both talked non-stop. When they reached Patrick's house he said, "I'll make drinks. I know you're tired from the flight."

"That sounds like a good idea. I need to freshen up a little and then I'll be good as new," Faith said as she headed to the bedroom Patrick had decorated for her. Finally, he had removed most of

Olivia's belongings and made it look like a guest bedroom. Each time Faith stayed there she couldn't help but think about the little girl, her half-sister and how she wished she could have known her. Patrick had told her they shared many similarities, each being cheerful, friendly and engaging. When he said they both had eyes like his, his speech became weak, his voice shaky…

Faith looked around the room. The only reminder that this space once belonged to a five year old was the small easel in the corner with an unfinished painting of a harbor, a big dog and a little girl. Faith could tell that Olivia had possessed artistic talent. "I wonder what she would be like today," Faith found herself saying softly, knowing only that Olivia would have been almost fifteen.

"Okay, what's to drink?" Faith asked, walking into the kitchen where Patrick was standing at the counter.

"How about a Cape Cod?"

"That sounds refreshing," watching him pour vodka over cranberry juice and 7-Up.

As he handed it to her, he said, "Let's go outside for awhile. I took the liberty of making a reservation at Vincent's on the Bay for 7:30 p.m. Think you can manage a lobster?"

"Maybe. It won't be easy, but I'll try," she said with a laugh. She liked lobster almost as much as her dad did.

When she sat down in one of the worn, but comfortable wicker chairs on the veranda, Faith said, "It is always so beautiful here."

"Yes, even in winter when it is bitterly cold and bare, this part of Maine has a distinct charm; it's still captivating. I really thought I would move, maybe even leave the area completely after Carol and Olivia were killed, but I couldn't ever make myself go through with it. Then, I spent so much time at Harvard that I was rarely here for those three years. After that, it just seemed easier to stay. I really don't know how I would have survived somewhere else. My friends here and the people at the church have been so good to me."

"Speaking of, what are you going to do about the church while we're in Boston?" she quizzed.

"I've asked for a six month leave of absence. I told them this would be the last time I would ever ask for special consideration. Tomorrow, I'm going to explain what is about to happen when you and I get to Boston. Of course I'll request they keep the information confidential, if they will, until we go to the authorities."

"So who is taking your place for six months?"

"A young woman who has recently been ordained. She finished at the seminary in Bangor and liked the area. I met with her a couple of weeks ago, a nice person, very enthusiastic and excited about her first ministry. I really think she is just what the church needs. I'm afraid I have neglected it somewhat lately with my speaking engagements and I feel badly about that. I think a little infusion of new ideas would be good here. I hope they are ready for a female clergy because she'll bring a new youthful spirit."

"Do you honestly think you'll come back in six months?"

Patrick looked stunned. How did Faith, who had only known him seven years, read him so correctly, so easily? "You amaze me, Faith," he said, not explaining. He figured he didn't need to. "I honestly doubt I'll ever come back as the senior minister, but maybe they will allow me to fill in when I'm needed. I enjoy my travels and speaking, and I also guess you can tell that I'm in somewhat of a transitional period." He stopped. "Faith, this is really hard for me."

She looked at him and smiled, waiting. Finally, she said, "Well, go ahead; tell me you would like to see my mother."

He shook his head in disbelief. "You're scary, nobody should be that perceptive."

"Was I right?"

He looked away for a split second and then softly said, "Yes, Faith, you were right on target. Would you attempt to find out if she'd see me?"

"I'll try, although you know she's dating someone. He seems nice enough, but I think he's a little bit of a nerd. He's some kind of engineer, yet he likes the arts so mother enjoys him."

"Maybe we could never rekindle anything, Faith. We've been out of each other's lives for so long. But, she was my first love and I have never forgotten her. I remember thinking about her on the very night I gave Carol the information about our honeymoon."

"But you did love Carol, didn't you?"

"Yes Faith, I loved her very much. I would never deny that to anyone, but there is something about Sue I never got over. Maybe it was our youthfulness. She was the first girl I was ever really with, if you follow me. I know I was her first as well."

Faith smiled. "In other words, you were both virgins, and then here I am."

He could always expect Faith to cut to the chase, to get to the bottom line and say exactly what was on her mind. It confounded him, the New Englander, but it was what he loved about her. Laughing, he said, "Well, my little love child, I guess you have described it well."

She had lightened his mood. "Okay, I'll see what I can do, but neither of you has been too forthcoming in the last six or so years. Several times I've tried to arrange your being together and both of you balked."

"I know we're both stubborn, especially me. And I know I hurt her beyond description. I'll understand if she doesn't agree to see me."

"Whatever happened to the guy just calling the girl and saying, hi, wanna go out?"

"I know I'm being silly Faith, but I would just feel better if you asked her. Maybe if she said no, your breaking it to me would ease the hurt."

"Okay, just be careful not to crush this cupid's wings. I'll give it my best shot, with my arrow, of course," she added sarcastically.

"You're impossible, but I do love you," Patrick said, now standing. "I'll make another Cape Cod and then it will be time to go to the restaurant."

"Make mine a double. You're stressing me."

He was so glad she had come into his life and although he knew he didn't deserve her love or understanding, he knew he had both.

They sipped the next drink in almost silence, but it was a comfortable and easy silence, with father and daughter gazing at the water below, their minds probably on the same wave lengths, thinking the same thoughts.

Chapter 2

Always an early riser, Patrick was often drinking coffee by 4:30 in the morning, but this Sunday he was awake before 3:00 a.m. Taking his coffee cup he walked outside where the moon glistened on the water. The sun would soon take its place; the sun came up early in these parts. He walked down to the water where he had lovingly cast the ashes of Carol and Olivia almost ten years ago. It seemed impossible to him that they had been gone that long. His thoughts took him back to the first long lonely winter he had spent in this remote part of Maine before he met Carol and to the first one after her and Olivia's deaths. He still missed them terribly. He never looked at this scenery that he didn't see Carol sitting before her easel painting broad strokes of every tint of blue on the eggshell colored canvas. Now, the colors of the light blue sky touched the deep blue shades of the vast ocean, making the view a monochromatic haze of memories. Even the sea of flowers on one side of the yard leading down to the water couldn't bring enough contrast to the landscape to enrich his life or lessen his sorrow. Against that backdrop he had played Frisbee with Rocky, the Irish Setter she had given him as a wedding present, as Olivia sat close by mimicking her mother's talent. Peri, all whiskers and fur, curled around Olivia's tiny feet, purring softly. Now the only things remaining in this picture were the sky, the ocean, the flowers and him, but he had changed. It was probably time for a shift in scenery.

He was glad Faith was still asleep when he quietly went back inside the house to shower and dress for church.

~

When Patrick stood behind the pulpit as he had for so many years, he found comfort. This place was in so many ways his cocoon, and these people his family.

Faith sat in the front row and that, too, gave him strength. He remembered another time when she had sat there and he had introduced her as his daughter, the daughter he had never claimed until she found him. She was the strong one; he admired her strength, her persistence and determination. Today, he would be strong because of her.

"Ladies and gentlemen, I have no sermon today, only a story. A story that could almost begin with, once upon a time in a far away land ... but it is no fairy tale. Sadly it is a true story of a little boy who grew up to be a man, a man who stands before you today. Thirty-five years ago as a boy of ten, I had a new watch and a used duffle bag that had belonged to my brother, and I was so excited to be going to camp for the very first time. I was an altar boy in the Catholic Church and altar boys my age from my parish and others were meeting in the wilderness of Massachusetts to swim and hike and play like only boys of ten could.

"It was an innocent time of life, a time without worry or sorrow or shame, until the priest whom I admired and trusted, in the darkness of night came into my small tent and changed my life. Twice he broke my spirit; twice he took advantage of my youth. I was never the same. Maybe that was my fault. I knew I was not to blame for the awful acts that took place, but, perhaps, I should have handled the aftermath differently. I could have gone to my parents or to the church authorities or to the sisters who were my teachers. I was ten, a mere boy, but they, the adults, the ones who could have helped me, loved Father Michael. They would not have wanted to believe me; I didn't think. They certainly would not have wanted to deal with the situation. Telling would have been difficult; not being believed, heartbreaking, their covering for him, unbearable. So I promised myself I would keep it a secret as long as I could. It haunted me for years and in my childish mind I tried to find ways to make it right. Finally, I decided that I would become a priest, a better priest than Father Michael, a godly one. But that was before I knew what it was like to fall in love. And that I did, with Faith's mother.

"We were young, in college. Neither of us had experienced these feelings before and I fought it because I kept going back to that night and my decision to become a priest. Finally, my broken spirit got the best of me and I broke off the relationship. I didn't know at the time, that she was two months pregnant with my child. I found out when the authorities contacted me about her disappearance.

"The baby, only four days old, went to live with her aunt, who I must applaud for providing Faith with a wonderful upbringing, for teaching her values, love and tenacity. Faith had a good life, but there was always something missing, along with unanswered questions. And I was not around to answer anything. Her mother was missing, her father absent. The next three years I bounced around in college like the basketball with which I played, managing to graduate and then head to Rome to study at a seminary there, still determined to be a priest.

"In less than two years I found myself confused, again fighting an internal demon. The Catholic Church was a disappointment to me, as I probably was to it. Being a priest was not going to solve my problem, only compound it. I had become, if nothing else, a rebel in a robe. Leaving Rome, I returned to Boston. It was the openness, the democracy of the Congregational Church that led me here. But because I had internalized my feelings for so many years, I continued to be bothered by forces I could only fight, never conquer. Meeting Carol and our having Olivia helped me, and although I loved them very much, I never shared this past with anyone.

"It wasn't until Faith came into my life that I realized that so many of my mistakes were indirectly related to my going this alone. Her probing for answers made me realize I could continue to hide behind this, or I could step up to the plate and play the game, whatever the final score. Faith convinced me that it was time to face it all, head on. I promised her then that I would do that only when my father passed away for he continued to be very close to Father Michael.

"I had waited all these years; I could wait a few more, if she understood. In the seven years since she and I first discussed this, a great deal has happened. Faith has received her undergraduate degree at the University of Texas, as well as her law degree. Just last week she received word she passed the Texas bar as well as the Massachusetts bar. She has also built a relationship with her biological mother."

Immediately Patrick could see confusion on the faces of many in the congregation; there was an audible exchange among a few people. He stopped and then continued.

"For years, everyone assumed that Faith's mother, Sue, was dead. I held that belief until one day just a couple of months before Carol and I were to be married, she shared a story with me about a magazine photo assignment entitled 'Women of God' that she had completed several years before we met. She had spent weeks talking with and photographing Baptist missionaries in Mexico, a Mormon Relief Society President in Utah and three nuns in a cloistered convent in Wisconsin.

"Carol described each woman so eloquently, relating their experiences and backgrounds. I knew the moment she characterized one of the nuns and told me her story that Sue was not dead, but somehow had fled to that convent. Seeing her photographs, although only silhouettes, confirmed my suspicions. I said nothing to Carol. This was a chapter of my life I had never mentioned before, and I thought it best to leave it that way. But when Faith found me, I knew she should be told. Shortly after she left here she went to the convent to see her mother for the first time since she was four days old. Three months later Sue left the convent and went back to the town where she had grown up. I have not seen her but, perhaps, that will happen someday, when we are both ready.

"As all of you know, my father recently passed away. So tomorrow, Faith and I will go to Boston where I will explain to authorities what happened to me so long ago and reveal the person who was responsible for these terrible acts. Maybe, nothing positive will come from this, but it must be done.

"Most of all it must be done, because I made a promise to Faith. You may read about this in the newspaper or see something on the news because Father Michael is a powerful man in the Catholic Church, very well known in Boston. He has been there a long time. So, that is why I tell you this today, asking for your prayers and understanding. This will not be easy after all these years, but healing is often neither easy nor without risks.

"But tomorrow I will do what I should have done thirty-five years ago. Perhaps, a lot of lives would be different if I had chosen that path." He paused. "Thank you for giving me so much love and understanding these years as your minister. I trust you will keep this confidential until after my initial disclosure."

He stopped to look down at Faith, who was smiling. No one moved except to look at Patrick and then to Faith. Finally, Patrick directed his gaze to the audience and asked them to join him in a prayer.

When the service was over, everyone in the church rushed forward, stopping to say something to Faith as they waited in line to give words of encouragement to Patrick. After more than an hour, Patrick and Faith were finally able to go home to pack.

Chapter 3

The next morning they left early for the drive to Boston.

"I don't think I'll ever be one of those people like you who wakes up early and is cheerful," Faith said with a half-hearted laugh.

Smiling he said, "I guess I'm lucky. I've always been a morning person."

"I don't know what I am. I like to sleep late and don't really stay up all that late either. I guess I'd better get used to rising early. Most law firms don't look too kindly on the lawyers coming in at 10:00 a.m. I doubt Jackson, Henry, Jackson would be any more understanding," she laughed.

"Are you excited about going to work for them? We've been so busy I haven't even asked you about the firm."

"Yes, I consider myself really lucky. It's one of the most prestigious firms in Dallas, and there are a lot of firms, that's for sure."

"It didn't hurt any that you edited the law review and were first in your class."

Faith blushed, "Now you're sounding like a bragging dad."

"Well, it's true and you know it. Now, tell me a little more about the firm."

"Mr. Jackson and Mr. Henry are the two main senior partners. Mr. Jackson's father is also, but he rarely comes in, I understand. I think he must be pretty old, but he still has an office. There are two junior partners and then ten other staff lawyers. I think I am the only female of those ten. I haven't met anyone but

Mr. Henry and Mr. Jackson. They hired me at the first interview. When I told them about my needing and wanting to do this, they said no problem; take as long as needed and then get there as fast as I could. They seem really nice, but I've heard they can be tough as nails in court, which of course, is good."

"Good if they are on your side," Patrick added. "I see you the same. Nice, but tough."

"Do you really?"

"Absolutely."

"Good. My clients will deserve that."

They drove, talking about Faith's duplex. She explained it was close to downtown in an old, but safe part of the city. The area had seen a revival in recent years as more young professionals moved closer in and wanted something other than the concrete jungle of repetitive apartments. Faith was determined to keep the conversation light so Patrick would not think too much about what awaited him.

"We're almost there," Faith said as she caught a glimpse of the harbor, admitting she was excited, though feeling a little guilty because she doubted Patrick shared her sentiments.

Patrick maneuvered easily through the traffic, knowing his way around the city. In no time, he pulled up to the main police station and found a parking space.

"Okay, let's do it," he said, with determination in his voice.

Faith was a little surprised in his mood, but relieved. She thought how relaxed he looked. She had worried that he would be tense, but he actually seemed upbeat and happy.

"I'm in," Faith said, picking up her briefcase that she was carrying for no good reason. She had a youthful bounce in her walk and her stride gave a look of confidence as she followed her dad into the station. She had looked forward to this day ever since he had shared his story with her.

Immediately a young lieutenant introduced himself as Lt. Hank Farley. Patrick introduced himself and Faith as they each reached to shake the officer's hand.

"Are you related to Joseph O'Brien who used to be a cop in Boston?"

Patrick smiled, "I am, indeed. He was my father, but you look a little young to have known him."

Lt. Farley laughed, "My dad and my dad's dad were all cops here. Guess I was destined to be one, too. Anyway, I never met your father, but I've heard my dad and grandfather mention him. They always talked about the 'brotherhood.' Maybe that is another reason I was always drawn to this job. My grandfather used to tell me all kinds of stories. Apparently he and your father worked together for awhile. Anyway, how can I help you?"

"This is going to be a long story," Faith offered, "So do you have a place we can sit and talk?"

"Certainly, follow me." They entered a small, dingy room. In it was an old, square, maple table marked with coffee stains.

"No wonder they confess. I would, to get out of this room," Faith said, frowning but with good humor.

"My lawyer, lieutenant," Patrick said smiling, nodding to Faith.

"Are you really? I thought you said she was your daughter," as he motioned for them to sit down.

"Well, I'm a lawyer, too."

"So, what's this long story?"

Patrick began telling his story, taking the police officer back thirty-five years. The lieutenant listened intently, making notes.

When Patrick finished he leaned back in the one straight oak chair that didn't match anything else in the room, and looked at Faith. She smiled as if to say good job, but said nothing, waiting for Lt. Farley to speak. He didn't for what seemed like an eternity. Finally, he said, "Son of a bitch!"

"My sentiments exactly," Faith added, quickly.

"I'm not Catholic, you see, so you probably came to the right person. I need to contact the police department of the county where this happened. I know you are aware of the Massachusetts statute," he said, turning to Faith.

"Yes. We're a little late, huh?"

"Right, normally I'd just tell you that, but I think my captain should get the paperwork on this, if you get my drift. He can send it to the district attorney for the last word. Guess you know the beat reporter will see this if that happens."

"That would be too bad," Faith winked. "I would hate for anyone to read about this," she added sarcastically. The lieutenant was playing into her plan precisely.

"Exactly. I seriously doubt you were the only victim, Dr. O'Brien. Maybe your coming forth will encourage some others, if that's the case. If not, the only thing we will have done is expose this guy. I guess expose is not a good word. Sounds like he enjoys that," Lt. Farley said. He quickly added, "Sorry sir, I didn't mean to sound trite or trivial about this. It is just that I have such disdain for anybody who does this sorta thing to a kid."

Patrick smiled. "Not a problem, plus it helps some to laugh."

~

Just as Faith had hoped, a story ran in the Boston Globe.

Maine Minister Accuses Local Priest of Child Molestation

Maine Minister and Harvard graduate Patrick O'Brien, after years of secrecy, has come forward and claimed that well-known Father Michael O'Mallory physically abused him as a ten year old altar boy…

Faith thought it was a decent story since it included Father Michael's name and most of the details, indicating that the priest refused comment. The reporter had contacted Patrick late the night before so there was a lengthy quote from him. The best part, Faith believed, was that the story ran on the front page. It was not in the most prominent place, but rather, in the bottom left hand corner; still it was front page news.

By 4:00 p.m. Faith had talked to the reporter twice and he told her his phone had been ringing all day. Although many of the calls were in support of Father Michael, he said, there were at least 20 people who called wanting to know more. The most interesting call, he added, was that of a young man who had told the reporter "he might call back with some news of his own." When pressed, he had hung up.

"I don't know whether it was a prank or legitimate. This could get interesting," the reporter told Faith.

"I hope so," she replied.

Because they were having trouble finding enough to keep them busy in the hotel suite, Patrick said, "Let's take a walk, Faith. This waiting around is driving me crazy. I'd leave and go back to Maine so you could go to Dallas, but I'm afraid if something breaks we would just have to return," Patrick said.

Faith quickly added, "Let's at least stick around a few more days. If someone else comes forward, we would want to talk to them. Also, I just feel better hanging around, if nothing else to keep the heat up. Who knows what will happen tomorrow when we meet with Cardinal O'Leary. That could be really telling."

"Or, he may be very tight lipped and withdrawn. I don't know what to expect, but I've heard he can be a little distant and not exactly forthcoming."

As they were about to leave the hotel the phone rang again.

"Just let it go Faith. You need some fresh air."

"No way. It may be big news."

"Okay, I'll be in the lobby. I need to talk to the desk clerk a minute anyway."

Faith picked up the phone as the door was closing and was glad Patrick was gone when she heard her mother's voice.

"How's it going?"

Faith quickly explained everything that had occurred since they had arrived in Boston. "I have this gut feeling that something big is going to happen. I think somebody is going to come forward," she added.

"There was a blurb in today's Dallas Morning News, a short associated press story that mentioned the charge, but we're not getting much news here, Faith." She paused, "I would like to come there for a few days if you think it would be all right."

"Sure, but you are going to have to see Dad. I can't go back and forth between you two. Can you do that?"

"Yes, Faith, I've given it much thought. I think I'm ready to see him. If it is too uncomfortable for anyone, I'll catch the next plane back."

"Okay, so when do you want to fly up?"

"I have a ticket to arrive there at 5:00 p.m. tomorrow," Sue said, laughing because she knew Faith would have something smart to say.

"Well, don't let me sway you one way or the other, or rush you either," Faith teased.

"I knew you would give me a bad time."

"I'm really glad you're coming, Mother. I know Dad will be, too."

"How do you know that?"

"Because he asked me this week if I could talk to you about seeing him."

"Really?"

"Yep, I feel like a matchmaker, cupid, for two teenagers."

"That's what we were the last time we saw each other, two teenagers. It may seem like a time warp, but our ages will quickly dispel that."

"I'll be at the airport to pick you up, and then we'll get together with Dad. I'll get another room at the hotel for you, unless of course you want to stay with him."

"Shame on you, Faith. I said I wanted to see him, not... well, never mind."

"I'm glad you didn't feel that way twenty-five years ago. I'd be zilch, never here. Hey, before you hang up, how's Mom?"

"Great. She is so head over heels about that new doctor in town. Did she tell you about him?"

"Not really. She just said she was going on a date with someone who had recently been widowed and moved to town. That's all. I tried to quiz her, but she said she'd tell me more after the date. I've been in and out so much I haven't talked to her since. I should have called her." Faith said, in a regretful tone.

"You probably couldn't catch her. They've been together the last three nights. Apparently, he...his name is Ben, had a thriving practice in Shreveport when his wife died. His kids are grown and he wanted a change, so when the Chief of Staff position came open at Glenview Memorial, he applied. That's about all I know, but I so hope he and Alice hit it off. She deserves it."

"Yes, she does for a fact. I'll call her tomorrow morning, but if you talk to her before then, tell her to be ready for twenty questions."

"I'm sure she won't be surprised, but I'll give her a heads up. See you tomorrow, Faith. I'm excited, but nervous."

"Just be cool. Everything will be fine; this little matchmaker will do her best."

When Faith hung up the phone, her mind was racing. She was excited that Sue was coming to Boston and that she and Patrick would meet again. In some ways she dreaded it, fearful that it might not go well, but she wanted them to at least try. However, more than Sue coming to Boston, she was especially excited about Alice.

When she had talked to her a few days ago, she had barely mentioned the upcoming date. Faith reasoned that Alice didn't want to get her hopes up or Faith's either. Faith desperately wanted Alice to find someone and have a companion, someone to grow old with. She had spent almost twenty years tending to Faith's every need, rarely taking time to do anything for herself, especially date or go special places. Now that Faith was grown, she knew her Mom was lonesome, even though Sue lived only twenty-five miles away in Rose Hill.

As happy as Faith was to have her biological mother back in her life, she knew that Alice would always hold the special place in her heart as her "real parent," not the aunt. They had bonded from the beginning and that wasn't going to change, no matter how many other people came into Faith's life. Alice was Mom; Sue was her mother, but Alice was the one who had been there all those years. When Faith fell off her new bicycle without training wheels and scraped both knees, it was Alice who picked her up, wiping away the tears and kissing her scratches. Alice had put her arms around Faith and consoled her when her best friend stole her boyfriend in tenth grade. Alice had explained the facts of life when Faith asked where babies came from and tried to lessen her hurt when Faith asked about her father and mother.

Alice was the one who had stayed up worrying about Faith when she was out too late, car pooled her to school, chaperoned parties, wiped away her tears and cheered her on in her goals and dreams. Faith loved her for all those things. Everyone who knew Faith and had known Alice and Sue as young girls said Faith's personality was much more like that of Alice than Sue. Even Patrick said that.

A tap at the door startled Faith from her thoughts.

"Yes?"

It was Patrick coming back to the room.

"Are you okay?" he asked.

"Yeah, I was just on my way down. Sorry it took so long, but that was Mother on the phone. She's coming here tomorrow."

Patrick looked stunned and then a big grin formed, although immediately his face changed to a concerned look. "Will she see me?"

"Yes, she will see you, though through no efforts of yours," she shamed him.

"That's great news. Let's walk and you can tell me about the conversation." He took Faith's hand as they got in the elevator.

Although it was July, there was coolness to the night air around the Boston Harbor. Faith wished she had brought a sweater, but because she was used to Texas heat, it didn't even cross her mind that it might not be hot or muggy or humid everywhere else in the world.

"It's not always this way this time of year," Patrick reminded her. "This is a little unusual, but you never know. Last week it was much warmer, the cashier at the newsstand said, but a front went through with rain, so it's nice. We can go back to the hotel if you're too cool."

"No, I'm fine, but I guess I'm just surprised. Actually it feels pretty good not to burn up in the middle of summer."

"Good, then let's get a burger or something."

"Sounds good, I'm hungry."

"You're always hungry, but you never gain an ounce, no matter how much you eat."

"Mom says it's my nervous energy that eats all the calories. Speaking of, let me tell you the latest," and she began relating to him what Sue had just told her.

"I hope this will work out for her." For years Patrick had felt that Alice never liked him while he dated Sue. To compound things Alice had always resented Patrick for leaving Sue, but lately they had talked on the phone when Faith handed it to one or the other, and if for no other reason but her, they had become friends, *buried the hatchet* as Alice described it.

After a burger and fries, Faith said, "I'll pick up Mother at the airport tomorrow. I read about Anthony's Pier 4. It sounds like a good quiet place. If things don't go well, neither of you would feel comfortable yelling in there."

Patrick smiled, "I doubt you have to worry about that, and it's an excellent choice."

"Remind me to get her a room when we get back to the hotel." She wanted to tease him, too, but restrained herself since he already appeared nervous.

When she returned to her room, the phone was blinking to indicate a message.

"Hello, this is your newest friend, Jeff, from the newspaper. Listen Faith, call me. There's some guy named Dr. Michael Kennedy from California trying to reach your dad. I need to know if it is okay to give Kennedy his number. So call me. I'm working late. Its seven o'clock now, but I'll be here until about ten."

"That was Jeff," she said.

"Faith, don't you go falling for some poor newspaper guy. Alice taught you better," he teased, sensing Jeff might be interested.

"Hey, this is serious. He said there's a man in California named Dr. Michael Kennedy who wants to talk to you. Do you know somebody by that name?"

Patrick thought for a second trying to recall the name. "I don't think I know anybody in California well enough for them to call." Then remembering, "It must be Mikey. I didn't recognize him calling himself Michael. But then, he's forty-five years old. What else did Jeff say?"

"He wants to know if it is okay to give him your phone number."

"Sure, tell him I would love to talk to my crimson feather friend."

"Huh? Mikey?"

"I'll explain after you call Jeff."

Faith returned the call, telling him to give Kennedy the number. "Thanks Jeff. You've gone above and beyond to help this story go forward. I appreciate it. I think this is going to be good for you in the long run. I really believe there is much more to come. Please keep in touch and I'll let you know how our visit goes tomorrow with the Cardinal. Can I take you to lunch or would that compromise your story?"

"I think I can be objective, Faith. Lunch would be great. What time?"

"Our meeting is at nine o'clock in the morning. I'll call you after that. I don't know what to expect."

"No problem. I'll probably come in late since I'm working late, so anytime is fine."

"I'll call. Take care, and again, tell Michael to go ahead and call. Thanks Jeff. Good night."

"Good night, Faith."

"Okay, so who is this Michael Kennedy?"

"Gosh, Faith, to tell you the truth, I haven't thought about Michael Kennedy in thirty something years. Had no idea where he was. I just remember him as a nerdy little kid with an overprotective mother. I never called him anything but Mikey, nobody did. I guess not many people were very nice to him. I felt sorry for him because his mom never let him do anything. On our camping trip he couldn't swim because she had never let him learn, so he just had to sit on the bank. I remember him sitting there all pitiful, pale and puffy fat, soft and delicate. Nobody paid him much attention. I tried to include him whenever I could, but it was hard because he was such a baby. Anyway, we were put together on a scavenger hunt, and we won. I'll never forget the look on his face when Father Andrew said we were the champs. I don't think he had ever won anything in his life, but he found the crimson feather that gave us the edge. He really won the competition. And I hadn't even wanted to be his partner. Anyway, I saw him some after camp, but not often. His mother just wouldn't allow him to go many places." As he was talking the telephone rang.

"I'll get it. It may be him."

"Patrick?"

"Yes."

"This is Michael Kennedy, Mikey as you probably know."

"Hi Mikey, Michael, I guess I should say. How long has it been?"

"Long enough that I'm bald headed and slim. Can you believe the last part?"

Patrick laughed. "How have you been?"

"Really well, Patrick. My mother read the papers and called me. I want to help you if I can."

"How's that Michael?" Patrick asked, confusion in his voice.

"Well, I wanted to talk to the reporter and tell him what I saw that night. You've talked a little about it in your quote."

"What do you mean?" Patrick asked, more puzzled.

"Patrick, I don't know if you remember or not, but I asked you if you were homesick while we were on the camp out."

"I guess I don't understand."

"I saw Father Michael leave your tent and I heard you crying afterwards. I thought you were homesick and that he had come to comfort you. When my mother called and told me about the article in the paper, it hit me right in the face. He was not in your tent to comfort you. I figure it might help if you had someone to verify your story."

"Thanks, Michael. I can't believe you can remember that, and yes it might help. Actually the statute of limitations keeps my case out, but I'm hoping if there is someone else out there who has experienced this, they will come forward. I truly hope no one else had to go through this, but if there was just one other, maybe my coming forward will help encourage him."

"What made you decide to tell after all these years?"

"Oh, Michael, it is such a long story; I hate to keep you on the phone that long."

"I need to go visit my mother. It's been almost a month since she was here. I think I'll fly there on Tuesday. Could we have lunch or something?"

"That would be great."

"I'll call you, Patrick, when I get there. In the meantime, I'm going to tell the reporter what I know. Perhaps, if he puts what I saw and heard in a news story, people will realize that there was someone else who can corroborate the events."

"I appreciate that, Michael."

"Patrick, it's the least I can do. You were about the only boy who ever spoke to me back then. I'll never forget you. See you soon, good night."

"Good night," Patrick said, softly, closing his eyes as if to close out the past.

~

The next morning Patrick and Faith met with Cardinal O'Leary. As Patrick had been led to expect, the Cardinal was less than welcoming. The conversation went nowhere, leaving Patrick frustrated and Faith angry. Over coffee at La Latte' near Harvard, Patrick said, "I warned you, Faith. They stick together. I learned that in Rome. Everyone is afraid of what the Vatican will think or do."

"I know you tried to prepare me, but I guess I still had some trust in the basic decency of human beings."

"Right now we have to give him the benefit of the doubt. The Cardinal may be completely innocent of knowing of any wrong doings. We are assuming he is covering something, and we may be wrong, Faith."

"True, but if he isn't aware of anything, he certainly was cold and removed. I wouldn't want him giving me Last Rites."

Patrick laughed, "I don't think you have to worry about that. Anyway, we weren't expecting cooperation exactly, so we're no worse off."

"Then I guess we'll chalk this up to effort. I need to call Jeff about lunch. What will you do?"

"I think I'll walk over to campus and see a few old friends. I understand Dr. Mata, who was my favorite professor, is thinking about retiring. I'd like to see him. You take the car and I'll meet you back at the hotel mid-afternoon. Okay?"

"Sure. Remember, I have to pick up Mother at the airport at five o'clock, so if I miss you, we'll be at the restaurant. Do you mind taking a taxi?"

"No, that works for me."

When Faith called Jeff, he answered excitedly. "Hey, I've been trying to call you. I knew you were probably not at the hotel, but can you pick me up now? I'll be outside the newspaper office, wearing a blue shirt and khaki slacks"

"Yes, Jeff, but what's up?"

"Just hurry, come on. I'll tell you," he said, excitedly.

"I'm in a silver Chevy, more like a tin can. I'll be there in 15 minutes."

Jeff looked like a big kid standing outside the newspaper office. *He wasn't exactly good looking* Faith thought, *but he had a clean cut, all-American look; the kind of guy you trusted and talked with easily.* His blond hair was too short for Faith's liking, but his polo shirt was pressed and his Dockers starched crisp, which she thought was unlike most of the young reporters she had seen. Remembering he had said he had a degree in journalism from the University of Missouri, she decided he was probably from the Midwest. That would answer why he appeared more conservative than she would have expected a journalist in Boston to be. She had not completely stopped the car when he jumped off the curb and began opening the door.

"Whoa, I've heard of you guys needing to make deadlines, but why so fast? You are Jeff, I hope. You could be a serial killer for all I know."

He reached quickly to shake her hand, and then started talking. "Faith, I have some news, not something we can use, but a start," he said, settling into the passenger's seat without further introduction.

"What?" she asked as she drove off slowly. She had never been patient, but law school had taught her some restraint; several years before, she would have stopped the car and demanded he hurry with his story.

"I received a call this morning. The woman wouldn't give me her name, but I think she was for real. She said six years ago her son attempted suicide at the age of fourteen. She and her husband were devastated, but relieved that he had lived. After he recovered from slitting his wrist, they took him to a counselor, but he wouldn't open up. He wouldn't say what was so bad that he felt he needed to end it all.

"After three or four sessions and no resolution, he started crying on the way home from the last session. His mother said he cried and cried and just couldn't seem to stop. She drove around, choosing her words carefully and softly explaining to him how much she and his father loved him. 'Why would you love me? I'm bad.' The mother was near a park so she pulled over and killed the engine. She asked him why he thought he was bad…what had he done that could be that awful?

"Finally, he just blurted everything out. He told her that he had let their priest fondle him, and then it had led to more. He knew it was wrong, but every time he was around the priest and no one else was there, the priest had molested him. It had gone on for two years. The mother was shocked but tried to console him by telling him it wasn't his fault. He was a kid she told him. But he said he had let him and that made it his fault. The mother and son talked for another couple of hours, alternately crying, and just sitting in the car, staring out the windows."

"Hey, wait Jeff. Who was the priest? Did she say?"

"Bingo, your guy!"

"Keep going," Faith had stopped the car in the parking lot of a small restaurant so she could listen better.

"Well, apparently, the good priest was filling in for another priest, as the principal or whatever, for a short stint at a Catholic school. This kid was having problems, especially in math. His teacher was exasperated with him because his learning problems had extended over into disciplinary ones. Finally, she took him to this Father Michael guy. The priest told the boy if he would behave in class and stay after school he would take him for treats and buy him things. The family wasn't very well off financially and the dad had lost his job a few months earlier, so this sounded pretty good to the kid. The boy didn't get much better in math since the tutorials were obviously not in numbers, but his behavior improved, thus everyone was pleased. Over the months, the kid got a stereo and new clothes from the priest, but his parents began to notice he started to withdraw, become depressed and sullen, and then he slit his left wrist. When his mother found him in his room, he had lost a lot blood, but the doctors were able to save him. Anyway, after the son spilled his guts he made his mother promise to not tell anyone, but of course she told his dad who became enraged. He went straight to the priest and then to the Cardinal."

"So he did know something, that sorry bastard."

"Excuse me?"

"Nothing, we'll come back to that!"

"The dad told the priest he'd cut his balls off if he ever touched his son again and then he told the Cardinal he wanted the priest removed from the school and their church. The Cardinal agreed to take him out of the school, but said it would not be acceptable to take him out of the church where he had been for so long. There would be too many people upset. Anyway, as it turned out, the mother is having second thoughts. Right now, she doesn't want to do anything, but she said she might, she just needed to think."

"Did you get a number or anything?"

"Nope, she wouldn't give me a clue."

"Damn!"

"That's what I said, but if we just had a little more from someone else, maybe she would crack."

"Did Michael Kennedy call you back after he talked to my Dad?"

"No, I haven't talked to him, but there were a few messages on my desk of calls I missed while I talked to this woman. I didn't have time to read them before you came. Maybe he was one of them. Why? What did he want?"

"He can corroborate my dad's story," Faith said.

"How's that?"

Faith explained and also told Jeff that Kennedy would be in town on Tuesday.

"If I can get a quote from him, I can at least keep the story going."

"That's what we need. This monster has a lot of heads I'm guessing. He didn't just molest my dad thirty-five years ago and then lay off until this kid," Faith added.

"Right, but if this mother would come forward, you've got one within the ten year limit."

"Hot damn, things are looking up. I've never heard of this restaurant, but let's go in and I'll buy your lunch."

"You got a deal, Faith. All this excitement has made me hungry."

~

After lunch, Jeff was anxious to get back to his office. Faith told him she would be driving to the airport to meet her mother's plane so she wouldn't be near a phone.

"If you haven't heard from me by the time you leave the hotel, call me," he told her. "I may not have anything new, but then I might. This is moving forward. I'm not sure where it's going, but it's going somewhere."

"Okay. We'll talk later."

"Thanks for lunch," Jeff yelled back at Faith.

She waved and drove back to the hotel. Although hoping Patrick would be back, she found the hotel suite empty and decided this was the perfect time to call Alice.

"Oh, I'm so glad I caught you at home," Faith said when Alice answered.

"Hi, Honey. It's good to hear from you. Sue told me you might call. I wanted to drive her to Dallas, but she said she'd leave her car at the airport since she wasn't sure when she'd return."

"What's this about a doctor?"

"I haven't been sick, Faith," Alice teased.

"Come on, tell me everything."

"Where should I start? With his nice looks, his sexy body, his great personality, or his intellect? Oh, and did I mention he has a condo at the beach?"

"Mom, he sounds wonderful."

"He is. I'm having such a good time. We're going to the casino in Bossier City late this afternoon, since he has a long weekend.

He lived in Shreveport for a long time, you know, so he knows some fabulous restaurants there."

"I'm so happy for you."

"It may not be the real thing, but I'm going to enjoy it while I can," Alice said, wistfully.

"Good attitude," Faith replied.

"So, what's up there?"

"A lot, hey, listen to this," and Faith went immediately into telling her the story Jeff had related.

"Sounds like this could heat up."

"Yeah, I hope it gets so hot it burns the old pervert's testicles right off."

Alice laughed, "Well, that wouldn't be a pretty sight, but it would probably be okay with him as long as someone grabbed them and put the fire out slowly."

Laughing, they talked for more than twenty minutes. When Patrick came in the suite, Faith was just hanging up the phone.

"Hey, have I got news for you!" Faith said and started telling him the story immediately before he'd had a chance to ask anything or sit down.

In the middle of her relating the incident, Jeff called.

"Faith, I talked to Kennedy. Watch for a story tomorrow."

"Great."

"Later."

"Bye for now."

She quickly started telling the rest of the story. When she finished, Patrick was still smiling but suddenly his smile turned to a frown.

"Amazing how a man could get away with such things for all these years, but that's my fault."

"Don't start beating yourself up again," Faith warned. "So how were all your old friends at Harvard?"

"Oh, fine and very supportive. Dr. Mata was thrilled I had come to visit, telling me he was worried after he read the newspaper. He called the house and couldn't reach me."

"Were they surprised?"

"You mean that I came forward or that Father Michael would do such a thing?"

"Both."

"They were shocked when they read it in the newspaper, but Dr. Mata said, there had been undercurrents about the priest's behavior for years, but everyone hoped they were just bad rumors. He said this had rocked the church, he hears, and everyone is scrambling right now, especially Cardinal O'Leary. I told him about our meeting and he said if the Cardinal knew of a problem he would keep it from being made public. O'Leary has dreams of becoming the Pope someday, but we all know that isn't going to happen because he's almost eighty years old."

"He doesn't look it," Faith offered.

"All that clean living," Patrick said with a crooked half-smile.

"Interesting day, but I need to freshen up and get to the airport. I didn't realize it was so late."

"It may be an interesting night as well," Patrick reminded her.

"That it might!"

Chapter 4

Sue stopped talking mid-sentence. Glancing at Faith's expression she knew Patrick must have walked into the restaurant. As she turned to look, he walked to their table, looking strained and less confident than normal. Stopping, he leaned down and kissed Faith on the cheek. Hesitating for a second, he glanced down and then turned to look at Sue directly. Softly, but haltingly, he said, "Hello, Sue."

"Hi, Patrick," she murmured, trying hard to look at him, but wishing she had not agreed to let Faith get them together. Tension hung in the air like a heavy black cloud.

"You ladies look nice," he offered.

"Not bad, for a forty-five year old, huh?" Sue said, more as a statement than a question. There was a trace of bitterness in her voice that she couldn't conceal, and she knew her strained expression showed a glimpse of what she felt. She had longed to see him throughout her stay in the convent and wished for this night as she lay awake in her dark, drab and scant room, but she couldn't help but think he had stolen her best years. He had left her only with the words 'nothing could change his mind.' She realized there is a thin line between love and hate, but she also knew nothing could make her hate him. She had tried, but those feelings wouldn't come. How she had tried. He deserved it she thought, but she knew she couldn't see inside him. Maybe, there had truly been demons he couldn't shake. Maybe, he had loved her, if only for a little while. Now, he was here, sitting at the same table, with their daughter between them, looking a little like he had the first time she met him, tentative and uncertain. Pausing, she added more softly and with honesty, "It's nice to see you, Patrick. You don't look so bad yourself."

He smiled, becoming more comfortable. "You've lost your accent," he said.

"Well, I guess I'm lucky to have a voice at all if there is any truth to the 'use it or lose it theory.' Almost twenty years of saying very little in a cloistered convent takes away more than an accent," she said, sadness returning to her voice, unable to relax. But try as she may, she could not resist his allure; she had loved him for so many years, had given up everything because she couldn't have him. She suddenly felt more alive than she had for so long, but a voice inside said *be careful.* He had walked away seemingly so easily before, and that fact hung heavy in her memory.

Feeling the tension, Faith jumped into the conversation. "Hey, how about let's order a bottle of wine?" knowing her dad would like that since he had become a connoisseur. Turning to him she added, "You select it and you can even pay," she teased.

Happy with the diversion, Patrick motioned the waiter to the table. "Could I see the wine list, please?"

"Certainly, Sir," the waiter said, handing him a black leather bound menu of more than fifty selections.

"What would you suggest, Faith?"

"Oh no, you're not going to trick me into selecting and making me pay," she countered.

"That's the bad thing about lawyers, they are always so suspecting, so accusing," he winked at both Sue and Faith. "This could take a few minutes."

"Save time and trouble, order one of each," laughed Faith, trying to lighten the mood more.

Sitting quietly watching the easy banter between father and daughter, Sue was surprised, but glad the two got along so well. Actually, she thought Faith got along well with everyone. Sue marveled how grounded Faith seemed and credited Alice for raising her well.

"Would you prefer red or white, Sue?" Patrick asked.

"Well, I've grown awfully fond of red I must admit after all those years of communion," she added, smiling and becoming more at ease. "I can't say it was exactly aged to perfection in oak barrels. Whatever you choose will be excellent, I'm sure. Faith has taught me a little about how to taste the different flavors and grapes. You have been a good influence on her."

"My friends, Stefano and Carmella from Italy have taught me well." He found himself now falling into an easy conversation with Sue. "You would like them. They are special people… they've been like family to me."

For the next twenty to thirty minutes Patrick talked about his Italian friends, describing them and their estate in Tuscany. Sipping a Super Tuscan, in their honor, the three seemed to unwind, lighten up, and enjoy the exchange of stories.

When they had finished dinner, Patrick suggested they return to the hotel bar for a nightcap. After two Irish coffees, Patrick asked softly and tentatively, "Would you tell me a little about the convent, Sue?"

For the longest, she paused, and then slowly began. An hour passed as she talked, remembering the years of silence and reflection. Finally, she said, "I think I feel better, just telling someone about the entire experience. You know, they were wonderful to me, but I just always felt so hollow."

"Do you miss any of the women?" Faith asked.

Thinking, Sue said, "There were so many sweet people there, but it's strange the way relationships don't develop as they do outside the walls. There is forever that feeling that everyone is holding something back. Perhaps, that is because the other women were committed to the calling, and I never was. I suppose for that reason I could never identify completely.

"And because they were truly devoted, and I never shared that. I probably only miss Ginger, who was my closest friend. I think she had some doubts, but I could never crack her mystery. I never told her mine, either," Sue added.

When Faith noticed that the two were talking comfortably, she saw the chance to allow them time alone.

"I think I'll go up to my room. Are you staying here for awhile?" Faith asked.

Patrick quickly looked at Sue, his eyes searching for a sign. "I'm afraid this coffee has wired me a little. I don't think I can sleep just yet."

Sue smiled slightly, trying to hide her agreement. "I'll stay a few minutes longer."

The next morning Faith slept until almost 9:30. When she noticed how late it was, she quickly washed her face, combed her hair, pulled on a bathrobe and ventured into the small living area of the hotel suite. To her happy surprise, Patrick and Sue were talking.

"Good morning or should we say good afternoon," Sue teased.

"Hey, it's only ten o'clock."

"We've finished two pots of coffee from room service," Patrick said and quickly added, "Check this out, Ms. Attorney," tossing the morning paper onto the table near where she was standing.

Renowned California AIDS Doctor
Says O'Brien's Accusations True

Michael Kennedy, M.D., formerly from Boston, and now one of the foremost doctors in AIDS research in California,

says he was on the camping trip where Patrick O'Brien claimed he was molested years ago by Father Michael O'Mallory.

Kennedy attested his tent was next to O'Brien's and he saw O'Mallory crawling out of O'Brien's tent late in the night of the second night of the altar boy wilderness event. He heard O'Brien whimpering and thought he was homesick and that the priest had been there to console him.

"Neither of us had ever been to camp, and I was homesick so I just figured Patrick was, also. But, looking back on it now, I know no grown man is going to crawl on his hands and knees out of some ten year old's pup tent in the middle of the night if he is legitimate. The priest kept looking around as if to see if anyone were watching. He never did stand up and walk; he just crawled for what seemed forever to his own tent."

When asked if he actually saw the priest do anything to O'Brien, Kennedy said, "No, but I know what I saw that night and I know Patrick O'Brien to be a man of integrity. He was the nicest, most caring young person I knew. If he said it happened, then I know it did. I'm still a very devout Catholic; this is not easy for me, but wrong is wrong, no matter what. It didn't take anything but reading the bare facts for me to figure this out."

The Sacramento physician said his mother, who still lives in Boston, called to tell him what she read in the newspaper and asked if this was the Patrick O'Brien he once knew. "Although I haven't seen Patrick in more than twenty years, hearing her recount the article, I remembered that night as if it were last night. I haven't been able to get it out of my mind since all of this surfaced. I have treated people who were victims of child abuse, and I know what lasting scars it can leave. I remember Father Michael and I've been back to Boston enough to know he remains a powerful man. Power is not always positive. Perhaps, that is the problem. I know he is known and liked

in Boston. I know he has great stature in the church, but no matter what, what he did he was wrong."

Kennedy left the Boston area years ago after completing his education at Johns Hopkins University and beginning his residency in San Francisco. He is one of only two physicians in the United States who together have developed the most promising medicines for AIDS.

Calls have been pouring into the Globe over the last two days in support of the local priest, although some callers have expressed concern and given information to the contrary. Neither the Cardinal nor the priest named would respond to the allegations.

O'Brien's daughter and lawyer, Faith O'Brien, is pleading with anyone who has experienced abuse at the hands of O'Mallory to come forward. "This is the time," she said. "No person should be afraid now to step forward and tell the truth. Now can be a time of healing."

Looking up, Faith said, "Not bad. That should create a little interest, don't you think?"

"I hope so, but I'm in no hurry now," Patrick said, looking over at Sue.

"Well, good for you, but I need to get to my real job pretty soon or register for food stamps," she said, smiling, obviously glad her parents were getting along. "What are you two planning for today?"

Patrick looked at Sue, as she gazed back at him. "I don't know. It's probably going to be slow today since it's Saturday. What's your plan?" he asked.

"If I had a plan it would have been to sleep later. Now that I'm up, I'm negotiable." At about the time she finished her sentence, the phone rang.

"Hey, Faith, how are you?" Jeff asked.

"Good, actually I just woke up."

"Glad I didn't call earlier. I've been up a long time and even been at the office awhile. I was wondering if I could interest you in a baseball game tonight. I'll also treat you to a nice dinner if you agree."

"Jeff, that sounds great. It's Saturday. Why are you working?"

"Well, a certain attorney lady I know is stirring up things in the city, which means a humble journalist has to cover all the aspects. But, I'm not going to work here all day. I have a few errands to run. Haven't taken care of much this week, so if I don't get to the cleaners I may have to wear dirty jeans."

Faith laughed, "Well, if you were staying in a hotel like I am, you could just send your jeans out and they bring them back, clean. Going to be hard on me when I get back to real life. What time can I expect you here at the hotel?"

"How does 5:30 sound?"

"I'll be in the lobby; I'm looking forward to it."

"See you then, Faith."

"Well, I guess you guys are on your own," Faith said, smiling, looking at Sue and Patrick.

"That's a real shame," Patrick said with a big grin on his face. "I sure hope we can find something to do, don't you Sue?" looking over at her with a genuine look of love in his brilliant blue eyes.

Smiling back, "I think I'll go shower and get ready. I don't want to miss anything."

"Good, you two hurry up and get out on the town so I can lounge around here, maybe read or nap. A nice long bubble bath might be in order," Faith said more as encouragement to them than out of laziness on her part.

"I know when I'm being run out of my own hotel suite. How about lunch, Sue? Then we'll take in some of the sights. You've never been to Boston, right?"

"No, and I want to see as much as possible."

"Then I'll be down to your room at noon if that's enough time."

"I'll be waiting," she said as she closed the door behind her.

Faith looked at Patrick, "Well, does cupid get a thumbs up?"

Looking happy, but serious he replied, "A thumbs up with fingers crossed. Faith, you know I never stopped loving your mother all these years. Sure, had Carol lived I would have never left her, because as I've told you, I loved her, also. Now, I know more than ever, because of her death, we have to live in the moment. I'm afraid though, because I know Sue still has anger and resentment toward me. I need to give her time to work through all this. I would not blame her if she can never forgive me."

"Mother is a very forgiving person. She's healing; be patient with her and she'll come around. I think you need each other now much more than you did the first time; I know there is a lot of water under the bridge and you may have burned a few of the same bridges, but now you're wiser."

"You're the wise one, Faith. The best thing we ever did together was having you." He walked over to give her a big hug. "If we never do anything again, that was worth it all."

Faith could see tears in his eyes. "You both have beaten yourselves up for too many years. It's time for you to get out there and live. So get your shower and your wallet and show her the time of her life."

"I'm on my way," he yelled back from his room.

Faith turned on the television to CNN. Although she wasn't paying much attention as she flipped through the hotel tourist guide to Boston, she heard…"allegations against a Boston priest appear to be heating up as a well respected doctor collaborates the accuser's story." Putting down the book, she listened, instantly noting that the story had become national news.

When Patrick left, Faith decided it was too pretty outside to stay in the hotel, but she took time for a bubble bath and tried to clear her head of all that was happening so fast. Realizing she was starving, she quickly pulled on a pair of jeans, a hooded sweatshirt, and ruffling her hair, gave it a lick and a promise as Alice would have said. Make-up could wait. She was in search of a restaurant that served clam chowder and had a water view. That wasn't difficult to find. After the steaming bowl of chowder with her favorite little oyster crackers she began walking aimlessly, enjoying the day. Noticing a quaint little corner book store, she decided finding a novel would be a nice treat, realizing it had been longer than she could remember that she had read anything for pleasure.

Sitting in a big overstuffed chair in one corner of the shop, she skimmed through book after book, finally deciding on a murder mystery. Occasionally taking time to look around, she saw an older gentleman with a cloud of white hair, wearing a torn, yellowed shirt that had most likely at one time been white. His dingy olive colored trousers were held up by striped red suspenders. He scanned the shelves along side two teenage girls, sporting MIT sweatshirts, and a studious, well-dressed, bespectacled middle-aged woman who appeared to be on a mission to find just the right cookbook. The older man, looking as tattered and worn as the books he removed, poured through a small section of used books while the girls giggled and pointed at pictures in a movie magazine they shared. Faith found herself wondering about him and the others. How did they get here, what fates had life given them, and in the case of the two young girls, what futures would they have?

For a few minutes she tried reading her book, but her thoughts returned to Patrick and Sue, somewhere in the same city, walking, perhaps holding hands, trying to put together the pieces of a broken past.

Looking at her watch, she realized time had escaped her; she had stayed longer than she had planned. She quickly paid for the paperback and headed back to the hotel so she would have plenty of time to freshen up and fix up for her date. Though she was not really attracted to Jeff, she was anxious to go out, laugh and have a good time.

~

When Jeff walked into the lobby, Faith thought he looked cute in his faded, yet starched blue jeans, multicolored polo and deck shoes. Since they were going out for dinner before the game she had opted for a simple, sleeveless coat-dress.

"You look beautiful, Faith," Jeff said, obviously smitten with her.

"Thank you. I wasn't sure what to wear since we are doing both dinner and a ballgame. It was difficult to pack for this trip," she joked.

"Well, I wouldn't know that by the way you've looked every time I've seen you." Faith blushed as he took her hand.

"What are you hungry for?"

"Anything. I didn't eat breakfast and only had a bowl of clam chowder for lunch, so I'm famished."

"I'm used to brown-bagging it, eating junk at my desk or on the run, so I'm starved for something good in a place with tablecloths and real silverware. More than that it will be nice to sit at a table and talk with an intelligent, beautiful woman," Jeff offered, opening the car door for Faith.

"You like your job, though, huh?"

"I love my job. And I'm really lucky to be working so soon for such a prestigious newspaper. The University of Missouri has an outstanding journalism department so that helped me immensely. The pay's okay, too. I knew when I was going into this field I would probably never get rich, but it sure is exciting."

"I have a job waiting for me in Dallas with a really good law firm. I'm anxious to get there and get settled in," Faith added.

Looking disappointed for a minute, he added quickly, "Dallas is a nice town. I did an internship there one summer at The Dallas Morning News, but it certainly was hot and humid."

"I guess I'm used to the heat. I've lived in Texas all my life, so I don't know how my dad stands living in Maine in the winter. I couldn't take the extreme cold."

"It gets pretty cold here, with occasional snow."

Pulling into a quaint little Italian restaurant in an old warehouse building, he said, "I've been here once before, and they had really good pasta. If you like seafood and pasta, that's the house specialty."

"I love any kind of Italian food, so this looks great."

"Good." Finding a parking space near the door as a car was leaving, "We're in luck. The last time I almost never found a space."

Jeff jumped out of the car, hurrying around to open the door for Faith who stood and immediately took his arm as they walked the few feet to the massive wooden door. Once inside, a hostess led them down a winding staircase to a dimly lighted dining room. Atop a long sideboard, candles burned in old Chianti bottles, casting a golden glow on aged photographs of Italian landscapes. Baskets, bottles and other memorabilia hung from the low and slanted beamed ceiling. Creamy white tablecloths covered the tables, giving an elegant and uniformed look to the otherwise different shapes, sizes and styles of antique furniture.

Choosing a corner table for the couple, the hostess, who spoke with a strong Italian accent, directed their attention to the nightly special entrees on the first page of the menu as she handed the wine list to Jeff. Faith thought the woman seating them looked like Carmella from one of the photographs her dad had shown her. Her jet black hair, was pulled back and swept up tightly in a bun, and she wore a long, flowing skirt and white ruffled blouse that showed her ample cleavage.

"Your server will be with you momentarily," she said with a smile, turning briskly and walking back up the stairs.

"Did you see anything upstairs? I mean another dining room or something?" Faith asked, looking puzzled.

"There is a tiny bar off to one side, but I think that's all. See that door?" Jeff said, pointing. "One of my reporter buddies told me this place was designed like this, so that if the cops came in upstairs, there was time for a gangster to escape out the back. I don't know if there is any truth to that, but it makes for a good story.

"I do know this is an old family-owned place. I was told the grandfather came here from Italy and started this restaurant right after World War II. He handed it down to his daughter who has run it ever since. I think that's her husband there and her son, too," Jeff motioned.

"It really is charming, Jeff. I love the feel of the place. How did you find it?"

"At the newspaper you get to know about everything and every part of the city, or at least you better. Some of my colleagues have lived here all their lives, so they've helped me a lot, plus I've taken time to drive all over to get better acquainted. Boston is an interesting city, with its old buildings and the history. History was my minor." Pausing, he asked, "Faith, would you like some wine?"

"I would love some wine."

"I don't know much about wine. Nobody in my family drinks, but I'm beginning to like it, especially with Italian food."

"I never drank it growing up. My mom liked gin and tonic, but I've really learned a great deal about wines from my dad these last few years."

"I'm a little confused about your family, Faith."

"I can understand why. It is a bit screwy to say the least. My mother and dad dated in junior college, in East Texas, in my mother's hometown, where my dad, who is from Boston, was on a basketball scholarship. They fell in love and that was when the priest abuse stuff really began bothering him. He decided to become a priest in an effort to compensate for everything. That's when he left my mother, not realizing she was two months pregnant with me." Seeing the waiter approach, she paused.

"May I suggest a wine?" the tall Italian waiter asked, handing a list to Jeff.

Turning to Faith, Jeff said, "Would you like to select it."

"No, let's see what he says."

The waiter pointed to a 1996 Chianti Classico on the wine list and said, "This is a medium-bodied wine, superb fruit character and modestly priced for such fine tannins and clear finish."

Worried that it might be more than Jeff wanted to pay, Faith interrupted, "We could have a carafe of the house wine."

"No, this will be fine, don't you think? This is a special occasion," he said, looking a little embarrassed, "I mean, this is your first time here and it has been an exciting week for me, with the story and all." He stopped short of saying *and meeting you.*

When the server walked away, Jeff said, "Okay, back to your story."

"Oh, I guess I should say this is off the record, huh?" Faith laughed.

Jeff said in a serious tone, "Even for an award winning story I would never betray your confidence."

Faith thought to herself how young, naïve and innocent he appeared. Knowing from law cases how the newspaper business can be cut-throat and harsh, she hoped he had it in him to be tough, not brutal, but tough enough to be successful in a very competitive field.

"When I was four days old, my mother disappeared and everyone thought she had committed suicide. My aunt raised me. I call her Mom. Anyway, long story short, my dad changed his mind about the priesthood, and I later found out that my mother wasn't dead but had fled to a cloistered convent."

"Why?"

"Why he changed his mind, or why she left?"

"Both."

"For him, he told me he felt at odds with the church, believing the overreaching power and control of the priest was a mistake that led to some of the problems that the church fails to address. As for my mother, it was two reasons. First, it wasn't exactly acceptable then in a little town for a young woman to have a child and not be married. Second, she could shield her identity in a cloistered convent, and feel close to my dad who she thought was a priest. Anyway, today they are spending their first full day together in twenty-five years. I hope it goes well for them because they both deserve happiness. Now, that's enough about my dysfunctional family. Where are you from?"

The server approached the table and showed Jeff the bottle. He nodded as the waiter uncorked it, handing the cork to him. Just as he was about to pour Jeff a taste, the young reporter stopped him. "Let the lady try it first."

After swirling the liquid slightly, Faith took a sip, "Mmm, this is quite good," and then waited until the server poured a glass for Jeff. Immediately he clinked his glass against hers and made a toast.

"To victory for you and your dad and award-winning journalism for me. I saw how to do this in the movies," he added with a grin.

He took a long drink. "This is nice."

The server returned, bowed slightly and asked, "Are you ready to order, sir?"

"We haven't looked at the menu. Could you give us a few minutes?"

He nodded patiently, apparently accustomed to people taking their time in an atmosphere conducive to quiet conversation and slow decision making.

"What will it be for you?" Jeff asked.

"The lasagna sounds really good. I think I'll go with that. And by the way, I normally would tell the server I have a brain and he can ask me questions also, but since this is a traditional old country Italian place, I'll be nice and adjust," she said, winking at him.

Although he didn't know Faith very well, he had already figured out that she was definitely her own person and certainly not timid or saving of her opinion. Jeff laughed, "Not one for chauvinism, I see."

When the waiter asked for their choices, Jeff said, trying hard not to smile, "The little lady here will have lasagna and I'll have the shrimp and linguini."

When the waiter turned around, Jeff said, "How was that?" as they both laughed.

"Okay, now about you, Jeff."

"It's not really very exciting. I'm the baby in the family and only boy. My two sisters and I grew up on a farm in Iowa, with chickens, corn, and pigs, whatever. My father wanted me to take over the farm someday, but I hated it. To me, the pigs smelled, the corn rotted and the chickens pecked, ugh. It was just depressing with no day being different from the day before.

"My mother stayed home and canned everything she could stick in a jar while my father worked outside, coming in at sundown, tired and dusty. He's probably not read anything but the local newspaper and Farmers' Almanac in fifty years. At night, they watched a little television, that is, when we finally got one. My father would doze off while my mother quilted or mended socks or sweaters. She never threw anything away that I can remember. Then they would go to bed early and get up before the sun came up.

"It was always the same, except on Sunday, the only day he didn't work when we all went to the little Methodist Church in the town, near our farm. My sisters are both married and still live in the area. My oldest sister's husband took over the farm, although my father still pretends to be in charge. Thank goodness for Henry, my brother-in-law who took the pressure off me, but my dad really never got over the fact I wanted to leave."

"Why journalism?"

"I worked at the little county newspaper in high school writing birth announcements and obituaries and everything in between except women's garden club stuff. Thankfully, a little old woman had done that for years. I even threw a paper route on top of everything else. My high school counselor helped me get a scholarship to the University of Missouri and now here I am."

"Do you go back home much?"

"Only when I have to or I start feeling guilty."

"But what made you interested in newspaper work in the first place?"

"I guess because it was the only exciting thing in town. It allowed me to chase ambulances once or twice a year if somebody was hurt or killed in a wreck and report all the local scandals, although there were very few. I played Little League as a young kid, but then I had rheumatic fever and the doctor said it had weakened my heart and I shouldn't play sports. So I started reading about them and then that love for reading spread to other subjects, especially history. I became the sports editor for the high school newspaper so I could at least travel with my friends on the team.

"I think the doctor also made my father think farming might be too hard on me, but, I had a complete physical a couple of years ago and my heart couldn't be stronger. Looking back, I realize that doctor didn't know if the fever had affected me or not. He just guessed because that's what everybody thought then."

The waiter placed a salad in front of each of them.

"Did you know that in Italy they don't serve the salad first?" Faith asked.

"No, I've never been out of the United States. I traveled a couple of weeks after I graduated, before I took this job, but it was just down the East Coast to see Charleston and Savannah."

"I haven't been to Italy, but my dad lived there for a couple of years, and he goes back to see friends. That's how I know."

As they finished eating the salads, their dinners were served in large, elaborately painted bowls, accompanied by a basket of hot bread.

"I really like this place," Faith said, midway into her meal. "This is a special treat."

He smiled. "I'm glad you like it. It's nice to come out and have such a pretty lady to look at over all this rich linguini."

Blushing slightly, Faith asked, "So how long have you lived here in Boston?"

"Two years. It will actually be two years this month."

"And no one special in your life?"

"No, I really haven't taken the time to meet many people. I wanted to make an impression at the newspaper, so I try to work as much as I can, which doesn't leave much time for socializing. I've dated a few nice girls, but they were all still in college. Once you're out, it's just different, you know? You're not part of the scene. What about you, Faith?"

"I had numerous male friends in college and law school, but no real steady. We all hung around together, which was fun and probably less stressful. I had definite goals, and I guess I wouldn't allow myself to get serious about anyone."

"That's the way I was," Jeff said. Maybe it sounds selfish, but I didn't want anything to threaten or compromise my success."

"Could I interest you in dessert?" the waiter asked.

"They have outstanding tiramisu," Jeff offered.

"You don't have to twist my arm. That sounds great."

"We'll each have one, please," Jeff said. "Oops, I did it again. I ordered for you. Sorry," he said, smiling.

Faith winked at him, "Hey, for dessert I'll let it go."

When they had finished, she added, "I really enjoyed this. It was so relaxing and peaceful."

"You know what, Faith. I know a really neat little jazz bar not far from here. If you don't mind missing the ballgame tonight, we could go hear the music and then to a ballgame tomorrow afternoon. That is, if you don't have plans."

"No, I don't have plans for tomorrow and the jazz bar sounds fun. I haven't been anywhere to listen to music in ages."

Inside the dimly-lighted lounge, the young couple found a table close to the nondescript stage where three musicians were performing the soulful music so connected to their heritage. Like thick fog, cigarette smoke filled the warm, stale air that smelled of a mixture of tobacco and sweet perfume.

Looking at the black, concrete walls and exposed ceiling of what was once a thriving warehouse, Faith thought how the setting created a perfect mood for the music. "If I didn't know better, I'd expect "Jelly Roll" Morton to walk in here any minute. This atmosphere makes you feel like a holdover from the 1920s, lost in some old speakeasy along the Mississippi River. Have you ever been to New Orleans?"

"No. I'd like to go, maybe someday during Mardi Gras. Who is "Jelly Roll" Morton?"

Faith laughed. "He was a well-known early jazz pianist in the South. I listened to some of his music when I was a kid. My mom had all kinds of old records and loved jazz. She would put a stack of records on the player and start dancing in the living room, and finally after a few minutes of prodding, I would join her. That's how I learned to dance."

"So, I guess you have been to New Orleans."

"Twice. When I was little I went with Mom, and she let me see parts of Bourbon Street, and then I went again with college friends and took in the whole flavor. I love the French Quarter where they have great jazz bands, especially those that play Dixieland jazz—my favorite. You can walk along Bourbon or Canal Streets where the doors of most places are open and the sounds from the bands fill the night air."

Melancholy and hauntingly soulful sounds were emerging from this unlikely trio: a middle-aged saxophone player, an older, graying clarinet player and a skinny boyish-looking individual whose youthfulness contrasted sharply to the other band members and to the yellowed keys of the worn piano he played. Faith looked around the dingy room noticing the eclectic combination of cultures represented, all gathered to listen to the rhythmic blend of blues and swing.

When the band took a short break, Jeff asked, "Well, what do you think?"

"I think they are wonderful, but most of all I like the mixture of people. It looks like a United Nations delegation in here. Everyone is smiling and friendly. I've heard music is an international language and I think that's probably true."

"Do you think we have time for one more set?" Jeff asked.

Faith answered, a sleepy "Yes."

"I'm not too convinced, but we'll stay a little longer anyway," Jeff said, laughing. "I'm not a person who needs much sleep, so sometimes I have to be reminded that others do."

"I'm enjoying this so much I don't want to leave," Faith said, suppressing a yawn.

Standing, Jeff walked over to the piano player who was taking a short break, stopping to drop a ten-dollar bill in the Mason jar, which held other tips. "When you finish your break, could you play a little Dixieland jazz for that nice southern girl?" he asked, turning, so the young musician could see Faith.

Smiling, the piano player nodded as he gently twisted and crushed the stub of his cigarette into a metal ashtray and walked back to the stage. The band then played a heartfelt rendition of "Basin Street Blues," followed by a soulful, "When the Saints Go Marching In."

A few minutes before midnight, Jeff whispered, "I guess I'd better drive you to your hotel."

"I may have to throw these clothes away," Faith said, as Jeff started the car.

"Yes, I know what you mean. We don't smell too fresh, do we?" bringing his wrist to his nose. "Even though I didn't notice that many people smoking, you could still cut the air with a knife."

"I think some of it comes from a lingering effect, like it has been trapped in there for decades. Their ventilation system, I noticed, consisted of a tiny window they had opened slightly. But it was worth it."

Driving up to the front of the hotel, Faith observed, "Jeff, I know it's late and you have to get up early. You don't have to find a parking space and ride the elevator up with me. I know that's correct by today's etiquette standards, but I assure you, I'm fine."

"You're positive?"

"Very."

"Okay then. He reached over and kissed her on the cheek. Then I'll see you tomorrow."

"Good night, Jeff, and thanks for a wonderful evening."

He waited until the doorman let her in and then drove away. "This is not good," he said to himself softly, wishing he weren't falling for her. Knowing she would be leaving, going to Dallas as soon as everything settled down with the priest, he couldn't help himself. He already looked forward to tomorrow.

Faith opened the door to the suite slowly and carefully so as not to wake her dad. But she need not have worried. He wasn't there. "Hmm," she said under her breath as she undressed for bed. *Wonder if he's in her bed.* She stopped, not wanting to speculate and realized how sleepy she was. *I'll know in the morning,* she thought. Quickly she dressed for bed and as soon as her head hit the pillow she was asleep.

When Faith woke the next morning, she pulled on her robe and went out into the little room that separated the two bedrooms. There she found Patrick at the little table drinking coffee and reading the morning paper. He had already been to early church and was still dressed in his suit pants and pressed shirt with his tie loosened.

"You going somewhere?"

Patrick laughed, "No, I just got back from church, and just haven't changed into my casual clothes. I needed another cup of coffee, so I just stopped here first. You want a cup?" He reached to pour her some of the strong coffee that he liked before she could answer.

She took it from him and added a packet of sugar and a few drops of cream, and joined him at the table. Tasting the hot drink, she made a face, and added more cream.

"So how was the ballgame?"

"We're going this afternoon. After we had a nice meal at this small quaint place in Little Italy, we both felt more like jazz than baseball. Since they're playing this afternoon, we decided to wait, and now about your day, and night? You were out late, huh?"

He smiled, "It couldn't have been better. We went to the New England Aquarium and then saw some of the historical places along the harbor, and had a drink at the Cheers Bar. Then we had a nice dinner and talked for hours. Maybe she will tell it differently, but I think we both had a great evening."

"That's good. I'm delighted."

"We're driving over to Newport today and were going to see if you wanted to go, but it appears the young reporter grabbed you first."

When the phone rang and Faith answered, Jeff's voice was filled with excitement.

"Faith, the baseball game may have to wait."

"Hey, that's okay. Is everything all right?"

His voiced raced. "You know that woman who called the other day, the one whose son tried to commit suicide? Well, she called back." Not even giving Faith a chance to answer, he continued, "She wants to talk to me right after she leaves church; she said she goes to the second service, and would come by then. I'm thinking she might want to ask you questions or you might want to hear what she says. I don't know quite what to expect, but could you come to the newspaper office?"

"Sure, when?"

"Just come as soon as you can."

"Okay, but it will be at least and hour before I can get there."

"I'll tell security to let you in."

He hung up without saying anything else.

"Hey, listen to this," she said to Patrick as she related what Jeff had just said. "This could be the break we need."

"I hope she doesn't change her mind."

"Well, apparently she's thought about it for a couple of days."

There was a gentle tap at the door and Faith opened it to see Sue, smiling and dressed in a mint-green summer pantsuit, sporting emerald loop earrings. Faith couldn't help but notice that her mother still had a really good figure and not so much as a single grey hair. She looked happier than Faith had seen her in over six years.

"Wow, don't you look smart!"

"Well, thank you, my dear."

"Guess what?" Faith again related the story from Jeff.

"Do we need to stay here?"

"Heavens no, you two go and have fun."

"If we leave now, maybe we can get there in time to get a good table at Christie's. It overlooks Narragansett Bay. Just give me a minute to change into something more comfortable, as he tugged quickly at his tie. You ladies excuse me."

When he was out of sight, Faith looked at her mother questioningly, but before she could ask her anything, Sue smiled.

"You don't need to worry Faith, I'm fine. I've never been better. We'll just see where this all goes." The two women hugged. Their relationship had grown strong over the last several years after Faith came to a better understanding of her mother. It had not been as hard for Faith to forgive as most would have expected of a young woman whose mother had left her as a baby because she had always loved Alice and never felt alone. Although she had some difficulty forgiving them both, she had come to grips with their decisions. She figured they sometimes had a harder time living with their choices than she did accepting them.

Patrick came back into the room smiling. After reaching for his windbreaker and sunglasses, he took Sue's hand and turned to talk to Faith. "We'll be anxious to hear about your day when we get back, but it may be nine or ten o'clock."

"I better hurry; Jeff is waiting. I don't know what my day will bring so if I'm going to be later than 10:00, I'll call the room and leave a message."

~

Although Jeff had told Faith security would let her in, he was waiting downstairs at the front door.

"Is she here?"

"She and the son are in my office. She got here earlier than I expected so we have talked quite awhile"

"I'm sorry I'm late. I didn't think I would have to wait so long for a taxi on Sunday. How did it go?"

"Really well. They're ready to go to the authorities, but they need to ask you some questions."

"I can't wait."

Faith saw them sitting quietly in Jeff's office. The mother was small and frail although, Faith could tell she couldn't have been older than her early forties. Looking through the glass partition at him, Faith thought that the son might not be the best of witnesses. With scraggly long, dirty hair, he wore a black tee shirt with an emblem of a little known rock band. *Maybe we could clean him up,* she mused, but she hesitated to draw more conclusions until she heard him talk.

"Hello, I'm Faith O'Brien," extending her hand first to the woman.

The woman took her hand and held it for a few lingering seconds and then suddenly hugged Faith tightly. The son stood, looking embarrassed at his mother's actions, and reached his hand to Faith. *Well at least he has some manners.*

Pulling up a chair for Faith, Jeff said, "This is Mrs. McGee and Rick," after noticing that they had not introduced themselves.

"Faith, they have detailed for me Rick's abuse and have some questions for you. I'm sure you have some for them as well," Jeff explained.

"Yes, thank you, Jeff. I'll have many questions about the incident itself, but I'll just start with a few preliminary questions. First, let me say that I am a lawyer, but I am not representing you.

I am merely here to lend additional support before you go to the authorities tomorrow."

"But Ms. O'Brien, we thought you would be our lawyer," Mrs. McGee quickly countered.

"I'll help anyway I can at no fee to you whatsoever, but once the complaint is filed it will go to the district attorney and a prosecutor from that office will handle the case."

"But Jeff said you are a lawyer and are helping your father and that you passed the state bar here in Massachusetts."

"True, however, Mrs. McGee, I'm still not a prosecutor for the state. Besides for me, the most important thing in this case was for my dad's story to draw attention to what we guessed was not an isolated event. He is forty-five years old; his abuse happened when he was ten. We knew going into this we couldn't jump the hurdle presented us by the ten-year statute of limitations. For us, this is a cleansing process, but we hoped that someone would come forward who was within the statute, and get the district attorney's attention, win the case and put this evil priest away.

"You and Rick have the opportunity to do this. I'm just out of law school, and although I would like to think I'm smart enough and shrewd enough to tackle the civil case that may result after the criminal, I know I don't have the experience. I'm concerned for Rick and any other person whom we may discover to have had the misfortune of being in the close presence of this terrible man. You… they, will need the most seasoned, toughest son of a bitch, excuse my language, that you can get to represent you because I assure you Father Michael will have one to match."

"But Ms. O'Brien, we are not wealthy people. My husband finally found work three years ago, after not working for so long, we've depleted all of our savings, and all the hush money the church paid us. Now, Rick lost his job a month ago."

Faith looked over at Rick, noticing that in spite of his unkempt appearance and faraway look in his emerald green eyes, he was handsome. Looking down, cupping his hands in his lap, he sat silent.

"Mrs. McGee, I have taken a job in Dallas with a well established firm. The senior partners have many connections. I'll call them tomorrow and see if they know a lawyer here that might help us. I'll do everything I can, one way or the other, please know that, but if the D.A.'s office takes this, they'll take care of Rick. We're talking about two separate cases: a criminal case against O'Mallory, and a civil one against O'Mallory and the Archdiocese of Boston, possibly even the Cardinal, for his conduct in covering for the priest."

"I'm going to trust you Ms. O'Brien. Jeff tells me you are a sincere person with compassion. It is very hard for me to trust anyone anymore, after Father O'Mallory and Cardinal O'Leary."

"I understand completely. Turning to Rick, Faith continued, "Why are you willing to go public with this?"

He sat there for a long time as if giving her question much thought, although Faith knew he had probably been through this many times in his mind the last couple of days.

"If I say because I hate him so bad, would that be wrong?"

"No Rick, I don't think so at all, but is that enough to carry you through what may be a long, messy trial?"

"I…I think so. Whatever this is, it's taken me over. My therapist says I've got to get it out, or I can never begin to heal."

"Your therapist is right, Rick."

"This has screwed up my whole life. I know I'm weak, but I just can't get a grip anymore. I can't focus."

"Rick, when this is over, you will know that you are not weak, not at all, but a very strong young man."

"I hate him, I hate myself more," Rick said, putting his head in his hands and crying softly.

For the first time, Faith saw the scars on his left wrist. They were deep and ugly, a constant reminder to him, she guessed, of when it had been so bad he wanted to end it all.

"How long have you been back in therapy?" Faith asked, assuming from what Jeff had said, that he had been in and out since the incident.

"Just a couple of months, I was doing better I think, but then I lost my job."

"What happened?"

"I just didn't show up one day."

"Why not?"

"I don't know. I just didn't feel like it. I went to the park."

"You didn't call in or anything?"

"No," he said, seeming much younger than his twenty years.

"Do you know Rick that if we go to trial and you don't show up, we could lose the whole case?" she said, wanting to impress on him how important his behavior would be.

"Yes, I don't want that to happen."

"Would you do me a big favor?"

He looked at her startled, wondering what that could mean.

"I guess…no, I mean yes."

"Before you go to the police station, would you cut your hair and wash it so it will shine and accent your beautiful eyes?"

"How short?"

"It doesn't have to be short. Not like his, pointing to Jeff, but a little off your shoulders. And maybe wear just a regular shirt, one that buttons and tucks in, because you'll have to do that for court."

"Okay, but why does that matter?"

"Because it just does Rick; this trial is not going to be easy. Even though you are not the perpetrator – the bad guy, the other side will try to make you look like you are. They will do everything they can to make you look bad, to look unbelievable. That's their only hope, so you have to look like someone the jury will believe, someone they can connect with."

"So, why can't I wait to cut my hair?"

Beginning to think this was like dealing with a thirteen or fourteen year old, as if Rick stopped maturing back during the molestation, Faith, tried not to reveal her frustration, and calmly replied, "Because we need to be good from the very beginning. We want to impress the police and everyone else. Besides, Rick, how much trouble does it take for you to be handsome? Very little." She patted him gently on the knee. "The girls are going to want to wait outside, on the courthouse steps, just to get a glimpse of you."

He smiled faintly, but said nothing.

She pressed, "Will you do that for me? There's probably a place at the mall where they cut hair on Sunday."

Finally he mumbled, "Yes."

We'll have to work on enunciating too, she thought, but decided not to push it any further.

"If you would like, I'll meet you at the police station at nine o'clock in the morning to file the complaint. I'm sure everything will have to go before the grand jury first. The grand jury doesn't decide guilt or innocence," she explained. "Your attorney will present facts about the accusation and then the grand jury will decide if there is enough evidence to warrant criminal charges. If at least twelve jurors agree that there is cause for indictment, then that is returned to the Judge."

"So, all twelve jurors have to agree?" Mrs. McGee asked.

"No, grand juries are different from regular juries in that they can have up to twenty-three members. You may be called as a witness, Rick, we'll see, but we're getting ahead of ourselves. I just want you to be informed, not to be hit blindside by something."

"Ms. O'Brien, will you just think about representing us? I know you can do a good job. We're comfortable with you. Please, will you just think about it?"

"I appreciate your confidence in me, Mrs. McGee and I will think about it." Standing and reaching to shake their hands, she said, "I'll meet you in the morning."

Without further conversation, they walked out, leaving only Faith and Jeff in the office.

"Well, what do you think?" Jeff asked.

"I think the unholy priest is in deep poop," she said, smiling. I suppose you'll stop by the police department sometime in the morning?"

"Exactly, and before you arrived, Mrs. McGee and Rick both agreed to being quoted. It's going to be quite a story." He stopped and after a long pause insisted, "Faith, will you think about staying and being their lawyer?"

"I'll think about it Jeff. I really will. But I need to talk to Mr. Henry or Mr. Jackson. I'll know more tomorrow."

"Guess we missed the ballgame, huh?"

"It looks that way." Glancing at her watch, she saw it was almost four o'clock. "I need to make some notes while things are still fresh, Jeff, or I'd treat you to a burger," remembering she hadn't eaten all day.

"Hey, I understand. I've a couple more hours of work to do here, myself. Maybe later in the week?" he asked, hopefully.

"Sure, soon, I hope," she nodded, gathering up papers and her briefcase. "I need to call a cab."

"I'll take you." Jeff offered.

"No. A cab is fine."

"Okay. I'll call if anything else comes along. Wait, I'll walk you out and be sure you can get a cab. Think about staying, Faith."

"I promise I will. There is a lot to consider with my job and everything, but this case right now is the most important thing in my life. We'll see. I'll do what I can."

~

Faith was on the couch, painting her nails when Patrick and Sue arrived back at the hotel.

"Hurry, sit down. Let me tell you the big news," Faith said, explaining every detail.

"So, are you going to represent him?" Patrick asked when Faith had completed her account of the day's events.

"I don't think so, Dad, but we'll see. I don't think he needs me. The state will take care of him. I just worry that he'll crumble if the D.A. isn't gentle with him, and without him, there isn't a case."

"Faith, you know you can do it."

"Oh Dad, I'm afraid this is bigger than I am."

Sue interrupted before Faith could go any further. "That doesn't sound like the Faith I know."

"I'm worried, I guess. This kid, well, he's actually twenty years old, but he's not that age emotionally. He's very fragile so he needs badly to win this. I would feel terrible if I did something stupid."

"Faith, that's not going to happen."

"If I got out-lawyered in my very first case, it would, and then I'm afraid I might lose my confidence."

"And if you win it, you'll be famous."

"I'm going to talk to one of my bosses tomorrow if possible to see what they suggest. Maybe they know some good lawyers here. Now tell me about your day."

Chapter 5

After the complaint was filed at the police station, Faith knew it would be just a matter of time before Father Michael would be arrested. Doubting that he would appear in district court, but rather have his lawyer there representing him, she also figured he would be released on his own recognizance. The fact that he was seventy-three years old and had a faithful following would garner him some additional sympathy.

Needing to talk to her bosses, she returned to the hotel and waited impatiently for the switchboard to open. Finally, she was able to get through.

When Mr. Jackson came on the phone he seemed delighted that she had called. "Faith, how are you? We've been trying to keep up but haven't seen anything in the papers here this weekend."

"Well, there will be tomorrow," explaining the details. Pausing in an effort not to sound over anxious, "They want me to be their lawyer, Mr. Jackson, but I told them I felt like I would be over my head, and that I need to get to Dallas and get started in my practice with y'all. Besides I explained that the state would represent Rick."

"Faith, this is a once in a lifetime trial for you. This is big. I can send another lawyer up there if you like, but I really think you can handle it. You are in this whether you know it or not. The only problem you may have is that you are emotionally involved because of your father, but I think you can handle that.

"Look, tell you what I'll do. Of course I'll have to talk it over with Alfred, but we'll start you on the payroll and pay your expenses. Whenever possible use the name of our firm. If you get anything out of this, you can pay back the expenses. If you don't, then we'll chalk it up to advertising. I know you must be a little worried about finances."

"Yes sir, I am, more than a little, but I'm more worried about who the Archdiocese will get to defend this priest. The kid I'd be defending has no money; the mother has already pointed that out."

"Number one, Faith, if the Cardinal paid off the parents and you can show that, maybe the state can get a plea. Secondly, if you win a civil case, this kid will have money. Set up your percentage on that and cut your losses on the criminal one. Let's play this day by day. If it keeps getting bigger, I'll either send someone up or call a friend I have there who is a super attorney. But right now, let's hang in there, Young Lady. You were the best in your class. You can do it. I believe in you. Besides, you'll get a lot of exposure."

"Mr. Jackson, I really appreciate this. How do you want me to keep you informed now that I'm on the payroll?"

"I've got a really talented young man here, name's Tyler England. He's been with us about four years, came to us right out of Tulane Law School. I'm going to put him in charge from this end. You keep him informed and if you need help, he'll get you answers and brief me. But Faith, you're the one who passed the Massachusetts bar. Just remember that."

"Yes sir."

"And Faith, don't hesitate to call me, either. I'm just setting you up with Tyler because he may be easier for you to reach. Good luck, you hear?"

"Thank you, Mr. Jackson," but the phone clicked before she finished.

Within an hour Mr. Jackson had called Faith again.

"Listen, Faith, I think Alfred and I are on to something. Stay where you are. I'll call you back hopefully, later this morning."

"May I ask what you're referring to, sir?"

"Oh, I'm sorry Faith. I guess I got ahead of myself. Okay, here's our plan. You're familiar with pro hac vice, right?"

"Yes sir."

"Well, even though you passed the bar there, you're not a resident so this rule probably needs to be invoked anyway. But Alfred suggested we take it a step further. I know the D.A. there. Nice guy. Went to law school with him and saw him a couple of years ago at a conference. Although we haven't talked in awhile, I think I may be able to convince him to go along with this."

She wanted to interrupt, ask him what in the world he was talking about, but she refrained and anxiously remained silent.

He continued, "You're the one who knows everything about this case, the one who is passionate about it and the one who has developed rapport with the complainant. I'm going to ask Marvin, the D.A., Marvin McChristensen to allow you to apply for pro hac vice status and then for him to appoint you as a temporary prosecutor for the state. If he wants to assign some young assistant from his staff as the chief prosecutor for political correctness, that's fine, but he needs to give you free reign for the most part. Anyway, that's the jest of my request. Are you okay with that?"

Catching her breath, Faith found herself unable to speak for a minute. After an obvious and embarrassing pause she replied, "But Mr. Jackson, are you sure? I mean, do you really think I can do all this?"

"Faith, if I didn't, I wouldn't be doing this. I'll call you soon."

~

Faith paced the hotel room, unable to calm herself. She began making notes, information she might need to share with the district attorney. Startled by the phone, she answered "Hello" on the first ring.

"Faith, that was easier than I thought. I explained everything to Marvin. Although he was torn in wanting one of his assistants to take the case and receive positive publicity with a win, he understands that there's a chance someone with less commitment could lose it. Also, he's totally understaffed with overloaded dockets. He wants to talk to you and then he'll decide. Sounds like a done deal because I know after your conversation with him, he'll be even more convinced. I've made you an appointment for 1:00."

Shortly before one o'clock, Faith arrived at the district attorney's office, nervous and not knowing what to expect. Assuming she would have to wait, she had brought work, but at exactly the appointment time, a gregarious man with a shock of wiry red hair opened the door.

"Ms. O'Brien?"

"Yes. Hello, I'm Faith O'Brien."

"Hi. Marvin McChristensen, call me Mac. My secretary's still at lunch so come on in," he directed politely, stepping aside for her to pass in front of him. "Please sit down," he said, closing the door.

His calm demeanor had settled Faith's nerves because she had anticipated a more formal, rigid individual to greet her, as she waited for his next move.

"Well, my old friend Henry tells me you are a bright, up and coming legal expert."

Smiling, Faith answered, "I'm not so sure about that sir, but I know a great deal about this particular case. To say I'm apprehensive or uptight about the trial would be an understatement, but I do believe we have a strong case if we can get the facts across."

Appearing relaxed and casual, the district attorney encouraged her, "Tell me about it."

As Faith explained the events beginning with her father, she lapsed into an easy conversation, answering his questions and indicating to him her knowledge of the legal implications.

When she had finished, he said, "As much as I would like one of my seasoned assistants to run with this, I know Henry's correct in that you are ready to proceed and quickly, if necessary. It would be nice not to drag this one out, which unfortunately, happens to be a pattern with so many cases and so few staff attorneys.

"I have a new lawyer on board who has yet to try a case, Jason Pacheco. He wouldn't be intimidated by your leading this and I believe he could learn from the experience. Basically, he'll accompany you as a procedural maneuver.

"If you don't mind, I'm going to highlight my appointment of you as a way to save the state money and resources. Our department has taken heat lately for being slow to react. Of course, that could backfire in this case because O'Mallory's a popular figure in Boston. There may be a following who want to sweep this under the rug.

"One never knows, but I'm hoping this is a win-win. Let me call Jason and introduce you two. You can explain the case to him, but I'll ask that you be the person who talks to the media. If you need him to do anything to help you, you're certainly free to ask him; otherwise, he'll be there as support from my office."

Reaching for the phone, he dialed and spoke softly to a secretary. "Tell Jason I need to see him if he's free."

Within minutes a young, lanky attorney appeared at the D.A's door. "Yes, Mac? Jackie said you wanted to talk with me."

"Yes, Jason. This is Faith O'Brien from Texas. Let me tell you what I have planned."

Faith and Jason spent an hour going over the logistics of the case with her outlining her next steps.

"I'll keep you posted everyday, Jason. I know this may not be a comfortable position for you, but I'll make every effort to make it satisfactory."

"Faith, I want to work my way up the ranks here. You won't hear me complaining. Mac is a super lawyer and great man. If this is what he wants me to do, then I'm fine with it. In the long run, it will be the best for me. Besides, when I grow up I want to be just like him," smiling modestly.

"I'm happy that you feel that way, Jason, I didn't ask for this, but our two bosses apparently believe this is the way to tackle the case. I trust mine completely and it appears as though you do as well."

"Absolutely. Mac is one of those people who is totally at ease in his own skin, and has very little ego. What you see is what you get. That's what I like about him, a rare personality for an attorney, don't you think?"

"Yes, I was surprised when I met him."

Laughing, Jason said, "Most people are, but you should see him in the courtroom, not the same individual. He looks more like a man on fire with his red hair blazing, his nostrils flaring. People see him as loose and easy and that catches them off guard. Then, Bam! He hits them right in the gut. He has perfect timing, terrific delivery so don't be fooled by his good ol' boy approach."

"Glad you told me, but I had a feeling there might be an animal inside waiting to pounce. Everyone says my boss is the same way. I wouldn't want to be on the receiving end, but that is what makes him so good. I hope I can be half as good as he is someday." Pausing, she continued, "So you're okay with my taking charge?"

"Not a problem. I'll have my day. Just be certain you win," he added with a half-smirk on his boyish face. "Seriously, it is obvious that your bosses have a lot of faith in you, no pun intended.

I'm sure I'll learn from you, and that's what I need right now. I need to watch, internalize and learn."

"I love the no pressure encouragement I'm feeling these days. I'll be in touch, and thanks, Jason. I hope I don't let you or anyone else down. Some days I feel this will be the biggest trial of my life. It's scary, but exciting."

Her first stop after the meeting was the bank where Mr. and Mrs. McGee had deposited their money from the Cardinal seven years ago. Knowing that even if she got a record of the deposit, it wasn't proof without a check or way to make a connection, it wouldn't help a lot, but it might raise suspicions among the jury, since Mr. McGee was out of work at the time. She could show that he hadn't inherited any money and hadn't been charged with any theft. Although the bank had changed ownership and names twice in the last six years, Faith was in luck; the deposit was on microfiche, $25,000 dated March 3, 1991. She called Mrs. McGee to tell her that not only would she be Rick's attorney, but she explained the arrangement she and the district attorney had agreed on. "We need to work out an agreement. I'll do this criminal one pro bono and take thirty-five percent of the civil settlement, if we win. If we lose, I get nothing. When we meet I'll bring some paperwork you can sign, if you agree."

"That's more than fair, Ms. O'Brien. Thank you so much. Where should we meet?"

"If it's all right, I'll drop by your house. Rick needs to be there to sign as well. What time would be okay with you?"

"We'll be here all day."

"Then I'll be by sometime in the morning."

~

The afternoon newspaper headlines read:

MICHAEL O'MALLORY, BOSTON PRIEST ARRESTED FOR CHILD MOLESTATION

Father Michael O'Mallory was arrested late this afternoon in his office after being accused of molesting a then thirteen year-old boy in the school where he was serving as principal. Rick McGee who is now twenty years old filed charges today saying that the abuse went on for over a year. McGee's attorney, Faith O'Brien from the law firm of Jackson, Henry, Jackson in Dallas, said this complaint stemmed from an earlier one filed last week accusing O'Mallory of the same charge more than thirty-five years ago. "My client came forth yesterday in order to begin the healing process. I won't be surprised if this doesn't start a chain of events" she said.

O'Mallory is set to appear in district court on Wednesday where he will be arraigned and bail set, according to a court spokesperson. In an unprecedented chain of events, Boston District Attorney Marvin McChristensen has appointed Ms. O'Brien as a temporary prosecutor under a little known legal rule, pro hac vice, meaning in Latin, "for this occasion." McChristensen has assigned assistant district attorney, Jason Pacheco as co-prosecutor. Explaining, McChristensen said, "This office is answerable to the people of the state and I believe this arrangement best serves their interest. Ms. O'Brien passed the Massachusetts state bar and is well versed in our laws. Furthermore, she knows more about this case than anyone else. Having her on board will save the state money in research and time because she will be serving pro bono."

O'Brien also said she expects to soon file civil charges against O'Mallory for molestation and the Archdiocese of Boston for covering up the actions of O'Mallory. O'Mallory, 73, has been a priest in Boston for forty-seven years.

On Wednesday, Faith reported to the district court at 10:00 a.m. anxious to see if Father Michael or his attorney would be appearing in court. Having learned on Tuesday that O'Mallory had secured the services of long-time Boston attorney, Fred Stevens, further investigations revealed what she had feared. Stevens was tough and unscrupulous, and ill-mannered.

As expected, Stevens, all three hundred and fifty pounds of him, was there to represent the priest. Faith thought, *he may be outstanding, but he is gross.* Wearing a too small, tan leisure suit frayed on the legs and obviously left over from the seventies, with a half smoked cigar sticking out of the breast pocket, Stevens, who appeared to be in his early seventies, nodded an unfriendly hello toward Faith. Immediately, he asked the court to release his client on his own recognizance and then waived his client's right to a preliminary hearing.

Expecting the request for no bail, Faith was surprised by the waiver of the right to a preliminary hearing, which meant that the case wouldn't go to the grand jury, but directly, to the superior court.

After the court agreed to both requests, Faith walked over to the disheveled defense attorney.

"Hello sir, I'm Faith O'Brien and I'll be representing Mr. McGee."

"And so you are, Young Lady. I'm pleased to meet you," sounding more like a southern attorney than a Bostonian. "I hear you aren't from these parts."

"No sir and you don't sound as though you are, either."

"Been here thirty some years, can't seem to lose this damned old accent though." Although he didn't indicate where he was from, Faith guessed South Carolina, Alabama or maybe Georgia.

"I understand this is your first case, Young Lady."

"Yes sir, it is," now standing as straight as she could, glad she was wearing high heels today that gave her at least two inches more height than this broad, squatty man.

"Well, I've been checking around about you. Good firm you're from in Dallas, but I hear you've got a dog in this race."

"If you're referring to my father, sir, I suppose I do."

"Well, I've always thought it best for a lawyer not to get personally connected or emotionally involved in a case, but I guess I'm from the old school."

Faith knew the strategy he was using. "Well sir, I do believe I can be most objective in the case of Mr. McGee. I suppose we all allow our emotions to influence us some in the cases we elect to take. Personally, I abhor child abuse and believe someone should help those who are innocent and so betrayed. If I didn't feel strongly, I would, perhaps, be on an airplane back to Dallas. But instead, I plan to be here for the duration."

"Well, I respect that Young Lady, and I'd like this to be over as quickly as possible."

"Good, we agree on that. When would you like to have a pretrial conference?"

"Let's get it set up," he said gruffly, turning to walk away without so much as another word.

In spite of Stevens' condescending tone, and his displeasure in the Judge for agreeing to allow Patrick as a witness, Faith felt the first meeting went well. The trial was set for the first week of September, giving her time to go to Dallas and get a few things settled before she had to return.

Although she had rented a small house near downtown and work, she had not had time to do more than put her clothes and furniture there. Her office still needed attention.

Returning to the hotel, her first action was to call Tyler England.

"Hello, I've been expecting to hear from you. Mr. Jackson said you would be calling," he responded in a friendly and casual tone.

"Hi, I really meant to call before now, but things have been hectic." Faith began explaining everything that had transpired since she talked to their boss. "I'm going to wind things up here and then fly home Friday. I'll be in the office Monday."

"Oh. Well good. I didn't think you would be out of there so soon."

"I'll have to be back here in about three and a half weeks but I'm extremely anxious to get back to Dallas."

"We're anxious for you to get here."

She liked the way he sounded, low-key, but sincere.

"Then, I guess we'll see you Monday."

"Okay, 'til then, bye."

She called the McGees to tell them her plans and that she would be in touch. When she called Jeff, she could hear the disappointment in his voice as she told him she would be in Dallas until closer to the trial.

"I had hoped we could get together again," he said.

"I'm coming back a few days before things start up, so maybe we can do something then."

"Okay, but will you keep in touch?"

"Of course I will. I still think this is going to get bigger than it is."

"Yes. I do too," he said, wishing that she were referring to their relationship rather than the case.

~

Walking into the hotel suite, holding hands and looking genuinely happy, Patrick and Sue were surprised to see Faith packing.

"Where are you going?" Sue asked, unable to hide her surprise.

"Hi. Hey the trial's been set for September 4, so I need to get back to Dallas for a few weeks. Good news, Dad, Judge Ford is going to let you testify. Long story. I'll explain later."

"That happened quickly."

"Well, O'Mallory's attorney wanted to get it all set up as soon as possible and apparently over with the same way. You should see him. He's crude and unkempt and well, I'm not sure what else to think about him yet. Anyway, I'm outta here Friday morning." Looking at her parents, she asked, "What's your plan?"

"Well, it just so happens I've been invited to speak at Oxford on the nineteenth of August, but I didn't give them my answer because I wanted to see what your schedule was for everything. Now that this has turned out like it has, I can call them and accept," he responded, looking at Sue. "So will you go?"

"I promised you twenty-five years ago, I'd follow you anywhere. Do you remember?"

"Yes, I do," he said softly, and then turned and looked at Faith, "Then I guess I'll get tickets to Rome as soon as we can. I thought about going to Italy first if all this worked out. I want Sue to meet Carmella and Stefano. Then, perhaps, we can see some of the sights, go to England for my meeting and then spend another week or so around that part of the world before we get back for the trial."

"You don't have to be back for the trial."

"I wouldn't miss it for anything," he said.

"Nor would I," Sue added.

"Good, then we'll plan for you to be a witness mainly just to show a pattern or common scheme. I'm sure from what the Judge said to me he'll give the jury specific instructions about your testimony. Tomorrow I'm going to file the civil charges on behalf of you and Rick. They'll toss yours I'm sure, but then again, the

Archdiocese may want to just settle all of this quickly without any kind of proceedings."

"Can your packing wait?" Patrick cut in.

"Sure. Why?"

"I'd like to take my two favorite ladies for dinner and drinks."

"Good, I'm famished."

"What else is new?" He looked happily at both Sue and Faith.

Chapter 6

Faith knew the minute Tyler smiled at her that she was hooked. "He is the most gorgeous guy I've ever seen," she told Alice on the phone.

"Did you talk to him?"

"No, he apparently had been in court all day. I was about to leave at six when he rushed by me to Mr. Jackson's office, smiling and waving as if he knew who I was."

"He may be married, you know!"

"I know. I didn't want to ask anybody, but I looked in his office and didn't see any photographs or anything."

"Well, I hope he lives up to that smile. I'll call you tomorrow night to see what progress was made. Now, tell me about the rest of your day."

"Well, I set up my office and tried to get organized. The Scales of Justice you sent me look magnificent on my credenza. I love them, Mom. They are perfect, and mean so much coming from you. They are so feminine in the yellow and pink."

"Yes, and they say it all. You are Lady Justice—one tough, yet feminine young lady, and you will always weigh the evidence and support the truth. That much I know. Now, you have already told me that you love them 100 times. What else did you do?"

Faith laughed. "There you go exaggerating. I do love them though. Okay, let's see. Well, Tyler, Sid, another young lawyer, and I share a secretary. She seems nice enough, a little flaky maybe. Mr. Henry and Mr. Jackson were both really nice to me, even sent me flowers with a card welcoming me."

"Are you going out tonight?"

"No, I'm just making a sandwich for here. I'm tired from all the excitement; you know setting up my office and everything."

"I'll bet."

"How's the good doctor?" Faith asked.

"Wonderful! I met his son Sunday. He seems to be a really nice boy, a senior at Texas Christian University, who wants to be a doctor also."

"What about his daughter?"

"I haven't met her. She may be a little less endearing. Girls who lose their mothers at that age rarely like to see their fathers interested in another woman. But it's been five years. Ben says she's okay with it. We'll see. She's a sophomore at Texas Tech. Neither comes here often. After all, it's not really their home, and they don't know anyone here."

"So what are you doing tonight?"

"Ben may come over later, but he has a late meeting. We're going to dinner tomorrow night. Not having to cook is wonderful," Alice said, laughing. "Actually he likes for me to cook, but I think he feels bad sometimes expecting it and wants to treat me. After his day I know he's tired, so the least I can do is cook something. We're talking about coming to the Dallas/Fort Worth area next weekend, not this one. Do you think you'll have some time?"

"I'll make time, Mom. I want to meet this guy who may become my step dad or something like that."

"Who knows? We'll see."

"Do you two want to stay with me?"

"I don't know the plans yet. I'll let you know. I'll call you tomorrow night anyway."

"Okay. Good night."

~

The next morning he stuck his head in Faith's office. "Hi, I'm Tyler. So you're the Boston Strangler," he said, grinning. "I was anxious to put a face with the voice, and a nice face it is!"

Speechless for a moment, Faith sat at her desk, staring like a stargazing teenager at her tall, lean and tanned colleague. "Thanks," she stammered. "I'm glad to be here even if it is only for a few weeks..."

Rushing into his question, Tyler asked, "Do you have plans tonight?"

Before she could reply, he blushed and then in a serious tone, said, "Well, I guess I should first ask if you're involved with anyone?"

"No on both counts," Faith answered.

"Good. Would you like to go to dinner? We probably should talk about what you're doing with the trial. I mean, if you don't mind sharing some info with me."

"I'd love it. Besides you are my contact, and Mr. Jackson gave me strict instructions to report in," she said smiling.

"Where do you live?"

"Do you know the M streets?"

"Sure. Which one?"

"Martel. Third place on the right."

"Great, I live on Merrimac. Can you believe I live so close? Cool area, isn't it?" He didn't wait for a reply before he asked, "What about 6:30? Is that too soon after work?"

"No. That's perfect."

Grinning broadly, he moved his mouth funny, as if to blow his hair up and out of his eyes. Fly away, clean, straight and chestnut brown, his hair had a slight part in the middle and was collar length in back. In his blue tailored suit, starched white shirt with initials on the cuff, red and blue striped tie, he appeared professional and poised, but Faith couldn't help but notice a relaxed, easy-going side to him.

For a few minutes, Faith could think of nothing else but him. When Linda, the secretary, came in her office, Faith was so absorbed in her thoughts about him she was startled when Linda asked if she was going to lunch. Throughout the day, Faith could not get this handsome, athletic young man out of her mind.

When she returned to her duplex, Faith showered and changed into a pale blue sundress. With the temperature in the high nineties all day, she was having difficulty adjusting to the heat after being in New England. The light weight cotton fabric felt nice and the sandals, especially good after having worn heels all day. Faith couldn't remember being this nervous before a date. Waiting for Tyler to arrive, she called Alice.

"We're going to dinner!" Faith yelled, excitedly, the minute Alice picked up the receiver.

"We, who?" Alice asked, pretending not to know that Faith was referring to the young lawyer.

"Mom! Tyler, you know, the attorney I told you about."

"That didn't take long. You've already put your spell on him, huh?"

"I don't think so, but he did seem interested. I am so nervous."

"Honey, that's not like you. Why?"

"I don't know. He's perfect."

"Settle down, Love. He may be Godzilla once you've spent some time with him. Go slow and be careful."

"I know, I know, but he sure seems nice."

"Where are you going?"

"Who cares? No, I really don't know, just somewhere for dinner."

"What are you wearing in this dreadful heat?"

"A new sundress. I don't think you've seen it. It was so damn hot today. I think I could have fried an egg on the sidewalk."

"You think it's hot there. We must have ninety-nine percent humidity. You know how the old oil roads outside town smell here when it is so hot? Well, I had to go out to visit an elderly woman I've been checking on while her daughter's out of town, and I swear I could hardly catch my breath. Her little shotgun house is set in a clump of pine trees and it must have been at least 105° in the shade."

"July in Texas, gotta love it. The Northeast is looking better."

"Yeah, until the first blizzard."

"Right, I'd hate that. I guess I'd better finish my lipstick and such. Wish me well tonight. I'll probably fall off a curb or something."

"Faith O'Brien, now don't even talk that way. You may knock him off his feet, though."

"Talk to you later. Love ya."

"I love you, Honey. Now go out there and charm that guy right out of his pants. Oh, no pun intended. Bye." Alice said, giggling.

"Bye Mom," Faith said, hanging up the phone and laughing. *Leave it to her to lighten things up.*

He was at her doorsteps at 6:30 on the dot.

"Hi, Tyler, come in."

'You look, well...," pausing, "tremendous."

"Thank you. I wanted to wear something cool."

"Yeah, me too. I meant to tell you very casual, so I'm glad you didn't dress up," Tyler said, wearing tight starched jeans and a red, white and blue striped Izod.

"You like red, white and blue, I've noticed."

"Oh yeah. Call me Mr. Patriotic," he grinned. "What kind of food do you like?"

"Just about every kind."

"I thought we might go to a little Tex-Mex place not too far from here. Does that sound all right?"

"That sounds great. I love Mexican food and I haven't had any in a month. Boston may have lots of good food, but the Tex-Mex there leaves a little to be desired."

"You're a Texas girl, through and through aren't you, Faith?"

"Absolutely, and proud of it."

"I'm proud to be from Texas, too."

"What part?"

He had made himself comfortable on the couch and she across from him in her favorite chair. "West Texas...Midland. And you?"

"East Texas, Townsend. I guess we're both used to oil wells, although I certainly don't own one."

He smiled. "Nor do I, but my dad has been in the business for years. My mom's a teacher at one of the middle schools."

"What subject?"

"Music."

"Not one of my best. Mom made me take piano lessons for what seemed like years, but they didn't exactly take."

"Yes, mine tried that, too. I balked after a year, and my dad took my side. I don't think he wanted his son playing the piano anyway. My sister's really good at it. I can play the guitar, even the fiddle a little."

"Really? I guess you like country western music?"

"Is there any other kind? What about you?"

"I like it all. I don't exactly have a great amount of rhythm, but I like music, even a little classical, as long as I don't have to hear it for a couple of hundred miles in the car."

He laughed. "Speaking of, I guess we'd better hop in mine. I could sit here and talk, but we had better go eat."

"I'm ready, just let me get my purse."

Thinking it told her something about a person, she was anxious to see what kind of car he drove and was not surprised to see a white Chevy Blazer in her driveway. Opening the door for her, he then came around and jumped in the spotless vehicle.

"I really wanted a pickup," he offered without even knowing she was interested in his automobile choice.

"So why didn't you get one?"

"I decided that this better fit the city. I had a truck in high school and I loved it, a 1983 blue GMC. I worked in the oil fields two summers to get enough money to buy it. She was my Baby Blue, my pride and joy."

Faith laughed, "You're almost a cowboy, I've decided."

"Well, I had a horse, too, but after I got my truck, I gave my horse to my little brother because I wasn't riding her anymore and he wanted her." He pulled into an open parking space and quietly announced. "We're here."

The sign announced "The Blue Tortilla" and there were young people in their twenties standing around the door, in the patio and along the curb.

"Popular place," she said.

"Very, one of those yuppie places, but it's really good. Let me give them my name. Would you like a margarita or maybe something else?"

"I would love a margarita."

"Frozen or on the rocks?"

"Rocks, with salt."

He guided her to a corner table in the patio where a couple was just leaving. "We're in luck!" he said, pulling out the chair for her. Within minutes he was back, holding the drinks and balancing chips and salsa on top. "I probably knocked off half the salt from around the rim, but they have great chips so I figured we could munch on them while we waited."

She took the basket from him with one hand and the drink in the other.

"To you and your big case in Boston," he said, touching his glass to hers, causing even more salt to fall.

"Oh, I wish you hadn't brought that up," she said shaking her head and smiling.

"Why?"

"Do you really want to know?"

"Yes, really."

"I'm nervous, scared to death actually. I'm afraid I'll lose, although the case is pretty tight. This kid, he's not really a kid, but he seems like it…well, I don't know what he will do, if we don't win. He's not stable, already attempted suicide once."

"But you have all that you need to put the priest away don't you?"

"On the front end, it's just the kid's word against the priest, but then the fact that the Cardinal paid off the parents, that's a big help, although I'm sure he'll deny it. I've got a deposit record for $25,000, but of course it was cash."

"What kind of witnesses?"

"His therapist, his mother, and the doctor at the hospital where he was taken after his suicide attempt. I've subpoenaed Cardinal O'Leary and the big news is the Judge is going to let me call my dad as a witness. My biggest worry is that with such a large Catholic population in Boston, there'll be bias in the priest's favor and it doesn't help me any that he's seventy-three years old. But then the kid is Catholic too, so I guess it all depends on how many good strikes I get with the jury. I need a few non-Catholics and some Irish luck."

"Are you Irish? Well I guess that's a dumb question; your name is O'Brien."

"My dad is, so I guess I can say I am. I'm not even sure what ethnicity my mom's side of the family is—East Texan," she added, laughing. "That is a nationality, you know."

"So, I hear. Hey, I know you initially went to Boston because of your dad. So what's the story?"

"There aren't enough margaritas in this place to tell that story, but I'll try."

"Okay, but wait a minute. Let's get a couple more. It looks as though we have a wait. I'll be right back. Don't go anywhere," he said with a wink.

Reaching to take her drink from his outstretched hand, she started her story. She was just finishing when they heard "England" on the microphone.

"That's us," Tyler said.

Faith thought, *I like the sound of that.*

"What a menu," she said, looking over the large number of entrée selections. "What ever happened to just enchiladas, beans and rice?"

He laughed, "Yeah, I know what you mean. We have a lot of little family-owned Mexican restaurants in Midland and all of them together don't have this many choices. So, what will it be?"

"I guess the Poncho Villa, although I hope that's not an omen. He lost, didn't he?"

Tyler laughed. "Yes, but he had a good run for a long time before he did. Maybe that's a good sign. Do you want some queso to start?"

"If you'll share."

"Sure. I never think I've had Mexican food if I haven't had chili con queso and pico de gallo."

Talking easily, as if they had known each other for a long time, it was obvious they wanted to know everything about each other. When they finished dinner, Tyler asked if there was anywhere else she would like to go.

"Hey, I'm new here. Remember? I barely know my way to work. Why don't we just go back to my place and visit some more?"

"Sounds like a plan."

When they arrived back, he took the same place on the couch he had earlier, seeming to feel comfortable.

"Faith, I'm going out to Frisco on Saturday to pick a Collie puppy from a litter a client has. Would you ride out with me?"

"I'd love to. What time?"

"I'll pick you up about 11:00. We can have lunch somewhere on the way. It's about an hour drive. Wear shorts or something comfortable."

"Do you have a yard for the puppy?" she asked.

"Yes. I bought a little house two years ago. I just couldn't stand living in an apartment any longer. It was a fixer upper, but I think I can double my money now."

"This area has really become a hot spot hasn't it? My rent's high, but I didn't want to live in an apartment either."

"All my friends still live over at The Village, but that's not what I wanted. It's a village all right, more like a city. Too much going on for me."

He looked at his watch. "I guess I'd better be going."

"Court tomorrow?"

"Yep, probably the rest of the week."

"You can tell me about it Saturday," she said, suddenly depressed that she wouldn't see him until then.

Almost immediately he asked, "Do I have to wait that long to see you?"

"No, I just figured you'd be too busy. I'm not much of a cook yet, but I could do burgers tomorrow night if you like."

"That I would like a lot. What time you want me?"

"Anytime after six. I just need a few minutes after work to run by the store."

"May I bring something?"

"No, I'll take care of everything."

"Okay, if I don't see you at the office I'll see you then," he said, standing. Taking her hand, they walked to the door, where he stopped and put his hand under her chin. Lifting it slightly, he kissed her gently. "I had a great night, Faith."

"Me too, Tyler. I'm already looking forward to seeing you tomorrow night."

He kissed her again, not wanting to leave; he stood there a few minutes before slowly opening the door and saying, "good night." When he had walked halfway down the sidewalk he stopped and turned around to see Faith, still standing in the doorway. Running back, he kissed her again and then walked quickly back to his car. Rolling down the window, he yelled as she still stood in the doorway, "Don't make me come back. Quick, get in the house and shut the door," he laughed.

At that she smiled and closed the door behind her, wishing it weren't after 11:00, so she could call Alice again.

~

Faith didn't see Tyler the next day until he arrived at her duplex. "Hi, long day in court, huh?"

"Very," he said, handing her a bouquet of yellow roses and a bottle of Chardonnay. "I didn't know if you liked wine or not."

"Oh, Tyler, the roses are beautiful. Thank you," she said, and then she kissed him on the cheek. "And I love wine."

"Really, do you really, or are you just saying that?"

"No, I genuinely do. Remember, my dad lived in Italy and he learned about wine there. He's taught me a lot about different wines."

"I'm a beer guy at heart, but I've learned to like wine because that seems to be the politically correct thing to order with clients these days."

"Somehow I figured that," she said, popping the top on a Miller Lite and handing it to him.

"Do you want me to open the wine for you?" he asked.

"Yes, please. I'll get a glass, but first let me get a vase for these flowers, so I can get them in water. You're a sweetheart. You didn't have to bring these, you know."

"I know, but I wanted to… for my yellow rose of Texas," and he blushed slightly. He was wearing khaki shorts and a beige and navy checked shirt, both crisp from the cleaners.

"Do you play golf?" Faith asked.

He looked at her, surprised. "How did you know?"

"You just look like a golfer."

"How's that?"

"I noticed it at the beginning. I don't know. Just the way you carry yourself and your athletic build, but today because of the way you're dressed, you look, especially that way."

"Do you play?"

"I was on the golf team in high school but I haven't played in several years. I did move my old clubs with me here, just in case I ever wanted to play. I figure that's an asset for an attorney."

"Yeah, me too. So, how about we play Sunday afternoon?"

"Promise you won't laugh?"

Tyler said, "No golfer should ever laugh at anybody but himself, because any day can be the bad one. Believe me, I know!"

By now both were sitting on the couch facing each other, Faith with her legs crossed Indian style.

"So tell me about this puppy you're getting."

"One of my clients owns land out in Frisco and has race horses. He also has registered Collies and Border Collies. He called one day about a month ago and asked if I wanted a pup. He knows how much I like dogs, always had one as a kid. So, I thought about it at least a minute and said, yes. It's probably crazy though, as much as I'm gone, but at least she'll have a yard."

"She?"

"I really would prefer a female. My client told me I could have the pick of the litter. It's probably my imagination, but I have always thought girl dogs make better pets and are easier to train, don't dig out, that kind of thing, but like I said, I'm sure there's nothing scientific about that."

After Faith went to the kitchen for another beer and to top off her glass of wine, they sat, talking about the day. "I'd better start the burgers."

"I'll help."

"Okay, but there's not much else to do, I've already chopped the vegetables. We just need to heat the charcoals for the meat." Opening the back door, she pointed to the new red Weber grill in a corner of the small red bricked patio and went to sit in a lawn chair while he lit the fire and then joined her.

"Besides being close to town, I think I chose this place for the trees, drawing his attention to the three large oaks. I wish there were a little grass in the back, but it's probably just as well. The front will be enough to keep."

"They've done this well though, the way they've bricked the patio and also around the trees. It looks fairly maintenance free except watering the boxwoods along the fence," he said.

"No yard is maintenance free to me, but it is worth it to have the trees. Do you want to eat outside?" she asked.

"We might as well. It's not so hot now. Besides this is a perfect place."

After dinner, Tyler helped her clean the dishes and put things away before they crashed on the couch in front of the television. With Faith sitting next to him, Tyler put his arm around her to draw her closer. Within ten minutes they had both dozed off. The chiming of the clock woke him at midnight as David Letterman was signing off. Trying to carefully remove his arm, Tyler realized it felt paralyzed from being in the same position so long.

When he moved, Faith opened first one eye and then the other and smiled.

"I guess we were both tired, huh?"

"Apparently."

He leaned down and kissed her. "I better get out of here quick, or you'll have to kick me out."

Thinking how much she would like for him to stay, she didn't allow herself to say it.

"Another hard day tomorrow?"

"Yes," he said, yawning, "But I think we'll wrap up the trial."

He stood to go, but then stopped. Leaning over he took her hands, pulling her up close. When he kissed her again, it was obvious that he didn't want to leave and that she didn't want him to go.

"Run me off, Faith," he laughed.

"Okay, but I don't want to," she said, taking his hand and walking him to the door.

"Bye. Another great night. I'll call you tomorrow."

"Thanks again for the roses."

"Sure," he said, getting into his Blazer.

After going inside, Faith checked to be sure her alarm was set for 6:30 a.m. Although she hated getting up early, she didn't like to rush getting dressed and she detested being late to anything.

~

Faith need not have worried about oversleeping. A loud ringing at 6:00 a.m. startled her from a deep sleep. Thinking it was the alarm she fumbled with it before she realized it was the phone. She answered sleepily.

"Faith, we know it's early, but we were afraid we would miss you," Patrick said.

"Oh, hi, what's going on? Are you in Italy?"

"Yes, we're at Carmella and Stefano's. Your mother is right here by me. We want to ask you something."

"It better be really good at this time of the morning," she said, laughing.

"Well, we think it is, and we hope you agree. We want to get married," he paused, waiting for Faith to say something.

She sat up in bed, stunned. "You don't need my permission, you know," she said, "but I sure like the idea. So, when's the wedding?"

"That's why we called. We would like it to be in just a few days, but we didn't know how you would feel about not being here. Although we may not need your permission, we certainly want your blessings."

"So, where's it going to be, and who is going to conduct the ceremony? Surely you aren't going to use a priest!"

"We're going to have it here at Carmella and Stefano's. They've encouraged us. Carmella and your mother hit it off immediately. Here, I'll let you talk to her for a few minutes."

"Hi, Faith."

"Mother, are you excited?"

"Oh, words can't describe how I feel. It's been many years, but I never stopped loving him."

"I know, Mother, now tell me about your dress and all that good stuff."

"Are you sure you're okay with this?"

"Yes, yes, now hurry and tell me."

"Carmella and I are going to Florence tomorrow morning to buy everything. Then, your dad and Stefano are coming after lunch so that we can choose a ring. From what Carmella says, the most difficult part will be narrowing down the choices because Florence has such wonderful jewelry. We don't have much time because Carmella wants to get back to help the housekeeper get everything ready for the small ceremony and reception."

"Who will be there? Dad didn't answer me about who is doing the service?"

"There is a civil official nearby who Stefano knows. He'll do the ceremony and they are inviting friends. Patrick knows some of the guests. They assure me that Italians love a good excuse to eat, drink and party, so they'll all show up," she said with obvious excitement in her voice.

"I'll bet the wine will be flowing!"

"Your dad said the same thing. He's about to take the phone away from me. I'll try to call you before all this happens, okay?"

"Okay, I'm happy for you, really happy."

"Thanks, Faith, we both love you very much. Any news there?"

"Not really, nothing that can't wait until all this excitement is over."

"Here's your dad. Good night Hon." Sue handed the phone to Patrick before Faith could respond.

Excitedly, Faith asked, "So you're finally taking the big step. Are you a nervous groom?"

He laughed, "No, but I am excited. This happened pretty fast, although I must admit I had given it hours of thought. When we get back to the States, we'll also have a very small ceremony somewhere there, with a minister and you, just to make it seem complete."

"Sounds great." She wanted to ask him if they were going to live in Maine or what other plans they had made, but she figured those questions could wait. "Good luck finding the ring and all that."

"I don't think your mother will sleep a wink tonight. We wish you could be here, Faith."

"I know, but just enjoy it and take lots of pictures."

"Okay, you get dressed, and have a great day. I am truly happy, Faith, and for that I thank you. Bye for now."

"You deserve to be happy, and so does Mother. You can wake me up with that kind of news anytime. Call me soon." Faith looked down at the tiny promise ring on her pinkie finger that her dad had given her mother so many years before. It was the one thing her mother had left with her in the crib before she fled to the convent. Faith had worn it since Alice gave it to her on her twelfth birthday because it gave her a feeling of connection to her parents during the years she had neither of them in her life. Now, at last, he was going to make good on his promise.

That night, Tyler had a late dinner with a client, but called to tell her good night. "How would you like me to bring over a pizza and a movie after work tomorrow? I'll see you at work, but I just wanted to ask before someone else did."

"You've got a date. I'll try to fight off all those other guys," she laughed.

"Talk to you in the morning. Try to get there a little early and we can have a cup of coffee before things get hectic."

"I'll be there about 7:30."

Their schedules were busy, leaving no time after coffee for them to talk. Although Faith wasn't taking a case until after the trial in Boston, she was researching information Mr. Henry needed for an upcoming class action suit and preparing her opening statements and preliminary questions for the abuse trial.

Mid-afternoon Tyler stuck his head in the door and with a wink announced "See you about 6:30."

~

Pulling her close to him, as they sat on the couch watching the movie *Pure Country*, Tyler told her, "This is one of my favorite movies, probably because I like George Strait and his music so much," he said. "When you get back from Boston, would you go country western dancing with me?"

"Sure, but I need to warn you. I'm not a great dancer; my dancing lessons come from Mom, although she's good, you'll maybe have to help me. I'll probably step all over your feet."

"Do you have boots?" he asked.

"No, in high school some of us went dancing every now and then, and I had a pair of red ropers, but I don't even know what ever happened to them."

"Well, we'll change that. We'll make a trip to Leddy's in Fort Worth and get you fixed up; a girl can't dance country without some pretty boots." He leaned over and kissed her. Before long, it was obvious that it was going further tonight. She stood up, took his hand and led him into her bedroom.

~

Trying not to wake Faith the next morning, Tyler eased out from the covers, taking his clothes into the bathroom to dress. When Faith heard the running water, she glanced at the clock and sat up quickly, forgetting it was Saturday. When she realized she didn't have to go to work, she sank back onto the pillow, closing her eyes to think about their lovemaking.

"Good morning," Tyler said, seeing that she was awake. "I tried to be quiet, but I guess I wasn't, huh?" Sitting on the bed, he leaned to kiss her. "How are you this morning?" he asked softly.

"Wonderful," she answered, smiling.

"You were, last night, as well," he said as he twisted her hair around his finger. "I am going to go home and change. Do you need more than a couple of hours before I come back, so that we can go pick out the puppy?"

"Do I look so bad that you think it will take me two hours?" Faith asked, frowning.

"You look gorgeous, but you might want to wash your face," he said, wiping the smudged mascara from under one eye.

"I'll be ready in an hour. I know you are anxious."

"Okay, I'll see you then," kissing her again.

~

Looking over the chain link fence, Tyler and Faith saw seven bundles of sable and white fur. The mother dog barked as Tyler reached over to pet the heads of two puppies that were jumping the highest to garner his attention. When the owner opened the gate to the large pen all seven puppies ran out, competing for the spotlight.

As Tyler turned to take one in his arms, another one sat and looked up at him with pleading deep chocolate eyes, her ears tipped forward and her head cocked slightly to one side. Reaching to pet her, he noticed the blaze of white stretching from the top of her head to her nose. Her markings were perfect with white around the chest and neck and on her feet and the tip of her tail. A lighter color than the other six, the puppy's fawn coat gleamed in the sunlight.

When Tyler stuck out his hand, she nibbled at it gently and made an ever so slight whimper as if to say, take me. "This is the one," Tyler said, looking up at Faith for approval.

"She's beautiful," Faith said, smiling.

By now, Tyler was holding the puppy that nuzzled into the crook of his arm.

"Then you've got yourself a dog," the owner said, beaming with pride, obviously pleased that Tyler was so happy with his selection. "Have you picked out a name?" he asked Tyler after corralling the other puppies and closing the gate behind him.

"Judge…I am going to call her Judge. Maybe she will listen to me more than those at the courthouse do."

Both men grinned as they walked to the car. "Thank you, Rex. You know I'll treat her well."

Slapping Tyler on the back, he said, "I'm certainly not worried. I know she is going to a good home. Just don't spoil her too much."

Placing the puppy in Faith's lap, Tyler turned to his client and with a wink said, "Now I've got two girls to spoil."

~

As Tyler drove back from Frisco, Judge nibbled first on Faith's fingers and then on the rubber toys she had bought.

"I want to show you my place, so if you like, we can take Judge back and get her acquainted with her new surroundings, and then I'll run to the market for some ribs. I barbecue some mean baby backs."

"That sounds delicious. I'll make some potato salad and baked beans, but I need to stop for the ingredients."

"I'll buy that, too, if you don't mind staying with Judge. First, you have to take the grand tour of my house. We're almost there, Judge," Tyler said, reaching over to pet the puppy's head.

When he turned into the driveway, he smiled broadly. "Well, what do you think so far?" Tyler said, visibly proud of his home and the hours of work he had given to renovate it.

"Tyler, it is wonderful, and so cute. It has the same lines as a few others on the street, but yours is the prettiest of all. Is there a name for the style?"

He grinned. "You aren't biased, are you?"

"No, I'm serious," Faith said, handing Judge to Tyler, who quickly set her on the grass, where she peed for what seemed like ten minutes.

"I think we got here just in time. Bless her heart. She must have held it a long time. Hope that's a good sign, but I doubt it." Faith said, first looking down at the puppy and then to the front of the house.

"I don't think she could have held it much longer," he said, laughing.

Standing in the front yard, Tyler said, "This is called Craftsman Style Bungalow. The one next door is Craftsman Tudor, which is more a combination of these early architectures. My house is older, built in the late 1930s. That one was constructed a few years later. Anyway, you can tell the main difference in these two by the pitch of the roofs and eaves, and of course mine doesn't have the ornate wood," he explained, as Faith studied the one and a half story house with its sloping roof line and wide sheltering overhang.

Supported by tapered, square posts atop stone columns, the over-sized front porch looked every bit an outdoor room, decorated with natural wicker rockers and giant green ferns, overflowing their containers.

"The one thing I couldn't change was the color of the brick. I would have preferred red instead of this sand color, but I really liked the street facing gables and dormers plus the pecan trees. I think the trees are what sold me, along with other aspects," he said, opening the front door of oak and leaded glass to the vestibule.

Surprised, Faith shrieked, "Tyler, did you do all of this?" pointing to the oak floor of the living room and the pecan balustrade along the stairway.

"The floor was here, but it was hidden under worn-out carpet. I had to strip it and refinish the entire downstairs. I don't think the old couple who had lived here since it was built, had ever done anything, except cover the floors. Can you believe they would put wall-to-wall carpet over this? I sanded and re-stained those glass-fronted bookcases and took out all the heavily embossed wallpaper in the dining room and floral paper in the baths. It was gaudy, to say the least."

Faith looked up at the coffered boxed-beam ceilings that gave the room an elegant, yet warm and cozy feel. "The ceilings are beautiful. I love the wood."

Two wooden columns, each less than 12 inches from the walls, were the only structures separating the living and dining rooms so the horizontal emphasis made the rooms feel open and larger than they were. Light flooded in from the large window in the dining room. Yet, the oversized fireplace of rustic river stone, framed by window seats on either side was the focal point.

"I found the wood for the mantle at a flea market. I think it came from an old saw mill that shut down in the 70's, and had been used as a beam at one time. Anyway, I cut the log so that the red heartwood would show and polished it. Then I used the rest of it to make the log supports." He explained, rubbing his hand over the smooth wood.

"They're two small bedrooms down here and one bath or powder room as they called it then," he said, pointing. "I laid the tile and designed it to go half-way up the wall to look like a wainscot. The kitchen is small, but workable. I wish there were room for a larger table, but this is okay for a quick breakfast."

Taking Faith's hand and heading toward the stairway, Tyler said, "I am most proud of the bedroom upstairs." Following close behind them, Judge tried maneuvering the first step, but missed, and landed on her butt. Faith leaned down to help, but Tyler said, "She needs to learn; she'll be okay in a few weeks; she's too little now, but she can keep trying 'til she manages."

Faith gave him a pouty look, but didn't interfere.

Once upstairs, Faith understood his pride as Tyler explained how he had expanded the room at the back and added the small seating areas under the slanted ceiling.

"Did you lay this tile, too?" she asked, pointing to the small white hexagonal floor tiles.

"Yes, and it took me two weekends."

"How long did it take you for the entire renovation?"

"Two years, and that was working nights and most weekends, but I enjoyed every minute of it," he said, leading her down the staircase.

"Tyler, I am so impressed. This is absolutely beautiful. How did you know how to do all of this?"

"Trial and error and lots of reading. I made mistakes along the way and had to tear out a few projects. The poor guy at the hardware store…I drove him crazy with all of my questions." By then they were back on the first floor and Judge was squirming for attention. Tyler reached down and stroked her head. "Good girl. You'll be up those steps in no time." The puppy wiggled with excitement. "Okay, okay," he said picking her up.

"Sucker! You are going to spoil her so bad." Faith said in a teasing manner and with a huge grin.

"Now, you've had the house tour," he said, walking into the kitchen and pouring each of them a glass of iced tea. "Let's go outside so I can show you my brick work on the patio."

"Tyler, you are so lucky to have these oak trees."

"Yes, but there is so much shade, the grass doesn't grow very well. I'm going to try some ground cover, but I just didn't have the time before the weather turned hot."

Noticing the large potted plants, Faith asked, "Did you do these, too?"

Smiling, he said, "I had a little help getting them started. My mother and sister did these and that flowerbed. Do you want to sit out here with Judge while I go to the store?"

"Sure, let me get her toys and I'll play with her until she's tired. She's probably going to miss her mother tonight. I hope you're ready for that."

Winking, Tyler said, "Yes, **we** probably won't get much rest. I did buy a cheap, noisy clock to put in her box so she can hear it tick. That always worked before when I had new puppies."

~

The next three weeks were a flurry of activities for them both, but they found time to be together every night. The night before Faith was to fly to Boston, they went to bed right after dinner, clinging to one another, dreading their separation. Tyler turned on the stereo so they could listen to the sound track from the *Pure Country* movie and they lay together just listening and talking, then making love.

When Judge woke, she began to whimper to be picked up.

"You know, as long as we are moving and whispering, she's going to cry," he said softly.

"Don't you dare stop moving," she said.

He smiled as his hands slid across her breasts. They were much larger than they looked in her clothes and he could not seem to touch them enough.

"You're a boob man, Tyler England."

"They're beautiful. You're beautiful," as he cupped her breasts, touching one and then the other, with his tongue.

When Judge's cries became so loud they drowned out the music, Tyler stood to take her and the box into the den. Faith liked to look at his sleek, nude body in the dim light, as he moved about, remembering their first night in bed when he had been gentle in his foreplay, yet forceful in his entry.

Easing back into bed, he murmured, "Poor Judge, she just doesn't understand that this isn't puppy love." Stroking Faith's hair, he pulled her close, feeling her heart beat.

"She can sleep with you while I'm in Boston, but tonight I don't want to share," tickling his back.

With a sigh he told her how much he would miss her, his breath warm on her face. She kissed him as he turned to cover her body with his.

"You'll have to stop this by sun up you know. Remember, I have to catch a plane."

"Don't talk about it now. I'm trying to forget." His hands were gentle on her, tracing the curves of her body. She trembled as he buried his face between her breasts and then slowly slipped inside her, filling her completely.

~

The thunder woke Faith before the alarm buzzed. Glancing up, she saw Tyler as he placed Judge on the bed. Immediately she tried bounding toward Faith, but her legs tangled in the covers. Faith picked her up, hugged her and then held her high above the sheets.

"If that dog pees in this bed, Tyler, you and she are both dead meat."

He grinned, as he sat on the edge of the bed. "I've been outside with her for ten minutes. She couldn't possibly have another drop inside of her. I should have named her Puddles. She must have held it all night because her box was dry."

About that time she wiggled under the cover and touched her cold nose against Faith's body. Faith yelled in surprise. The fur tickled her skin. "Look, you little ball of energy. I've been pawed most of the night. I don't need anymore," she said, smiling over at Tyler, who by now was lying on his back, holding up the cover with one hand and lightly patting the bed to get Judge to come to him, "here girl, here girl."

Faith moved to push Judge. "Are you calling me or her?"

"I'd rather have you. I've not been pawed near enough." By this time he had Judge propped up on his stomach and was laughing so hard the puppy was bouncing.

"If I'm going to catch an eleven o'clock flight, I'd best get a move on," she said, sliding into her robe. "Is it raining?"

"No, but I'm afraid it will start any minute. The sky is really dark."

"I hate going to catch a plane in the rain."

Tyler set the puppy on the floor and walked over to Faith, putting his arms around her. "I hate you're going anywhere, rain or shine, without me. There really is no sunshine when you aren't here. I'm going to miss you, Faith. I don't want you to go, but I know you have to." He paused. "I love you, Faith O'Brien."

She just stood there looking at him for a minute, tears welling up in her eyes, "Oh, Tyler, I love you so much. I've never felt like this. Before I met you, I never thought I could feel this way, never thought I could love anyone so much."

"I…I guess this is not very romantic, certainly it's not the love story we will want to tell our kids, but I have to know before you leave. Will you marry me?"

Faith put her head onto his chest and started crying, "Yes, Yes, Yes," she repeated.

Chapter 7

As Faith sat on the plane waiting for takeoff to Boston, her thoughts were on Tyler. A month ago flying from Boston to Dallas, she had never even met this remarkable man. Now, she was in love with him and he with her. It had happened so quickly that it seemed everything was in fast motion, her parents getting back together and getting married so soon afterwards, the trial. Everything.

The trial. She must concentrate on the trial. It had been her major focus until she met Tyler, but now she didn't want to leave Dallas. Next week she would be center stage of one of Boston's most talked about trials in years so she would have to be at her best, knowing Stevens would try his best to highlight her lack of experience.

She pulled out her notes and began to study. Although she had spent the last two workdays going over and over the case and Tyler had practiced with her playing the devil's advocate, she knew she could never be prepared enough for what might come her way. This was too important to lose, for her, for her dad and now most of all for Rick.

When she arrived at her hotel room the message light was blinking, and a dozen yellow roses were setting in a crystal vase by her bed. She smiled at what she knew was Tyler's thoughtfulness, but it made her suddenly feel lonely without him. She picked up the phone and pushed the message button.

Immediately she heard, "Hi, I miss you. Judge will be so sad when I get home without you. I love you." And then a loud click. The next message was from Jeff.

"Faith, hi, it's Jeff. Call me when you get in. Maybe we can grab a sandwich or something. Bye."

Frowning slightly, she realized she needed to tell Jeff about Tyler as soon as possible. When she had explained to Tyler about Jeff being the reporter who had helped break the story, Tyler had been understanding about their need to get together often during the trial. "Just don't get too close together," he had teased Faith after she related that she thought Jeff might have a crush on her.

Faith liked Jeff and didn't want to hurt his feelings. As she dialed the newspaper, she brooded over how she would break the news. Getting his answering machine, she left a message. "Hi Jeff, it's Faith. I received your message. I'll be around the hotel awhile. It's about 3:30 now. I just arrived. Had to get a rental car and all, plus that damn tunnel took forever. Call me, please."

Unpacking, she began to think about her mother and dad who would arrive from Europe tomorrow sometime late in the day. Patrick's car was at the airport so she didn't have to pick them up, but she hoped they would call today to let her know when to expect them because she wanted to make a reservation at On the Waterfront to celebrate. Tomorrow was going to be busy since she needed to buy at least another suit and heels and a few incidentals that she hadn't had time to buy in Dallas. As she started making a list, the phone rang.

"Hello."

"Hi, Faith. How are you?" she heard Jeff ask.

"Good, and you?"

"Great, are you game for a burger or some fish and chips?"

"Sure, my treat though. I need to pick your brain so I'll feel better if I pay," Faith told him, wanting their getting together to sound less than a date.

"I don't think that's necessary, but it will be nice to see you."

"Thanks, Jeff. Why don't we meet at Grill 23 about 6:30? That will give me time to do a few things around here."

"Sounds good. See you then."

When she had finished unpacking and writing her "Things to Do" list, the phone rang again.

"Hello...Hello," she repeated. Through the static, she could faintly hear Patrick on the other end.

"Faith?"

"Yes, Dad, talk louder. I'm having trouble hearing you."

"Okay, I'll be quick. Our plane arrives in Boston at 5:45 p.m. Just wanted you to know." The connection cleared.

"I'm glad you called. I was hoping you would. Can y'all meet me at On the Waterfront for dinner or will you be too tired?"

"Sure, we'll try to sleep on the plane. Coming through customs and then getting my car will probably take an hour. You know what a mess Logan is to get in and out of, so it may be 7:30 before we get there."

"No problem. I'll make a reservation for 8:00 and I'll wait in the bar," she said, straining to talk over the returning noise, which was hindering their conversation.

"Okay, your mother was going to talk, but we'll see you tomorrow night. She sends her love."

"Tell her hi. I'll see"...but their connection was broken.

After making the reservation for dinner, Faith decided to take a bubble bath. *What is it about flying that makes a person feel so grungy?*

Stretching out in a tub full of bubbles she thought of Tyler, wondering if he was still at work and what he would do tonight. Selfishly she hoped he might be a little lonesome.

Chapter 8

Jeff was watching for her at the restaurant and the minute he saw her walk in, he jumped to his feet, a big smile on his face. He reached for her, putting his right arm around her waist tentatively. She leaned into him slightly as a good friend might to another who had been away for awhile and then stepped back. Quickly she slid into the booth across from where he had been sitting.

He spoke first, "It's so good to see you, Faith. I've missed you."

"Thanks, Jeff. It's good to be back." She measured her words carefully, not to leave any room for misinterpretation, but almost immediately, seeing his expression, wished she had said something a little more personal if only to make him feel more at ease. "So, how have you been?" she added hastily. She could tell he was a little more guarded now.

"Busy, but okay. How about you?"

"Busy, very busy."

"I'll bet with your new job it's really been hectic. I tried to call a few times."

"I know, Jeff. I got one message shortly before I left and I apologize for not calling you back." She shifted her gaze and then looked him in the eyes. "Jeff, I want to be honest with you. I know we've become friends and I treasure that. I don't want to damage our relationship, but…" she paused and then started again almost as quickly as she had stopped. "I've met a wonderful man, a lawyer in the same firm. We're…we're in love with each other."

Jeff's eyes were wide with surprise and then he made a face as if taking it all in. His voice faltered, "So soon? Didn't you just meet him?" He was caught off balance and it showed.

"Yes, Jeff, it did happen fast, but it's as if we have known each other forever. I can't explain it, and I know it sounds sudden."

After sitting there for a long minute, he reached across the table for Faith's hand. "It's okay, Faith. I think…" he halted and then continued, "I understand. Sometimes a person meets someone and just knows that the person is the one." Before Faith could reply, his voice became more upbeat. "Hey, someday when I'm in Dallas on business, maybe I can meet this lucky fellow," willing himself, Faith thought, to relax.

"I'd like that, Jeff," patting his hand with the hand he wasn't holding. "You're a special person and loving Tyler doesn't change my feelings for you as a friend."

He smiled and took his hand away. "Okay, now that we have that out of the way, how about a drink?"

"I thought you'd never ask," she winked.

"What will it be?" Jeff asked, now sitting straighter in the booth, looking slightly more in control.

"I think I'll have a Cosmopolitan."

"That's a switch from wine," as he motioned to the waiter who had been watching them from around the corner, not wanting to disturb their serious conversation. "The lady will have a Cosmopolitan and I'll have a Scotch straight up." He looked at Faith, shaking his head and smiling, "There, I've gone and ordered for you again. Now I'm in real trouble."

She smiled broadly and exhaled, glad that the mood was lighter. "Scotch, straight up? I didn't think you were that big of a drinker!"

"Tonight seemed like a good time to start," he teased, but Faith knew he was trying to put on a good face.

"Did I tell you my parents married while they were in Europe? That sounds funny doesn't it, my parents getting married?"

"My, this has been a busy few weeks for you and your family. So, tell me about it."

Faith sank back more comfortably in her seat and began telling Jeff the saga. When the server brought their drinks, she took a sip of the cool reddish liquid and held it in her mouth. "Mmm," she swallowed. "That's good. I propose a toast to the big trial." As soon as their glasses clinked, she went back to her story. Before she finished, Jeff ordered each of them another drink. As conversation came easier, they laughed more. Faith was glad the tension had lifted and they could enjoy each other's company like they had their first night together.

When Jeff showed her clippings of a news article about the upcoming trial, their talk shifted to case strategies and expectations. Finishing their Lobster Newburg, Faith frowned. "I think I'm going to have to call it an early night. The plane ride and everything made me a little tired," but she didn't add that she had been awake most of the night before, lying in Tyler's arms, making love.

"I understand, but I'm really glad you agreed to meet me." He waved to the server to request a check.

"Oh, no you don't Jeff," as she reached to put his hand down. "I told you that this was my treat."

"Yes, well, you've told me a lot tonight so this is my way of saying, congratulations on your new life. I'm getting this. I think I'll stay and have another Scotch, but let me first walk you out."

"Jeff, are you sure you'll be all right going home. I mean, you don't usually drink this much."

"I'll be fine," he said, standing up. "See, I can walk," as he took a step.

"Jeff, I can get to my car just fine. Thank you for a wonderful evening." She reached over and glanced his cheek with a kiss. "Are you going to be at the trial on Monday?"

"I wouldn't miss that performance for anything."

"Okay, I'll see you then and thanks for being so understanding, Jeff."

"Sure, no problem," He said, his voice trailing off as he started to sit back down.

Walking toward the door, Faith turned around briefly to wave, but Jeff never saw her because his elbows were on the table, hands cupped around his head.

Chapter 9

Faith woke early Saturday morning to the ringing of the phone and the sound of Tyler's voice. She had tried to reach him the night before when she arrived back at the hotel, but there was no answer. "I was worried about you. I called until I fell asleep," she told him immediately after he said good morning to her.

"I should have left you a message, but I left in such a hurry, I forgot. When I went home, I felt empty so I threw a few things in a bag, picked up Judge and her bed and took off to Midland. I haven't been here to see my parents in awhile so I thought this would be a good time. So, that's where I am."

"Good. I'm glad you're there. I know they'll enjoy that."

"I've already told them about you, Faith."

"Oh, and what did you tell them?"

"Just that you are beautiful, witty and…"

"And what?"

"Well, I stopped short of saying sexy. They don't need to know everything."

She laughed. "Good, I want to start out on the right foot."

"My dad said, 'a new girl and a new dog all in the same month. Aren't you taking on a lot in a short time?' But he was smiling the whole time he said it. They're going to love you, Faith, almost as much as I do."

"Tell them I'm anxious to meet them. I love you, Tyler, and miss you."

"Did I wake you?"

"I was lying here in a fog, you know in that zone of almost awake, almost asleep. But, I'm glad you called because I need to get out of bed and dressed. I've several errands today, shopping, you know."

"Oh, I know," laughing loud enough for Faith to hear.

"So, what are you doing today?"

"I think I'll help Dad around the yard. Mom's wanted him to trim a mesquite tree that she hates. I'll do that and while I have the saw out we might as well go out to their little farm outside of town and cut some wood for their fireplace. It'll start getting cool here before I get back."

"Sounds like a work day for you."

"Yes, but I'll enjoy it, being outside and all and visiting with Dad. Judge will have some wide open space to run…"

"I miss her, Tyler. I have to admit I've gotten used to her whiskers tickling my face."

"What about my whiskers?"

"I miss everything about you, Tyler. I told Jeff about us last night."

"And?"

"I could tell he was a little upset, but he was sweet about it."

"How sweet?"

"Oh, you know what I mean," she said, trying to sound exasperated but smiling into the phone. "Will you call tonight?"

"Sure, when would be a good time?"

"I'll probably be back here by 10:00 or so. I know Mother and Dad will be tired. Just keep trying, okay, and remember it's an hour later here."

"Okay, be careful running around Boston today, and remember, I love you."

"You be careful with that chainsaw. I like your hands, you know."

"Bye, Faith."

"Bye, Love, talk to you tonight."

Faith stood by the phone for a few minutes after she hung up, just thinking about Tyler. Quickly, she showered and dressed.

~

Within minutes Faith discovered that both Newberry Street and Copley Square Mall were everything she had read and heard about as she walked from one pristine, upscale store to another, stopping at quaint little boutiques along the way. After only two hours she had found two suits, with lingerie and hose, three pairs of shoes and a pair of simple earrings. Her feet hurt from walking, so at one o'clock she stopped at one of the many small sidewalk cafes for lunch. After a salad and soup, she was ready to tackle a few more shops when she spotted The Pampered Pooch in the next block and decided to look for Judge a present. Immediately, she thought it was good that Tyler wasn't with her. He would have bought a lot more than a collar made of bandana fabric with leather trim that could be adjusted as the dog grew.

Inside the mall, Faith was like a kid in a candy store, shopping in trendy stores she had been intimidated by before she had her own job. Looking at her watch, she realized she was running out of time and money and was far from finished. She knew Tyler would admonish her for spending so much on him, but she bought him a Mont Blanc pen, a pair of Ray Bans and an Armani shirt and had each wrapped separately at a kiosk in the center of the mall. Needing to find something special for Alice, she hurried into Caché where she selected a pale blue silk gown and robe. While she studied the listing of stores at the information center to determine the best place for a wedding gift, a young woman standing near, noticed her quizzical look and asked Faith if she needed help finding something. After Faith explained that she was searching for the perfect wedding gift, the woman quickly pointed to Artful Hand Gallery.

"They have beautiful hand blown crystals, sculptures and wonderful gifts," she volunteered. Thanking her, Faith trudged forward, her arms again full of packages, although she had unloaded several shopping bags on an earlier trip to the rental car.

The store was, indeed, full of artistic treasures and Faith looked for almost an hour before settling on a pair of white doves on an ivory base as a gift for her mother and dad. She thought the piece was refined and simple, graceful, and a symbol of the feelings they must have shared deep down for each other all these many years.

It was almost six o'clock when Faith reached the hotel. She would have to hurry to freshen up and get to the restaurant. Slipping into the warm bath water she felt good as she leaned back against the tiled tub. Another minute or two and she might have dozed, but the phone startled her from her daydreaming. It was the desk clerk calling to say she had a gift at the front desk.

"Who is it from?" she asked.

"I don't know, ma'am. He didn't leave his name. A young man probably, in his late twenties. He said just to give it to you when you came in. I guess I missed you as you passed the desk. Shall I send it up?"

"Sure, but could you give me about fifteen minutes?"

"Not a problem. I'll send it by a bellman then."

Who could a gift be from, Faith wondered, out loud. Stepping out of the shower onto the plush mat she allowed the water to drip for a minute as she wrapped herself in the oversized velvety soft towel. She hurried to put on the hotel terrycloth robe and began freshening what little make-up she wore when she heard the knock on her door.

"Bellman."

When she opened the door, the young hotel attendant handed her a small package, wrapped in bright red paper, no bow or ribbon. Thanking him, she handed him a small tip.

Who could this be from? she asked herself again. *Certainly it wasn't in fancy paper, but maybe Jeff had sent something. It looked like something a man might have wrapped, but Tyler had already sent flowers.* She opened the envelope, which contained only a card with the word "careful" scrawled on it. Thinking it was referring to the contents of the box, she cautiously lifted the paper, gingerly opening the top flap. *Well, whatever it is must be small. All I see or feel is tissue.* By now she was beginning to grow more curious, and a little concerned. Finally, feeling something cold with a hard edge, she felt a tiny gold bent cross attached to a string of black beads with a note reading, "Say your prayers" in the same scrawl as the card in the envelope. Only half of the beads appeared to be together, as one lone bead fell out of the tissue. "*What did all this mean?*" A tingle went up her back. Though knowing she was being threatened, she had no idea who was behind it or what the symbolism of it meant. She knew enough, however, to know it was sinister.

She needed to talk to someone, but whom? She didn't want to dare say anything to her mother and dad and risk putting a damper on their homecoming or to alarm Tyler. Even though it was time to leave for the restaurant and she doubted he would be in his office, she took a minute and dialed Jeff.

"Hello."

"Oh, Jeff. I'm so glad you answered. I didn't really think you'd be there."

"Hi, Faith. Yes, I have a lot to do since I'll be out of the office next week covering the trial. Why the call? You sound in a hurry or something."

"Jeff, you have to promise me that you won't share this with anyone."

"What are you talking about, Faith?"

"Promise, Jeff. I mean this is important!" she rushed.

"Sure, Faith, what is it?" noticing something almost frantic in her voice.

Hurriedly, she described what happened and the contents of the box. "I don't want to make any big deal out of this Jeff, but I just needed to talk to someone."

"I'm glad you told me, Faith," trying to put the pieces together. "I think whoever did that is definitely serious. You need to be really careful. Maybe they're trying to get you to quit before the trial begins. Let me do some checking around to see if I can hear what's going on with those close to the priest, but everyone's been awfully tight-lipped lately."

Faith laughed for the first time since she received the box. "Love your choice of words. Too bad the old pervert didn't keep his lips tight before."

Laughing to lighten her mood, Jeff was worried. "You always find the humor, Faith, but this isn't a laughing matter. Please be careful. I'll call you tomorrow. Will your parents be staying at the same hotel?"

"Yes, right next door."

"Good, at least that helps."

"But, I'm not telling them about this tonight."

"I understand, but you are going to tell them, aren't you?"

"Probably, but I haven't decided. How do you think someone knew where I was staying? No one here knew my flight, hotel or anything."

"Maybe someone called all the major hotels downtown, but that's a lot of hotels or maybe someone was staked-out at the airport" he admitted. "I don't know yet, but I'm going to work on this, Faith. Try not to worry, but please look over your shoulder."

"I'll talk to you tomorrow, and thanks for listening, Jeff."

"Anytime, Faith. You can call me anytime."

Faith knew he meant it.

Shaking slightly, but beginning to regain composure, she asked the desk clerk to describe the delivery person.

"I told you all I remember about him. Just a young guy a little, unkempt. Was there not a card, ma'am?" he looked at her, incredulously.

"Well, yes, but I'm afraid he didn't sign his name. I just wanted to know whom to thank, so if he should come back would you try to get a better description? The delivery person and the giver may not be the same, but perhaps I can make some connections."

"Certainly, and I'll make a note to the other desk clerks if I am not here."

"That would be nice. Thank you," she said as she walked toward the parking garage, feeling more than a little unsettled.

Chapter 10

Faith rushed through the restaurant door and stopped. Her parents, the newlyweds, were perched on tall metal bar stools looking on top of the world, leaning in toward each other, whispering, smiling, separated only by their martini glasses and the glow of the flickering candle. Looking around the room, she saw men in dark suits standing huddled over smartly dressed women sitting at the long cherry wood bar. A steady hum of conversation was interrupted only by occasional, spontaneous laughter. Other couples sat at the tall round tables that lined the wall of windows overlooking Boston Harbor, the lights from the boats and a last quarter moon reflecting on the smooth dark waters. She glanced again at her parents just as they noticed her. Patrick jumped to his feet and embraced her. Faith leaned over and kissed her mother on the cheek.

"Hi, I'm so sorry I'm late. Boy, do y'all look like two happy people!"

"We are, indeed, Faith," Patrick said, bending to take her hand and then Sue's.

"Now I have my two girls with me. I hope you didn't mind, but we went ahead and ordered drinks."

Faith seemed not to even hear him as she turned to Sue. "Oh Mother, I'm sorry. I was just so glad to see you, I forgot about your ring." Taking Sue's hand in hers she said, "It's beautiful, really beautiful."

"I wanted a plain gold band, but your dad insisted on the three diamonds, one for each of the three of us. It is perfect, isn't it?" her eyes glowing, a look of total contentment in a smile that reinforced the beginnings of tiny lines around the mouth.

Faith couldn't help but notice and think about the years Sue had waited for this ring. She started to say something about the wait, hesitated and sighed, "It is perfect. Now tell me about the wedding."

Before Sue could answer, Patrick broke in. "Hope this champagne is okay with you, I told him to bring it as soon as you arrived."

As the server approached the table with three fluted glasses and a bottle of champagne in a crystal wine bucket, Faith said, "I don't think I'll complain," noticing it was Cristal. She remembered that Patrick's first wife had a cat named Peri after her favorite champagne, Dom Pérignon and was glad he hadn't ordered it. She shifted her gaze to the door.

"Are you all right, Faith?" Patrick asked.

"Oh…sure," she protested. "I've just been running all day. You know how I hate to be late."

He shook his head, "Just wanted to be sure; you just act a little edgy or something."

"Nonsense, I'm just frazzled. I'm so glad you're back. Now, am I going to hear about the wedding or not? And, how about pictures?"

Sue reached for her oversized purse. "Okay, you asked for it," she said, laughing and pulling out a bundle of photographs.

"I almost had to get a loan to get all those developed before we left Italy, but we didn't want to wait," Patrick said.

"I love your wedding dress. Did you get this in Florence?"

"We bought everything in Florence. You should have seen Carmella and me rushing from place to place. There are so many choices and everything is splendid."

Patrick interrupted, "I hate to bother you two, but I'd like to make a toast."

"Oh, I should be doing that," Faith said quickly as she held up her glass. "To promises kept. Congratulations and many happy years together." Just as she sat down her glass she handed Sue a tiny box. "I think you should have this back now. It was special to me for many years because that's all I had of yours. Now it's time for it to be returned." Inside was the tiny promise ring Patrick had given her when they were teenagers. A tear ran down Sue's face as she stared at the ring, unable to speak.

"It's okay, Mother. You have the ring and you have him. Sometimes a promise takes a while to be fulfilled. What counts is that it is."

Patrick looked at Sue and smiled. "I can't think of a better toast. To promises kept, indeed."

Tears welled in all their eyes. Faith grabbed the photographs, overcome with emotion and continued to sort through them, asking question after question. When she came to the one with Sue placing Patrick's ring on his finger, she stopped. "I'm sorry, Dad, I didn't even think about your ring."

He stuck out his hand and shrugged, "Just chips, couldn't afford anything else after your mother's," he said, winking, teasing Sue.

His was a yellow gold band with three smaller diamonds that matched Sue's. Although Faith had never seen him wear his earlier wedding ring, she had seen photos and knew it was platinum. *He's doing everything different. I'm glad about that.*

"Not bad, not bad, but I'm more interested in the rest of the wedding," she said turning back to Sue and the pictures. Patrick made a mock frown and took a sip of his champagne.

By the time Faith had looked at all the photographs and drank two glasses of the champagne, she was feeling less tense. "What are your plans, now?" Faith asked, looking first at Patrick and then to Sue.

His forehead wrinkled slightly and then he said, "First we're going to be here until the end of the trial, maybe see some of the sights on the weekends. When that's over, Sue is thinking about going to Dallas and looking for a house for us while I go back to Hidden Harbor, put the house up for sale and officially resign from the church. I'm not sure how long all that will take."

"Did you say Dallas?" Faith asked in astonishment.

"Can you believe I'm getting him back to Texas?"

"Well, but at least it's a city, not some…never mind," he countered, making a face while he reached over to pinch Sue's cheek.

"But what will you do in Dallas?" Faith's eyes were wide. She was obviously glad about their decision but surprised.

"I've applied at Southern Methodist University for a professorship in their theology department. I saw the opening when I went over to Harvard to see Dr. Mata. I didn't think much about it then, but when I saw Sue, I went back and checked on it and it was still open. When we decided to marry, I called about it from Italy. Fortunately, I have a few connections so they want me to fly down for an interview, but I told them I couldn't until the trial is over."

"Why don't you fly Monday? Nothing will get going for a day or so. Besides, you can miss some, it doesn't matter."

"No, Faith. I have to be here. Remember this is all about me. You wouldn't be doing this if it weren't for me."

Sue looked at Patrick. "But Patrick, you really should go. I'll stay here with Faith."

"I'll call you as the next to last witness. That can't possibly be until the middle of the week or later. Is there anyone you can call tomorrow to set something up for Monday?"

Patrick thought for a minute. "I have the Dean's name. Maybe I could call him. I know they want to settle this soon so the person they hire can start second semester."

"I don't want to put a damper on your plan, but what happens if this doesn't work out? I mean, you might even decide you don't want that job," Faith inquired.

"We're moving to Dallas either way. There are plenty of opportunities there, though probably not as a Congregational minister."

"Sounds great to me," Faith said without hesitation.

"Are you ready for your table?" the server asked.

"Yes. I think everybody is hungry," Patrick said, eyeing Faith and Sue.

In all the other excitement, Faith had forgotten about the mysterious package until she stood up. Looking around quickly, she followed her mother into the dining area, feeling good that Patrick was behind her. She knew she had to shrug this off because she didn't want to be thinking about it during the trial.

When they were seated, Faith started talking immediately. "I have a little bit of news myself."

Patrick and Sue looked at each other. "Well, let's hear it," Patrick nudged.

"I've met the guy I'm going to marry."

Now it was their time to look amazed. "Tell us, Faith. I'm dying to know," Sue encouraged.

For the next five minutes Faith described Tyler, and how they had hit it off from the start.

"So, when do we get to meet Mr. Right?" Patrick teased.

"I guess as soon as we get back to Dallas."

"How long do you think this trial will last, Faith?"

"I'm hoping it will go fast. Who knows? I think a week and a half at the max."

"That's not so bad," Patrick offered.

Faith frowned. "Easy for you to say."

Patrick nodded. "Yes, I'm sorry you have to do this, Faith."

"I'm not, not one bit. I do miss Tyler, but I want to nail this guy," determination and resolve in her voice.

After their meal, when Patrick asked about dessert, they declined, admitting to being tired and ready to retire. "Guess we do have a little jet lag, huh Sue?"

"I have more than a little jet lag! I didn't notice it until I ate. I'm sleepy."

"I'll check in and then you can take your small bag and get started for bed. I'll go get the other bags after that. Why don't you ride with Faith and I'll follow you."

Faith was glad to have her mother's company and even more relieved that her dad was following them.

~

Faith woke up early Sunday morning and couldn't get Tyler off her mind. They had talked on the phone for more than an hour last night and she missed having him by her in bed. She thought how quickly she had grown used to him, how perfectly she fit, her back curved against his taut stomach as they fell asleep. They had talked about wedding plans and agreed they wanted something simple, maybe right before Christmas. With a new job and so much going on in her life, it was going to be important to have as little further complication as possible, and she was happy that Tyler felt the same.

When she had told him about the package, its note and contents, he was obviously concerned, reminding her over and over to be cautious. Though she was not easily intimidated, this had frightened her, probably because of what it didn't say, more than what it did. Knowing she must get focused, after her shower, she dressed and took out her notes for the trial.

The only break Faith allowed herself during the day was to have a brief lunch with Patrick and Sue in order to give them their wedding present. Handing the gift to Sue, she said, "I didn't really have any good ideas as to what to get y'all. I mean you both have everything in terms of household things. I wanted it to be just something special, commemorating your getting back together."

"You didn't need to do anything, Faith. Come on Sue, open it," Patrick said, turning to her.

"It's beautiful," Sue said, and as she read the card she started to cry.

"Don't start that or you'll have us all doing it," Faith said, quickly.

"Read this, Patrick. You'll see why I'm crying." She handed him the card and he began reading:

The moon is high, the tide low,
A gentle breeze is blowing,
So many years have gone
It seems their youthful pledges overslept.
The days have a way of passing,
Alternately fast and slowly,
Just when we cease to ask,
We find: promises kept...
Love, Faith

"Yes, I understand." Patrick chimed in as tears gathered in his eyes. "This is truly special, Faith. You're truly special. Did you write this? I didn't know you wrote poetry."

Faith smiled, a little embarrassed. "Seeing you two together just reminds me of poetry. I try my luck at it every now and then—a little creative outlet. Hey, I've got to get back to work." She stood to leave as they both wiped their eyes.

"Can you wait just five more minutes?" Without waiting he rushed on, "We both forgot to tell you this last night. There was so much to tell. As a wedding present Carmella and Stefano gave us 65 hectares of their land, which is equivalent to about 160 acres in the United States. The landscape is beautiful, but one of the most unbelievable things about it is that it has the huge olive tree where I sat and thought about your mother on my first trip there. I'll never forget how I felt that day. And now all these years later it is our tree, together," he said, taking Sue's hand and leaning to kiss her.

"Enough of that stuff," Faith teased. "But what will you do with it? I mean you're thousands of miles away. It's not like you can go for the weekend."

Patrick laughed. "Leave it to you. We'll spend some time there in the summers probably and maybe even half of the year when I retire. We really don't know yet. I think Carmella and Stefano wanted to be sure we would visit often. They're getting up in years. Stefano would love for me to take over everything, but I told him I could never do that. Although he's slowing down, he still has Enrico to help."

"What about their daughter and her husband?"

"They will never leave Milan, Carmella and Stefano said, but they have designated the remainder of everything, about 130 hectare and the main house, in their will to Elisabette. They have also given 65 hectares to Enrico and Claudia."

"We were so touched with their generosity. They didn't even know me and they still gave it to us," Sue added.

"They fell in love with you instantly," Patrick said, turning to Sue. "You and Carmella hit it off like two little girls sharing ice cream!"

"Speaking of, Faith, the gelato in Italy is so delicious. You wouldn't believe it."

"Well, I hope someday to know first hand."

"We hope so, too. Soon!"

"The best part...I haven't been able to finish this story, is that it even has a bungalow on the property. Maybe someday we can add to it. It's small, but it is very nice with a magnificent view of the Tuscan landscape. We're so anxious to get back, but it may be awhile. I need to make some money, I'm afraid," he said, frowning. "I certainly hope, if I do get the position at SMU, that I will be able to continue some of my speaking engagements."

"I'm really happy for you both. You didn't take photos of the place?"

"We did, but we still have a few rolls to be processed and those are on one of them. Hopefully, I will have a chance to take those somewhere this week," Sue answered.

"Put them in your purse and if we see a photo shop, we'll stop," Patrick told Sue. "You can get back to your prep for tomorrow, Faith. We just had to tell you. And thank you so much for the figurine and the poem." He kissed her on the cheek and then hugged her tightly.

Sue rose and drew Faith close. "Thanks for everything, Faith. You are the most wonderful daughter anyone could ever even dream of having."

~

Around 9:00 p.m. the phone rang but no voice came on the line. Three times the same thing happened, but on the fourth time a voice came on the line: "I'll be watching you tomorrow," and then click. Faith put down the receiver. *Whoever this is isn't going to give up,* Faith thought, *but we've waited for this a long time so neither am I.*

When she slipped between the cool sheets and reached to turn off the lights, she felt a chill, alone with her thoughts and fears.

Chapter 11

Jury selection took the entire day and as soon as they were seated, Judge Ford recessed. Tired, but relieved that this process was over, Faith felt good about the jury of seven women and five men plus two alternates, both women. The pool included a teacher, stockbroker, fireman, nurse, two retail managers, and a day care worker, along with a computer analyst, real estate salesperson, used car salesman, sales clerk and a bartender. Faith had used one of her strikes on a retired woman who appeared to be in her late sixties, fearing that her age might make her sympathetic to the aging priest and another for a church secretary. Nine of the twelve were Caucasian, two African American and one Asian. The majority were in their forties and fifties, except the bartender who had recently turned thirty.

The trial was scheduled to start at nine o'clock the next morning. Faith had heard that Judge Ford was a stickler about punctuality and noted he had warned the jury about this at least three times. She was always early wherever she went, but she wondered about Stevens, who moved at a snail's pace. She hoped he would be tardy just once and maybe give her an edge.

Returning to her hotel room, she noticed Tyler had left two messages. Anxious to talk with him and tell him about her day, she called him at home. When he finally answered, he was out of breath.

"Hi. I was outside feeding Judge. I thought I heard the phone. Anyway, I ran. Guess I'm not in as good a shape as I thought. So, how did it go?"

Faith provided a play by play, describing every juror, leaving out no details of the day. "I wish you could see Stevens. He is so gross. He had on the same stained leisure suit he wore when I met him and it wasn't any prettier today and certainly no more pressed."

After listening to Faith and asking questions about the Judge, Tyler's voice turned more serious. "Faith, I asked Linda if anyone had called for you in regards to where you were staying. At first she said no, but remembering a reporter had called last week, she checked her records, which showed the call came in on Wednesday. You said it couldn't have been Jeff, because he knew where you would be staying, but do you think it could be someone at the paper who heard him and perhaps sent that package?"

"Tyler, I really don't think it was anyone from the paper. Maybe someone took his name from a byline from one of his stories on the trial."

"Linda knew I wasn't too happy about her giving out that information, but she just kept saying she knew from what you had told her, the reporter was a friend, assuming it was okay. I told her if anyone else called for you she was to transfer them to me."

"It's okay. Tell her, will you? Whoever is doing this would have found me one way or the other. I think he is following me. I just had that feeling when mother and I drove into the garage. I saw a truck circling the garage but I didn't get a description of the driver. It may be my imagination, but I was glad Mother was with me anyway."

"Faith, maybe you should not park there. Is there valet parking?"

"I'll check, but maybe I'm just paranoid. I'll be careful, Tyler."

"Well, check on that. If nothing else, arrange for the bellman to park it. Would you do that for me, please, Faith?"

"Okay. Now tell me about your day," Faith said, trying to change the subject.

When they had talked for more than half an hour, Tyler wished her luck for the following day.

"Give Judge a big kiss for me."

"What about me?"

"Tyler, I send you my love a thousand times."

"Not enough, but a good start. Bye for now."

"Bye."

Faith called Jeff first at his apartment, but after no luck, tried the newspaper office. "Jeff?"

"Oh. Hi, Faith. I'm glad you called, because I wanted to know about the jury selection."

"We finished, and start the real thing tomorrow morning at 9:00, but I also wanted you to know someone is probably using your name to get information about me." She explained about the call to her secretary and the story Tyler had relayed.

"I am really sorry about that, Faith."

"It's no one's fault. It just comes with the territory. The crazies come out with trials."

"This isn't just any trial either; this is the biggest trial Boston has seen in years. You really need to be extra careful, Faith. Don't get careless. Okay? I wish I could say it was me so you wouldn't worry, but it seems someone is determined to scare you off." There was obvious worry in Jeff's voice and it caused her to shiver.

"Yeah, I'm afraid you're right."

"I had to leave early. I guess you know that, though. My pager kept going off. Lots of things going on so I had to get back here," Jeff added.

"I did notice, but I figured it was pretty boring today for you."

"I'll be there in the morning though, expecting lots of action," he remarked.

Faith laughed. "We'll see. I'm a little nervous."

"You'll do great. Faith, please be careful and don't let down your guard. Thanks for calling. See you tomorrow."

"Thanks, Jeff. Maybe I had better say my prayers. Later. Bye."

~

Tuesday dawned cool and gray. *I hope this is not any indication of the way my day or the trial is going to be,* Faith thought as she stepped out of her car at the courthouse.

She had rehearsed her opening statements so many times she couldn't count them and had them timed down to the second. Fifteen minutes wasn't much time to say what she wanted to get across to the jury, but that's all she was allotted. Stevens talked less than ten minutes.

Feeling relieved when the opening comments were finished, Faith called her first witness: Rick McGee's therapist, who was poised and articulate, a good witness, Faith thought. She didn't talk too much, which was always a fear, and she came across intelligent and caring. Stevens asked very few questions under cross-examination, which surprised Faith. Rick's mother was the next witness, and although Faith had some concerns since Mrs. McGee was timid and withdrawn, this was Faith's chance to introduce information about the payoff from church officials. Stevens tried his best to show that the bank statement proved nothing, stressing there were no cancelled checks, or paper trail. Still the statements from the testimony were on the record and the jury was aware of them.

Faith watched the panel carefully, making an effort to analyze expressions, body language, any movements that might indicate an opinion or thought by any juror. Most she couldn't read, their emotions in check, but the daycare worker, a pleasant rotund middle-aged woman frowned several times during Stevens' questioning and once, Faith noticed tears welling up in her eyes as Mrs. McGee described the changes in Rick's behavior. The woman had a sweet face and wide hips that looked as if they might easily hold a baby if one needed carrying. Faith hoped that because of her job, this juror would be sympathetic, an advocate for children.

Faith was especially interested in the demeanor of a female stockbroker who would become the jury foreperson and who both days looked like a fashion statement from Vogue Magazine. Today she wore a long wool skirt of bold plaids, a blazer and high heel suede boots. Her shoulder length hair was pulled back loosely. High cheekbones accented her dark, almond eyes that were now squinting behind round tortoise shell glasses. Her lips were pursed and her eyes flashed as she watched Stevens move closer to Mrs. McGee. Faith scanned the others' faces. The real estate broker, a balding, sixty-something man with bushy eyebrows, beady eyes and a full mouth never changed his expression, and the computer analyst looked lost in some high tech dream world.

The next witness, Cardinal O'Leary, had been subpoenaed to testify and Faith was anxious to see how he was going to maneuver out of her questions, or if he would perjure himself. But, before he took the stand Judge Ford recessed for the day, leaving Faith's curiosity waiting. Driving home from the courthouse, she looked in her rear view mirror and knew she was being followed.

Back at the hotel garage she again noticed a guy in an old green Ford pickup drive through and stop, but when he saw Patrick get out of his car four spaces down he drove on. Because Patrick had flown in a few minutes before the court recessed and arrived at the courthouse just as Sue and Faith were leaving, Faith had insisted her mother ride with him to learn how the Dallas visit had gone. She was glad he was here now.

~

The morning of day three brought no real surprises. The Cardinal, indignant in his manner, did what Faith had guessed and said the Archdiocese paid Rick not because they thought the priest was guilty, only because they didn't want negative publicity. There wasn't much Faith could do to his story, and she thought it best not to come down too hard on him, expecting it could backfire.

When she called Patrick to testify, the Judge gave special instructions to the jury, explaining cautiously, "the defendant is not charged with committing any crime other than those specified in the indictment, which I read to you at jury selection and that will be submitted to you at the end of this case for a verdict. As you hear mention of any other acts allegedly done by the defendant, you may not consider such evidence to demonstrate the defendant's propensity to assault boys sexually or substitute it for proof that the defendant has a criminal personality, bad character or who has an inclination toward criminal conduct."

The Judge continued, "You may consider the testimony as permissible to show a pattern, a course of conduct, a modus operandi, a common scheme or plan and to corroborate the plaintiff's testimony. You may not use it to conclude that if you determine the defendant assaulted another that it must inevitably follow he committed the same with the plaintiff."

Stevens had strongly contended at the pretrial hearing that Patrick's allegations were not sufficiently similar, too remote in terms of time and that the prejudicial effect outweighed the probative value. Judge Ford had not been swayed.

Though Faith had won on her request for Patrick's testimony, she had not convinced the Judge to allow the arresting officer to testify about the pornography found in the priest's house. Judge Ford referred Faith back to the wording on the indictment and suppressed her claim that this too showed a pattern.

Sitting tall and straight in the witness chair, Patrick looked relaxed, controlled and distinguished, Faith thought. His once auburn hair had turned a spicy nutmeg, a tinge of gray around the temples, but his eyes were the same brilliant blue she remembered when she first met him. Earlier in the morning, he had been so pleased and touched when he walked into the courtroom to find all of his brothers and sisters waiting for him, especially his sisters who he had feared would be angry with him for going forward. Their presence and Sue's support gave him needed resolve.

Faith had purposely not practiced with Patrick, feeling certain that he had prepared this moment in his head for years. Whatever he said, however he said it was what he needed to do, because this was more about his healing than winning a case or putting someone behind bars.

In order to counter concerns a juror might have about her relationship to Patrick, which Faith knew Stevens would bring up in cross-examination, she quickly asked Patrick if he were serving as a witness on his own free will. Next, she asked him to explain the statute of limitations as he understood it and reminded him that he was under oath, as a simple precaution, to reiterate the integrity of his testimony.

"Dr. O'Brien, will you please tell the court your occupation, age and place of residence," Faith began.

Patrick's voice was strong and steady and he looked at the jury when he spoke.

"Would you please tell the jury how long you have known the defendant and what that relationship was," Faith implored.

Patrick relayed his family's ties with the priest and how much his parents had loved and trusted him, and how he had once felt the same.

"What happened then to change those feelings?"

Patrick turned and shifted his gaze to the priest who now was looking at the floor. "He robbed me of my innocence, he changed my life when he came into my pup tent and touched me in places he should not have touched and had me do the same to him."

"And how old were you then?"

"I was ten."

"Why did you not go to your parents or someone about this?"

"We had a family that Norman Rockwall could have painted. You'll notice there aren't any monsters in his paintings, and I grew up with parents who didn't believe there were any monsters in the Catholic Church, certainly not Father Michael. I was afraid that they wouldn't believe me, or even worse, that they would blame me and not him. It took a lot of years to realize that bad things happen to the innocent, sometimes."

"So, why now?"

"Grief and acceptance have their own timing. When my father died, I was no longer worried about hurting anyone. Plus, I made a promise that when that time came I would come forward."

"So, how over the years did this abuse affect you?"

"Objection, Your Honor. That is irrelevant to this case."

"Your Honor, I am trying to show that when young people suffer from this type of abuse, there are lasting effects and those effects trickle down, causing hurt not just to the victim but others who are associated."

"Overruled, but please be brief Dr. O'Brien."

Patrick began again, "I made many poor choices because I could not make sense out of this pain and shame. I couldn't talk to anyone about it so it became an internalized demon. I hurt a lot of people who loved me. I let boys like Rick McGee down by not coming forward."

"Have you forgiven Father Michael?"

"Your Honor," Stevens said as he jumped to his feet. "This is ridiculous."

"Sustained."

Faith nodded to Judge Ford. "I only have one more question for the witness, Your Honor."

"Proceed."

"Dr. O'Brien, did Father Michael O'Mallory sexually abuse you on two separate occasions at a wilderness camp for altar boys when you were ten years old?"

Patrick looked first at the jury panel and then squarely at the priest who at this time was staring straight ahead. "He did…he did…and I have never been the same."

"Thank you. Your witness, Mr. Stevens."

Faith couldn't have been prouder of him when he finished. Patrick held his own against Stevens and Faith thought he scored some extra points with the jury by being calm when Stevens appeared to get scurrilous. She knew she could have objected to several of his questions and sarcastic comments but she refrained, knowing Stevens was being unsuccessful in showing Patrick as a prejudicial witness.

The next witness, the physician who treated Rick in the emergency room following his suicide attempt, did not present crucial testimony, but he was able to describe the extent of Rick's self-inflicted injury and the demeanor he projected in the emergency room. When Stevens finished his cross-examination, the judge recessed for the day.

The sun was setting when Faith walked to her car. Out of the corner of her eye she saw a green pick-up truck turning into her lane. When she parked in the front of the hotel, she noticed the pick-up's license plate number and jotted it down quickly. Not wanting to appear aware of the truck, she strolled slowly, but purposefully into the lobby and called the police.

Chapter 12

"I can explain, man, I was just doing it for a friend."

"Whose pickup truck?"

"A friend's. I was just doing what he asked."

The cop popped the cuffs on his wrists. "Yes, well you can do your explaining downtown cause it looks like you're in a heap of trouble. What's your name?"

"Pete…Pete Wheeler."

"Let's go." They drove in silence to the police station.

When the sergeant walked in the interrogation room, he said, "Well, well, a familiar face. When did they let you out, Petey?"

The ex-con grimaced, but said nothing.

"You'd better chirp or you'll find yourself right back in your cage, Petey," the sergeant said, with a hint of malice.

"What difference does it make? You'll put me back, no matter what."

"Officer Cruise said you could explain. So let's hear it. By the way, where's your priest buddy. Don't you want to call him to see if he can get you out of another mess?" As he finished his sentence the connection occurred to him. He stopped, and walking over, sat down close to the skinny man, whose hardened face betrayed his youth, his arms scarred by tattoos that he or someone even less experienced had carved into the sallow skin.

"Okay, Pete, give me the story. I'll talk to the young woman you've been stalking. Maybe we can all cut some kind of deal. You want a lawyer?"

"Naw, I don't need no lawyer, but I need a beer and a cigarette."

"Can't get you that right now," as the cop looked at Pete's nicotine stained teeth, "but let's make this easy for everybody, huh? What do you say, Pete?"

The young man, looking much older than his years stared down at the floor, a hopeless beaten expression on his face. For a split second, the seasoned tough sergeant felt a little sorry for him.

Pete started slowly. "You know the priest?"

The officer nodded.

"Well, he's helped me out of a lot of scrapes. When I was released from the pen, he helped me get a job at a little diner. Not much, but at least I get my meals and make enough money in the kitchen to buy cigarettes and whiskey. He even convinced a halfway house to take me in."

"Go on."

"About a month ago he came to see me, asked me to do him a favor. He put a hundred dollar bill in my hand and told me to deliver a package for him."

"And you did?"

"Yeah, nice hotel he sent me to. Then he said he wanted me to follow this woman, watch her close and make it obvious, but not where she could really tell who it was or why. Hell, he even gave me a truck to use. Not too bad, either."

"And how did he tell you to follow her and scare her?"

"Different ways. He gave me directions. Be here or be there. If she goes to a restaurant, I'm supposed to slide in and pay the bill and have the guy at front give her a note."

"What did the note say?"

"I don't know every time. I only read one and it said, 'Say your prayers."

"Did you think that had any significance?"

"Huh?"

"Did you see that as a threat?"

"No, but I never did know why he wanted me to follow her. He said be like a shadow, but don't go too close. I didn't get it, but I never asked."

"How did you know the priest to begin with? I mean, years ago, when you first started getting into trouble."

"I lived with my old man in a two bit apartment not too far from his church and school, across the highway. I used to mow lawns in the nicer area closer to the church. I asked him one day if he needed any yard work there and he let me make a few bucks, but I only had to pull some weeds."

The officer met his eyes. "Did he ever touch you? Did he come on to you?"

"Oh, once when I first started hanging around there, he slapped me on the butt and told me I was a good boy. I knew that wasn't true since I was stealing hubcaps and siphoning gas out of cars. I just looked at him and said 'I don't let nobody touch me' and he never did again, but I know he did other boys."

"How do you know?"

"I seen him."

"You saw him do what?"

"You know, man."

"No, I don't. What?"

"Sex stuff, except these were just kids, a lot younger than I was. I used to laugh and say I was the only Peter he didn't want," he said sheepishly with a twisted grin.

It was the only time the sergeant had seen Pete's face change expressions. "Did he know that you knew?"

"Yeah, he caught me looking one time."

"Did you know the boy?"

"I wasn't exactly looking at his face."

"How long ago was this Pete?"

"About seven or so years. Right before I first got caught stealing."

"Is that why he helped you out with your problems with the law – to keep you quiet?"

"Yeah."

"Well, that's just changed."

"What do you mean?"

"Did he tell you this woman is a lawyer?"

"He didn't tell me nothing but what to do to scare her."

"How long have you been out, Pete?"

"About two months, why?"

"Did you know about his trial?"

"I heard at the diner that he was in trouble about abusing a boy a few years back. I ain't surprised about that, but I didn't know what she had to do with it."

"You know stalking, harassing this lady, leaving threatening messages and such can put you right back, don't you? You're on probation aren't you?"

"Yeah, what can I do, man? I can't go back."

"I'm not sure. We're going to keep you right now. I'll talk to her. Maybe she won't press harassment charges, but you're going to have to sing in court, I'm afraid, and it isn't going to be pretty for your old buddy."

"It's my ass or his, I guess."

"That it is, Petey. That it is," the officer said, picking up the phone to call Faith.

"Is this Faith O'Brien?"

"Yes, it is. Who is this?"

"Hi, Faith. This is Sergeant Castillo, Boston P.D. I think I have some good news for you. We caught your boy, the one who's been following you, and guess who was pulling his chain?"

"Don't tell me it is the Famous Father!"

"Yep. Petey spilled his guts. Said he wasn't going to go back to the big house. He'll talk in court if you don't press charges."

"Tell him he's got a deal, if I can convince Judge Ford that his testimony is relevant at this stage of the trial. The witness list had to be filed before the trial started. I'm sure Stevens will have a fit. But I'll give it my best try. I want to talk to him. How long are you going to keep him?"

"He'll stay until you get here."

"Do you think there's a chance he'll run then?"

"No way. He knows that if he did, when we catch him, he's in the slammer. He won't go anywhere. He's broke, living in a halfway house. He doesn't even want them to know or he'll get thrown out of there. No…our boy will sing, but he's going to need some clothes for the trial."

"No problem. I think we can manage that. I'll be there in less than an hour. And thanks Sergeant. You've been great. Thank the patrolman, will you?"

"Sure, Faith, see you in a little while."

Talking with Pete, Faith decided he probably would be a suitable witness if she could convince the Judge. She worried a little how he would handle cross-examination, knowing that Stevens would bring out the fact he had been in the penitentiary and attempt to destroy his credibility, but it would be worth it in order for him to tell his story.

Then practicing with him, Faith stressed how he should deal with Stevens. "If Stevens asks you what time it is, don't tell him how to make a watch," she instructed him, trying to impress on him just to answer the question, in as few words as possible. That had gone right over his head. *I hope I'm making the right decision,* trying to reassure herself.

Doubting that Judge Ford would allow Petey, as a witness, she still gave him fifty dollars to buy a new pair of jeans and shirt. "Just a plain button down, long sleeve shirt. No t-shirt," she instructed him. "And be at the courthouse by 11:00 a.m. sober, or the deal's off."

He nodded that he understood.

"Oh, and Pete, if you get to testify look at me, okay? No looking down. Eye contact. You understand?"

"Yeah."

"Yeah is okay tonight, but tomorrow, it's 'Yes,'" she said, pronouncing the word slowly, for effect. "I know you can do this right, Pete. Here's your chance!"

"I'll try."

Seeing him smile for the first time when he answered, Faith reasoned, *he probably could have been an okay kid if anyone had ever given him a chance, ever cared, but there is too much water under the bridge now.* Her bet was he'd be back in the pen within a year.

Faith arrived at the courthouse early the next day and gave the bailiff a note to give the Judge asking for a quick conference with him and Stevens before the proceedings began.

Stevens eyed her suspiciously when they were requested in the chambers and said, "What's up your sleeve now, little lady?"

"I just have a slight request."

After the Judge listened to Faith, he scratched his head and thought for what seemed to her a long time. "Can't do it, Ms. O'Brien. You should have been luckier and found this guy earlier."

"Yes, sir. Thank you just the same."

Stevens' face changed to the acrimonious, smirking smile that Faith had grown accustomed to seeing.

"Nice try, little lady," he taunted.

Faith turned to reply, stopped, smiled and walked on.

Later in the morning when Faith saw Pete, she bragged on how nice he looked in his clean jeans and ivory oxford shirt, and then told him the Judge's reaction. "Keep those clothes clean for a few days Pete, and don't stray far from the diner or the halfway house in case something comes up."

"Like what?"

"I don't know right now, Pete, but hang tight. Okay?"

"Does this mean the deal's off?" he muttered.

"No, Pete. It doesn't, but until the trial is over, be available."

"Yeah; I mean Yes," he stammered.

When she saw the unsettled look on O'Mallory's face as he noticed Pete, Faith concluded, *if nothing else, parading him in the courtroom was worth that.*

Her last witness was Rick, looking small and frail. Faith decided his eyes looked especially weak today; the color of swamp water and his voice thin, but steady.

"Rick, is the person who molested you in this room?"

"Yes."

"Would you please point him out?"

Rick pointed to O'Mallory. "That's him, over there," his voice gaining strength, but still full of despair.

"Would you explain how your relationship started and then what happened after that?"

"You mean everything?" the color rushed to his cheeks.

"Do the best you can Rick to explain to the jury what this man did to you."

Rick picked at his hair, wrapping it around his fingers. He looked off into the distance, hesitated and then began describing the relationship. Faith knew it was painful for him to relate the events and noticed how his face had gone pink as he told how the priest had touched him.

"Why did you not tell anyone, Rick," Faith pressed.

"I was ashamed," he stammered, "and scared."

"That's all I have, Your Honor. Your witness, Mr. Stevens."

Though she had practiced with Rick again and again and warned him about Stevens' mode of attack, she was nervous.

"All I can do is tell the truth, Ms. O'Brien," he had told her when she had asked him repeatedly if he were going to be strong.

"That's exactly what I want you to do."

When Stevens stood to cross examine, Rick shifted in his chair, sinking down slightly. He looked at Faith and she pushed her shoulders back, in an exaggerated manner, reminding him to sit tall.

He straightened. Faith knew he was straining to listen and think about all the things they practiced. *Just tell the truth,* she wanted to remind him, but she just sat and hoped for his sake this would not last long.

"You say Mr. O'Mallory gave you gifts. Why did you accept these if you thought he was doing something wrong?"

Rick lowered his gaze. "I wanted nice things, I guess."

"You were caught shoplifting once weren't you, Mr. McGee?"

Rick looked at Faith who wasn't expecting this question because he had never told her about his youthful arrest.

"Answer the question," Stevens said, sternly.

"Yes sir."

"And you didn't want your parents to know, right?"

"That's right."

"What did your parents do when they found out?"

"My dad whipped me."

"You mean with a belt?"

"Yes sir."

"What was your relationship like with your dad?"

There was a look of puzzlement on Rick's face. "What do you mean?"

"Did you and your dad get along? Or did you fight?"

"Some of both. When he was working, he wasn't around much and it was okay, but once he lost his job, he was home all the time and he rode me about stuff."

"So, was this when you started spending more time with Father Michael?"

Rick hesitated, "I…I guess."

"So, were you still shoplifting then?"

Faith was seething, both at Rick for not telling her about his record and at Stevens for taking this approach. "Objection, Your Honor!"

"I can show a connection, Your Honor," Stevens added quickly.

"Overruled."

"You didn't want your parents to know that you were still stealing. Am I correct?"

"Yes sir, no sir. I mean no I didn't want them to know."

"So, you told them Father Michael was buying you all these nice gifts didn't you, so they wouldn't know you were stealing. Didn't you, Mr. McGee? You lied to your parents, like you're lying now? You made all this up."

"No, I mean…" Rick was obviously flustered and Faith knew it. "Yes, I lied to my parents about some of my stuff but the stereo and most of the clothes, he did buy for me. I didn't make that up."

"But you lied didn't you, Rick?" Stevens drilled, pressing him hard.

Rick looked down but didn't answer.

"Answer the question, son," Judge Ford said, softly.

"I only lied about some of the stuff I stole."

"That's all the questions I have," Stevens drawled, a faint, half smile on his face.

Faith knew he had greatly injured Rick's credibility with the jury and left some lingering doubts about his story so she asked for one question in redirect examination. "Rick, you have just told Mr. Stevens you lied about some of the gifts. I want you to look at me and listen carefully when I ask you this one question. You must be honest. Did you tell your parents the truth when you described the abuse by Father O'Mallory?"

"Yes," he said, firmly.

Turning to the judge, "No other questions, Your Honor," Faith said with a considerable sense of relief. Knowing Stevens had only three witnesses to call, she surmised, *win or lose it's only a matter of time.*

Stevens called his first witness right after lunch. At Stevens' prodding he described himself as a third generation Catholic, a retired state Senator, and a pillar of the community, who had known Father O'Mallory for more than thirty years. "I've been to the church during the day and stopped by the school any number of times. I've never even seen any young boys hanging around talking to Father Michael. I've never witnessed any impropriety in Father O'Mallory's behavior."

Stevens pushed harder asking more questions along that line.

"I've talked to many people and they've never seen that happen either," the witness reiterated.

"Hearsay, Your Honor," Faith interjected.

"Sustained."

As she began her cross-examination, she was thrilled Stevens had taken the witness this direction and Faith asked two questions, both in regard to his statements about never seeing any young boys in Father Michael's office or even working on the grounds. Again he stuck to his version of events.

"No more questions, Your Honor, but may I have permission to approach the bench?"

Judge Ford motioned her forward.

Quickly she indicated that because of this testimony she now wished to bring Pete as a rebuttal witness.

The Judge gestured for Stevens.

Faith explained her request again as Stevens listened intently.

The Judge began, "I am going to allow you to call this witness, Ms. O'Brien, but you cannot mention the stalking, his being hired by O'Mallory or any of that. You can only question him about what he saw when he hung around the church and school where O'Mallory worked."

"But, Your Honor," Stevens interrupted.

The Judge frowned, "Mr. Stevens, Let me remind you that your witness clearly pointed out and then reiterated that there were never any boys hanging around. You pounded that home. Ms. O'Brien says her witness can rebut that."

"But..."

"My decision stands. She can call her witness at the end."

Suppressing a smile, she noted there was no little lady remark this round.

Although it was not quite two o'clock, when they returned to their seats, Judge Ford recessed for the day.

Leaving the courtroom, Faith's spirits soared.

"Let's change clothes and go down to the harbor to celebrate," Patrick said as they stepped outside and Faith told them her good fortune.

"It's a little premature for a celebration, I'm afraid, but it would be nice to get away from all this for awhile. First, I've got to call Pete because I may have to go find him to tell him he needs to be down here tomorrow."

Because Faith usually took the parking garage elevator, Patrick had asked her to stop by the desk to pick up a delivery for him. She thought it was strange that he had asked, but the minute she turned the corner she knew why. In a chair, smiling broadly, sat Tyler, who jumped up as she shrieked his name.

"Tyler, how did you get here?"

He enveloped her in his arms and kissed her repeatedly. "On an airplane," he teased.

"We nearly went from the courthouse straight to the harbor. I would have missed you. I'm so glad..." She stopped mid-sentence remembering how odd Patrick had acted about coming back to the hotel, asking her to get his package, and wondered if he knew Tyler was coming, but that didn't make sense because they had never met.

"I called your dad last night. I just decided I'd introduce myself and see if he would help me pull this off. He was great, like we had known each other for years. I didn't think you'd be here this early, though."

"You mean you didn't call Judge Ford and include him in your scheme?" Faith asked, her face beaming.

"No, but Mr. Jackson is in on this. After I told him about us, he said with a wink that I should go check on you."

"What did you tell him?" Faith asked with a little surprise in her voice.

Smiling, he paused, hoping the wait would peak her curiosity.

"Tyler, I know you didn't say what you are implying. Now, tell me," she said, pinching him on the arm.

"That we are dating. I went in early in the week explaining to him, I was in love with you. I didn't want him to think we were trying to hide anything. I told him if I needed to resign and look for a job elsewhere, I would."

"So what did he say?" Faith quizzed, anxiously.

Tyler laughed. He said, "Boy, you sure work fast," mimicking Mr. Jackson's drawl. Then he said, "If you think I'm going to give up a good lawyer just because of that, you're crazy, Boy. I'm happy for you both, and I'm not worried. You're both professionals. I think he wanted to tease me and say a few more things, but he restrained himself. Next time he's had a few drinks after golf I'm sure it will get a little more graphic."

"I bet it will. I'm glad you talked to him, Tyler. That was thoughtful. You never cease to amaze me."

Dismissing her compliment, he continued, "Anyway, he knew I wanted to fly here so he came in Wednesday morning and reminded me that I was your contact person at the firm. 'Don't you think you should fly to Boston on Thursday and see how our newest attorney is faring?' he asked me. I told him it sounded like a great idea to me, so here I am. I have the room on the other side of yours. Your dad worked that out for me, too. I thought that might be best this first time I meet them," he offered.

"I can't remember if there is a door into that room from mine. If not, I guess the hotel won't mind if we knock out the wall," Faith said. "Don't think you're going to sleep without me."

"Well, I admit I was hoping you might consider sneaking around. Now, what do you say, you introduce me to your parents."

"I'd love to," Faith said, taking his hand as he reached for his bag with the other.

"Will it make you nervous if I go with you to court tomorrow?"

"Probably, but that's okay. I think it's going pretty well. I'll tell you all about it later. Stevens sure isn't too happy."

"Hey, where's Judge?"

"Sid's taking care of her. Actually he's staying at my place since he doesn't have a yard. Shea's coming tomorrow for the weekend so I'm sure Judge will get plenty of attention."

Faith had only met Sid Davis once because he had been on a case in Louisiana most of the time she had been with the firm, but she knew he was Tyler's best and most trusted friend, and the only African-American attorney, at Jackson, Henry, and Jackson. He was handsome by anyone's standards. He wore his dark hair cropped short. A thin, neatly trimmed mustache and soul patch accented his complexion that reminded Faith of the heavily creamed coffee at the famous Café du Monde in New Orleans. Tall, an easy inch more than Tyler, his muscular build made him look more like a body trainer than a highly regarded young environmental lawyer, the only specialist in that field for the firm. One night early in their relationship as Faith and Tyler lay in bed, Tyler had told her all about Sid, how his interest in conservation and the atmosphere evolved from growing up along the Texas Gulf Coast where oil refineries lined the bays and their foul odors permeated the air. His dad had worked in one of those refineries for almost forty years and his mother cleaned houses for several of the executives.

Tyler told her that Sid had related to him that his parents had encouraged him and his sister to get an education and a career that allowed them to give their children more than they had been able to do. He said he never thought they were poor, but he hated to see how hard his parents worked, how dog-tired his mama came in, after cleaning and cooking all day and then she would start over at their house. It was always important to Sid and his older sister that they never disappointed them. When the opportunity came for him to play football on a scholarship at the University of Houston, he grabbed it. Today his sister is a professor at Texas Southern University, just a short distance from his alma mater.

Sid's only regret was his failed marriage to his high school sweetheart, Vanessa, Shea's mother. He said he should have known early that it wasn't going to last, Tyler explained. Although they were only thirty-nine miles from their home in Texas City, Vanessa missed her family and never liked the city. Law school at Tulane was worse, and Tyler saw it coming long before the actual separation. After Vanessa moved back home and took the baby, Sid and Tyler started going for pizza and beer about once a week. Sid's last year of law school, they rented a small house together so when Sid took the job in Dallas, he talked Tyler into applying there when he graduated a year later.

Chapter 13

The headlines in the morning paper grabbed Tyler's attention. "Look at this. It's getting more exciting by the day," Tyler said, handing the paper to Faith who had been leisurely drinking coffee. She began reading the story.

Grand Jury to Convene in Archdiocese Probe

Prosecutors are preparing to convene a special grand jury to investigate how the Archdiocese of Boston officials responded to allegations of sexual abuse involving Father Michael O'Mallory.

Civil cases are pending against O'Mallory and the Archdiocese according to Faith O'Brien who filed the charges on behalf her clients, Rick McGee and Patrick O'Brien. O'Mallory is currently on trial for indecent assault and battery and criminal sexual activity. According to a spokesman for the court, the trial is expected to last several more days.

The scope of the grand jury investigation including who may be called to testify is unknown since grand jury proceedings are secret.

"This is great news, but I'm ready for this excitement to be over so I can go home to Dallas. I'm glad you talked me into setting the clock early or we probably wouldn't have had time to read the paper. Oh, Tyler, it was so wonderful to be with you all night."

He smiled and leaned to kiss her. "You want to go back to bed for awhile, just to be sure?"

She slapped his arm. "That's cruel. You know I have to get ready now, but I think the offer was nice," now patting him softly on the same arm. "There's a really good chance this could go to the jury today, you know."

Tyler smiled, "That would be a nice way to start the weekend, knowing it won't be much longer. I'm really surprised that it has gone so quickly. I expected his attorney to call more people, but when you think about it, it doesn't sound as if there are many people to call. Do you think if they lose, which I know they're going to, the Archdiocese will settle?"

"I'm certainly hoping. Right now, I don't think O'Mallory even has an attorney for the civil case. Stevens hasn't mentioned it, and I think he would," Faith said, standing. "I need to get dressed and so do you, if you're going with me. I can't lollygag around here drinking coffee and making love all day. There's a major court case to be won," she said, as she wrapped her arms around his tall athletic body. "On second thought, maybe we should lollygag," she teased. "You want to take a shower? Just a shower, though."

"I'll take the crumbs. That's better than nothing," as he stripped off his robe and headed into the shower after her.

After Stevens had called his last witness, the Judge allowed Faith to call Pete as her rebuttal witness. Faith was pleased with the way Pete had cleaned up and even with his testimony. Although Stevens had hammered him, Pete held his own, looking relaxed, his hands clasped in front of him, answering the questions calmly. She noticed his eyes met O'Mallory's once and he glanced down briefly, but only for a second, and then when he was finished he smiled, a genuine smile as if he had finally done something right. The Judge called for a twenty minute recess before closing arguments.

When Stevens stood to present his closing remarks, he didn't look any better than he had throughout the trial. With his frayed suit clinging to his middle and his buttons looking as though they were hanging on for dear life, what he lacked in style he made up in shrewdness. "Ladies and gentlemen of the jury, I am going to forgo my closing…"

Faith was stunned. But before she could think any further he continued…

"I think it might be nice if I stepped down and let Father Michael give his own closing. You haven't heard from him and you need to know what he has to say." He was looking squarely at the jurors now. Then he turned to look at Faith with a slight smirk, out of the jury's sight, and signaled for Father Michael to proceed.

Faith shot a glance at the Judge who nodded for the priest to begin. Then she cast a worried look at Tyler who was sitting next to Patrick. She noticed immediately that Patrick's face had gone cold, his eyes narrow. *Damn.* Stevens had done what she had feared all along; he had outsmarted her. He had nothing for a case and now he had made it everything. He had blindsided her, but it was legal. She had only known of one other case – a case she had studied in law school where a lawyer had stepped down and let the defendant deliver the closing. She knew that Stevens would have never let O'Mallory take the stand because she would have been able to cross-examine him. This way, that was impossible.

Now, the once somber priest who had sat stoically throughout the trial was standing before the twelve people who would decide his fate. He looked regal somehow, courtly and dignified, his thin grey hair framing a soft saccharine face.

His voice started off weak, bordering a whisper, but as he straightened his rounded shoulders his speech became more pronounced, determined and fervent.

Damn him, damn him, and Stevens both. Faith gave a fleeting look at Tyler and then watched the expressions of the jurors.

O'Mallory was speaking eloquently, much like Faith supposed he had sounded in front of a congregation of believers. His voice made her sick. She wanted to yell, to stop him, shout what an imposter, a fraud he was, but she managed to sit quietly, poker-faced, looking squarely at each panel member, carefully rearranging some of her closing statements in her head. She thought his thirty minutes would never end, but in other ways she wasn't sure she wanted them to. She was going to have to summarize and overcome the significant gain the priest had just made, and from the looks on a couple of the jurors' faces she had a major hurdle to jump.

Arousing her from her thoughts, the judge spoke firmly: "Ms. O'Brien."

Standing, Faith turned to the jury. "Ladies and gentlemen, you have just heard the pleas of an old man, I do not say, gentleman, you will note, but rather a pretender, a phony who has the talent to persuade, the rhetoric to convince, the poise to unbalance you. Please do not be deceived."

Her voice rose and then fell as she then began speaking slowly from the heart, as she put away her notes. One quick look at Rick, his parents, and then her father, and she was completely absorbed in bringing the priest down. One hand went in her pocket for an instant. She felt the tiny broken cross and it gave her added strength and spark. Dangling it indiscreetly, she glanced at the priest, whose grimace told her he had noticed. She knew she couldn't mention it, but she could certainly use its power as she made eye contact with every single juror. She noticed that the bartender who had been hunched over slightly was now sitting up erect, the teacher had stopped taking notes and the fireman's expression was serious. She hoped she was reading them correctly, that maybe she had turned a corner. Off to her right side, she saw Jeff smiling, not something he was prone to do in the courtroom. She kept her pace, reminding the panel of the reprehensible behavior of the defendant.

"He may look sad today, old and afraid, but he hasn't always been that way. He wasn't when he was enticing Rick McGee with expensive stereos and giving him money. He wasn't when he targeted him, preyed on him for his sick sexual episodes. He has hidden behind that collar for too many years and he is still hiding. You may think it quite clever that Mr. Stevens stepped down so that Father Michael could speak. Generally, when someone wants to speak to the jury, they play fair and take the witness stand. The only problem with that is it allows the opposing lawyer to cross examine the witness. That way you hear the whole story, the good, the bad and the ugly, but as always, Father O'Mallory wants you to hear only his side. Now you can put a stop to this hiding. You can put a stop to him so that no other young boy will have to suffer demons because of this man. You have the power to start the healing process. It's time for power to be used in a positive way. You have that opportunity. Thank you." And then Faith sat down, tired, relieved, a bundle of emotions.

Judge Ford gave the jury their final instructions, reiterating their responsibilities and cautioning them again about Patrick's testimony. He explained they would be given a written copy of the indictment, that their decision in a criminal case would have to be unanimous and that they were not to discuss the events of the trial with anyone other than other jurors.

Faith glanced at the clock. It was ten minutes after three. She was betting the judge would recess and bring the jurors back Monday morning for deliberations. Instead, he sent the jurors off to the jury room. Faith stood and began organizing and putting page after page of yellow legal sheets into a briefcase so new it hadn't even a minor scratch in the black Italian leather. Patrick had given it to her as a graduation gift and she was pleased with its feminine styling. She picked up the small packet of Kleenex and orange highlighter and placed them neatly into zippered compartments. She hadn't looked up after the jury left the room, but now turning to find Tyler, she almost bumped into him. He wanted to kiss her, but he reached out his hand and shook her hand.

"Nice job, counselor. Very nice."

She smiled shyly. "You think so?"

"Without a doubt."

Patrick and Sue stood back and watched, giving the young couple a few minutes before they approached Faith with similar compliments.

"Well, I guess we'll know how good," she said to their comments. "The jury will let us know eventually, but it's going to be a long weekend."

"I hope so," Tyler cut in.

Faith took his hand and squeezed it. "Let's get out of here."

As they started for the door, three gentlemen, who Faith guessed to be in their mid-thirties, approached her. "Ms. O'Brien, could we talk to you a minute?" one man asked.

Faith glanced at Tyler who was now studying the three. "Could I ask what this is about?" she requested.

The tallest and oldest of the three started to answer, then paused, "It's…it's about us," he stammered, "We were abused too. We would like to talk with you about a civil suit."

"Was it O'Mallory?"

"Yes," another of the men answered. "Ms. O'Brien, my name is Gary Casey. This is Ron Kelly and Joe Navarro." Each man reached to shake her hand.

Faith studied the men for a minute before talking. Casey was a square of a man with curly brown hair and intense, reflective green eyes. Ron, who had been the first to speak, had a craggy, acne scarred, studious looking face, slightly betrayed by a constant twitch.

Before Faith could answer, Joe Navarro cut in. "There's more of us. We're just the ones who were at the trial today. I can't believe how that Son of a Bitch O'Mallory could even look at those jurors, must less talk," Navarro's eyes were as cold as a mountain blizzard and there was certain hardness in his voice. Faith thought he was almost handsome, although a little rough around the edges; someone, she guessed, who was probably more comfortable in a dingy, smoke-filled bar, slugging down shots and dodging cue sticks and insults than in a courthouse.

"Let's go some place where we can talk," she broke in quickly. "This is Tyler England, one of my colleagues at the law firm. He'll be joining us." She looked at Tyler who was now motioning for the three to lead out.

"Why don't we go to the hotel? We can talk in my room," Tyler offered as he gave the men directions.

~

"Well, my dear, it appears you have a big job ahead of you," Tyler began as soon as he opened the car door for Faith.

"Tyler, what am I going to do?" she asked worriedly in a voice out of character for her.

"You're going to take their case and make a slew of money for Jackson, Henry, Jackson."

"Oh, Tyler, I wanted to go home, now this could mean a lot more time away from you."

"We'll manage. Look, I'll talk to these guys while you call Mr. Jackson. He'll need to give you some directions. We'll figure out our situation later tonight," he said calmly, reaching over to pat her leg.

Faith gazed out the window. It was now early September and some of the trees along Beacon Street were beginning to show signs of change. There was definitely no warmth in the sun this afternoon, but Faith wasn't sure if it was the chill that caused her to shiver or the look she had seen in the eyes of Joe Navarro.

"I'd say Joe is plenty angry, wouldn't you?" Faith asked, flatly.

"And bitter. Did you notice his eyes? I'm anxious to hear his story," Tyler added.

"I'm not sure I am. O'Mallory is, indeed a monster."

~

First thing Monday morning, the jury asked Judge Ford for a written definition outlining the six points that must be satisfied for a conviction of indecent assault and battery charges for someone less than fourteen years of age. The foreperson read the statements out loud to the other jurors: "The alleged victim must be under fourteen at the time of the incident, the defendant intended to engage in the touching, the defendant touched the victim, however slight, the touching was harmful or offensive, the touching was indecent as judged on a scale of common understanding and practice and the touching came without justification or excuse."

Within three hours, they sent a note to the judge that they had a verdict.

When Faith heard the words, "Guilty as charged," she wanted to shout. Judge Ford set the penalty hearing for Thursday. She looked at Patrick quickly and then at Ricky, her eyes meeting his, a wry smile on his lips. With tears running down his mother's cheeks, they both rushed forward. Patrick mouthed a simple "thank you" and held back.

"Ms. O'Brien, I can't thank you enough. You have given Ricky his life back," Mrs. McGee said in a hushed tone, pressing her rosary. Rick stood silently beside his mother.

"Hey, Ricky, what's this I hear about a new girlfriend?" Faith asked breaking the silence.

He smiled a crooked smile and shrugged. Faith hugged him gently. "You take care of yourself, you hear?" Turning to his mother she asked, "You will you be back for the penalty stage?"

"Indeed, the hard part is over. That will be, hopefully, the icing on the cake. What do you think, Ms. O'Brien?"

"I wouldn't guess, but he could get the maximum of ten years. Let's hope so. He's almost seventy-four years old so that could be a life sentence. We'll keep our fingers crossed."

Chapter 14

Waiting was not something Faith did well, but with four days until the next phase of the trial, she decided to fill her time planning for when she returned to Dallas. Thinking about the next couple of months ahead, she began to make mental notes, lists in her head. In law school, she had almost become compulsive about this. The first thing she wanted to do when she had a free moment was to see Alice. She missed her and had been so busy of late that their conversations had been short or not at all, but Alice was her understanding and sacrificing self. Faith was happy that her mom's relationship with Ben was growing and there was even some talk of a wedding in the late spring.

The wedding, her own wedding, that was the next important event, and she hoped she and Tyler could talk about it when he returned from shopping. She had tried to not allow herself time to think about it during the trial. If it were to be a December wedding, they didn't have much time to make plans. So far they hadn't even had time to buy rings, but she wasn't worried. Keep it simple had become her motto. What she didn't know was that Tyler had already checked into a number of options and cleared two weeks for their wedding and honeymoon with their bosses.

She was surprised when the phone rang, since she had already talked to Jeff and Alice and she couldn't imagine who else would be calling.

"Hello, Ms. O'Brien?" Stevens' voice was quickly recognizable.

Why would he be calling her this morning? "Yes, this is she."

"Sorry to bother you."

She knew he wasn't in the least but was still curious about his intentions.

"We need to talk. The Archdiocese has retained me in this civil suit. I don't think they want a long drawn out trial and a bunch of dirty laundry aired that is nobody's real business, so I think, perhaps, we can work this out and be done with all this foolishness, if you understand?"

"Are you telling me they want to settle, Mr. Stevens?" Faith asked with some firmness in her voice. Stevens no longer threatened her confidence; mostly he just repulsed her.

"Maybe, we may can come to some resolution," being careful to not obligate himself early in the process.

"Are we talking about all concerned to this point, Rick, Dr. O'Brien and the three latest gentlemen who have filed?"

"I'm not sure about your dad."

"Then no deal, Mr. Stevens. It's all or nothing," Faith said emphatically, knowing, however, she was trying to play a hand with no hole cards. She was taking her chances because at this point they knew she was serious and her dad was in essence, her most important client. At first she figured there was no chance of him receiving anything in the case since it had been so long ago, but the Archdiocese knew that this is where it had all started. He was the true strength behind this entire confrontation and that Faith O'Brien had become a force to be reckoned with.

"Well, maybe we can work something out. Let me talk to my client again. What about meeting me at Delmonico's about three o'clock?"

"Tyler and I will both be there…" The phone clicked before she finished. *He's such a pompous ass.*

Because Mr. Jackson had encouraged Tyler to wait until the proceedings were complete, he had gone to purchase more clothes and was taking longer than Faith anticipated. Though knowing it was premature, Faith decided to call Mr. Jackson to tell him what she knew from this morning's conversation with Stevens.

Mr. Jackson had encouraged her and told her to continue being tough. "You can make some good money for yourself in this deal and it won't hurt my feelings either," he had said. She really didn't have any idea what kind of settlement they might offer, but the possibilities made her giddy.

After showering and dressing, she put her things to do list on paper, along with questions for Stevens. When Tyler arrived back to the hotel, he was noticeably upbeat, whistling as he came through the door. Faith ran to him telling him about her conversations.

"Then I guess we had better get a bite to eat and think about our strategy, huh?"

"It's almost one o'clock. I certainly don't want to be late."

"Just let me put all this away and I'll be ready. I've made a reservation for dinner. I thought it might be nice if we went out someplace where the atmosphere is pleasant and the food delicious."

"That's great. Today seems full of surprises."

Tyler smiled to himself, knowing the ring might be the biggest surprise of the day.

~

Stevens was waiting in a corner booth in the expansive bar. Seeing him waiting impatiently, Faith was amused since he was rarely punctual.

"Good afternoon, Ms. O'Brien." he said, struggling to remove his large frame from the compartment where it was wedged. Watching him, she was careful to hide her enjoyment, yet reveled silently in his laborious efforts. Obviously he hadn't thought of the awkward position he had put himself in when he chose this arrangement, Faith surmised.

She turned slightly to look at Tyler who was composed and reserved, acting as if he hadn't noticed any problem.

"Okay, I'll get right to the point," Stevens said, somewhat out of breath and reeking of cigar smoke, once more pouring himself into the small space. "My client wants to be done with this mess. We'll pay each plaintiff a million each to drop the case and cease with any more claims."

"Not enough, Mr. Stevens." Faith couldn't believe the words were even coming out of her mouth. That was more money than any of these five people had ever seen, would probably ever see. "These men are scarred forever. Some have lived with this shame for years. That's miniscule compared to their years of suffering. Admittedly, money is not going to make this go away, but at least it will allow them to feel somewhat vindicated."

Stevens' face turned red, as perspiration was beginning to collect on his forehead. "Ms. O'Brien, don't be so cavalier. You and I both know this is all about money now."

"I do not know that, Mr. Stevens. That is simply not an acceptable amount. If you want to discuss this further, we'll be happy to stay; otherwise, we have a great many other responsibilities."

After a lengthy pause, she cut a quick peek toward Tyler who was trying to hide an amused look.

Stevens was obviously battling frustration and annoyance, and Faith knew from his behavior that he had been sent here to cut a deal and it wasn't going at all as he had hoped. She pushed it a step further.

"Well, Mr. Stevens, do you wish to continue this conversation?"

His eyes looked menacing as he stared icily at Faith. "Well, little lady," he drawled sarcastically, "what do you think would be fair?" He hadn't called her that since the middle of the trial, but instead of infuriating her as it once had, it buoyed her, knowing she knew she was getting under his skin.

"Well, sir," as she exaggerated the enunciation of sir. "I could sit here and pull large unreasonable numbers out of my hat and we could spend the remainder of the afternoon negotiating, but we have a dinner to attend so I'm just going to cut to the chase. My clients will accept nothing less than two million each. We expect nothing more, nothing less. Now, my offer is on the table."

By now Stevens was sweating profusely and Faith, though enjoying it, was beginning to become embarrassed for the old overweight attorney.

They all sat waiting while Stevens thought, pouring over his options.

"I think I'll get everyone a drink after all," Tyler said, jumping to his feet. Earlier they had declined when the server came to get their order. "What will you have, Mr. Stevens?"

"Make mine a JB and water," he barked, looking relieved for the diversion as well as the liquid.

"Ms. O'Brien, you are being ridiculous."

"Mr. Stevens, let me remind you that my clients didn't ask for this abuse or the subsequent cover-up by the Catholic officials. Ten million dollars is a drop in the bucket for the church. That's the bottom line. If you want to sit here and argue, my amount will just continue to rise."

Tyler was back at the booth with a Scotch for Stevens and two glasses of Chardonnay.

Stevens gulped his and then sat it down loudly on the walnut table top. "You drive a hard bargain, Ms. O'Brien," and then motioning his glass at Tyler, he ordered, "I'll take another one of these."

Thinking how uncouth he was and how condescending he sounded as he growled his drink order to Tyler, Faith was happy the atmosphere was becoming more palatable with a little Scotch in Stevens' fat belly.

More relaxed, he said, "Now, Ms. O'Brien, you know my clients can't pay that kind of money."

"Then I suppose we don't have any more to discuss. We'll just finish our wine and be off."

Tyler was back with Steven's second Scotch. This time she noticed it was a double in a tall glass. Stevens reached for it without as much as a muttering of appreciation. This time he drank it slower, but nonetheless purposely.

Faith heard a less than repressed belch. She was beginning to lose patience when Tyler patted her leg under the table as if to say, be cool, we've got him where we want him, just hang on.

"Please excuse me for a moment," as she rose to go to the ladies room, feeling bad for leaving Tyler alone with this corpulent ogre.

When she returned she could tell he was enjoying himself, almost baiting Stevens with his zealous pleasantness. They were talking shop, Stevens feeling better and now bragging about some earlier case.

"I see you two are having a good time, but let me remind you that we are here for business."

"Well, let me buy you one more drink Mr. Stevens and then we'll be out of your hair."

"Sounds good, young man."

Although Faith knew Stevens was nowhere close to being drunk, he was definitely feeling more comfortable, but she was less. She didn't want him to later accuse her of playing unfairly.

"I don't think we need to stick around, Tyler. These kinds of decisions should be made with a clear mind."

Stevens stiffened, "I'll have you know, little lady, that I was holding my liquor before you were born," motioning Tyler to go ahead.

"Well, I'm running out of time."

Tyler handed him the glass and this time Stevens grumbled something inaudibly.

"Okay, I'll tell you what I'll do. We'll pay your two million apiece, but I don't want to hear another word from you Ms. O'Brien. Nothing, you're done here. If anyone else comes forward, someone else will have to do their dirty work."

"I take offense to your calling it 'dirty work.'"

"Well, get over how you feel. Do we have a deal or not?"

Faith looked at Tyler while she tried to do the mental math. Her firm would make almost two and a half million from their take, she would have about $700,000.00 from the agreement she made earlier with the McGee family and Patrick could take his money and spend as much time as he wanted in Italy. Besides she was ready to get home and settle into her routine.

"Could you excuse my colleague and me for a moment to discuss this?" Normally she would expect Stevens to show some manners and get up, leaving them to talk, but she knew that wasn't going to happen, so she tapped Tyler on the shoulder to indicate they would walk away for a few minutes.

As soon as they were out of earshot she said, "Tyler, I just didn't want to do anything without talking to you."

He grinned. "You want my opinion?"

"Yes, please."

"Take the deal and let's go home. The penalty phase will be over Thursday. Everybody you care about will have been taken care of. Who knows if anybody else will even come forward?"

"I was hoping that was what you would say," as they walked back to the booth.

"You've got yourself a deal."

"Good, I'll draw up the papers and have them ready for all the signatures Thursday morning. Have all your people there."

Faith reached to shake his hand while Tyler paid the tab. Stevens stuck his hand out begrudgingly, but then softened.

"You just might make a damned good attorney someday, Ms. O'Brien. And by the way, that friend of yours, colleague, whatever you call him, nice fellow. I saw the way you looked at him. You can't fool an old fool," and then he winked.

For a slight second, Faith almost liked him. She smiled, turned and walked toward Tyler. When she stepped outside, she gave a slight scream, "Yes!"

She took Tyler's hand and told him how Stevens had finished the conversation.

"He's a piece of work," Tyler said, laughing. "We make a pretty good team, don't you think? You doing the mediating, me buying the drinks. I like that."

They rushed back to the hotel to change clothes for dinner.

"Let me see if Mother and Dad are back before I change." She knocked on their door excitedly. "Open up, I've got news!"

Patrick opened the hotel room door. "Are you okay?"

"You better sit down. I'll bet you remember that old television show, 'The Millionaire.' Well, she just came to your door."

"What in the world are you talking about, Faith?"

"We settled, with the Archdiocese. You're getting two million smackaroos."

"Are you serious?"

"Yes, I'm serious. You think I would be running around like a wild woman just for my health?"

"But...I didn't think they would do anything for me."

"First Stevens said everybody but you, and I told him the deal was off. I knew they had sent him to settle, so I pushed the envelope."

"Then he agreed to one million and I said no deal. So Tyler proceeded to get him drunk." She looked at Tyler, who was now sitting on the couch, and giggled.

"Come sit down, Faith," motioning with his hand on the couch. "No, Patrick, she did everything. She settled it all. I simply bought the portly ol' barrister a few Scotches."

Patrick looked over at Sue who was pale. "I can't believe it," she muttered.

"I won't believe it until it's a done deal," Patrick added.

"Well, we shook on it, plus Stevens said for all the parties to be at court early Thursday to sign the papers he is having drawn up. I'm telling you it's settled. I could just tell the big shots had given him some latitude and this is how it went. Now, you can add several rooms to your bungalow and spend plenty of time in Tuscany."

Patrick turned again to Sue. "How do you feel about that?"

"Favaloso!"

Everyone laughed.

"I have no clue what you said, but it sounds positive," Faith said.

"Carmella was teaching me a few words. It means 'Wonderful!' if I have it pronounced correctly, which I doubt."

Patrick continued to look stunned. "I'm so grateful to you Faith. It's not just the money, although it will certainly be nice to have. But you've given me back my soul and my heart. He rose and went over to sit on the arm of Sue's chair and put his arm around her…and the love of my life." Tears welled in their eyes.

"I'm getting out of here before everybody's crying. This is supposed to be a happy time."

"Wait, Hon, it is. We're crying tears of joy," Sue said quickly.

"I know. I'm teasing. But I need to call Mr. Jackson and then we're going out to dinner, some fancy place Tyler won't even tell me about."

Tyler winked at Patrick. "Some things the lady must not know until it's time, don't you agree?"

"Totally."

Patrick stood and hugged Faith tightly. "Thank you, Faith, for making me strong."

She smiled and turned, walking out the door.

When she reached her boss on the phone, she repeated the story of the settlement.

"Nice job, Young Lady. My partners will be very happy. So, he told you that you might be a damn good lawyer someday, huh? Well, you could tell him I said you already are. We're anxious to get you back here."

"I think we may wrap everything up and be home Friday or Saturday. It's hard to tell, but I can't imagine the sentencing taking very long. Neither of us is bringing witnesses so it appears to be prison or probation."

"I'll keep my fingers crossed. Is my golf buddy around? I need to talk to him."

She motioned to Tyler. "Sure, hold on."

"Faith, congratulations. I'm proud of you."

"Thank you, sir. See you Monday, I hope." She handed the phone to Tyler.

"Hello, Mr. Jackson."

"How are you, My Boy?"

"Doing well."

"I'll bet you are. Got the ring yet?"

"Uh..." he stammered. "Yes sir."

"I read you. You haven't given it to her yet?"

"Correct."

"Well, what are you waiting for?"

"Soon, very soon."

"I see. Okay, just checking. Sounds like you're doing good work there."

"Faith is. I'm just tagging along."

"Well, with that kind of money for the firm I can afford to let you tag along. You take care and hurry up and give her that damn ring. Sara and I haven't been to a wedding in months. Oh, yes, we'd like for you to have the reception at the country club. We'll pick up the tab. You two talk it over after you give her the ring."

"That's really kind and thoughtful of you both. I'll talk to you about it Monday because I'll be back whether Faith is finished or not. I've got the O'Neil case coming up."

"Later then." Jackson hung up without further comment and Tyler was left holding the phone, hoping Faith had not heard the conversation from the other room. Fortunately, she had gone out of the room for most of the conversation.

"So, what did he say?" she asked, curiously.

"He's very proud of you. Mainly, he was wondering when I'd be back. I told him Monday, no matter what. We should be getting ready or we're going to be late for our reservation."

~

"Tyler, this restaurant is beautiful. I love the rich olive colors and the dark woods. How did you know about this place?"

He smiled. "I asked around. Your dad gave me several names for places in the North End. He said he came here once when he was in graduate school and that it was really romantic except for one problem; he was by himself."

"It's nice and quiet, too. We have our own alcove. Pretty cool, pull the drape and it's just us," Faith whispered.

"Yeah, you want to fool around?"

"Tyler, shame on you. You bring a nice girl out to a fancy place and try to take advantage of her. I've heard about guys like you," she teasingly scolded.

As she finished her sentence, a server pushed back the long, velvet drape, holding a dozen yellow roses. "I believe these are for you, Miss, from the gentleman here."

"Oh, Tyler, you think of everything. When did you arrange for me to get these?"

"You ask too many questions. You must be a lawyer or something," as he leaned to kiss her. "What would you like to drink?"

"I think a very dry, dirty martini would be a nice beginning. What are you having?"

"A Crown and water; I hear it goes with your Esteé Lauder."

Faith laughed, "Aren't you the poet?"

At that, he handed her a gift box of Private Collection perfume. "See, not just a poet, but a deliverer of gifts."

"You know I love every perfume Estee Lauder makes."

"So do I. I love the way you smell." The room was dimly lit with a low hanging antique chandelier and the glow of votive candles scattered around in frosted glass holders. The light cast a luminous glow on their faces as they looked into each other's eyes.

"Why don't you open the box," he suggested.

Faith released the bow and gently lifted the box from the heavy ecru colored paper. When she raised the bottle out, another tiny box fell on the table.

A look of puzzlement was on her face. "What is this, Tyler?"

"I don't know," he said trying to hide his excitement. "Why don't you see?"

When she opened the box, she gasped. "Tyler, I've never seen a ring so beautiful." She sat stunned for the longest time.

"Do you really like it?" he asked with a tinge of hesitation in his voice.

"Tyler, how could I not love it?"

"I wasn't sure about mixing the yellow diamonds with the white, but the jeweler assured me we can change them out…I…I just like the yellow because they're fitting for my yellow rose of Texas," he blushed as he said it.

Faith was crying now. "See what you've done. You've made me cry."

Tyler took her hand. "Is it happy crying or sad crying?"

Brushing away a tear, she said, "Happy, Happy, Happy!"

"Is it bad luck to try on both the engagement and wedding?" he asked.

Faith was already slipping them on. "I have to see if they fit, silly." They did. She looked at the engagement ring and smiled. "It is gorgeous and so big," she said emphatically.

"I know you don't wear much jewelry, but I wanted it big. Besides when I told my dad he said remember it needs to show her how much you love her…"

"The reason I don't wear much jewelry is not because I don't like it. I've just never had the money." She continued to stare at the rings. The engagement ring held a two carat white emerald cut diamond with two smaller yellow diamonds surrounding a small white diamond on either side, set in yellow gold. The wedding band held three rows of six white and yellow diamonds, set alternately.

"Okay, give me back the band," he grinned holding out his hand. "You can't see it again until December."

"Oh, Tyler, you're mean!" She reached to hand it to him and squeezed his hand. "I can't quit looking at it. How did you know my size?"

"I didn't. I called your mom in Townsend, introduced myself and told her I wanted to marry her daughter. First, I needed her consent and then I needed to know if you had a high school class ring she could measure for me. She was so neat. She talked and talked and was so excited. She promised she would keep it all a big secret. You know the last thing she said to me was to be sure and ask Patrick and Sue for their approval. She must be a hell of a woman."

"That she is," Faith said with tears in her eyes. She has been the best mom a girl could ever have. She sacrificed a lot for me. I'd like her to walk me down the aisle."

"You mean, like give you away?"

Faith grinned through tears. "You know me better than that, Tyler England. Not exactly give me away, accenting the give. Slavery is over, but you know…represent the exchange of love from one person to another."

"I should have known my 'Little Yellow Rose' would have her own ideas. I'll bet you want us to write our own vows, too," he teased, lovingly.

"You got it right."

"Actually, I was a little nervous to pick out the ring by myself. I wasn't sure how you would feel about not picking it out, but you've been so busy with the trial and I…I wanted you to have it."

"I'm thrilled you did. So when can we have the wedding?"

"How about December 21? That way we can couple it with Christmas if you don't mind being away from your family. We could have longer for the honeymoon."

"Tyler, I love my family, but you are the most important person to me now. I love the thought of it being just you and me for our first Christmas."

"Have you thought about where you'd like the wedding?"

"Remember, I don't know much about Dallas, just somewhere small and simple. Are your parents going to be okay with that?"

"My parents will be okay with whatever we choose. They're not fancy people; they would probably prefer the simplicity. You want your dad to do the ceremony don't you?"

"Is that okay with you?"

"It's great. How do you feel about Sid being my best man?" he asked a little worriedly.

"If you think I care because he's black, you've got me figured all wrong. I may be from East Texas, but that's not me. I'm anxious to get to know him."

"Any special place you'd like to go for our honeymoon?"

"You told me once you used to spend Christmas some at your parent's cabin in New Mexico. Could we do that?"

"You mean Ruidoso?" he looked surprised and pleased. "You mean you would really like to do that?"

"Yes. I've never been there. Think we might have a white Christmas?"

"It's been known to happen. I can't think of anything better than to be snowed in with you," he said looking very pleased.

"Do you think your parents will mind our using it? What if they already have plans to go?"

"I'll call tomorrow. I know they will be pleased we want to stay there. It's been years since they went there for Christmas, but I'll check to be sure. If you like, we could spend a few days after that in Santa Fe."

"Oh, good. I've never been there either and I've heard about the adobe houses and the Indian jewelry."

"Then, is it okay if I take care of everything…I mean reservations and all?"

Faith was staring at her ring again. "Tyler, you can plan my entire life if you do as good a job as you did on this ring."

Smiling, he kissed her again. "I think it's time for a bottle of wine," pushing a small button at the tiny side table for the server to come. "This is good. I think I'll get one of these buttons when we get married."

Jabbing him with her knife, she said, "Don't even think about it, Buster," leaving them both laughing as the server walked in.

~

Propped up on his elbows, lying next to Faith, Tyler asked, "What are we going to do today?"

"Look at my ring all day."

"You really do like it? You're not just telling me that, are you?"

"Tyler, you know I love it. Well, first I want to call Alice and scold her for keeping secrets from me, and then I want us to go buy the wedding band for you that matches mine. Hey, what did you do with my band?"

"Don't you worry your beautiful little head. I have it until December 21, and then you can wear it forever."

"Today's our last free day in Boston. Anywhere you want to go?" Tyler asked.

"I wish we had more time so we could go to Cape Cod."

"If we drag ourselves out of this bed, we'll have time. It's only seven o'clock. By the time we're dressed it will be okay to make your calls, and then we can run by the jewelry store. If we leave here about 10:30 we can be to the Cape for a late lunch. We might be late getting back though."

"That's okay. I don't think tomorrow will be that hard in court. I'm ready for everything. I'm hoping the judge will be brief and then it will be over."

"Sounds good. I'll bet Sid is ready to stop dog sitting. I'm ready to see that little pooch."

"If we fly out of here Friday, why don't you invite Sid for dinner Saturday night? You could grill some steaks and I'll do the rest."

Kissing her, "You're a doll. I need to let him know something. I'll call him tomorrow just to let him know what we think is going to happen."

~

After lunch at a small waterfront café in Falmouth, the young couple drove as far as Hyannis Port, trying to get a glimpse of the Kennedy compound.

"Now, we're regular tourists," Tyler said. "Nosy tourists."

"I know Tyler. I know you don't like stuff like this, but I've always wanted to see where they lived."

"Well, now you have seen it, sorta."

"Is that as close as we can get?"

"I believe it is, without getting arrested."

"Okay, but at least I know what the roof looks like. You know what? This whole Cape is nothing like what I expected."

"What do you mean?"

"I guess I was just thinking there were going to be rows and rows of quaint little cottages. You know, Cape Cod style, all along the water. Hell, you can't even see the water most of the time. I wasn't expecting an interstate through a bunch of trees with nothing on either side," she said, wishing they had time to drive to the end.

"Maybe we can come back someday. I understand Provincetown at the very end is the prettiest part, but wouldn't you get jealous if some cute guy pinched me on the rear?" Knowing she didn't know anything about the area, he continued to tease her. "P-town, as it is called has a huge population of gay guys and even more who visit. We could probably get there by nightfall if we press on."

"Never mind, I don't like to share."

"Then I guess we'd better turn back. It will be late either way. And tomorrow will be here before you know it. Aren't you a little excited about the sentencing?"

"Yes, but I guess I'm trying not to think about it much. If he gets probation I'm apt to choke someone."

"I'm glad you warned me."

"The most important part was the conviction," she admitted, but "I want him to have to suffer more than that."

"I understand, but you need to be prepared."

"I'm talking to myself as we speak," she said a little sarcastically and smiling as she put her hands together in a choking position.

~

The courtroom was packed with curious onlookers and journalists. At least five different television vans were parked outside, and cameramen stood on the steps.

"How are you feeling about all this Ms. O'Brien?" one reporter asked as he stuck a microphone in her face.

She stopped, smiled and said, "Why don't you ask me that when we know the penalty? Right now I'm just like you, waiting."

Prompt as he had been throughout the proceedings, Judge Ford had the priest stand, and began reading the decision almost before everyone was seated. "Michael O'Mallory is hereby sentenced to nine years in the state penitentiary." He looked directly at the defendant. "You will be eligible for parole in six years. At the time of your release, you will be on probation for life and face strict monitoring." He motioned to the bailiff to take Father O'Mallory away.

Looking stunned and even frailer than at the beginning of the trial, the priest put his head down, and then saying nothing to Stevens, slowly walked with the bailiff, his hands now in cuffs.

When the court was adjourned, several reporters made a beeline to Faith. The same one, who had asked her earlier, repeated his question.

"I'm pleased with the sentence. I believe it was the fair and right decision."

"Ms. O'Brien, you say that. But this man is 73 years old. He may never leave prison alive. Isn't that a little difficult for you to deal with?"

"He dug his own grave if that's the case."

She heard one of the reporters ask Stevens to comment. "I have no comment except to say that I believe the sentence is extreme."

"Will you appeal?" another reporter asked him.

"I haven't had a chance to talk to my client. Obviously we're both stunned."

Swarming the courtroom, media people talked to each lawyer and then Patrick.

Finally, Faith turned to Tyler, motioning to Patrick, said, "Let's get out of here. I want to pack and go home. We no longer have unfinished business in New England."

Walking out of the courthouse, Faith noticed two television vans surrounded by cameras and heavy cables. A group of people applauded when they saw Faith. Touching her lightly on the back, Tyler walked down the courthouse steps behind Faith with Jeff at her side.

Jeff turned to Tyler. "Take good care of her, you hear. Because if you don't, I'm right behind you… waiting."

Tyler hit him lightly on the arm. "You're a good guy, Jeff. Thanks for all your help. Will you come see us sometime?"

"Yes, Jeff, please," Faith added.

"I'd like that. I'll miss you, Faith. Selfishly, I'm sorry the trial is over."

A single bystander shouted, "Go back to Texas, bitch."

"Can't please them all, I guess," she said, smiling at Tyler as she ducked into a taxi.

~

The next morning Tyler read the two brief stories about the criminal case and civil case to Faith.

O'Mallory Convicted, Sentenced to Nine Years in Prison

Father Michael O'Mallory, after a week of testimony, was sentenced yesterday to nine years in the state penitentiary.

Reporters, photographers and camera crews from as far away as New York City, representing CNN, ABC News, Court TV as well as every local news agency were outside the courtroom to catch a glimpse of the seventy-three year old priest.

Rick McGee, the plaintiff in the case declined comment, but his lawyer Faith O'Brien said that justice had finally been served.

The case actually resulted after O'Brien's father, Patrick O'Brien, filed charges against O'Mallory, but the statute of limitations prevented his case from going forward. Due to the publicity, McGee filed the sexual assault and battery case that led to O'Mallory's conviction yesterday.

According to police records three other adults have accused O'Mallory of molestation and they were in the courtroom to witness the proceedings, not to testify.

Patrick O'Brien did testify against the once-beloved clergyman.

Archdiocese Agrees to Settle Abuse Charges

Boston, September 12 – The Archdiocese of Boston has agreed to pay an undisclosed amount to settle at least five cases against a priest accused of molesting young boys during the past thirty-five years.

The agreement, which was signed yesterday, settles cases against Michael O'Mallory and the Archdiocese. Officials said

O'Mallory would also be defrocked following his criminal case completed earlier this week where the priest was found guilty and given a nine-year sentence.

Faith O'Brien, the lawyer for the plaintiffs, said she was prepared to go to court over the abuse and the Archdiocese's subsequent cover up of at least one of the cases, but was glad the officials agreed to settle.

Just last week prosecutors in the Boston Commonwealth said they were preparing to convene a grand jury to investigate how the Archdiocese of Boston responded to the early allegations of sexual abuse by Father O'Mallory.

A spokesperson for the district attorney's office said there has been no determination made at this time, as to whether that investigation will be halted due to today's settlement.

Ignoring the stories, as if in a daze, Faith said, "I've never seen checks for this much money, Tyler."

"No, me neither."

"I really didn't want to take any from dad, but I know he wouldn't have it any other way."

"That's right. He told me that one way or the other he was going to give you the same amount as the McGee's agreed to pay. Besides, he would have never had any had it not been for you. But I'm glad you only took half of it. That way he and Sue can get on with their lives. Maybe he won't take the job at SMU after all," Tyler said.

"He told me he plans to talk to the Dean tomorrow. He hates to back away from his agreement, but I think he'd like to propose teaching less than full-time. I hope they can work something out. That way they could have an apartment in Dallas, but he would still be able to travel for his speaking engagements and spend time in Italy."

"What are you going to do with your money?"

"You mean, what are we going to do? We need to talk about it. I guess CDs or something safe. I'm not a fan of the stock market. What do you think?"

"Maybe we should talk to a financial guy, although that scares me too. We should probably diversify it; you know some bonds, or other things as well as certificates."

"I hate all that. Will you check around and see what you can find out, Tyler?"

"Sure, you make it and I'll invest it," he teased.

"I'm almost finished packing, Tyler."

"You mean, you've tossed most of your things into the suitcase," he winked at her.

"Whatever. I'm anxious to go."

"So, your mother's not flying back with us?"

"No, she said they needed to figure everything out first, since the money has put a new light on things. Even though Dad needs to go back to Hidden Harbor, she said she is prepared to go with him. Whatever, they'll have to face that together, and they will. Hurry, let's not be late for our plane."

Chapter 15

Handing Sid a beer, Faith said, "Tyler tells me you have quite a handsome son."

"Well, I think he's pretty special and awfully cute. He favors his mom."

"You're being too humble, My Man. You know he looks like you," Tyler interjected.

"Oh, you know what they say, we all look alike," Sid said, grinning. "Oh, the latest, Shea told me his mom is now living with a guy who works offshore. This is her third since we split, first the shrimper, then the mechanic, and now the driller. She's set her sights pretty high, huh? Of course she blames it all on me."

"How does she figure that?" Faith asked.

"Oh, she says if I had cared enough about her I would have stayed there. I guess I thought if she cared enough she would leave there. I never imagined she'd be like she is now. She's settling for whatever, whoever. It's really sad, but nothing I can do. We're done. I feel bad for Shea, but he's a good kid. He'll be okay," Sid said with sadness in his voice.

Faith looked at him. She could see he still had some feelings for her, but the emotions were raw and there was a hint of bitterness in his voice.

"It's too bad she didn't know what a good thing she had going," Faith said.

With a noticeable change in his demeanor, Sid said, "Oh well, there's a woman out there somewhere for me. After all if

Tyler can get a woman like you, surely I can get someone," he said frogging Tyler on the arm and winking at Faith.

"Yeah, well, maybe if she's blind and deaf," Tyler said, returning the jab.

Obviously, they liked each other and their verbal sparring was all in fun.

"Hey Man, I'm being serious now. What do you say; will you be my best man in the wedding?"

"Really?" Sid asked seriously.

"Sure."

"I'd be honored," he said looking at Faith to watch her reaction. "Are you okay with that?" sounding skeptical.

"We're the honored ones, Sid. It's going to be December 21. Is that a problem for you with the holidays?"

"Not a bit. I wouldn't miss it. Where's it going to be?"

"We're not sure yet, but it's going to be small," Tyler said, changing the subject. "Now, let's get the steaks on, Buddy. I'm starved."

"I'll be out in a minute. I've got a few things to do here. You better take an extra beer..."

They were already out the door before she finished her sentence and began setting the table.

~

The remainder of September and all of October passed in a flurry of activity.

Since Alice had invited everyone to Townsend for Thanksgiving, Patrick and Sue decided it was the perfect time to repeat their vows in front of an American minister and their family.

"Did I tell you, Tom, you know your dad's best friend from Hidden Harbor, is coming for the wedding?" Sue asked.

"No. Is his wife?" Faith asked.

"He says she has to work because the library is going to be open for the holidays. Besides she and Carol were close, I know it would be hard for her. Tom, I think he is more curious than anything. He tried to get away to come to the trial but he had some big case going there. Patrick is, of course, thrilled and anxious to see him."

"So, where will he stay?"

Sue said, "Alice is getting him a room at The Derrick. I'll bet he'll be really impressed." She and Faith laughed at the same time. "Those amenities will carry him away, don't you think, as will the chipper personality of the owner old man Green. Alice says he's as grumpy as ever. Patrick said we'd stay there, too, just to make him feel more comfortable. Besides the young couple will be moved into my house by then anyway."

"So what are you wearing for the wedding?"

"I bought an A line soft wool in whipped mint. I think it's really nice. I found a shirt almost the same color for Patrick with a darker tie of the same hue."

"Have you told Mom what color?"

"Yes. We talked last week. I'm sorry I didn't tell you earlier."

"That's okay. I haven't had time to shop anyway. I'm going this weekend. I'll try to find something to complement those colors. Tyler will probably have to wear a white shirt. I'm not sure I can talk him into anything green."

"White will be fine. Patrick hasn't had a chance to ask Tyler if he minds Tom standing up with him, too."

"Tyler will be fine. Tell Dad not to worry. That's really better since you have Mom and me."

"We thought so too, but I know Patrick wanted to ask Tyler anyway."

"When are you going to Townsend?"

"We're leaving Wednesday. Since this will be Patrick's first trip back, there are a couple of places we want to see."

"Do you think that will be hard for you both? I mean, well, I'm just a little worried that it might open some old wounds."

"Faith, Honey, those wounds have long healed. Sure, a part of this weekend will be bittersweet. Actually, I'm looking forward to our being there together again. This time I think we'll do it right."

"How do you think Dad will handle it?"

"We've talked about it. At first he was a little hesitant, but once I assured him that I was okay, he was, too."

"Good, I've worried about it."

"Well, you can stop worrying. We're doing good Faith. We really are."

"We're driving down early Thursday. Mom said she absolutely did not want any help with Thanksgiving. Ben's on call so she said she hoped she would have the whole kitchen to herself."

"Well, too bad, because I plan to be right there, in her way, making pies," Sue said.

"Good luck. You know how territorial she can be," Faith said. "We'll see you around noon. I've gotta run."

~

Out of Dallas, the landscape changed from concrete and tall buildings to long stretches of nothing but pine trees and an occasional leafless crepe myrtle.

"Don't you think it's pretty here, Tyler? When I finished junior college, I couldn't wait to leave the piney woods, and I would never want to live here again, but I do think it's pretty."

"Yes, but you're talking to a West Texas boy who until I moved to Dallas was happy to have a few mesquite trees in the yard."

"Well, at least you didn't have to rake leaves or pick up sweetgum balls. Yuck!"

"I don't believe I've ever seen a sweetgum ball, not that I feel deprived."

"Well, obviously you didn't have cool Christmas decorations in West Texas like we did in East Texas. After all, what's a holiday centerpiece without toothpicks stuck in a few sweetgum balls to look festive then spray-painted red and sprinkled with gold glitter? Now that, My Love, is an ornament."

Tyler laughed, "Sorry I've missed those. Maybe you can make me one while we're there."

"Only if you are really nice and act right."

"I'll be at my best," he grinned.

~

"Mom is in a complete tizzy," Faith said. "I knew she would be this way, but she wouldn't hear of my help."

"It's fun to watch her spin, but I think I'll excuse myself to the den for a little football. Okay?" Tyler asked.

"I think that's a great idea. I'll probably join you in about five minutes. I'm sure I'll be kicked out of the kitchen."

Walking into the den laughing, "What did I tell you? She wants to do it her way," Faith said.

"Must be a family trait."

Throwing a pillow at him, "Remember, if you're not nice you won't get your sweetgum ball ornament. I think I'll take Judge for a walk. You want to go? She probably does not understand why she's been relegated to the back yard."

"Sure, just let me grab my windbreaker. It's a little cool. I'll get yours too."

~

The dinner was just what Faith expected…large. Alice had cooked a twenty pound turkey and a ham, mashed potatoes, sweet potatoes, green bean casserole, Waldorf salad, corn salad, giblet and brown gravy, two heaping bowls of dressing, Parker House rolls, a pumpkin pie, a mincemeat pie and a pecan pie.

Faith looked in the kitchen on her way to the dining room. "You've got to peek in there. Every pot and pan is dirty. There is something on every inch of the counter. She didn't want my help preparing, but I'll bet I get to clean up the mess," she whispered to Tyler.

The family was relaxed, talking easily and laughing at the stories Alice told. Pride and love showed as she described some of Faith's antics as she was growing up.

"I wish you had told me some of this before now, Alice. I mean, before I proposed, now I'm way too committed," Tyler teased, looking at Faith.

"You hardly knew her name before you proposed, Sonny Boy. Nobody had time to warn you," Alice jabbed at Tyler.

He blushed. "I guess you're right."

"I see the Pizza Joint is still here. I think that's where Sue wants to go after the wedding tomorrow," Patrick chimed in.

"You've got to be kidding," Alice said, aghast, turning to Sue. "That place is a bigger dump than it was thirty years ago."

"That's okay. Patrick and I went there on our first date," Sue said, defensively.

"Well, Honey, you'll probably have the same oil they used to grease your pizza pan back then. Nothing has changed there except it's more run down than ever. There's tomato sauce on those walls that has been there since the week it opened. It was old when we were in high school. Do you really want to go there?"

"I really do," Sue said, beaming.

"Well, we'll have to come home to change clothes first. I'm not sitting on those chairs in my new dress. It would never be the same, and I love this sage color."

Tyler grinned at Alice and whispered in Faith's ear, "Talk about a character, your mom is one of a kind. I like her spunk."

~

The wedding ceremony lasted less than fifteen minutes. "And to think, I shaved my legs for this," Alice quipped as she hugged first Sue, then Patrick.

"It's been a while coming, huh Alice?" Patrick asked.

"You mean the wedding or my legs?" Alice paused then added, "I'll say, but better late than never. Guess we'll go change for this big celebration at the Pizza Joint. Are you sure you don't want to wait and go there, just you and Patrick tomorrow night, for a nice romantic meal? Sue, I'm sure they will stick a new 50¢ candle in one of those old Chianti bottles for you. Come on, let's all go to the best restaurant this area has to offer, Johnny Cace's, my treat."

Sue looked to Patrick for direction.

"I was planning on leaving in the morning, but what's one more day, if my bride wants a bowl of spaghetti at The Pizza Joint, that's what she will get. We'll stay and go there tomorrow night."

"Thank goodness," Alice said. "I can leave on my panty hose and fancy dress. You know I don't get out much," she said, slapping Patrick on the back.

He laughed, knowing she talked that way just to aggravate him, but he loved her just the same, because she was Sue's only sister and Faith's favorite person.

"I never would have believed she would have gotten me in a Baptist Church," he said, turning to Alice.

"Scary, isn't it? Next thing you know you'll be singing 'Bringing in the Sheaves' instead of that stiff stuff you're used to."

Faith looked at Tyler and just shook her head as if to say, sorry, but she is who she is.

"Hang on. I'm going back in the church, and call Ben to see if he can meet us at Cace's." Looking at Patrick and Sue, she continued, "Why don't y'all go on and get us a big table? I'll ride with Faith and Tyler if they'll wait."

"No problem, Mom, take your time." She and Tyler held hands and walked to the car.

"I'm glad that's over," Faith said, acting relieved.

"Why?"

"I don't know. I guess every kid doesn't get the opportunity to see her parents get married. It's just strange after all these years."

"Were you ever mad at them for the choices they made?"

"Mad? I was totally pissed and bitter. If I hadn't had such a wonderful life with Mom, I don't know that I could have ever forgiven them. That's why I love her in spite of her antics. She loved me unconditionally so I feel the same toward her."

"How did you work through it all?"

"With maturity I realized everyone makes mistakes. I think I was more hardened toward my mother when I realized she out and out deserted me. All those years I thought she was dead, so when I found out she wasn't, I was so glad to have her in my life. Then it all came tumbling down—that she had left me, a baby. I still have moments when I am a tad resentful, but those thoughts fade quickly now. Mom, though will always be my real parent. She was my rock. For years I was really mad at my dad, although I understand now that his bad choices, bad decisions are what caused the house of cards to fall. It's still sad we all have so many lost years. But you can't bring them back. That's just life."

Alice came running, "I'm on my way, hold on. Sorry it took so long, but I couldn't find Ben. Turns out he had to go to the hospital, some problem, but he can leave now, so he's going to meet us."

"Slow down, or you'll be at the hospital."

"I'll have you know, Young Lady, I'm in tip top shape and can run circles around you."

"No doubt, but just in case you are overestimating yourself, we have time. You know, Mom, I really like Ben, He's good for you and you for him." Faith said.

"I like him too." Alice actually blushed when she said it. "No fool like an old fool, huh?" poking fun at herself.

"I'm sure glad you talked them into going somewhere besides the Pizza Joint from what Faith has said about it," Tyler said.

"Yes, me too, but I want to take Tyler by for a quick look around tomorrow before we leave. It's like a historical marker here, you know." Faith added.

"You mean, hysterical marker," Alice said, winking at Tyler.

~

When the dinner was over, Ben stood. "I'd like to make a toast if I may, to the bride and groom."

After he said a few words to Patrick and Sue, he continued. "I also have a request…this one is for Faith," who suddenly looked puzzled.

"Maybe this is not the typical or traditional way to do things, but there is nothing typical about this family." With everyone laughing, he said, "Faith, I would like permission to marry your mom."

Turning immediately to Alice who was smiling a broad smile, Faith jumped up to hug her. "Oh, Mom, I'm so happy for you." Then she looked at Ben who was still standing.

"You know you're getting the best, most giving woman in the world, don't you? Just treat her special – that's all I ask," wiping away a tear. When she looked around the table, there were no dry eyes.

~

The next morning as Faith and Tyler were leaving, Alice said to Faith, "We're not sure exactly when we want our wedding to be, sometime in late spring or early summer, we think. It's going to be at South Padre Island. You remember Ben has a place there. Anyway, I want you to be my matron of honor. But you know what, you have to go barefooted."

"Huh?"

"Yep, we're going to tie the knot right on the beach. I'm gonna wear a long linen dress with a flower in my hair and put my toes in the sand. I've got to leave my footprints somewhere, Love."

"You've already left them all over my heart, but are you serious?" Faith asked, knowing full well she was.

"As a heart attack. You can't wear shoes either."

"What did Ben say to all of this?"

"Oh, Ben, he's so laid back. I don't think he was too keen on the idea, but he said I was the bride so I get to choose. I think he'll end up wearing a pair of sandals though and that's okay. I may get him in one of those Hawaiian type flowery shirts or something beachy. I'm going to keep working on him."

"Okay, Mom, just give me plenty of notice so I can paint my toenails and buy a sundress."

"Honey, when we get to the island, we'll get pedicures, massages and the works to get us ready. The wedding will be real simple with just a few of us, and the preacher. Ben and I will be standing in the sand, water lapping up on our feet, saying our vows. This time, it'll be right Faith. I won't be marrying a spoiled brat who wants to fool around."

"Do Grandma and Grandpa know?"

"I've hinted a little to get them prepared, but they want me to be happy. They know they'll always be special to me. After all I was their only daughter-in-law, until their lousy son screwed it all up. No man is going to change how I love them; their own son didn't. I'll see you in a few weeks, Sweetheart, for your big wedding. I can't wait. You'll be the prettiest bride ever. Don't you think she will, Tyler?"

"Without a doubt, Mom. Is it okay that I call you that?"

"I would be honored," Alice said with a slight blush.

"It was a great Thanksgiving. Thanks for including me. Faith loves you so very much, and I see why. You make it easy," Tyler added.

As Faith was stepping up into the truck, Alice said, "You've got yourself a good one, too, Faith," kissing her on the cheek and hugging her. "Call me when you get back just to let me know you're safe." Looking in the cab, she noticed Judge. "I see she's comfortable and ready for the ride. Sweet dog. Bye, Hon."

And with that, Faith, Tyler and Judge drove by the Pizza Joint for a quick look and then out of Townsend.

Chapter 16

December dawned colder and wetter than usual for North Texas. Rain had fallen every day the first week creating driving havoc for the beginning of the holiday shopping rush. Faith had hoped to finish her own shopping early and to begin moving a few larger items to Tyler's before the wedding grew closer, but both the soggy weather and her hectic schedule were less than cooperative. She was only able to sort through her belongings and determine what she wanted to take and what would be donated to one of the local shelters for abused women.

Tyler was so busy winding up a case until four days before the ceremony that Faith hardly saw him. Due to his workload, he was even late to one of her bridal showers. He apologized profusely while Faith excitedly showed him new kitchen gadgets and lush monogrammed towels.

"I don't see a hyphen on this towel she teased." She had been nervous to talk to Tyler about hyphenating her name to Faith O'Brien-England after the wedding for work purposes, but he had quickly assured her he thought that was smart.

"You're not mad, Tyler?" she asked. "I mean when we have children I want them to be just England, but I just thought for my work that…"

He cut her off quickly. "Sweetheart, I'm not bothered or threatened by that. I realize I'm a little traditional, but that's what people with careers already in place often do. Now stop worrying and please don't ever be nervous about asking me something. That's not even like you."

She smiled meekly and confessed that she wasn't nervous any more, but that the idea was a selfish thing on her part and she felt guilty, she guessed, for wanting to do it.

~

Faith's friends from the university began trickling in for the pre-wedding festivities. Almost six months had passed since Faith had seen many of them, although they had talked on a few occasions. After the tenth visitor arrived, the girls changed the plans for the bachelorette party, deciding that rather than go to a fancy restaurant and lounge, they all preferred to stay at Faith's, order in pizza, tell stories, share memories, drink wine, each give Faith a "dirty gift" and have a slumber party. They agreed that everyone should be asleep by two or three o'clock "…so Faith's eyes wouldn't be puffy at the wedding." Faith had declined a luncheon in hopes of keeping the entire weekend as simple as possible. The reception was not in her control. Mr. Jackson had insisted that he and his wife were doing everything including the decorations, the band and the bar. But knowing that Mr. Jackson had circuitously quizzed Tyler about colors Faith wanted to use, she didn't worry.

~

The morning of the wedding day could not have been a more gloriously beautiful first day of winter. The sun shone and gave warmth and brightness to the cool, cloudless blue skies. Being the first to wake, Faith stepped over bodies stretched from wall to wall of her den. This was her big day and she wasn't about to miss any of it.

She called Tyler. "I'm not supposed to talk to you, right?"

He laughed. "I think that's what they say, but since when have you followed tradition?"

"How was your party?" she pried.

"Okay, we did the usual bar detail. 'HOOTERS' as you would guess. It was really pretty mild. I guess we're past going to the real titty bar joints."

"I should hope so. Are you excited about today?" Faith asked.

"Very. I'm ready."

"Me too. I've missed you. Gosh, we've been busy." Noticing her friends, she stopped talking to Tyler and laughed. "I see a few of my friends are slowly pulling themselves off the floor holding their wino heads. I've already set aspirin out on a tray. Guess I better hang up and soothe their aching heads with a few Bloody Marys. See you tonight. I love you."

"Okay, Hon. It won't be soon enough. I love you, too."

~

Standing before Patrick, Faith looked both classy and radiant in her creamy winter white silk shantung suit, offset by Tyler in his winter white linen dinner jacket. Alice, who had walked Faith down the aisle and Sue, her matron of honor, held petite bouquets of yellow roses and white orchids with a wintry mix, and looked stunning in cinnamon A-line silk dresses. Faith's nosegay, was all yellow roses to match the single yellow roses worn by Tyler, Sid, Evan and Patrick.

Patrick began the service by saying a few words about the importance and sanctity of marriage. When Patrick turned to Tyler, the couple had never taken their eyes off each other and Faith continued to gaze lovingly as Tyler began repeating the lines from their favorite song, "I Cross My Heart." When he had recited the entire song, he stopped, blinking back tears.

Faith began, forcing back her own tears, her voice quivering slightly: "I use a favorite poem to answer the question of how

I love you. 'Let me count the ways. I love thee to the depth and breadth and height my soul can reach, when feeling out of sight, for the ends of being and ideal grace. I love thee to the level of every day's most quiet need, by sun and candlelight. I love thee freely, as men strive for right; I love thee purely, as they turn from praise. I love thee with the passion put to use in my old griefs, and with my childhood's faith. I love thee with a love I seemed to lose with my lost saints – I love thee with the breath, smiles, tears, of all my life! And, if God choose, I shall but love thee better after death.'"

Turning to Tyler, Patrick asked, "Do you Tyler take Faith to be your wife for better or worse, in sickness and health, in riches or hardships as long as you both shall live?"

"I do."

Patrick then turned to Faith and repeated the same.

"I do," she answered softly.

After they were pronounced husband and wife, they kissed quickly, and smiling to the audience, Faith took Tyler's arm, stopping just long enough for her to kiss Tyler's mother on the cheek and hand her a single yellow rose. She then handed a rose to Tyler's sister, Libby, on the next row.

Mr. Jackson and Sara looked pleased as Tyler and Faith entered the ballroom of the old, extravagantly embellished country club that smelled of wealth and old Dallas tradition. Tonight, the band was playing country western music and the tables were detailed in China, white linen table coverings and snowy orchids in ornate porcelain vases. Yellow roses filled tall urns placed strategically throughout the room.

When the band began playing, "I Cross My Heart," from which Tyler had said his vows, the young couple took to the dance floor for the first dance, absorbed in the rhythm of their bodies against one another and in the words of the song. Patrick hesitated to cut in and waited until the next song to dance with Faith while Tyler danced first with Alice and then Sue.

After a brief time, Mr. Jackson asked Faith to dance a slow waltz and to Faith's surprise he was a good dancer. He didn't seem the dancing type, but he often destroyed perceptions; this much Faith knew. Early in his adult life, he had been sold short, but had proven the skeptics wrong every time. Slight in height, but sturdy in build, the sixtyish attorney was not a handsome man, but just the same, he wasn't unattractive. His hair had receded leaving only a patch of unremarkable brownish hair circling his head. Being a good two inches taller than her boss, Faith thought he looked a little like a larger Danny DeVito, but his eyes were more piercing, although they could be gentle looking as well. Over time he had developed an intense look as a defense attorney in the courtroom. Tyler had told her that according to legal legend when he first began practice, some of the more distinguished lawyers, failing to notice his brilliance and determination, thought him a laid back pushover because of his outgoing friendly personality and wicked sense of humor. Within only a few years, he had become an attorney to be reckoned with, and along with his father and quiet friend and colleague Alfred Henry, had built one of the foremost legal firms not just in Dallas but, in all the state.

His wife, Sara, an equally extroverted, genial person, was stylish and pretty as well as highly respected in the upscale social circles where she often led fundraisers and charity benefits.

"Thank you so much for this wonderful reception," Faith said when the dance was over.

"It is our pleasure, Faith. You know I would do anything for that boy, and you are becoming just as special because it's obvious to Sara and me that you love him genuinely."

She blushed slightly. "Yes, I do and it only took a second, it seems."

He smiled, "Sometimes that happens, but life goes fast so you need to grab it while you can." Taking her arm through his, they walked back to the table where Tyler sat talking with Sid and his date. "I guess I'd better return her before you start to get jealous," he teased Tyler.

~

When it came time to leave the reception, the parking attendant pretended to be unable to find Tyler's Blazer. In a look of panic, he explained he would search one last time. This time he drove up in a new white Dodge Ram extended cab truck with "Just Married" written on the back window.

"It appears, sir, that someone traded vehicles with you."

Looking puzzled, Tyler flashed a glance at Faith.

"Surprise, Tyler. Happy wedding day."

Dumbfounded, he exclaimed, "I can't believe it…a new truck."

By now a crowd had gathered and were cheering and clapping. Faith tossed her bouquet to Alice and shouted, "You're next."

"Well, are you going to drive it or not?" Sid yelled, obviously in on the secret.

Turning, Tyler smiled and opened the door for Faith, helping her in. He then gave the crowd a thumbs-up and waved as he opened the driver's side door, squared himself in the seat beside his bride and drove away.

~

When they reached their hotel room, Tyler unlocked the door and opened it, reaching to draw Faith up in his arms. "Across the threshold, My Love."

On the bed lay a Ranch Mink jacket and matching hat. "It's not a truck," he said, almost apologetically, "but I thought it might be cold on our honeymoon."

"Oh, Tyler, it is gorgeous…And I know that this is a special kind of mink. You shouldn't have, but I love it" she paused and kissed him, "but as long as I have you, I'll feel warm all over."

Chapter 17

They sat on the well-worn brindle brown leather couch in the Ruidoso cabin, huddled beneath the radiant red wool Indian blanket, sipping Merlot. Except for their own breathing, the crackling fire was the only sound Faith and Tyler heard. Flickering candles illuminated either side of the room and added a fragrant hint of vanilla to the air that smelled heavily of piñon from the burning logs and fresh Christmas tree, coupled with the old timbers that shaped the A-frame structure.

"This is nice, Tyler," Faith said almost in a whisper.

"Yes, I've spent some nice Christmases here, but this is definitely the best ever. We did a good job on the tree don't you think?"

"I think it is wonderful. It was fun cutting it down and doing it all ourselves. That friend of your dad's is a true western character, isn't he?"

Tyler laughed, "Yep, Zeke is something of a mountain man, a true free spirit. He's broken horses for over half a century. The only thing that's broken him was a woman. My dad said she tore his heart apart when he first came to New Mexico and fell in love with the Indian woman. She thought he was her ticket off the Mescalero Reservation into the city lights, but all Zeke wanted was a little warm cabin, a few acres, his horses, and her. When she realized he wasn't going anywhere, she did. He never got over it. For a while he drank himself to sleep every night, or went over to a little tavern at the edge of the village. One night he'd had too much to drink and he fell asleep at the wheel and hit a tree with his pickup. He was bunged up pretty badly and they thought he might lose a leg. Dad said he never drank another drop of whiskey after that, but he became even more of a recluse. Everybody up here knows him though. He still goes to the Log Cabin Café for breakfast once in awhile and of course he still breaks horses for most of the ranchers around Ruidoso, Nogal and the Carrizozo areas."

"I thought he was really sweet," Faith said.

"Yes, he's a Gentle Ben of a guy, probably too good for his own good, but that's okay, you could tell from his place he doesn't require much, huh?"

"Yeah, I thought how simple but sad his life was, just he and his old dog sitting in that little adobe house nestled in the trees."

"He does have a beautiful view of Sierra Blanca, doesn't he?"

"Yes, but it seems such a waste to watch the sun fading behind it every day all alone."

"I guess he's used to it by now," Tyler muttered, drinking his last sip of wine. "I'd better throw another log or two on the fire. We've about let it die to ashes. It's getting colder," he said, pushing back the blanket and walking over to the fireplace of smooth river rock. The logs caught immediately from the hot embers.

Sitting on the hearth he looked lovingly at Faith, while the twinkling lights from the tree danced on the bearskin rug at her feet. "I could look at you forever."

"I'm glad, but I sure wish you would get back here under this blanket. I can feel air coming in from somewhere."

Tyler smiled, "We never quite got all the logs chinked enough, but I think most of the draft comes from around the windows. You sound like my mom. She claims she is cold from the minute she gets here until she leaves, summer or winter. Needless to say, my dad likes it better than she does."

"I love it. It's beautiful, but the thought of a bath scares the hell out of me," Faith said, laughing as she put her cold hand on Tyler's face. "How's that My Love?"

"Yikes."

"This may be the world's fastest shower," she said as she grabbed her robe and sleep clothes.

"I'll help warm it up," he said, tossing his clothes in the clothes hamper and reaching for a towel. "Hurry, start the water. It takes forever to get hot."

"I'm freezing, Tyler."

"Well, as soon as we are out of the shower we can get under some big covers upstairs. Bet you didn't know you can see the stars from the loft."

"Tyler England, I've seen stars ever since I met you."

~

They lay together in silence, long after they had made love.

"I've never told you about my granddad, Daddy Ty, have I?"

"No."

"He was a quaint little guy, not one for many words, shy and introverted. Anyway, I always think of him this time of year because he loved Christmas. You know my mom was an only child. My grandparents had wanted a houseful he had once said, but he quickly added they were blessed with one who filled the house. I guess Christmas was quieter for them than they had wished so when we all came along; Christmas was a special time for him. He picked pecans on his farm and shelled them all year for my mom. He always put them in quart Mason jars and tied a big red ribbon around them. We kids always got money from him and I loved that. We never knew how much, so before we opened the packages, which Daddy Ty wrapped himself, my dad would bargain with us. Of course, he knew how much we were getting. I'd be so tempted to take his offer, but was always afraid it might be less, so I never did. I was never sorry. Daddy Ty didn't have much money but his gift was always more than my dad agreed to give.

"But, what I recall most is no matter what time one of us got up in the middle of the night on Christmas, he was always sitting there awake in a chair right by the tree. Ever since I can remember he had a cloud of white hair and a sheepish grin. I can honestly say his eyes sparkled at Christmas. Sometimes I would get up at four in the morning, thinking I would be there before him. Maybe he had been there all night or maybe he had just gotten there, but no matter what, I never arrived first!

"He died in March the year I turned eighteen and you know what, before he died he gave my dad the money for our Christmas. That year we had his gift but not him and Christmas has never really been the same," his voice trailing off sadly.

"You really loved him didn't you, Tyler?"

"It's funny, I wasn't around him much, but the times I was were really special. Of course, I'm named for him so that makes it unique as well."

Faith turned to kiss him softly on the cheek. "You know you're a sentimental guy."

"You think?" He took a wisp of her hair and twisted it gingerly as he continued to talk.

"One time, I guess I was about nine and I wanted a baseball glove. I asked him if I could do something to earn money and he let me mow his yard. He had one of those old-fashioned push mowers, the kind with no motor. Have you ever seen one?"

Before Faith could answer, he continued, "Anyway he paid me five bucks and I took off to town walking the three or so miles. When I got to the little variety store, the glove was there, but I was short about six dollars, so I walked back and told him my plight. He said, 'Boy, here's three more dollars, that's the best I can do, maybe they'll take less.' So I walked back to town.

The store manager looked at me with sympathy, but told me he just couldn't take less than ten dollars, so I was still two dollars short.

"I walked home totally discouraged. Daddy Ty saw me ambling up to the house, kicking a can as I went along. He met me at the door and asked what was bothering me, and told me I looked like I'd lost my best friend. Again, I told him my story. He smiled and pulled out two more dollars and then, another fifty cents. 'Why don't you stop at Gentry's on your way, boy, and buy yourself a coke?' I never worked so hard for anything in my life, and I've never forgotten the smile on his face when he pulled the last two dollars and fifty cents out of his pocket."

"Tomorrow's Christmas Eve, our first together. Just think, Tyler, someday you'll be a granddad and the kid might be lying here talking about you."

"I hope so, Faith, and I hope we have a houseful of kids, too."

"Well, maybe not a houseful, but three would be nice, huh?"

"Three would be perfect. Good night, Sweetheart. I love you."

"I love you more, Tyler England."

"Not more, there's no way," he said, closing his eyes and wrapping his arms around her.

In a tiny voice, Faith asked, "Tyler, are you cold?"

"A little bit, are you?"

"I'm freezing! I thought warm air rose to the top. This loft seems to be the coldest part of the cabin."

"Did you say air rose or froze?" he laughed. "I know where there are some more blankets. I just hate to get out from under these. Let's flip to see who gets up."

"Your brain must have frozen," she said, pushing him out with her cold feet.

He hurriedly threw a blanket and an old worn, hand stitched crazy quilt over Faith.

"Help! Now I'm smothering from all this weight," she badgered him.

"We're going to smother together because this is wonderful," Tyler said, easing down into the deep covers. "I just hope I don't have to get up to go to the bathroom anytime soon. I should have put on some socks. That floor is ice cold!"

"I'm much better now. Tell me some more stories," Faith nudged, as she snuggled into Tyler.

"Once upon a time, there was a little girl who wouldn't go to sleep so her hubby said that if she would be good and close her eyes he would make her hot chocolate for breakfast and build a big fire and wrap a blanket around her..." He stopped and waited for her response. She was fast asleep.

"Tyler," Faith screamed. "Hurry, come here!"

"What's wrong, are you okay?" he called, running to her.

Faith was standing at the window looking out.

"There are deer everywhere. And it's snowing."

"Oh, I thought something was wrong," he said, looking relieved. "Yeah, there are always deer around here. Wait until we're here sometime in summer. Then you might see a bear!"

"A bear? A real bear?"

"Well, you might see a stuffed one, too, but I'm talking a real bear," he said. "They come down from the mountains looking for food. Late in the day they're usually scavenging in the trash cans."

"Look at those flakes, Tyler. They're huge. They look so pretty falling on the tall pines and spruce. I think it's beginning to stick. We may be snowed in for real. I hope we have enough food for a few days. Do you think we should go to the store just in case?"

"Why don't you pull on some sweats? I know a quaint little breakfast café, and then we'll get a pot roast or something that can slow cook all day. How does that sound?"

"Great, do you have a deck of cards?"

"My family's the world's biggest game players. You name the game, it's here."

"Good, I'm up for a challenge."

"This could be brutal."

Once, back from breakfast and the grocery store, Faith stood silent watching the sky unfold in white beauty and thinking that there is a blissful sweet calmness that mesmerizes the soul of one who takes the time to watch the earth undergo this pearly metamorphosis. The green pines and blue spruce were transforming into tall alabaster pyramids springing up among mounds of indistinguishable life right before her eyes. Tiny finches forged the ground for seeds Faith had lightly tossed into the snow, waiting now to be plucked from the soft canopy. The purity of the landscape was tranquil and serene. She was suddenly startled from her thoughts when Tyler wrapped his arms around her from behind.

"You certainly are quiet. You're like a little girl who has never seen a snowfall."

"I haven't seen many. It is so peaceful, Tyler. It's almost scary how pristine everything seems. I remember as a kid how much we wished for snow, mainly because we would miss a day of school, but how much we loved to step in its freshness, touch it. Just looking at it makes me feel like a kid again. Hey, I think I vaguely remember, before I fell asleep, something about hot chocolate."

Tyler smiled, "Coming right up. Pull that rocker over by the window. I'll bring the chocolate to you there."

"Growing up in East Texas, we didn't see much snow, maybe a few flakes every two or three years. If we had anything, it was usually ice, but no matter how slippery or slushy dirty it was we loved it. From the time I can remember until junior high I had a little boyfriend, who I would call the minute I saw a flake. He would do the same if he saw one first. Mom used to tease me about Timmy calling."

"So, where is this guy?" Tyler pretended to be jealous.

"You don't have to worry. I hear he's gay now."

"Whew, that's a relief. From the look on your face awhile ago when you were in a trance at the window, I thought you might leave me for a memory."

"Not a chance." She leaned down to kiss Tyler, who now was propped up on two large pillows beside her rocker. "You even thought of the marshmallows."

"No, they were in the pantry from about two years ago."

Faith screwed up her face, and then as soon as she saw Tyler's grin, she knew he was playing another joke on her. She slapped him lightly on the arm. "Tyler England, you drive me crazy."

"How crazy? Crazy enough to go back to bed with me?"

Now it was Faith's time to grin. "Well, you know what they say in East Texas about the snow. It's like sex. You never know how much you'll get or how long it will last."

"Let's go do some research," Tyler said, taking her empty cup in one hand and her hand in the other.

~

"Tyler, it's after one o'clock. We must have fallen asleep. I was supposed to put the roast in the crock pot when we returned from breakfast."

"It's okay; we'll just cook it on the stove later. It'll be just as good."

"But I was going to use my famous onion soup recipe," she said, looking disappointed.

"You still can, but we can do that later. Let's get dressed and go play in the snow. Look, it's still falling."

Both were bundled up in coats, gloves and hats as they tramped through a half foot of fresh powder.

"I almost hate to disturb it," Faith said.

"Yeah, but I don't know my way around here, so unless you brought some bread crumbs we might not find our way back without the shoe prints."

"There you go again. Do you ever tell me the truth?"

Tyler stopped and hugged her, the bulk of their heavy coats preventing them from coming close. Suddenly serious, "Yes, always when I tell you how much I love you." He kissed her icy cold lips and pushed some loose wisps of her hair under her furry hat.

"You want to build a snowman?"

"Only if we build a snow woman, too. When am I going to train you to be politically correct?"

"I'm learning. I'm learning," as he clumped a handful of snow and tossed it straight at her stomach.

"Okay, Buster, you've done it now." She scooped a handful of snow and headed toward him, just as he tackled her gently and knocked her to the soft ground.

He fell to her side and allowed her to rub his newly stubbled face with the coldness. "You win, you win," feigning surrender.

They built two small snow figures and stood admiring their creations. Just as Tyler turned to walk away, he heard Faith giggle. He spun around and broke out laughing.

"I just thought he needed to be anatomically correct."

"You're awful. Mr. Snowman is quite a guy, I'll admit."

"Some guys just have it."

"Oh, thanks a lot," trying to appear hurt.

She took his hand. "It's okay. You'll do in a pinch."

They walked back to the cabin, happy and cold, but warm on the inside.

After a warm bubble bath that smelled of lavender and mint, Faith felt rejuvenated. She hurriedly dressed to find Tyler, freshly showered and changed into jeans and a mock turtleneck, putting the roast in a pan that obviously had cooked its share in previous years.

"Hi, I thought I'd help out. You can peel the potatoes and carrots though, while I add a log to the fire. It's beginning to get cold in here. Did you have enough hot water, Princess?" He smiled, poking fun at Faith's lengthy, luxurious bath.

"Not bad for a primitive soak. Are we going to open packages tonight or in the morning?"

"I don't know. What did you do as a kid?"

"We always opened all the family type presents on Christmas Eve, although Mom would never let me open a single gift until after the sun went down and my grandparents arrived. Well, they weren't really my grandparents. They weren't even Mom's parents. They were her ex-in-laws. They always came over for soup and sandwiches and then we read the Christmas story and opened presents. During the night, Santa came so I had more packages on Christmas day."

Tyler looked momentarily surprised. "I had forgotten she had been married. I remember now that she mentioned him once when she was talking about marrying Ben, but I don't think I have even heard his name."

"Dwayne. They split up before I was born. What a jerk and a loser. I mean, he wasn't always that way, well, at least not a loser. I understand from the stories he was 'the catch,' holding up her hands to make quote marks around 'the catch,' in high school, but then after they got married he started running around, sleeping with a floozy," she said smiling.

"Another one of those terms I never heard growing up," he mocked.

"Anyway, his parents more or less disowned him and took Mom's side. They always treated me as their granddaughter."

"What about your real grandparents?"

"I never knew them. They died before I was born. On my mother's side, my granddad was killed in a fire. He was a volunteer fireman and my grandmother died soon after with cancer. Mom said she didn't want to live anyway after their dad died. So, that's why it was just Alice and Sue by themselves. Confusing, isn't it? I only met my dad's dad once, a couple of years before he died and his mother had already died."

"Why didn't your grandparents come to the wedding?"

"They're both in really frail health. I miss them too. You know how you said you always think of your granddad at Christmas? Well, I guess I feel the same way about them. When did y'all open your presents?"

"We did everything Christmas morning. We always went to church on Christmas Eve and then drove around to look at the lights. Then, we'd go home and eat pie and cake before my parents made us kids go to bed, which wasn't an easy task. We always left a piece of cake and milk for Santa; did you?"

"Yes, except it was usually cookies. I was big into collecting autographs, so one year I left out the usual cookies and milk and when I woke up the next morning, Santa had left me a personalized thank you note. It just so happened that Christmas was on Sunday that year so I took my "autograph" to Sunday school and showed it to all my friends. A couple of them snickered and one finally told me there was no such thing as Santa Claus. I was crushed.

"I remember I cried and when I saw Mom afterwards I asked her if that were true. I'll never forget. She looked me squarely in the eyes and said, 'No, Faith, your little friends are wrong. There is a Santa Claus and he lives in all of us. He's always been and he always will be.'"

"So, do you still believe?" Tyler quizzed.

Faith laughed, "I was in the third grade. I'd heard rumblings for several years and couldn't quite figure out all the details, like how he could deliver all those presents in one night and those kinds of things. I had asked a few things like that. Mom always had an explanation like when it's night here it's day across the ocean. But to answer your question, I still believe."

"That's what I love about you, Faith. You're so strong and can be really tough, but in many ways you're childlike. Don't ever lose those characteristics."

"I don't think that's going to happen. I've always said you might have to grow old, but you don't have to grow up."

"Why don't we open one gift tonight and let Santa bring the rest?" he offered.

"I'd like that. So, when can we open?"

"Not until it gets dark."

~

Ripping off the paper, Faith gasped and said, "Tyler, they're gorgeous."

"Well, my mom said every lady lawyer needs pearls. Now, I don't know how she knows that. I guess from watching Court TV or something."

She jumped to her feet to give him a hug. "I'm sure changing my look with my big ol' ring and now pearls." She held them up to her neck. "What do you think? Am I sophisticated or what?"

"Well, maybe if you didn't have on those fuzzy puppy house shoes," he said, looking down at her feet.

"Okay, smarty, it's your turn." She handed him a large box.

"This is heavy. I can't imagine." He slowly took the paper from the box and folded it.

"Oh for heaven's sake, Tyler. Just tear it. You are too neat," but secretly that was something she admired in him, something she wasn't. She teased him often about his drawers and closet. Everything was neatly folded and hung by color and clothing article. She knew her closet drove him crazy. He couldn't imagine how she could find anything. He had asked her early in their relationship about it. "I just dig," she had told him.

His kitchen was the same, with pots and pans arranged perfectly and the spices in alphabetical order.

"Come on, hurry up!"

He was opening the box even slower now to torment her. A look of total amazement came on his face. "How did you know I wanted these?"

"Because when you took me to Lucchese's for my ropers, I saw you looking at these. I knew you wore black full quill ostrich so I just thought you needed a pair of these. Don't they call these, peanut brittle?"

"Yes, I love them. They will look really nice in the spring and fall. They look good now too, but they will look especially good then. We'll have to come back here in October for the Cowboy Symposium."

"What's that?"

"It's a long weekend of singers and guitar pickers and fiddle players. I've only been a couple of times. They have booths set up with western clothes and accessories. For three days different musicians take the stage and play western swing and country music, and they have a dance every night."

"Sounds like a lot of fun."

"Yeah, we'll have to get you a big hat before we come back. You'll look really cute. Also, I had hoped we could go to the casino at the Inn of the Mountain Gods and to the Texas Club for dinner one night while we're here, but we're running out of time. They have great steaks. We'll go the next trip."

"The Texas Club in New Mexico?" Faith asked, looking incredulous.

"Oh, half the people who come here for the weekend or even for the summer are from somewhere in West Texas, Midland, Lubbock, or San Angelo. I once saw a sign in Colorado when I was in college on a ski trip and it said, 'If God had meant Texans to ski he would have made bullshit white.' Ruidoso isn't that way. They cater to Texans, but it still has the great New Mexico flavor, too, which makes it special."

Trying on his boots, he announced, "Perfect fit. You've been in my closet checking my size, huh?"

"Well, it wasn't hard to find them. I just looked under B for boots and BL for black," she teased.

They sat close together admiring their gifts and the fire.

"Are you hungry?"

"Yes, that roast smells so good; I've been thinking about it for a couple of hours."

"You want to eat it here in front of the tree and fire?"

"Yes, I'll fix our plates. You just sit still so I can play the good little wife."

"As it should be," he taunted.

~

Waking first, Tyler watched her sleep. She was beautiful to him and he had to restrain himself from touching her face, her complexion flawless and more satin than ever against the dull, lackluster pillowcase. He lay there for more than thirty minutes just looking at her, thinking about how much he loved her, how perfect their world was. The oversized window framed the glow of the morning sun glistening against the snow covered branches. The light poured through and he wondered how she slept. Because he was enjoying the quietness of her steady breathing against his neck, thinking about their life together, he didn't dare stir, fearful he might disturb her.

When she turned, he was looking in her eyes. "Tyler, have you been awake long?"

"Oh, not too long, half an hour or so."

"Why didn't you wake me? What time is it?"

"It's 6:20. Because I love watching you sleep."

"Yeah, I'm sure I'm sexy in flannel pajamas and four layers of cover," she said kissing him on the cheek. "Did Santa come?"

"I'm sure he did. Didn't you hear the reindeer on the roof last night?"

"I slept so sound after all that roast and potatoes and good wine that I didn't hear anything."

"That's too bad, because they made a lot of noise. I guess you missed the ho, ho, ho, part too."

"Yep, that too. You're going to make such a good dad."

"So, when can we start making this baby?"

"I thought we already had. I stopped taking the pill last week, actually on our wedding day."

Tyler was stunned. "Really? You mean you would be okay to be pregnant this early in your career?"

"Why wait? Besides, don't you think a jury would be more sympathetic to a pregnant lawyer? How can I miss, waddling in front of the jury box looking radiant as they always say one looks in that fat unattractive state?"

"You would never look unattractive, but I can't believe you got off the pill. You've given me a Christmas gift just telling me that? You want to see what Santa brought?"

Although the gifts had been under the tree all along, Tyler had slipped out once Faith was asleep and rearranged them as if to indicate Santa had been there. Then, on a napkin lying on a small red plate he had scrawled – "Thanks Faith, Always Believe!"

Her eyes shone like a child's when she saw the plate and the reorganized packages. "You're first as she handed him a little red and green sack with a ribbon tied through the top."

"Well, it's not another pair of boots; that's for sure."

Inside was a smaller box with the words Rolex inscribed in gold. Shocked he said, "Surely you didn't," but when he opened it there was a gold watch with his initials engraved on the back. Placing it on his wrist he fixed his eyes on it smiling. "I had no idea. I've looked at these, too." He reached to kiss her and retrieved a package for her from under the tree.

The box was big, but feather light. She tore the paper off in her usual manner and opened the box to find another smaller box. Twice more she did this, only to find empty boxes. Displaying fake exasperation, she said, "You're mean," when suddenly she opened another box to find a black velvet case holding a Lady President Rolex. She looked at Tyler in stunned disbelief.

"I guess we think alike," he said, grinning sheepishly. "I thought for a minute when I saw mine that the store had made a mistake, but I knew I had wrapped yours. I couldn't figure it out."

"Now, I'm really sophisticated, cheesy shoes or not. Now, we can't spend any more money on us. We have to save everything for the soon baby-to-be."

"Sounds wonderful to me. I have everything else I want right here in this room."

~

"Do you think we can still go skiing this afternoon?"

"If we walk to the shuttle and ride it up the mountain. I don't think the pickup is a good idea since I don't have chains or snow tires. Are you up to walking a half mile or so?"

"Sure, that will be fun."

"I had hoped to rent our skis in the village, but we can get them when we get up to the mountain. Let's try to catch the 11:00 one. Will that rush you too much?"

"No, let me get breakfast on while you put up our gifts and get rid of all that wrapping paper. It's only 8:30."

After a leisurely breakfast of ham, eggs, and biscuits, they dressed in their ski attire and headed for the shuttle where they waited with six other eager skiers. The man who appeared to be the father of some of the kids told Tyler that the mountain had received more than 10 inches of snow in the last two days, and according to the highway report the mountain road appeared to be clear of snow, but there were still some hazardous areas. He had also planned to drive, but decided against it, and had tried to talk the kids out of going, but they would hear nothing of it.

Faith and Tyler and the other adult climbed into the seats behind the driver, as the kids all clamored to sit at the back. At the next stop, a teenage boy piled in with a snow board, and took the last available seat. Faith relaxed as she saw how clear the road was to Ski Apache and pointed to the snow drifts all along the way. What she didn't know and Tyler didn't tell her was they hadn't began the 12 miles up the mountain, but within minutes it became obvious that the rest of the way was not going to be an easy or uneventful drive.

"Holy crap," Faith whispered to Tyler. "I can't watch." She turned her face from the window and buried it on his shoulder. Gripping his hand, she said quietly, "Oh, my heavens, if I had known it was going to be like this, I would have never agreed to this trip." At that moment, the van slid and fishtailed and the kids yelled, obviously enjoying the danger.

"Tyler England, I'm going to kill you. Did you know it was going to be like this?"

He smiled sheepishly. "Why do you think I didn't want to drive? It will be okay. These shuttle guys drive it like this all the time. He's taking it pretty slow."

Briefly, Faith let herself look out the window and wished she hadn't. Her death grip on Tyler's left hand steadied her momentarily, but still she was pale with fear. "Tyler, there aren't even any guard rails on this road!"

"It is pretty though, isn't it? Look at the snow on all those trees."

"There is nothing pretty about how I feel right now. All I can see are the tops of trees and 100 feet straight down. I think I am going to be sick."

"Let's think about something good, something we enjoy. We only have about four more miles to go."

"Why are these other vans going down the mountain? It wouldn't be so bad if we weren't meeting cars. Plus that idiot who passed us. We may see him hanging from one of these trees and I wouldn't even care. Is that it? Are we here?"

"Yep, and we survived."

"Yeah, now all I have to worry about is getting back down."

Tyler took her hand and helped her out of the van, coaxing her to stay calm and enjoy the afternoon. As soon as she got on the lift, she began to relax and marvel at the beauty of the scenery.

"You know I don't know much about skiing. I've only been twice. The first time I had lessons, and the second time I wished I was on the bunny slopes instead of the intermediate runs."

"You'll do fine. I've never seen you be anything but good at whatever you do."

"Yeah, well, get ready. Best I remember the worst part was getting off the chairlift. One time, they had to stop the whole lift because I didn't hop off in time, and when I did, I slid right down the little slope."

"That's what you are supposed to do."

"Not on your butt, Tyler."

"No, that would not be the best start." He smiled and took her free hand. "Okay, tips up, polls high, get ready."

"Now, you did great. The rest is downhill from here," he said with a big grin.

"Aren't you too funny? Race you to the bottom."

~

There were still patches of snow all along the road from Ruidoso to Carrizozo, the back route to Santa Fe. Tyler had timed their leaving so they could stop at The Outpost for a green chili cheeseburger and French fries.

"This will be the best burger you've ever eaten. And if you think the Pizza Joint was rugged, you're in for a big treat."

"Looks interesting all right," Faith said as they drove up to the little white building that once had been a post office. Painted illustrations of huge burgers and mugs of sudsy beer along with signs saying TRY OUR FAMOUS GREEN CHILI CHEESEBURGER and COLDEST BEER IN TOWN adorned the sides of the flat structure.

Blinking to adjust her eyes from the bright outdoors to the dim interior, Faith smiled, "I don't believe I've ever seen so many trophy mountings in an eating establishment. I think I'd prefer not to sit under one. They look a bit old, as if the hair might fall off."

Tyler laughed, "I warned you; let's sit by the fireplace anyway."

The small black metal pellet stove was surrounded by dozens of sacks of wood pellets on one side and a video hunting game on the other. Two pool tables took up one end of the eating area. Hardly a ten inch space on the walls was not covered with various memorabilia including cow skulls, posters, cue sticks, wagon wheels and other taxidermy.

"Nice springs in this booth. One is right in my butt," Faith noted as she studied the stuffing sticking out of the faux red leather wrapping the seat.

"But the music's good, huh?" as an old Hank Williams tune played on the jukebox. The music videos showing on the televisions hanging from chains overhead seemed anachronistic in the old rustic setting.

"Well?" said the skinny waitress who was missing several front teeth.

Tyler looked at Faith. "I think she wants our order. Do you know what you want?"

"Uh, yes…I guess if the burger's what they're famous for… that's what I'll have."

"Yeah, me too…two green chili cheese burgers and fries."

"Drink?" she muttered, looking at Faith.

"Cold beer, whatever's on tap."

"Don't have tap, just bottles."

"A Miller Lite, please."

"Make that two."

When she left their table, they both giggled like two children who had just peeked through a hole in the neighbors' fence.

"This really is fun, Tyler. I could just sit here and look at the ceilings and walls for a couple of hours. There is stuffed stuff everywhere."

She read aloud the sign over the bar, "If you need credit, you don't need a drink, you need a job. My sentiments exactly," she added.

The waitress appeared back at their table with two icy cold Miller Lites, adding "Here's the condiments," while slapping down the salt, pepper, ketchup and Tabasco in a metal holder.

"Good cold beer, that's for sure," Tyler said after taking a long swig from the frosty bottle.

Faith nodded, "Interesting place, a real mixture of people," as she looked around at the two older middle class couples sitting juxtaposed to a young Mescalero Indian, in his dirty worn work boots, who obviously was employed in ranching or construction. A guy at the bar in a quilted vest and weathered cowboy hat talked easily with the bartender about the snowstorm that had hit the high desert ranching area that sits in a valley shadowed by the Sacramento mountain range.

"I think I need a few more napkins," Tyler said, trying to catch the drip from the juicy burger.

"Here," Faith mumbled, her mouth full, as she passed him a handful of thin paper beverage napkins and added, "This is the best burger and fries I think I've ever eaten," she said when she finished chewing.

"I told you so," Tyler grinned and wiped his face again. "Doesn't get better than this, huh?"

~

The terrain had become more horizontal and flat as the newlyweds approached Santa Fe. Buffalo grass, chamisa and other native vegetation blotted the long stretches of drab soil, marked with an occasional ranchito or pueblo. Buff colored adobe structures took the place of wooden or brick houses, creating a dull monochromatic panorama, broken up only by the rise of the Sangre de Christo Mountains, rising against the white clouds and pale blue winter sky.

"What are those, Tyler?"

"What?"

"Those funny bee-hive shaped adobe things out in the middle of that field, close to their huts or whatever."

"Oh, those are called hornos. They are ovens where the Indian women bake their bread."

"Still?"

"Yep, if you visit one of their reservations, you would see that not much has changed in hundreds of years. They're still living the same ways as their ancestors, believing in the identical mythology, same superstitions, weaving their baskets and molding their pottery."

"But why?" Faith asked in disbelief.

"They're very proud of their traditions. Many could live differently in the modern world, but they don't want that. They are content with their lives."

"I guess there's nothing wrong with that except they look so poor. It makes me sad to see the poverty. They appear to lead such a meager existence, which seems strange in our modern technological world."

"They're changing slowly. Many of the young people are leaving for the cities, but the old ones wouldn't know how to live anywhere else. Some still speak their native language, which no one other than those living on the reservation would understand."

"I can't believe they live like this in this century."

"Hey, did you know that Santa Fe is called the 'City of Holy Faith?'"

"How do you know all this stuff, Tyler?"

"Research, My Love, research."

"Oh, I'm disappointed. I thought it just came to you in a dream or something. Oh, look Tyler, an outlet mall, out here in the middle of nowhere it seems."

"I can't see it," he teased, speeding up his truck. "It must be a mirage."

In less than fifteen minutes they were at the Inn of the Anasazi, only a half a block from the historic plaza. Hand carved doors set in a heavy wood and stone façade welcomed them into the lobby and reception area filled with locally woven baskets, earth tone leather chairs and a massive kiva fireplace. Sandstone walls reflected the warmth of the spacious room, accenting the indigenous hand woven rugs in deep reds and rich browns as well as the authentic Southwestern art. The handsomely dressed desk clerk handed Tyler a key.

Opening the door to their room, Tyler said, "Look at this bedroom."

"It is so romantic…our own kiva fireplace."

A four-poster bed covered in a colorful textile filled a corner under the traditional Santa Fe ceilings of vigas and latillas. Hand-woven Navajo rugs dotted the wooden floors. Plush ecru bathrobes hung in the bath area alongside organic toiletries created with native cedar extract.

"If I didn't want to see the plaza and all the shops I think I could just stay in here for two or three days."

"Well, I could buy a guidebook of the city and we could lie in bed and look at pictures," Tyler offered, feigning seriousness.

"You wish. I want to see the Palace of the Governors. Hurry. We can unpack later," Faith said, tossing her make-up kit on the tiled dressing table.

But Tyler was already busy hanging clothes and carefully placing their shoes within easy reach.

"Come on. I'm anxious."

"Do you want to see the inside of the Palace and the museum or just the jewelry the Indians are selling on the porches?" Tyler quizzed.

"Oh, just the jewelry…you can tell me all the historical stuff later."

The crisp air smelled of piñon as the setting sun cast shadows on the mountains. Faith took Tyler's arm and they were soon in step together, walking along the rough pavement to the main center of activity.

Because it was late most of the Indians had gathered up their jewelry and handmade pottery, but there were a few still sitting, bundled up next to their blankets that held row after row of earrings, tie tacks, bracelets and other pieces made of silver, each marked or engraved in some way to indicate the artist.

"Look Tyler, I want to buy you this silver guitar pick as a souvenir."

"Let's wait until tomorrow when this area will be lined with vendors. The competition encourages better prices. They'll deal better when it's crowded."

"Okay, but don't forget."

"We won't," he guaranteed, not bothering to tell her that the Indians sitting here tomorrow wouldn't necessarily be anywhere near the same spot as today or in many cases, they wouldn't even be the same Indians. "There will be plenty of choices, I assure you."

"I want to take back gifts for friends and family."

"We'll have plenty of time. You can shop all day tomorrow. It's getting colder. Would you like to go over to the bar at the Pink Adobe? I believe it is called the Dragon Room and it's known for its margaritas."

"Sounds fun."

The blustery wind had died down, and although the night air was dry, it was chilly as they hurriedly made their way to the oldest part of town in the center of the historical barrio area.

Inside, a warm fire awaited them as they sat at one of the rose colored wooden tables not far from the massive wooden bar. They each sipped a Rosalita margarita named after the woman who established the now world-known bar in the mid-1940s.

"Do you remember that we drank margaritas on our very first date?" Faith asked, softly.

"I do, and I remember that I didn't want to go home that night, but I dared not push my luck. I think I was already falling in love with you."

"I have you beat. I told Alice before we even had a date that I had fallen for you."

"Really?" he asked, obviously touched by her sentimentality.

"Really, like love at first sight."

He reached and took her hand across the table. "You've made my world complete."

Sitting in silence, mesmerized by the glow and crackle of the fire, Tyler broke the quietness, "The restaurant next door has an extensive menu, steaks, chicken, lamb, all kinds of cuisine, but I like the Mexican food the best."

"I definitely want Mexican food."

"It's New Mexico style with lots of red and green chiles and blue corn tortillas."

"You're making me hungry. I thought I'd never eat again after that hamburger and French fries, but that seems like days ago now."

"Let's have another margarita and then we'll go over to the Pink."

~

As they walked back to their hotel after a huge serving of green chile enchiladas and an after dinner drink, the starless night was lighted by farolitos lining driveways and courtyards, and the hundreds of twinkling Christmas lights that hung from trees and outlined the old adobe buildings.

"It's magical. It looks like a picture postcard, only a card couldn't capture this. I love the luminarias everywhere. I wonder if they have them anytime other than the holidays." Faith asked.

"I've seen them here even in the summer, although not as many. You know, here they call them farolitos, whereas in southern New Mexico and in Texas they are called luminarias, like you said. Let's ride around the plaza," Tyler offered, waving to hail a venerable Mexican man holding the reigns of the horse drawn carriage. "Are you too cold?"

"No. That spiked cocoa warmed me."

"This is really the only time I drink peppermint Schnapps, but it warmed me too," helping her as she stepped up into the carriage.

"You want the fifteen minute ride?" the driver asked unenthusiastically, a result of endless, monotonous many trips around the square.

"Whatever you suggest; we're on our honeymoon."

The old man grinned, a toothless grin with a knowing look on his wise, wrinkle-etched, and earthen face. "I once was married a long time ago" his expression changing, a hollow sadness in his voice. "A long time ago," his voice trailing off into the night.

~

"This is my favorite breakfast place in Santa Fe," Tyler told her as they rounded the corner to Café Pasqual's. A long line curved around the building and it was only eight o'clock in the morning.

"Looks like you're not the only one who likes it."

"I'll go in to give them my name and get a couple of Mexican hot chocolates. They're worth the wait."

Returning, he handed Faith a steaming tall Styrofoam cup topped with a huge dollop of whipped cream and cinnamon.

"Oh, this is good," Faith said after she sipped the warm drink. "Mmm, I can taste the cinnamon. Yummy!"

"I don't think it will be long, maybe fifteen minutes at the most. I brought a menu for you to see, because they don't give you much time when they come to the table. I guess that's what keeps this line moving, though."

"Ohhh, this sounds good. Listen, Tyler, chili relleneos, omelet style with two eggs on top, a drizzle of tomato jalapeño salsa and black beans. Oh but, this does too – breakfast quesadillas made of whole wheat tortillas, filled with jack cheese, guacamole and scrambled eggs with salsa fresca and apple smoked bacon."

Tyler was laughing at her. "I like the home fries with red or green chilies, cheese, sour cream and scallions, topped with an egg and served with a tortilla. But sometimes I order the whole wheat pancakes with maple syrup and apple smoked bacon," he said, tormenting her.

"Well, maybe I'll have one of each."

"You're not pregnant yet, are you?"

"Why? Just because I like to eat for two?"

"Hey, that's our name they're calling. You better make up your mind."

~

As they had finished breakfast, Tyler said, "Let's drive out to the Tesuque Pueblo. You seemed intrigued by the people who live on the reservation. It's only about ten miles, and then we'll come back and do the plaza."

"Oh, I'd like that," Faith replied.

The pueblo sat in the reddish contestoga foothills of the Sangre de Christo Mountains, south of the Camel Rock, a natural sandstone formation having taken that shape after thousands of years of erosion by rain and wind.

Standing in the large central plaza, Tyler explained, "Historians believe this has been the focal and gathering point of the pueblo since the thirteenth century. Although this is one of the state's smallest pueblos, home to just eight hundred Indians, it encompasses more than 17,000 acres."

Then reading from the brochure, Tyler said, "The name Tesuque is a Spanish variation of the Tewa name, Te Tesugeh Oweengeh, meaning the 'village of the narrow place at the cottonwood trees'. Even today, the people here speak their native Tewa along with English and some Spanish."

Browsing around, Faith noticed a group of the Indians selling traditional clothing, pottery and paintings.

"I think we should buy something, don't you Tyler? After all, we're intruding into their domain."

Tyler smiled, "You're a pushover. That's the idea, but I agree. Pick out whatever you want."

"I like this little bowl. I can even put it in my office. Do you think I could take a picture of the artist holding it?"

"Generally, the pueblos don't allow photographs or at least that's what I've read. You can ask. Every reservation has their own set of laws and visitor policies; actually each pueblo and tribal reservation is a sovereign nation."

"Oh, I don't want to even ask them, it might offend them, and I sure don't want to do that. I'm glad you know all this, Tyler. I'll just buy it."

"They're really sensitive about things like that. For example, their tribal dances are religious ceremonies, not public performances so they frown on applause, yet in contrast they own the Camel Rock Casino that includes a gift store. There's also a huge market up on Opera Hill. It's weird, but this is their home so everyone has to respect their privacy."

"This is interesting. I'm glad we came."

"I thought you'd like it. I guess we should go back to the more civilized world, so you can shop, although I've noticed you can spend money in the most primitive of places."

She made a face and stuck out her tongue at him, then reached to take his hand.

They spent the remainder of the day visiting the Georgia O'Keefe Museum, walking along Canyon Road, stopping at the galleries and specialty shops. At the Palace of the Governors, Faith bought something for everyone she could think of: a silver golf ball marker for Tyler and his dad and Sid; a piece of Navajo pottery and hand woven basket for his mother; a money clip for Patrick; a bracelet and earrings for Sue and a turquoise and orange coral squash blossom necklace with earrings to match for Alice. Each piece was marked regarding the heritage and tribal affiliation of the artist or craftsperson.

"Oh, I forgot Ben."

"Does he play golf?"

"A little when he has time, but I think I'll get him a money clip. I think they're pretty with the unique symbols and designs."

"Maybe we should get all of the bosses one," Tyler suggested.

"Oh, that's a great idea. I'm so glad you thought of them."

"I'm about shopped out," Tyler said after they finished buying the jewelry. "I know you want to look in some of those dress shops so I think I'll sit on one of these benches like the rest of the old men while you shop your little heart out."

"Why don't you go back to the hotel lobby and watch football? Surely there's a bowl game on."

"Hey, I haven't even thought of that. Do you mind? I mean, walking back by yourself and all?"

"Not a bit."

"Okay, take your time. Tonight we'll go to the Bull Ring for a steak, if that sounds good," appearing excited that he had received a reprieve from shopping, and especially happy to go watch football. "Better buy all you want. Remember we're leaving before daybreak in the morning."

"How could I forget?" She blew him a kiss as he turned to grin at her.

Chapter 18

Tyler's parents were the newlyweds' first houseguests when they visited in late February. Weeks earlier, Faith had asked her mother-in-law to bring recipes of Tyler's favorite foods so the first afternoon the two women sat in the kitchen drinking hot apple cider and pouring over recipes, with his mother giving Faith little pointers about each special food. An instant rapport had developed between them and Faith enjoyed her mother-in-law's company.

When Faith had asked what to call her, Tyler's mother had responded quickly with, "anything but Mrs. England." Laughing, Faith had told her that she would like to call her Mom but she already had so many mothers that it would be too confusing.

"Would Joy be okay?" Faith had asked, referring to her given name.

His mother had smiled and readily agreed, "And you can call his dad Tom just like everyone else does."

As the two giggled like schoolgirls, Faith said, "Let's go to the store to get the ingredients for these chicken enchiladas. I'll cook and you can watch and tell me what I'm doing wrong."

"That sounds like fun. I'm sure our two guys will be starving after eighteen holes of golf."

At Central Market, Joy pushed a cart down every aisle, amazed at the abundance of products.

"Faith, what I would do to have a grocery store like this in Midland. Would you look at this?" she said in her West Texas drawl, pointing at the spices. "I have never seen so many. There are things here I've never heard of, much less used."

"Wait 'til you see the bakery. They have every kind, shape and size of bread you can imagine."

"Look over there, would you? They've got tortilla chips in blue, green, red, you name it."

"Let's get some red ones for tonight. They'll look pretty with a green salad and guacamole, don't you think?" Faith asked.

Joy looked at her watch. "Faith, we've been here over two hours. If we're going to cook tonight, we better get going, but I want to come back."

"I'm glad you liked it."

"Liked it? I loved it!"

When they drove in the driveway, Tyler and his dad were already home, sitting in the den, drinking beer.

"Well, well, here come our little shoppers," Tyler said, obviously pleased that Faith and his mother got along so well. It would be hard for them not to, both were so likable, but he knew he was prejudiced; he loved them both.

"I'll have you know we have been out hunting and gathering for your dinner. Right, Joy?"

"That's right, so you better be nice or you'll be taking us out."

Both men laughed.

"So, what's cooking?" Tom asked.

"Tyler's chicken enchiladas, Spanish rice and a salad. How does that sound?"

"Great," Tom said. "We've worked hard today."

"So, who won?" Faith questioned.

"Oh, we don't keep score," Tom said, quickly.

"Oh, not only does he cheat, he also doesn't tell the truth," Tyler jabbed at his dad. "Hey Faith, we made a tee time for 9:58 in the morning. Dad really likes that course. You'll drive his cart, won't you Mom?"

"Oh sure, I guess you'll want me to caddy, next."

"Would you?" Tyler teased. He knew his mother loved to ride in the cart and watch, and the weather was supposed to be in the high sixties and sunny tomorrow.

"Okay, you guys just put your feet up and rest. We'll go slave over a hot stove. And why don't I bring you another beer?" Faith said, already popping the top on one for her father-in-law and then Tyler. Judge was positioned as close to Tyler as she could get so he would rub her back with his foot.

"What a cozy, lazy bunch. Let's get out of here Faith before we catch whatever they have," her mother-in-law said, winking.

Later that night in bed, Tyler said, "Thanks for being so sweet to my parents. I can tell they really love you."

"It's no problem being nice to them because they're truly special people. They're easy to love."

"I told dad what a good golfer you are."

"Oh great! No pressure or anything."

"I told him you were good at everything," leaning to kiss her, his hands reaching under her thin gown.

"Oh, no you don't, Tyler England, not with your parents in the next room."

"Oh, come on, Hon. We'll be quiet."

"No," she said emphatically. "Now turn over and go to sleep."

"Okay," he said, sticking his lip out, "but you don't know what you're missing."

"Oh, yes, I do, but I'm sure your interest will return another night." She pecked him lightly on the cheek. "Good night."

"Good night, Sweetheart."

~

Tyler had told his dad correctly about Faith's golf abilities. After playing one of her best games, she was obviously pleased and relieved.

"I told you she was cutthroat, didn't I, Dad?"

His dad smiled. "She's quite the little pro. Lunch is on me. You get to choose, Faith."

"What sounds good?"

"Food…anything…that cereal is long gone," Tom said.

"How does TGI Friday's sound, Tyler?"

"Let's go."

They talked easily over lunch and made plans to meet in June in Ruidoso for the horse races. Thinking back about their honeymoon, Faith smiled.

"I wish you could stay longer. We could go back to the Central Market plus the mall and do lots of fun things. I'll take off work tomorrow," Faith said to Joy.

"Oh, my goodness, we have to get home. Didn't you know the earth would cave in if Tom England missed a day of work?"

Faith smiled, "Like father, like son."

Chapter 19

Spring came in like a lamb, mild and calm, light rain showers at night. Green was everywhere Faith looked. She knew Texas weather was unpredictable anytime, but especially in the spring when it can rain and be cold one year with tornadoes touching down often and the next year there's not a drop of rain for two or three months. This year it appeared as if it was going to be one of the wet ones, but warmer. So warm that the flowers took in the warm moisture before dawn and reached for the sun during a break in the clouds.

Every weekend in March, Faith and Tyler had worked in the backyard, with Tyler laying brick flower bed borders and using pavers to expand the walkway. In shorts and one of Tyler's old shirts, Faith helped him haul sand in the wheelbarrow and worked peat moss and vermiculite into the soil in preparation for the flowers she wanted to plant.

Meticulously, Tyler followed his sketches and designs that indicated his careful planning for every step of the landscaping while Faith pestered him to hurry. Slowly, and methodically a terraced garden emerged around the patio.

"Tyler, we have to put something around the trees so Judge will quit rolling in the dirt. What is it about that area?"

"It's cool to her tummy!"

Showing her the plans again as he said, "As soon as I complete the circular beds, you can plant the ground cover, maybe Saturday after next," he explained, wiping a mixture of dirt, sand and sweat from his brow. "I have the hangers ready. Do you want to go to the nursery later this afternoon? We can choose some flowers for the hanging baskets. Maybe that will help you see progress, my impatient little one."

"Great. It's looking wonderful, Tyler. I can't believe how well. If I prepare everything for burgers, would you be too tired to grill. I'd love to sit out here and enjoy our labors while the weather's nice."

"Sounds like a plan," he said with his arms full of brick. "Since you're anxious for this part, if you'll help me with these, we'll measure where they'll go around the first tree and I'll start digging the trench."

Dutifully, Faith loaded the red wagon with beige bricks. She had been excited when he bought her the shiny new wagon, but she laughed out loud now, realizing her earlier enthusiasm might have been misplaced.

"Put the stacks right over there," he told her as she tugged at the wagon. "You might try loading fewer at a time," he cautioned, grinning.

She turned and did a mock salute, pulling the empty wagon back through the metal gate, to the unattached garage where Tyler had stored his supplies. "Mr. Persnickety," she mumbled under her breath, not fazed by his suggestion.

Judge, disrupted from her spot now followed close behind Faith, who stopped to rest and pet her. Now almost a fully grown dog, she continued to exhibit puppy traits as she immediately rolled over for Faith to scratch her tummy.

"You are so rotten. I think your daddy is getting exasperated with me. What do you think?"

Judge rolled over, cocking her head as if she understood every word.

"Come on girl, we have to follow orders," Faith mocked, counting out the bricks as she haphazardly placed them in the wagon, knowing Tyler would have stacked them neatly. "Let's see if he notices."

He looked up, smiling as Faith approached. "I heard everything you and Judge discussed. That's much better. Now, next time, let's work on our arrangement of the brick," he teased as he rose to kiss her on the top of her head.

Smiling, she said, "I'll get a snack for us."

She returned shortly with a large tray stacked with ham and cheese on rye sandwiches, potato chips, brownies and iced tea, sweetened just the way Tyler liked it. "I didn't forget you, Judge," taking a dog biscuit from the tray. Tyler had refused to let her have "people food" so Faith was forever giving her treats, also to his dismay.

"I'll be right back. I need a pen and notepad," Tyler said hurriedly.

Returning, he sat down at the outdoor table where Faith had arranged their lunch. She looked at him quizzically as she handed him his tea.

"I want us to decide what we need at the nursery, and I'll make a list."

"I should have known. Okay, let's see if we can do it in alphabetical order. Hmm. I can't think of anything we need starting with an 'a'."

Tyler grinned and took a bite of his sandwich. "You make a mean ham and cheese—plus you are quick."

"Thanks, but what do you have in mind for the list, seriously?"

"Well, I've been thinking. See that one spot over there that actually gets afternoon sun?" He pointed to a small corner on the west side of the yard. "How would you like a little herb garden?"

Faith squealed with excitement. "Oh Tyler, you know I would love that. But I thought you wanted to plant a Bradford pear there?"

"I decided I would put it in the front yard. That would free up that space for you. So what herbs do you think you want?"

"Definitely basil, lots of it. Then she started laughing and singing 'Parsley, Sage, Rosemary and Thyme.' No, really I would like some parsley and oregano. Maybe one mint and one dill."

"You might want to put the mint in a separate pot. It tends to spread and there isn't that much space."

"Yeah, you are right. Let's get a terra cotta pot for mint—spearmint."

"What do you think about some hostas for that shaded area in the other corner? I think that is about all that will grow there. Anything else?"

"A couple of hummingbird feeders would be nice. Oh this backyard is going to look so beautiful." Faith said smiling. "What about the marigolds for the front yard?"

"Maybe in a couple of weeks, while you do the ground cover back here. I need to clean that front bed out completely. Before I do that, I want to get the pear tree in the ground. I think we can finish the brick work today, if we get busy," he said as he stood to help Faith with the lunch dishes.

"I'll clean up, and report right back to duty." Faith said with a big grin.

~

For Alice's wedding, Faith, Alice and Sue had decided to fly down early on Wednesday to South Padre Island, leaving themselves time to go shopping in Mexico, enjoy a spa day and spend time walking the beach before the men arrived on Friday afternoon.

Ben always left a car at the Harlingen airport to have when they flew in, so the three quickly grabbed their bags and found the white Dodge Durango. "Why is it that all the men I know only drive white cars or trucks? It looks like they would like to snazzy things up a little rather than have everything plain vanilla," Faith exclaimed as she lifted her suitcase into the luggage area.

"They depend on us to snaz up their lives. And of course we do," Alice said, climbing into the driver's seat.

"You're gonna love the island, girls. The sunsets are even better than Key West. I think it's one of the best kept secrets in Texas."

The forty-five minute drive from the airport took them past fields of cotton and sugar cane, tall yuccas bulging with puffy white blooms, and billboards in Spanish. The conversation was marked by giggles and girl talk.

"I see the bridge first," Alice screamed.

"I didn't even know we were looking for it. You need to explain the rules of your games," Faith said, feigning disappointment.

"Now, you know I don't do that or I'd never win."

"Look at the water. Oh, this is beautiful," Sue chimed in, as they drove the two-mile causeway over the Laguna Madre.

"If you look closely you also see the Gulf of Mexico from this bridge."

"I don't know what I was expecting, but it's much smaller; I mean the town itself. I guess I thought it would be like Corpus Christi or Galveston," Faith said.

"Oh no, not even two thousand people live here. It's only five miles long and less than a mile wide. That's one of the best things about it, that it's small, but there's so much to do."

"Are you hungry?"

"Starved," Sue replied.

"Me too."

"Then let's put our luggage up and go somewhere for drinks and fried shrimp. How does that sound?"

"Wonderful," Faith assured her.

The sun was a low red ball in the sky over the bay as they sat outside drinking wine and watching a few die hard fishermen and windsurfers.

"You're right about the sunset, Alice. It looks as though it might melt right into the water," Sue commented.

"I think I could sit here every afternoon and never get tired of watching it. Wait a few minutes after it sets and the sky will take on the most gorgeous pink glow."

"Are you too tired to walk the beach when we finish here?" Alice asked.

"Goodness no, I'll need to walk off this dinner. This is the best shrimp I believe I've ever eaten," Sue replied.

"I'm stuffed. Can we change into something more comfy?" Faith asked.

~

The moon was high when the three women walked back to the condo. They had wiggled their toes in the chilly water as the tide came lapping in and watched the glow off the waves rising and falling in the warm, humid night air. Now they were tired.

"As soon as I shower and get the sand off, I'm heading to bed," Faith said.

"Well, no one is going to have to rock me to sleep either," Alice yawned.

Sue was dozing in a chair on the deck overlooking the water. "Wake me when I can get a bath. Life at the beach is tough."

~

The dirty streets of Matamoros, Mexico, were bustling the next day when the women passed through security from the

United States. Although only 25 miles from the island and right over the bridge from the US border, Matamoros is a world apart. Lined with vendors hawking their cheap wool blankets, colorful baskets and various knock-offs of famous brand purses and t-shirts, the streets were strewn with plastic bags, crushed Styrofoam cups, bottle caps and other assorted litter. Young Mexican men manned make-shift wooden carts filled with shredded meats and tacos, ice cream, frozen fruits and pink candies. Unfamiliar smells of mystery meat mixed with the exhaust fumes from old trucks and taxis permeated the thick air of poverty as American tourists walked freely, spending more money in fifteen minutes than most of these people made in a day. Beggars holding paper cups and prostitutes in stiletto heels shared the same sidewalks as local businessmen and women.

The drab and dusty landscape yielded a hint of sadness and hopelessness, because unlike those who are poor in the interior of the country, the less fortunate here know what lies on the other side of the bridge in the United States. The bridge, a span of no more than a couple of football fields, separates two countries, two unique cultures, two languages, yet brings each together in an easy coexistence.

The first sights the three women visually absorbed were those of a boy about twelve years old juggling limes for a tip, an older man with a dirty rag washing the windshield of an old truck waiting in line to cross and a double amputee panhandler and a toothless woman crouched in the corner of two buildings speaking Spanish and hoping to score some change.

"Begging must be a universal language. I have no clue what they're saying, but I know what they want," Faith said as she threw change in each of their cups.

"Well, just remember, you can't feel sorry for all of them or you'll be broke before you get to Garcia's. Look over there; see those milk jugs on a stick? Those are from kids down at the bridge's edge holding them up for you to toss money in." Alice pointed out.

"Why aren't they in school?" Faith asked.

But before anyone could answer, Sue shrieked, "Look, there's a naked guy swimming in the Rio Grande. Do you think he's illegal?"

"I doubt it, I don't think he'd try crossing here where all the border patrol are swarming," Alice said.

"Well, he's holding his clothes over his head," Faith added.

"Who knows? It's a strange land; bizarre things can happen. After all, this is what we in Texas call, 'Old Mexico,'" Alice conceded. "Ben said to cross over and go straight to Garcia's and then if we don't find everything we want to catch a cab to the El Mercado for three dollars."

"I'm looking for bargains," Sue exclaimed.

"I want a margarita," Faith added.

Garcia's, a longtime family-owned establishment, houses a restaurant, bar, farmacia and shopping area, and comprises what would be a considered a city block in the states. Scores of trinkets, jewelry, and cheap booze can be found among the shelves and hand carved wooden furniture fills one room. Cabrito, frog legs and flaming cherries jubilee and bananas foster are available in the restaurant for the adventurous gourmand. During the day, tourists fill the well-known establishment, shopping, drinking and eating. But at night it is home to the locals as the live band plays traditional Mexican and Tejano music.

The women went straight upstairs to the lounge, where strolling musicians serenaded them as they ordered panchos and margaritas.

"Whew, this is one strong drink," Sue exclaimed.

"Good though, huh?" Alice asked. "The first time Ben brought me over here he warned me of its strength, but of course, I paid no attention. By the time I finished my third one, I was stone drunk. Thought he was going to have to carry me out. Sure was glad he bought my pretty gold choker first."

"Maybe you just drank them too fast," said Faith. "They don't seem all that strong to me."

Alice laughed. "Sweetheart, they'll jump up on you, I'm telling you. Oh, I forgot to order guacamole. I have to get our waiter back. It is the best you'll eat."

"Why do they call these panchos? I thought you were ordering a shawl or something."

"These are cheese and jalapeno nachos, and when they add refried beans they call them panchos."

Alice signaled for the young man in well-worn, black tux trousers, white pressed shirt and black tie to return to their table that overlooked the busy street below. The sharp contrast of the outside world of cheaply painted stucco buildings and their poor surroundings with the handsome, yet gaudy elegance of Garcia's mirrored the reality of the country and its culture – the haves and the have-nots.

"I'll have another margarita," Faith touched her glass, "and then I'll shop." And shop she did.

"I'm not sure I can carry all these sacks back across the border. They're beginning to get heavy," Faith said after a couple of hours of shopping.

"I'm in the same shape," Sue added.

"Alice to the rescue. I'll tote some of each, but we better start back before you both buy anything else."

The three trudged back over the bridge, cleared security and paid the attendant at the University of Texas/Brownsville parking lot near the Gateway International Bridge. Alice and Faith chatted continuously on the thirty minute drive back to the island as Sue dozed.

"You're going to love this spa I go to. They treat me like the queen that I am," Alice said, chuckling.

"Sounds good to me. I certainly don't mind a little pampering, right now I just want to put my feet in the cool sand when we get back and enjoy the beach a few minutes before dinner," Faith added.

"You keep walking in the sand and you won't even need exfoliating when you have your pedicure tomorrow," Alice laughed.

Waking from her nap, Sue asked, giggling "Won't the guys be pleased with all our purchases?"

"We're here sleeping beauty, time to carry your packages in. We've got other fish to fry."

~

When Tyler, Ben and Patrick arrived in the rental car the next day, the three women were sitting on the condo deck, sipping wine, their pampered feet on the rail.

"Well, guys, looks as though the women are slaving in the kitchen preparing our dinner," Patrick exclaimed.

The other two grinned, leaning over, giving Faith and Alice a kiss on the cheek. Patrick tapped Sue on the top of the head, ruffled her hair and began kissing the back of her neck.

"Watch it. I just had my hair done."

"Really?"

She turned, giving him a pat. "You're not too smart."

"Is that what it's going to be like to be married?" Alice said, turning to Ben.

Smiling, he said, "You've just got one more night to back out. Tomorrow's the big day. Oh, I almost forgot, we've got a tee time at ten o'clock. Is that okay? I mean, do you girls have something to do?"

"Are you saying we're not invited?" Alice asked, acting hurt.

"Uh, no, I just thought…"

She laughed. "I'm just teasing. We have plenty to keep us busy. If you've got the money, we've got the time…to shop that is."

Faith volunteered, "I'm not going anywhere, but outside by the pool. Although a decent tan is out of the question, maybe I can at least get some color before I wear my sundress."

"You have more than anyone here. I can tell you've been outside," Sue chimed in.

"Yes, but our yard is so shady, I never get much sun," Faith protested.

"While you girls are arguing about your bronzed bodies, I think I'll mix a drink," Ben added. "What will it be, guys?"

"Do you have any Crown?" Tyler asked.

"I have anything you want," Ben answered, opening the glass doors to a well-stocked bar and placing a bottle of blended whiskey, a fifth of Scotch and one of vodka on the counter." Make yourselves at home. If you want something else, it's here."

"I'll help," Patrick offered, reaching for the whiskey. "How do you want it, Tyler?"

"On the rocks with a little water, but I can pour."

"Done," Patrick said, handing the highball to his son-in-law.

As he poured himself a Scotch straight up, Ben turned to Patrick. "Do you need anything?"

"I'm good."

Faith walked in as her dad was unscrewing the cap of a bottle of tonic that sputtered and spewed fizz onto the counter. Seeing her dad's frustration, Faith pounced, "Hmm, you don't look too good to me."

Now smiling, Patrick asked, "Who invited you?"

She reached to mop the liquid with a paper towel. "Just walking through and noticed you might need some assistance," she taunted.

Tyler laughed. "Don't feel bad, it happens to me every time," passing Patrick a lime.

~

After a dinner of red snapper at Scampi's restaurant, Tyler and Faith walked the beach, hand in hand, the gentle waves lapping at the shore.

"I missed you, Faith," he said, stopping to kiss her, he then noticed the glow of the moon bouncing off her tousled hair.

"It's been fun having a couple of days with Mom and Mother, but I'm so glad you're here. It's not the same without you."

He leaned down to retrieve a broken shell. "I know it sounds corny, but I'm like this without you," He blushed slightly.

"Tyler England. You are the most sentimental, romantic creature in the whole world."

Silent, they strolled a deserted part of the beach down to the jetties where they sat on a granite slab to rest and watch the stars.

"When I was a boy, my dad would take me camping on our farm and we would lie in sleeping bags, looking up at the sky. In west Texas you can see every star clearly, like you can here. Even then, I wondered if they represented someone who had gone before. I remember thinking that the year Daddy Ty died."

To change the subject, Faith pointed, "Look way out there, Tyler. Can you see the lights of that boat? What do you think they're doing this time of night?"

"It's probably a great deal farther out than we realize, maybe a shrimper. They stay out for days and nights at a time."

"I'll bet it's lonely out there on the water, night after night, away from family."

"Yes, because you're surrounded by darkness, the sky, the seas, everything is black. Are you cold?" he asked, feeling a sudden chill.

"A little bit, the wind's kicking up, isn't it?"

"Yes, and I think it's pretty cool now. I guess we'd better head back to the rowdy group. Maybe they'll be asleep when we return."

"Don't count on it. I don't think Mom ever sleeps."

"Think we can slip in, unnoticed?" he asked, as arm in arm they walked back where lights of the long string of condos illuminated the glistening sand.

"Not a chance."

~

The sun poured through the open sliding glass door. In the darkness of night they had forgotten to draw the vertical blinds, and now the light hurt Faith's eyes.

"You don't need an alarm clock here do you?" Tyler asked, turning to Faith who scrunched down in the bed and pulled the sheet over her head. Joining her under the covers, he said, "I think I like it here," nuzzling his face into her hair.

"Shh, you'll wake somebody," she cautioned, as he slipped his hand beneath her satin gown.

She reached for him and felt his hard maleness.

For a long time after they had made love, they lay there in silence until Faith giggled, "That's a first."

"What?"

"Doing it, completely under the covers."

"Well, not entirely," he laughed, lifting the end of the sheet with his feet. "I needed a little more room."

~

When Faith and Tyler joined the others on the deck, it was after eight o'clock.

"Well, well, they did finally decide to crawl out," Alice chirped. "What time did you two come in last night?"

Turning to Tyler, Faith rolled her eyes without giving Alice an answer, "I think I've heard that question a few times. Here we are married and she's still asking me what time I got in."

"You certainly have heard that question, but don't worry. I always knew exactly when, whether you thought I did or not, Young Lady."

"I'll get the coffee, Tyler. Don't tell her anything," Faith teased.

When Faith returned with the two cups of steaming coffee, Alice said, "Guess what? Ben's kids called. They're flying in this morning. Isn't that great?" Turning to smile at Ben, she continued, "Now it will be perfect."

Looking pleased, he said, "It will be nice to have all our family. You want some breakfast? There are sweet rolls and fruit in the kitchen. Help yourself."

Just minutes before the sun faded into the horizon Alice and Ben exchanged vows on the sandy shores of the Gulf of Mexico. As the two kissed, a small crowd of onlookers joined family and friends in a cheer.

After gathering at the Sea Ranch dock, the small entourage set sail on a catamaran that Ben had rented for an untraditional reception. A one-man band played tunes from the sixties on the keyboard while a bartender mixed tropical drinks, decorated with tiny, fresh flowers.

"Better grab those hors d'oeuvres, before they get soggy," Ben reminded the happy party-goers, as he pointed to a buffet of peeled gulf shrimp and other appetizers.

"This is nice," Faith said, hugging Ben.

"Not a bad way to get married, huh?"

Chapter 20

Summer eased into fall without much notice, as it often does in North Texas. The weather was balmy until the end of October when the first crisp days gave way to chilly nights. Pumpkins lined the steps on most of the houses on Faith and Tyler's street and, orange and gold mums took the place of summer flowers. On Halloween, Faith made caramel popcorn balls and candied apples and placed them at the front door along with a heaping bowl of an assortment of single wrapped candies.

"I hope by this time next year we have our own little punkin," Tyler said, nuzzling Faith's neck as she sat down next to him on the couch to wait for the neighborhood kids.

"I keep thinking every day, we'll be pregnant. I can't figure it out."

"Patience, My Love."

"Oh no you don't. We have little munchkins coming for goodies. Be nice."

Just as she finished admonishing him, the doorbell rang, and he jumped up to pass out the candy. Faith smiled and thought what a great daddy he was going to be.

~

The first week of November Tyler began getting his guns and gear ready for deer season as Faith prepared to go to Austin to see her college roommate who had been living in Paris for the past four years. Both were excited to reunite with old friends and get away for the weekend, although it was rare that they were separated.

"Don't bring home a bunch of deer meat. You know I don't like venison."

Tyler laughed, "What if I get part of it made into sausage? You won't be able to tell it's venison. Besides it's good on the grill."

Faith made a face. "Oh okay, but that's all. And I don't like those little birds either."

"You are too funny, Faith," he said, wrapping his arms around her. "I believe those are called dove, and I'll give mine to one of the other guys. I guess this means you don't want me to bring home a wild pig?"

"Tyler England, don't you dare."

~

Football fever had ruled Friday nights during most of the fall, and occasionally Tyler and Sid found a high school team that they wanted to follow while Faith used her time alone to catch up on reading or to sit in front of the fireplace watching a sappy movie. The playoffs gave them a chance the week before Thanksgiving to go to Texas Stadium and watch three games. And although they didn't know a single kid playing, they ate hot dogs and popcorn and talked about when they were the kings of the field, each one trying to out story the other. When Tyler returned home, he found Faith in the den reading a knitting manual, surrounded by yarn and needles. She smiled as he came in the door and noticed the pile of yarn. Before he could ask, she began explaining that she had decided she needed a hobby and that one of her clients owned a knitting store, and had invited her to see it. Continuing, she told him how the cute little baby booties and tiny caps had caught her attention and once she started selecting yarn she couldn't stop.

"That I can see. So, have you thought about a lesson?" he asked, smiling, when it was evident from the looks of the frayed yarn that Faith had tried several attempts unsuccessfully and knowing how much she hated reading directions.

"I was hoping I would be a natural, but it doesn't appear that's the case. I've been working on this ever since you guys left for the games, and look this is all I have," holding up a limp chain of blue yarn. "Maybe this wasn't such a good idea. I had high hopes of making a baby blanket."

"Is there something I should know? Are you trying to tell me something?" He asked, anxiously.

Faith began to cry. "No Tyler, I'm lousy at getting pregnant and lousy at knitting."

He brushed away her tears. "Hey, best I remember it takes two to get pregnant. I'll try to help you out there," he said, taking her hand and pulling her up off the couch. "Now the knitting help will have to come from someone else."

She managed a smile as they walked hand in hand to the bedroom.

~

As their first anniversary and Christmas approached, Faith told Tyler that she thought it would be nice to spend Christmas with his parents and brother and sister. His mother had mentioned on the telephone back in September that they would love to have all the kids together, especially since it would be the last Christmas before Evan graduated college. *"Who knows where everyone will be next year," she had told Faith.*

Tyler smiled when she suggested it.

"That would be good," he said, smiling. "We'll celebrate our anniversary and then drive out there for Christmas."

"Maybe this weekend if we have a little time we could do a little holiday shopping. I need to mail gifts to mother and dad and since Alice and Ben will be at their place, I'll just send their gifts all together. Be thinking what we can get your family."

"It will be fun being there, Faith. Thanks for being so thoughtful. Heather will be almost four so that will make it special having a little kid around for Santa."

~

On Saturday, they awoke to strong winds and torrential rains, hard pouring rain, the kind that pelts the roof and racks the windows.

"What time is it?" Faith whispered, snuggling in close to Tyler. "I'm cold."

"I don't know. The electricity is off. It's still dark outside, but that may be from the storm."

"Do you know how long this had been going on?"

"I heard Judge crying at 4:15, and I got up to let her into the utility room. So the electricity must have gone off shortly thereafter. The rain was really coming down hard then. Didn't you hear the thunder?"

"I didn't hear anything, not even your getting up. You must have been really quiet."

"Not really. I talked to Judge, trying to soothe her and opened the refrigerator for a drink of water."

"I missed everything. I'm glad. I hate it when it's like this."

"Not as much as Judge does. Bless her heart she gets so scared. I'll build a fire so the house will warm up, then I'll see if my Boy Scout training helped any when I try to make coffee in a pot on the gas burner," he said, handing her a robe. "Stay in bed until I call."

"Tyler, you're so sweet," she said, her voice trailing off as she noticed he was already outside the room. Lying in the darkness, she felt guilty and dragged herself out of the warm bed.

When she met Tyler in the kitchen, he was lighting candles just as the electricity returned.

"Oh, thank goodness," Faith muttered, hearing the heat come on. "I wouldn't have made a very good pioneer, huh, Tyler?"

Grinning, he handed her a cup of fragrant hazelnut coffee, "Ignore the grounds. I'm afraid some may have slipped through."

Cupping her hands around the warm mug, she drew it to her mouth, "It's the best coffee, ever. I'll check on Judge."

Opening the door to the laundry room, Faith didn't need to call the Collie, who met her with her tail wagging. Crouching, Faith stroked the dog's long sable coat, "You okay, girl? I bet you need to go out."

By now the rain had lessened and the wind had died down as Faith opened the back door to the patio. "Go on," she nudged, "you can come back in."

Slowly, reluctantly, Judge sauntered out onto the wet brick. Within a minute, Faith heard her pawing at the door. "Okay, sissy, come on in, you big baby!"

Smelling the bacon frying, Faith said, "You're mister energetic, this lazy Saturday morning."

"Well, you cooked last weekend. Besides, if you want to go Christmas shopping, we need to get moving in order to leave soon."

"Let's clean the house after breakfast so we can be free when we get home. Okay?"

"Sure. Your turn to do the bathrooms," he said, mischievously.

Faith faked a pouty look. She said, "I thought I did it last weekend."

"Nope. I keep that on my calendar."

"You probably do."

~

The Galleria was bustling with shoppers as Faith and Tyler strolled along. Decorations of green, red and gold created a festive mood. The professionally designed tree, massive in its splendor and the smaller ones, embellished with ornaments by school children to reflect the holiday traditions of various cultures, added the finishing touches to a normally sterile retail center.

"I'm not sure what we are shopping for here. I think I just wanted to see the tinsel and lights, because the best place to buy Heather's present will be at Toys R Us. Then, we need to go to Home Depot for your parents' glass fireplace screen."

"I know, but let's walk around. We might find something unique for your folks. By then it will be lunch and we can watch the ice-skaters while we eat," Tyler offered.

"Oh, good. When we have children, you are going to be the one who takes them skating, Tyler. I did that once and almost killed myself and everyone else at the rink. I guess my ankles are weak, but probably it is my lack of coordination, because I was never a very talented roller-skater either. All my friends went to the roller rink on Saturday and did fancy twists and turns, skating backwards. I hated it, but invariably that was everyone's choice for their birthday party."

"I hate to admit, but I've not tried to ice-skate. There was never an opportunity growing up in West Texas and as an adult, it's not been a sport I have considered. I'll try, just not today."

"Tyler, I just thought of a Christmas gift for my mother and dad!"

"What?"

"Have you seen those new wine chillers? They look like a small refrigerator, but have a glass front and hold twenty to twenty-five bottles of wine. One would be perfect for their condo."

"Great. Where did you see one?"

"I haven't, only an advertisement in a magazine. We could check Home Expo."

"It's close. We'll go there when we leave the mall. That's a great idea, but don't you think we should mail something, too?"

"Okay, but it doesn't have to be anything major, just something to wish them Merry Christmas. If we find one, why don't we get Alice and Ben the same? I know they don't drink wine as much as Patrick and Sue, but they serve it when they entertain. It will be perfect for mother and dad. They will love it."

~

"We need to wind this up, Faith, if you want to have plenty of time to dress leisurely for The Nutcracker. We're supposed to be at Mr. J's at six and it is three o'clock, now."

"I'm ready. We can select a few incidentals for your brother before we leave for Midland. Other than him, I think we are finished. Do you have room for all of this in your storage area?" Faith asked, turning to look at the crowded truck bed, filled with gifts.

"I hope so. If not, we'll have to put some of them in the spare bedroom. If you know where Patrick and Sue might want theirs, I could install it next week-end and it would be a nice surprise when they return."

"We'll drive over some afternoon after work to take a look."

~

"I'm glad it's cold tonight so I can wear my mink. Unfortunately, there are not many occasions," she said, wrapping the jacket around her shoulders to show Tyler.

Smiling, he said, "You look like a Dallas socialite, Mrs. O'Brien-England."

"Well, you don't look too shabby in your new Armani suit."

As they were driving to the Jackson's house in Highland Park, Faith said, "I love going to their house to see what new accessories Sara has added. I can't wait to see the holiday decorations."

"I'm certain they will be elaborate. Mr. J told me some interior design guy decorated every room in the house for the holidays."

"Won't they be surprised when they come to our party? Designs by Faith won't exactly measure up."

"You make the house look homey and warm and that's what Christmas is all about," Tyler reassured her. "Besides, after some of my famous punch, they won't notice," he laughed.

Mr. Jackson greeted Tyler at the door with a Canadian blended whiskey and water. "Faith, I wasn't sure whether to pour red or white wine, so please excuse my slight in manners."

"Oh, it's okay, Mr. J, I know you're partial," winking, she continued, "but Sara and I will find a way to retaliate. I'll go visit with her this very minute," she teased as he took her jacket.

Before long, the house was packed with neighbors, clients and office personnel who had all been invited to join the Jackson's and then be their guests at the Majestic Theater where he had reserved fifty seats for the eight o'clock performance of The Nutcracker.

~

Sitting on the living room floor in front of the fireplace, Faith wrapped Christmas gifts as Tyler lay sleeping on the couch, one hand on Judge's back, the other on the TV remote. When he had begun to doze, Faith quietly muted the football game and switched to the stereo. Listening to Kenny G's newest Christmas CD and gazing occasionally at the twinkling lights on the Christmas tree, she felt peaceful and content.

First thing in the morning she had made a pot of cowboy stew that still simmered, the pungent fragrance of the various seasonings, filled the house. Actually it was more soup than stew with a combination of ground meat, vegetables and pasta blended with minestrone soup. Alice called it 'stoup' and had made it for Faith when she was a little girl. It was one of her favorite cold-weather dishes along with cornbread.

Faith had spent the remainder of the morning decorating the house, first stringing garlands of holly along the wooden staircase railing, careful to wind it through every spindle, adding large red velvet bows to the newels. She had not realized how difficult it would be to find fresh holly, but finally had been able to purchase just the amount she needed. She snatched it up quickly when she heard the supply was raided the very day it arrived at the nursery.

The mistletoe had been plentiful though and Faith couldn't pass up a clump to hang in the vestibule. Adding red tapers to the mantle and placing peppermint candy canes in the leaded cut glass bowl that had belonged to her grandmother, Faith thought the house looked festive. A hint of holly berry mingled with the scent of cinnamon, clove and citrus that filled the large bowl of fruit and spices, creating the centerpiece in the dining room. The pine Christmas tree reminded her of her childhood home, reminiscent of the times her "Pops" as she called Alice's father-in-law, took her with him to cut down a chosen tree on land that belonged to a friend who lived in the country, north of Townsend.

Though many of the ornaments were new, both she and Tyler had added a few special ones from their childhood, one of his a tiny porcelain Santa in boots and western hat, riding a horse and hers a ballerina slipper, holding a miniature package. The glistening tinsel caught her eye as it reflected off the thin silver icicles, which hung haphazardly from the tree. Knowing that it drove Tyler crazy when they were hung randomly in haste, she had tried to be accurate in her placement but her instincts got the best of her as she tossed them, smiling as they landed aimlessly on the limbs.

She was pleased with the way the house looked and smelled.

"You snored," Faith razzed, as Tyler opened his eyes.

"How long did I sleep?"

"I'm not sure, but a minimum of two hours. I finished all my wrapping."

"Really? Now, I'll never sleep tonight."

"Oh dear, that's not good news," she quipped.

"It sure smells good in here. It's making me hungry."

"We can eat anytime you're ready."

"No, let's sit here and watch the fire for awhile. I'll make drinks," he offered.

When he returned to the couch, he sat down next to Faith, putting his arm around her shoulders. "Would you like to go anywhere special for our anniversary?"

"Anywhere is great with me. When do you want to arrive at your parents?"

"I thought we might leave here on the twenty-first and spend three nights wherever we decide and arrive in Midland on Christmas Eve."

Frowning, Faith replied, "We need to be at your parents on the twenty-third, even if it is late, so I can help your mother the next day with meal preparations; otherwise, we'll get there too late to lend much help."

"Oh, okay. I hadn't thought of that. Well, are two nights somewhere enough?"

"Yes, especially if we leave here early on the twenty-first."

"What about Fredericksburg?" he quizzed. "Mr. J said there are several wineries in the area and all kinds of quaint shops in town. He also told me we shouldn't miss the LBJ Ranch near Stonewall, if we decide to go."

"Tyler," Faith exclaimed excitedly, "If we went to a winery in the Hill Country, we could send a couple of cases of Texas wine to Italy. Wouldn't it be fun for them to share with their Italian friends?"

"That would solve our dilemma of gifts," he responded.

"Then, let's plan it. We can look on the Internet and check about accommodations. Do you want to have our soup here in front of the fire?"

"Sure, I'll help."

~

For two days, they ate German food and drank Texas wine. When Faith decided on the second day to treat herself to a massage, facial and pedicure at the Herb Farm Spa, Tyler drove to Stonewall and then the few miles to the LBJ ranch. Always the history buff, he stood on the banks of the Pedernales River where another tall Texan had walked after serving as the thirty-sixth president of the United States. Watching the water gently spill over the smooth rock, Tyler thought how after criticism and controversy, Johnson must have basked in the solitude of his ranch, surrounded by his cattle under his mighty oaks. But having once visited the LBJ Library on the University of Texas campus and read about the complex personality of this fellow Texan, Tyler figured there were many days that the former president missed the limelight, power, the ultimate control over situations and people.

Not always in agreement with his politics, Tyler, nonetheless found Johnson fascinating because of his insatiable appetite for attention, his tremendous drive and ego. Their characters could not have been more at contrast, but that was not important now as Tyler studied the Hill Country ranch, so far from the lights and clout and dominance of Washington, D.C. Not unlike himself in his quest for perfection, Tyler decided Johnson was simply a man who wanted to be the best on whatever soil he stood in his lifetime.

~

Christmas in Midland was laid back and easy and as much fun as Faith had expected. The family played board games, allowing for no leniency in their competitiveness and stuffed themselves with turkey sandwiches, German chocolate cake, fudge, and divinity candy.

On Christmas day Tyler and Faith drove to the family farm where they walked for two hours, talking about their plans for the New Year. Resting under a gnarled old mesquite tree the two sat, absorbed in the possibilities that lay ahead.

"Someday, a third of this will be ours. Do you think you would ever be content to live here, after we retired? I mean, we could build a nice house and a barn for our horses and the dogs would have a place to run freely. Our grandkids could come and enjoy outdoors."

"You'd like that, wouldn't you, Tyler?"

"I don't think it would be a bad life after living in the city for more than thirty years, fighting the traffic and the concrete jungle."

"I'll be ready. We'll sit out on the porch together in our rocking chairs, asking each other where the years went, marveling how well we held up, never noticing the other's gray hair and wrinkles."

Chapter 21

Faith thought Tyler was unusually quiet during supper, but she knew that he had spent all afternoon at the courthouse and that was generally stressful.

"So, how was everything at the courthouse?"

"Faith," he said, looking pale and worried, "I. . .I didn't go to the courthouse. I went to a doctor."

"The doctor, what for?"

There was a lengthy pause and he sat down.

"Tyler, what's wrong? Are you sick? You haven't seemed as though you felt bad," her voice was notably panicky.

"The doctor thinks I have cancer."

"Cancer?" she said, louder than she meant to say. Now she sat down. "Tyler, cancer of what? How can that be?"

"That's what I've asked myself over and over since about 2:30 this afternoon." He blushed slightly and continued. "Just what every guy wants, cancer of the testicle." He looked down momentarily. When he looked up at Faith, who was sitting there in stunned disbelief, she noticed a tear on his face.

"What do we do now, Tyler? What did the doctor say? And how can he know that without a biopsy or something? Besides, how did you even know to go to the doctor?" asking one question right after the other, as she reached and brushed away more tears on his cheeks.

"About a month ago I felt a little knot, about the size of a pea and I noticed there was some swelling. I've watched it a couple of weeks, but I didn't have any pain there, no tenderness. But then, my lower back started hurting and I had shortness of breath, especially last weekend when I was playing golf. I really didn't think any of it connected, but I decided I'd better get checked out.

"First thing that happened was my doctor felt of my testicle and immediately called a urologist in the next building who said for me to come right over. After I waited there for about an hour he did a transillumination, where he shone a bright light at what he felt. The light didn't pass through so he knew there was a mass. Then he sent me for a scrotal ultrasound and blood tests.

"He'll have those results back in a couple of days but he said that ninety-five percent of these kinds of masses are malignant and that it is the most common form of cancer in men my age. They don't biopsy because if it is cancer, it can spread quickly."

"So, what do they do?" She was almost hysterical.

"They cut it off!"

"You mean your testicle?" she asked, looking horrified. She stood up and started pacing.

He couldn't help but laugh now at her reaction. "Yep, just like that! Scary isn't it? A lawyer without balls, talk about an oxymoron."

"Tyler, this isn't funny." She was crying now, but she sat down again as if to take it all in.

Consoling her he reached for her hand and said, tenderly, "No, it's certainly not, Hon, but if I don't try to see some humor in it, I might cry more, and I don't want to do that." "Besides," he said, "this kind of cancer is highly treatable, the percentage of survival is close to eighty-five to ninety percent, depending on if it has spread to the lymph glands or a major organ."

She could hardly catch her breath and her heart was pounding, but Faith managed to stand and walk around his chair and put her arms around him.

"Let's go in the den. These dishes can wait," he said.

While they were both sitting on the couch, she asked, "So when is the surgery?"

"As soon as he reviews the ultrasound and blood test results and can schedule it."

"But why so soon?"

"Because it's extremely important to get to this early before it metastasizes. It can be very rapid, invasive cancer."

"How long does he think you've had it?"

"We won't know much until after the surgery when it can be determined what classification of cancer it is. But there's something else we have to talk about, Faith."

Before she could say anything he continued, "There's a high probability that I'll have to have radiation or chemo afterwards and that could make me sterile. Or at least that's a possibility, so he wants us to think about sperm cryopreservation, which is just a fancy name for sperm banking."

"So, how does that work?"

"Well, the doctor said that I will strip naked and go into this dark, romantic room with about a hundred candles flickering and there would be at least ten beautiful naked women waiting to do all sorts of sexual things to get me excited…"

"Tyler! Stop it," dabbing her eyes with a tissue.

Continuing, his voice more serious, he explained, "Actually we didn't discuss that because he won't be involved in that part. But, I'm guessing it's like peeing in a jar, only not as easy. He did say I would probably have to do it several times. My sperm count's pretty low; he did a serum testosterone check, which explains why you haven't become pregnant which he said is not uncommon with guys who have testicular cancer. See, I'm able to say it easier already."

"Is…is there any chance it won't be cancerous?"

"Slim, very slim. He said he didn't want to give me any false hope. Either way, my little buddy comes off. Now you know everything I know. Let's finish the dishes."

ᘏ

The orchiectomy was successful and Tyler was able to leave the hospital the next day. Though sore from the incision, he otherwise felt good, but waiting for the lab report was difficult.

Four days after the surgery, they received the news they didn't want to hear. Tyler had a non-seminoma tumor containing embryonal carcinoma, a highly malignant cell type that had metastasized to his lungs.

His urologist sent him to an oncologist surgeon who immediately scheduled surgery to remove the small tumors on the lungs and the lymph nodes behind the abdomen where the metastatic cells were most prevalent. In an effort to explain the upcoming procedures to Tyler, the doctor described the systemic chemotherapy that an oncology radiologist would begin as soon as he was stronger and after the sperm cryopreservation.

ᘏ

During the six weeks of chemo, Tyler tried to remain upbeat, but the nausea made it difficult for him. He pushed himself to go to work, but when he arrived home each day, Faith insisted he take a nap before dinner. He was struggling she could tell, fighting the sickness and coping with the medicine that seemed to make him sicker than the disease that he was battling.

Every day was an ordeal for him because he was frightened, queasy and weak; it was the same for her because she hurt for him, but they both made every effort to make life as normal as it could be, given the circumstances.

"So tell me about your day," he encouraged, after an unusually exhaustive day for him at the office.

"Same ole stuff. I spent two hours at a 'prove-up' proceeding that should have taken fifteen minutes. The couple assured me they had agreed on the settlement of all the community property, and then we got before the Judge and they got in a huge fight. You know how that went over.

"Then this afternoon I worked on a will with an older couple who have 'yours, mine and ours,' who all despise each other. They aren't sure how they want to divide things, so we talked and talked, and got nowhere. You would think they would have this figured out before they came to me and paid big bucks by the hour. I finally sent them home and made another appointment for them next week. Told them they need to work it out in their minds before they arrived. People never cease to amaze me. What about you, what have you got going?"

"Still working on the Robertson bankruptcy case. That may go on another month. The good news is the ambulance company's deal went to arbitration. I'm glad to begin some semblance of closure with it. Why do mine always take so much longer than yours?"

Faith walked over and fell on the couch beside him, snuggling up against him. "Because I am just a better lawyer," she teased and took his hand in hers and kissed it.

"That you are."

"I am not, Tyler, and you know it. My cases are just different. When they involve children, we just try to push to a quick resolution if it is in the best interest of the child. But, remember that child custody case I had last year? It went on for over six months. And the one where the husband was a Mexican citizen, who actually lived in Mexico, but they married here. After a few months, she filed for divorce. There weren't any kids, but boy was there a lot of stuff—a lot of it he took with him. It took nearly eight months for us to finally get her all her assets. But your fraud cases are more complicated and involve a lot more people. At least mine tend to be confined to a few people."

"What ever happened to our being able to have lunch together at the office or at least coffee before the day gets busy?"

"I think those days are over. That was when I was a 'newbie' and you were so crazy in love that you shirked your responsibilities and snuck into my office."

"I'm still madly in love with you." He kissed her on the forehead. "I'm sorry if I've been a little cranky lately."

"You haven't been cranky. You've been sick. Can you imagine if I had been the one sick?"

He smiled his same endearing smile and didn't answer. "You want to watch a movie? Nothing sounds very good to eat, so let's have some popcorn, dill pickles and play like we are dating."

"Sounds like a plan to me. You pick the movie and I'll pop the corn."

~

When the Friday of his last treatment came, he couldn't hide his relief. Tired, but in good spirits, Tyler came in the door smiling. Faith was in the kitchen preparing food for Judge.

"Hi, I tried to call, but I just missed you I guess. You want to go to a hockey game?" He held up two tickets. "Mr. J. gave me four tickets. I gave two to Sid. Would you like to meet him and Sandy there?"

"Sandy?"

"Oh, that's his most recent flame. I haven't met her either. All I know is they've been out once or twice, and he seems head over heels about her. She's an elementary principal in Carrollton, I think, a couple of years older than Sid. He told me her husband was killed in Desert Storm the first month he was there. His helicopter crashed on a rescue mission."

"That's terrible. Do you know how they met?"

"At the gym, one Saturday morning."

"But the best news is it looks as though Sid is going to get sole custody of Shea. It appears his ex and her latest boyfriend got into some kind of trouble. He's supposed to know for sure next week."

"Do you think that will do the new relationship in?" Faith asked, frowning.

"Well, if it does, then he better run as fast as he can from her. That would mean she's not the one for him. Shea needs him and the kind of role model he will be. But she sounds pretty grounded."

"I agree that Sid would be good for him. Sounds like his mother is a piece of work—and I don't mean good."

"What about the game?"

"I'd love to go, but are you sure you feel like going?"

"It's been so long since I felt good, I'm not sure what it would be like, but I want to go. It's been a long time it seems since we've done anything fun."

"I can be ready in ten minutes. Do you want to get a bite of dinner?" Faith asked.

"How about junk at the game? I'm not sure I'll keep anything down anyway so you might as well enjoy some greasy fries and a hotdog."

"Did the doctor say how long it would be before you have an appetite or won't be nauseated?"

"He said in a couple of weeks, I should be much improved. Most of all, I want to feel like playing golf. I've missed my Saturday mornings with Mr. J. and the guys."

"They've missed you, too," she said, softly.

"How do you know that?" he asked.

"Because Mr. J. talked to me. He said he wished you would feel better and could play because it wasn't as much fun trying to beat anyone else," she teased.

He looked serious. "What else did he say?"

"Nothing really; he just wanted to be sure I told you that."

She didn't want to be dishonest with Tyler, but she didn't want him to know how worried his boss was about him and how often he came to her office, simply to talk and be reassured that Tyler was really doing okay. It was strange, but Faith found herself having to be the strong one for everyone; Tyler's parents, his boss, his friends at work, even her family who called almost every day for a report. Trying to sound upbeat to everyone because they needed that, inside she was a bundle of nerves, scared of losing Tyler, frightened that maybe neither could win this battle.

Before he could ask her anything else, Faith turned around to Judge who was waiting for her bowl to be placed back on the floor. "Okay, I'm hurrying," as she patted the dog's head. "Are you going to change into something more comfortable?" she asked Tyler quickly, to switch the tone that had become more serious than she wanted it to be.

"Yes, in just a minute. First, I need to call Sid."

Chapter 22

Clearing the dishes after dinner one evening in late November Faith asked, "Tyler, do you think it would be silly of me to try to become an expert on immigration law?"

Tyler looked up surprised. "Well no, but when did you start thinking about that and why immigration?"

"I'm already getting tired of family law. I think 'burned out' is a better word, plus no one else at the firm is doing immigration cases, which, as you know, is becoming a big issue everywhere, but especially in California, Arizona, and Texas. I've read several news articles lately about the human smugglers, they're also called coyotes, bringing in illegals from El Salvador, Honduras, Mexico, all sorts of places.

"These illegals save money for years, and then they pay the coyotes who take their money and just leave them for dead in the desert, or worse bring them as far as Houston or San Antonio in some locked 18-wheeler truck where they die from the stifling heat of the closed compartment. It's terrible and that's just one aspect of the whole immigration influx. I'm not saying that it's right for them to come in when they don't have papers, but in large part it is the fault of the greedy smugglers who prey on them, promising them a better life, then stealing their money and treating them terrible. There are no easy answers for how to keep the aliens out, but there are answers of how to treat other human beings decently.

"Anyway, I'm sick of dealing with one domestic case after another. Every once in awhile they're rewarding, but more than not it's always the same story: We're almost done with the divorce…I have the woman, the house, car and most of the money...he comes over, beats the shit out of her.

"When they release her from the hospital with a black eye, a broken arm and a concussion, she goes back to the son of a bitch! Makes no sense. I'd like to beat her up myself after that. I don't understand. Maybe Jason does. He seems to love dealing with those kinds of cases...not me! If I could just do adoptions like little Fu, I would love my job, but those don't come along very often.

"After September 11, there appears to be an emphasis on immigration legal training because of the terrorists who were here illegally and I noticed UT Law School is offering a three day seminar the second week in December, and I would like to attend."

"Then I think you should go for it. I certainly understand how you feel about the domestic cases. I don't see how Jason stands it either. I'm not cut out for that. He'll probably be glad you want to do other things since he's so damn territorial. Have you talked to Mr. J.?"

"No, I wanted to mention it to you first."

Chapter 23

"Tyler, Mom and Ben have invited us to go with them to Las Vegas for Christmas. Are you game?"

Thinking a minute, he said, "Sure, but when, exactly?"

"They suggested the twenty-third through the twenty-seventh because of Ben's schedule. He's working all of Thanksgiving so he can get away then. The doctor who covered for him last Christmas moved to another hospital and Ben is not as comfortable being gone an extended time with his new assistant."

"Those are good dates for us. Tell them we'll be packed."

"Oh, good! Do you think we should invite your family and mine for Thanksgiving, so we can send their Christmas gifts back?"

"That's fine with me, but have you ever cooked turkey and dressing?"

Taken aback, Faith said, sarcastically, "No, but there is a first for everything and I can read a recipe, you know!"

"Hey, I didn't mean it like that," he added quickly, noticing her tone. "I just meant..." his voice trailing off as she walked outside, slamming the door.

Following her out, he put his arm around her. "What's wrong? You sure seem edgy. Did I do something?"

Looking at him, she felt a lump in her throat and feared she was about to burst into tears. "I...I...I thought I might be pregnant, Tyler. I was nearly three weeks late with my period. I kept hoping, but didn't want to say anything to you. Then, this morning...well, I guess I'm not, after all," she said, in an unsteady voice.

"I'm sorry, Faith. I know how badly you want a baby, but it's not going to happen without the in vitro, and I just want to wait. I want to be certain that I am free of the cancer, I…" he paused, "please be patient with me."

"Oh, Tyler, I know," trying unsuccessfully to stop her tears. "I just got excited when I didn't have my period on time. I'm never late, so I thought there was a chance. I'm disappointed, but I'll be okay."

Taking her in his arms, he held her close, neither saying anything, as she buried her head in his chest. The tears rose to her eyes and fell on her cheeks, salty.

"I'm sorry, Tyler, I'm just a big baby."

Feeling a gust of air, he said, "Well, you're my big baby. Let's go inside before you get cold."

~

The next afternoon, Tyler told Faith he had to stay to meet with a client, so when he drove in the driveway only thirty minutes later than usual, she was surprised and met him at the door. Stepping out of the car, he looked at her sheepishly, holding a bundle in his arms. Before he could uncover the contents, Faith heard a faint meow.

"What in the world do you have, Tyler?" as she lifted the small white blanket to look at a tiny calico head, moving. Two dark, pleading eyes met Faith's.

"I thought maybe she might be extra company for Judge, plus Sid took one for Shea." he offered, hesitantly.

Although knowing that this gesture was a direct result of her actions the previous day, Faith kept her thoughts inside. "Oh, Tyler, she is so cute with her long hair, but so tiny. How old is she?"

"Six weeks, but she is weaned. Do you like her?" he asked, hopefully, looking worried.

Reaching to take her, Faith replied, "Of course I like her. What's her name?"

"That's your decision."

"Let's go introduce her to Judge. This may take a period of adjustment."

When Faith set the timid kitten on the patio, Judge hurried to investigate what appeared to be the newest member of the family.

"Easy, Judge," Tyler warned, as the Collie nosed the frightened feline who rushed to take cover under a lawn chair.

"As I said, this may take a while," Faith repeated, reaching to retrieve the kitten.

"Let's take them inside and sit on the floor. Maybe if she is in your lap she will be less afraid," he suggested.

Sitting on overstuffed pillows across from one another, Tyler petted Judge, who now yawned in disinterest, her tail curled around his leg, as Faith attempted to ease the kitten's fears. Soon a low, rhythmic vibration told Faith that the ball of yellow, white and black fur was becoming more comfortable. As the purring continued, Faith whispered, "My arm is going to sleep, but I'm afraid to move."

Easing to his feet, Tyler said, "I'll heat some milk. Maybe she'll drink and then sleep awhile. I bought some food. Do you think we should put a spoonful in a dish?"

"We can try, but see if Judge will go outside for awhile. I think that might help."

~

"Tyler, are you asleep?"

"Huh?" he muttered without opening his eyes.

"I thought of a name."

"Hmm," was all that came from his sleepy voice.

"How about Dusty? I'm afraid if I don't name something after your favorite movie character, you'll want to give that name to our first child." But she was talking to deaf ears.

"Okay," she said out loud, yet knowing he didn't hear, "We'll discuss this in the morning," as she reached to turn off the lamp and extend her hand to touch the kitten, sleeping in a box by the bed.

~

The first weeks of December flew by, giving Faith little time to think about Las Vegas. She had been at trial for two weeks on a case that involved a domestic distribution of property. Finally, the finding was in her client's favor, showing that she wasn't awarded a disproportionate share of the property, and that the division of community property was fair and reasonable. But it had taken an inordinate amount of her time, and had left little time for anything else. The night before they were to meet her mom and Ben at the airport at nine o'clock the following morning, she started packing, a task Tyler had completed the day before on their anniversary.

"Hell, I don't know what to take," throwing a blouse on the bed, in a slight tantrum.

"Settle down, Hon, if you don't have everything you need when we get there, we'll buy it."

"Oh, Tyler, I'm being a big boob and I know it," slamming her body onto the bed in exasperation.

Calmly, Tyler fell onto the covers next to her, "But I like your big boobs," tickling her and nibbling her neck.

Pushing him away, she yelled, "Stop! We haven't time for that stuff."

Undaunted, he continued. "We would have, if you'd packed when I did," lifting her sweatshirt to kiss her stomach. He had gotten the best of her and she knew it as she tried to roll over.

"Oh no, you don't. You're captured," pulling himself up enough to slide his body over hers, now more forceful in his pursuit. He covered her mouth with his and fumbling, found space to slide his hands down in her jeans. Before long, she succumbed to his undressing her as she reached to unzip the fly of his jeans. Hurriedly, he helped her, then reaching to dim the lights, he returned to touching her body.

Whispering, "You're going to have to help me pack, later, you know."

"Later…shh…just enjoy the moment," his breath heavy as his mouth found the center of her smooth, nude body.

Forgetting that she had fought his earlier advances, she begged him not to stop, her love for him swallowing her. When she could no longer stand the waiting, she pulled him up to her and he came inside her, giving a powerful surge of emotion and an orgasm like none she remembered.

Spent, but smiling, he reached to wipe her forehead, "If I don't win a dime in Vegas, I feel like a millionaire right now."

"Can we set the alarm for five o'clock? I don't have the strength to pack. I'll be quick in the morning."

Rolling over, he pushed on the alarm and kissed her damp face. "Good night, sweet dreams."

"Good night, Tyler, I love you."

~

When the alarm rang, Faith bounded out of bed, pulling her robe around her still naked body.

Tyler opened his eyes slowly, "Let's see how fast you can pack."

"Don't worry. I'll make it, but first, I'm going to take a shower. If I hang around here without my clothes on, you'll get other ideas and we'll miss the plane."

"How could you even think something like that?" Throwing off the covers, he rose from the bed, pulling on his sweats. "I best feed the girls and give them attention. They aren't going to be too happy when they see Sid today. I think they know the drill."

At five minutes until nine, they arrived at the terminal, suitcases in hand. Alice and Ben were waiting.

"We just need a minute to check in. The security people never go through Faith's luggage. If they opened it, they'd just figure someone else had already rummaged through it."

~

The lights of Las Vegas were captivating. As Tyler and Faith walked the strip on their first evening, they were in awe of the thousands of neon lights, the constant throngs of people in every color, shape and nationality, the steady hustle and the never ending excitement.

"Well, what's your game, Tyler?" as they entered Caesar's Palace.

"I think I'll try my hand at Blackjack, and you?"

"Slots. . .mindless slots. I'm going to take this roll of quarters and turn it into a hundred."

"You wish, but I hope you're lucky. Look, I'll be at that table," pointing to one where three people were sitting, seriously studying their cards.

"I'll find you, but if we get separated, meet me at 7:30 in the lounge. We're supposed to meet Mom and Ben back at the Golden Nugget at eight o'clock for dinner."

"Okay, good luck."

In less than ten minutes, Faith had lost her quarters. Not wanting to disturb Tyler, who appeared to be winning by the stack of chips piled in front of him, Faith strolled around the casino. Watching four Asian men in a high stakes game of Baccarat, she said, under her breath, "Too rich for my blood," and walked to the Keno lounge where she sat down to play a game. After choosing three numbers she waited for the little balls to pop up in the hopper, hoping the attendant would call her numbers. When the cocktail waitress returned with her drink, she studied the other people seated in the rows of chairs.

"Number three," the caller announced. Then, after calling several others, Faith heard, "Number twelve." Excitedly, she waited for the number six, but it didn't appear before the twenty numbers were called. *At least I pushed, or I think I did,* she decided.

On the plane, she and Tyler had studied the games and his careful explanations added to her knowledge. She had told him Craps was out for her. "Too fast," she had said.

Laughing, he had suggested Keno, as maybe more her speed.

After three more unsuccessful games, Faith went back to look for Tyler, whom she found sitting at the same Blackjack table.

Smiling, he said, "I'll be ready after this hand, which was quickly dealt. Blackjack! This is my lucky day, but I'm quitting while I'm ahead." Leaning over, he whispered in her ear, "I was lucky last night, too. Maybe you are my charm."

"I don't think so. I've lost at everything I've played. Well, I pushed once."

"That you did," continuing to tease her.

Standing, he took three black chips and cupped them in her hand. "Now, I've paid you well," winking.

"Tyler England, you're bad. How much money is here?"

"Three hundred dollars, now, how bad am I?"

Looking surprised, "How much did you start with?"

"Twenty dollars and I have two hundred in my pocket. What do you think now?"

"I think I'm going shopping."

~

"Would you rather see Siegfried and Roy or Wayne Newton tomorrow night?" Ben asked. "I'll make reservations."

"Makes me no difference," Faith shrugged.

"Me, either," Tyler agreed.

"What's your choice, Mom?"

"I've seen Wayne Newton and he does a stupendous show, but I'd really like to see the white tigers."

"That's really my choice," Faith confessed.

"Then the Mirage it is. Are you two still planning to drive to Hoover Dam? We don't need the rental car tomorrow."

"I'd like to," Tyler said, turning to Faith.

"History, you know," raising her eyebrows and frowning.

"I thought the same thing before I went with Ben. Lake Mead is beautiful. You'll enjoy it, too. Besides the light and fresh air are good changes from the smoky, dark casinos."

"Ben, what are you doing after dinner?" Tyler inquired.

"I may play Craps. You want to join me?"

"Sure, but what will you do, Faith?"

"Watch Mom lose nickels."

"Maybe you'll bring her luck, like you did me."

"I don't know about this gambling. I like to have something to show for my money."

"Relax, Faith. Life's a gamble. You just have to learn to play the hand you're dealt," Tyler said, almost wistfully.

Chapter 24

January and February were bleak and busy, and both Faith and Tyler were up to their necks in work. One particular fraud case was taking all Tyler's time and even then he couldn't seem to tie up all the loose ends. His own client wasn't even cooperating with him, much less the other attorney and his client. It all stemmed from a nasty divorce, but had taken another turn when the wife discovered her husband had fraudulently concealed assets, including a two million dollar estate in the Bahamas. Furthermore, he had hidden accounts in Switzerland that he had never revealed to her during the marriage. Another attorney in the firm had handled the divorce, but once the fraud complaints came forward, Tyler was assigned the case. It had dragged on it seemed for months, and the more Tyler uncovered, the uglier it got and the circle of people involved got wider. On top of that they had come home one Friday night late from a movie, and found their house had been broken into. Although nothing was taken, the intruders had decided to do as much damage to the home office as they possibly could. They took everything out of both filing cabinets and threw papers all over the room, knocked pictures to the floor and broke an urn that Patrick had given Faith from one of his trips to Italy. But what was the most disturbing to Tyler, was that they had carved the word, 'sucker' into his antique, cherry desk. He figured they had to have been in the house over an hour to do what they did. When the police came, they dusted for fingerprints and made a report, but seemed less concerned than Faith and Tyler had wanted. They did say that there had been no other reported break-ins in the area. Faith, who was normally strong, and tough, found herself for weeks unable to sleep through the night. Every little noise caused her to jump and cling to Tyler. If Judge barked, she checked the doors and windows, fearful the intruders were trying to break in again.

"I just feel so violated. Now, I understand better how some of the women I represent feel when they are so vulnerable."

"I know, Hon, but we have to get past this, and move forward. It was probably just a bunch of teenagers out on a spree who picked our house at random."

"But it seems odd they only went into the office and no other part of the house; well that we can tell, anyway. I am just so glad they didn't hurt Judge. Surely, she barked."

"She may not have heard them, since they came through the side door. She's not exactly a watchdog, I'll admit."

It took Tyler two weekends to sand and refinish the top of the desk and another to buy a new door and hang it.

"I'm so behind in this case Faith, I really need to go to the office."

"On Sunday afternoon when the Cowboys are playing?"

"I know, but the trial starts Tuesday, and I'm just not ready."

"Will you be late?"

"Probably not past 6:00."

When Tyler wasn't home at 7:30, Faith became concerned. She had tried calling him four or five times at his office and once on his new cell, but there was no answer. At 8:00, she called Sid and told him she was really worried.

"What if he got really sick or something. Maybe he passed out. What should we do, Sid?"

"Can I bring Shea over there? I'll go to the office. He may be in a conference or something. You say he's not answering either phone?"

Ignoring his question, she said, "A conference on Sunday night. He didn't say anything about meeting anyone."

"I'm on my way. Shea will be glad to have the chance to visit you and play with Judge."

Once he dropped off his son and tried to reassure Faith, he drove 80 miles an hour to the office. He had not wanted Faith to know he was worried, but he was. Tyler was the most responsible person he knew. It wasn't like him to be late. Sweat beaded on his forehead as he reached the double glass doors to the building. The security guard was asleep in a chair just inside. Sid pushed in his code and swung open the heavy doors. "Is Tyler here?"

"Yeah, he was. I ain't seen him leave so I guess he is." Sid rushed past the young guard, picking up speed as he approached the elevator. "Damn, come on you slow mother, get me to the third floor." He yelled as if the elevator could hear.

He grabbed the door and raced in hollering Tyler's name. No answer came. He ran into the next room and then the next. The place had been ransacked. Then he heard a low muffled moan coming from the closet. He opened the door. "Holy shit, Man! What's going on? Are you okay?" Tyler nodded his head yes as Sid untied his hands and gently pulled the duct tape off his mouth. "What in the hell happened to your eye? You've got blood on your face and your eye is all black and blue."

Tyler struggled to talk. "I don't really know. I was working and these two guys came in, both in masks. The only thing else I noticed was they each wore shirts with an electrical company's name on it. I guess that is how they got past the guard. Anyway, I stood up to approach them and that's the last thing I remember. They hit me over the head with something heavy and I was out. When I came to, I was tied up on the floor."

"I'll call the police, but we need to get you to the hospital. I'll call Faith to meet us there. She's worried crazy about you Bro."

"I'm okay, really I am. I've just got a powerful headache."

"You might need stitches. We need to clean that up to see. Wait here while I get a towel and water."

The police and Faith and Shea arrived within minutes of each other. Suddenly, everyone was talking at once and Faith was cleaning the wound and hovering over Tyler.

"Ma'am, we are going to have to talk to your husband. Could you maybe let us have a minute?"

"Sure, but just let me see if he's okay. I think we need to get him to the hospital. I'm no nurse. I can't tell for sure, so I think we should go to the emergency room."

"Wait Faith, let me answer their questions and then we can talk about seeing a doctor. You better call Mr. J. He needs to know what happened."

Mr. Jackson arrived within thirty minutes of the call with his neighbor, a physician. "I had a feeling he might fight you about going to the hospital, so I brought my friend Dr. Gardner to check him out. Where is he?"

"He's in there," Faith said, pointing to the next room. "The police are still questioning him and looking around. I'm sure he would like you with him. A detective just arrived, so I'm sure he's asking the same things again. Who do you think did this?"

"If I were guessing, the same people who broke in your house. Has to be related to the Ferguson case. Damn, I knew it was ugly, I just didn't know how ugly. We just may find out more about our friend than fraud. Appears he has some sleazy acquaintances, or should I say some sorry people on his payroll. He must really not want to share any more money with the missus. Sorry bastard. Of course, he may not be the one responsible for this, but that's my guess. Too many signs point to him. Makes sense now that they are scrambling for something we have. Did Tyler tell you anything about the case?"

"Mr. J., you know how tight lipped he is before he goes to trial."

"Yeah, I know, just hoping he knows something I don't."

"I do," Tyler said. "I overhead your conversation. As a matter of fact, I do know something, but I haven't figured out how to use it in this case. It has nothing to do with concealing assets. It's about concealing murder. As I was delving into his background, it appears he was held in the Bahamas for awhile on suspicion of murder, but the authorities there were never able to pin it on him. Anyway, I was going to talk to you about it tomorrow. I just got some more confirmations today. Seems that Ferguson must have thought I have known this for quite awhile when actually I didn't. Should we postpone the trial?"

"That depends on your injuries. If Doc here says you're okay, let's go after him and get the wife her due. Then the police can take over the rest. We'll press charges for the breaking and entering if we can prove the sonabitch was behind it."

"I'm okay, right Doc?"

"Good thing you are hard headed or they could have killed you. You are going to have quite a shiner for your court appearance, though."

"I've looked and felt worse. I can assure you."

~

One day in the middle of March when Tyler was behind closed doors with a client, Mr. Jackson called Faith into his office.

"Faith, I think you and Tyler need to get away for a trip. Tyler needs a rest."

She looked at him a minute. "Is everything okay? I mean is our work okay?"

"Your work, everything you both do is splendid. I'm just concerned about Tyler. When we were playing golf the other day, he seemed distracted, worse golf game I've ever seen him play. Then, afterwards, when we went for beer he hardly said anything.

That's just not like him. I know he's been working hard. That Berkley case has been rough and long, not to mention the Ferguson fiasco."

"Lately he's taken to those quiet moods at home too sometimes. He's the same sweet, thoughtful Tyler as always, just a little more introverted, I guess is the word."

"You've never used that trip to Italy, Faith, the trip your dad gave you for the wedding. It's been almost three years. I hear it's beautiful in the spring. Take ten days or so and enjoy yourselves."

"That's very kind of you, Mr. J. I'm worried about him, too. My mother and dad are actually in Italy now so it would be a perfect time to go."

"Well, I'd rather you make the suggestion then me, but if I have to, I will."

Faith knew Tyler was like a son to him. He had three daughters all of whom lived in other states and didn't visit often. His wasn't a close family and she could tell from little things Mr. J said that it broke his heart he didn't have a son, an attorney son, especially, to take over the firm someday.

"I'll try, but I can't be sure I can convince him. Seems lately he doesn't listen to me and I can't convince him of anything." Then spilling her feelings, she told her boss how Tyler was really the one who wanted children first. "I was fine with it, but he really wanted a baby as soon as we married. Now every time I bring it up, he says he's not ready. Sometimes I don't understand, but then deep down I know he's afraid."

"You're correct, Faith, he's still frightened. He's scared to death he'll get sick again and die, leaving you to raise a child alone."

"I know in my heart that's it, Mr. J, and raising a child alone would be difficult, but my Mom did it and I can too. It's the thought of losing Tyler that I can't deal with."

"It's been almost a year since the surgery, right?"

"It will be a year in May."

"Maybe when he hits that milestone, he'll feel better."

"That's what he's told me," Faith said. "I think when he gets a clean bill of health, he'll be ready. I'll talk to him tonight about the trip. I think he's relieved that case is over so that might make it easier to convince him to go away."

She paused. "Thank you Mr. J. I'd hug your neck if you weren't my boss."

He smiled a broad smile. "You're good kids, both of you. I wouldn't mind having a godson, you know. Now get back to work. I'm spending money on my own talk."

But getting back to work wasn't as easy as just saying it. Faith was excited about the prospect of going to Italy with Tyler, but worried about his reaction.

~

It had taken both Faith and Mr. Jackson to persuade Tyler he needed to take a few days for a vacation, because he had as many reasons not to go as they did to encourage him. In the end, Faith won out.

When they arrived in Florence, Tyler turned to Faith. "I'm really glad we did this. Now I'm anxious to see Italy."

"Me too," she smiled. "Dad has talked about it so much I feel like I've been here. Oh, there they are," she shrieked.

Patrick and Sue were standing behind the glass waving and smiling, both looking relaxed and tanned.

"Oh, it is so good to see you," Sue said, hugging first Faith and then Tyler.

Patrick embraced Faith and shook Tyler's hand, then pulled him forward in a manly clutch.

"Welcome to Italy!" Patrick exclaimed.

"Buon giorno," Sue said with an East Texas accent.

"Mama Mia, it's a long flight," Faith said, mockingly.

"Were you able to sleep?" Sue asked.

"Tyler slept most of the trip while I listened to some kid whine and cry and two old men snore. I finally went to sleep right before they woke us for breakfast; then the flight from Rome was so short, there wasn't time."

"You'll feel better after you've had a soothing bubble bath and an authentic Italian Cappuccino."

"You like it here don't you, Mother?"

Sue and Faith had fallen back several steps behind Tyler and Patrick who were talking about baseball. The women scrambled to keep up, and then decided it didn't matter.

"I love it, Faith. Italy is romantic, seductive; it has a poetry all its own. When we sit out on a moonless night under the tiglio trees, just the two of us, no one even near, the sky is as black as a tunnel, and yet I never feel afraid or lonely. The convent was always so dark, and always I was lonely. I thought I would never like the darkness again, but it's different here. And in the daytime, when all the flowers and herbs begin to bloom, the butterflies dance among the lavender…then I feel young again."

Taking her mother's arm, Faith replied, "I'm happy for you… both of you look well. I can't wait to see your place. I'm glad you decided to keep the bungalow and build a small manor of your own."

"Oh, I am too. Your dad has had such a good time having it built, which is not an easy task in these parts. Fortunately, Stefano knows everyone or we would never have it finished."

"Are you women riding with us?" Patrick teased as he opened the trunk of a silver Mercedes and reached to take the luggage Faith was pulling.

"I'll get that. I think she must be moving here or something," Tyler said as he hoisted her heavy bag into the truck. "Look at the difference in weight, as he casually lifted his."

"I couldn't decide what to bring," Faith said, defending herself.

"Obviously."

"You sit up front, Tyler. I'll sit back here with Faith," Sue said, opening a back car door.

As they drove the autostrada south Faith said, "I see why you love it here in spring. Well, I think I see. I'm not sure; we just passed a vineyard so fast the grapes are already aged wine."

"You have to go with the flow or you'll get run over."

Faith gazed out the window at the hilltop citadels dotting the countryside. The golden yellow of the barren earth was in sharp contrast to the palette of green landscape, full of trees and vineyards that lined the hills, meeting the sky that was as blue as a summer sea with clouds as puffy white as whipped cream.

When they arrived at their new home, Faith was astonished at the grace and style of the country chateau, but even more stupefied by its surroundings. She jumped from the vehicle the moment Patrick put it into park.

The lush landscape was a panorama of majestic color. Along one side of the manor was a pergola covered in a flowering canopy of violet vines.

"You need this in the summer when the sun bears down on you," Patrick explained, taking pleasure in showing off their little piece of land where Tuscany and Umbria seem to flow together.

"Here's your mother's herb garden and over there are the roses. Those ladies from East Texas sure like their roses. It's just a few weeks early for the full effect. Everything will be bursting in blossom in a very short time."

Sue rushed over, "I've planted Sweet William, fuchsia, white geraniums, lavender, basil, sage…I can't even remember what all. Carmella and her gardener Caesar helped me. I really didn't know where to begin. I wish you could be here when the red poppies are all in bloom." She stopped and smiled. "Now, Patrick must show you his pride and joy."

Grinning, he pointed to a brick wood-fired pizza oven with a stone dome. Together the four of them walked to the oven as Patrick explained. "Stefano and I built it from the ground up. We even gathered the rocks. The only help we had was setting the chimney. To get it just right, he had his friend Giuseppe help us. When we finished, Giuseppe insisted that we roast a piglet." He laughed. "After that I have stuck mainly to pizza and focaccias."

"Focaccias? What is that?" Faith asked, looking puzzled.

"A close cousin to pizza. I guess we would call it flat bread," Patrick explained.

"It is delicious the way your dad makes it. He adds rosemary and basil from my garden, olive oil made from Stefano's olive trees and lots of garlic. Then at the end, some mozzarella and pancetta top it off."

"It makes my mouth water just listening," Tyler said.

~

Quickly, Sue waved her hands as if to hurry them and said, "Patrick, I'll bet they're starved. We'll have plenty of time outside; let's go in. Let's show them the house and then have lunch."

The large sitting room off the main entrance hall was set in warm tones of verdant green, rich auburn and ocher and showcased a fireplace of dark walnut and Italian marble. A Persian rug, beautifully framed Renaissance art, and elegant woodwork and moldings finished out the setting.

The center of the dining room held a long wooden table with straight back chairs covered in fabric of woven tapestry. Two tall expansive windows allowed outside light to filter through the crystal prisms of the chandelier, reflecting the colors of the

Venetian vases on the wooden sideboard. Colors of gold, ivory and sienna dominated the room and the adjoining country-style kitchen. Simple wooden chairs with quilted fabric backing and a round table distressed by years of use filled the small breakfast area.

The master bedroom and bath carried out the theme of a country Italian manor with walls painted in rich earth tones borrowed from nature, just outside the draped windows. These complimented the luxurious duvet, the color of aged red wine that lay on the king-size iron bed. The interior of the bath was carved exclusively from Italian marble and the cream colored linens lightened the overall effect.

A smaller second bedroom and connecting library were highlighted in shades of smoky blue and ruby.

"You are certainly welcome to stay here, but we thought you might enjoy the privacy of the bungalow, and it has a small fireplace. This time of year the nights still get a bit cool."

"The bungalow sounds great, but your place is beautiful and I wouldn't change a thing."

"Do you mean it?" Sue asked. "It's the first new house for both of us so that makes it really special."

"Yes, it's gorgeous," Tyler chimed in.

"Wait until you see Stefano and Carmella's villa. It makes this look like the ghetto," Patrick said, laughing.

"I know you are both exhausted, but first let's have a bite to eat." Sue suggested.

"I'm more tired than hungry, if you can believe that," Faith said, but it was nearly lunchtime and she thought a taste of something might be good.

"I'm famished," Tyler said.

"Good, before you go clean up and take a nap, let me serve you a light Italian lunch," Sue encouraged. "I prepared melon wrapped in prosciutto, some marinated olives and crostini."

"I think I need a lesson in Italian vocabulary. What exactly is crostini?" Faith asked.

"Actually, it means 'little toasts'. The ones I make are little rounds of toasted bread topped with olives, peppers and mushrooms, and drizzled with olive oil."

"Mmm, that sounds great," Faith said.

They sat at the breakfast table, eating the Italian appetizers and drinking red wine.

"I'm ready for a bubble bath and a nap or rather a nap and then a bubble bath. I'm not used to drinking wine for lunch." Faith said, trying to suppress a yawn.

Patrick laughed. "You would get used to it if you lived here."

"Well, I'm ready for a nap and a shower," Tyler said, standing and pulling the chair out for Faith. "I'm beginning to feel as wrinkled and worn as I look."

She stood and kissed him on the check. "You could never look worn; you handsome, neat-freak devil."

Sue asked, "Can we all be ready to be at Stefano and Carmella's at six o'clock?"

"If that's the plan, we'll meet you here at 5:45, but you might want to call us about an hour before that to see if we're alive."

"I can do that. Now get some rest. You'll need it for Stefano and Carmella. They have boundless energy. I wonder sometimes where they get it. I have trouble keeping up with them, and you will too," Patrick said, shaking his head and smiling. "You are going to love them as I do."

"I can't wait to meet them. But for now… goodnight," Faith said, covering her yawn with one hand and reaching for Tyler's hand with the other. Within minutes they were inside the bungalow.

"We can look around later," she said to Tyler, "Sleep tight," as they fell onto the soft awaiting bed.

~

Carmella and Stefano were waiting for them on the veranda.

"Oh, my gosh, this looks like all the pictures I've ever seen of Tuscany," Faith muttered. "You were right Patrick, yours is the ghetto," Tyler teased.

"You haven't seen anything yet," Patrick replied, bringing his car to a stop. Carmella came running, with Stefano in tow. Since she had visited with Patrick and Sue the day before, she went straight to Faith, wrapping her arms around her in a colossal hug and taking Faith's face between her hands, slightly squeezing her cheeks.

"You are even more beautiful than your father described."

By now Tyler had met Stefano and was dutifully waiting his introduction to Carmella.

"And this is the handsome husband Ty, I presume," as she embraced him.

"It is a pleasure to finally meet you," he said.

Patrick laughed to himself; he had wondered how she was going to make their names Italian. He guessed the best she could do was shorten Tyler to Ty. It appeared Faith was going to just be Faith.

"Well, don't I get a hug?"

"Oh, Patrico, you always get a hug," as she buried him in her flowing silk caftan.

Carmella had changed very little since the day twenty-five years ago when Patrick had met her on the airplane on his way to Rome. Although he figured she was nearing seventy, she had aged beautifully; her soft raven hair still shiny and her ebony eyes bright. As always, there was a sparkle in her smile. Patrick had once described her to Sue as not walking and bending, but flowing and swooping.

Stefano was still a bear of a man, barrel-chested and no better looking than before. Patrick often remembered his first sight of this giant of an Italian and how shocked he was to see not a handsome, debonair, suave Mediterranean man, but a balding, slightly overweight average guy, totally dedicated to Carmella's every whim.

"What are we just standing here for? Where is the wine, Stefano? Or, would you like something else?" Carmella asked, looking first at Faith and then Tyler.

Faith answered, "Wine would be wonderful."

Tyler nodded in agreement.

"Then wine it is. Would you like to accompany me to the cellar and assist in the selection?" Stefano asked Tyler.

"Sure, it would be an honor."

Patrick's thoughts took him back to the first time Stefano had taken him down the long, winding stairway to the wine cellar, seeing the walls of ornately carved walnut and row upon row of wine.

Tyler's eyes were big with astonishment when he came out to the courtyard. "I've never seen anything like that," he said to everyone sitting in front of the oversized outdoor fireplace that was giving warmth to the chilly spring night.

"What did you select?" Patrick asked.

"A Brunello di Montalcino, whatever that is. I had a little help from Stefano," he admitted. "Also we chose two of his newer white wines."

Stefano had uncorked the three bottles and then joined them. "I'm making more white wine now than I used to. All of Italy seems to be joining the trend."

Pouring Patrick the first glass, he apologized, "I know it is rude to not serve my guests first, but I want Patrico's opinion before I pour any further."

Patrick swirled the pale wine and took a sip.

"This is excellent, Stef. What grapes are you using?"

"I thought you'd never ask," he winked as he poured the others a glass. "I used forty-five percent pinot Grigio, thirty-five percent Chardonnay, ten percent Viognier along with a little Sauvignon Blanc, Roussanne and Marsanne," his voice full of pride as he explained.

"Sounds like a lot of work," Faith added.

"Oh, but it is a labor of love, my dear. I am slowing down some and, perhaps, don't do quite as much as I used to, but I suppose I'll experiment with the grapes from my death bed."

"Yes, he'll try to kill us all before he goes," Carmella said, patting him gingerly on the knee.

Stefano smiled the same loving smile at Carmella that Patrick had witnessed now hundreds of times.

When they had each finished their first glass of wine, Stefano was instantly up pouring more. "This is more of the same; then we will have the red if you like."

The wine tasted good and Faith was beginning to feel warm inside. "I think I could get used to this, huh, Tyler?"

He laughed. "Not a bad life. No wonder you wanted to spend so much time here," he said, looking at Patrick and Sue.

"So what are your plans? What are you hoping to see?" Carmella asked.

"We'll be here four days and then we're taking the train to Venice for two days and on to Rome for the remainder of our time, about three days, I guess."

"One of those days here, we'll have to go back to Florence," Sue said. "Patrick was in such a hurry for them to see everything here they were not able to spend a minute in Florence," she explained to Carmella.

"Oh, yes. You must see Firenze. It is beautiful and the shopping is marvelous, too!" she said, as she winked at Faith. "Your mother and I have quite a wonderful time spending Stefano and Patrico's money."

Faith looked at Tyler and grinned, knowing he knew what she was thinking about spending the guy's money. Suppressing her ideas of new age female independence wasn't easy, but she managed.

"Someday you must go to Milan. Our daughter, Elisabette and her family live there. That is the fashion capital, where you find the Gucci bags, Prada heels and Vuitton bags. Although Firenze has its share of wonderful sights, Milan that is where it happens first."

"Shall we move inside and have dinner?" Stefano asked.

Everyone nodded in compliance.

"Carmen made us a wonderful basil and lemon chicken along with Risotto and red chard. I told her not to be too fancy, the Americans may not be ready for some of our amuse bouche or the like. Stefano wanted to drive to the coast yesterday and buy some fresh sea urchins, squid and eels for a tagliolini alla trigli but I told him, perhaps, another time."

Faith looked relieved. "What was the first dish you mentioned?"

"Oh, amuse bouche? Tonight, just a bit of fish roe served with tomato and basil."

"The chicken sounds delicious," Tyler said, as everyone laughed.

"We have the most wonderful food here. Since we live at the cusp of Tuscany and Umbria, we borrow from them both. Most of Tuscany favors the simple stews and pot roasts, whereas Umbria features the black truffles, the delightful peppery meats. Whenever we can acquire fresh seafood from the coast, we are happy."

Eating slowly and savoring the taste of the herbs and spices used to add the unique Italian flavor, everyone talked as Stefano slipped away for a minute only to return with more bottles of red wine.

"This is a special celebration. We should try this 1982 Solaria," as he poured a round into clean glasses before anyone could refuse.

While proposing another toast to Faith and Tyler, Carmella served a small helping of red peppers topped with melted cheese and then dashed with Balsamic vinegar, added as an afterthought. "Be sure to save room for the pear tart with mascarpone."

Patrick let out a moan, "You do this to me every time."

"Hush, hush, Patrico, the grappa will help settle all this," Carmella needled.

"I'll bet I sleep well tonight, after eating all this wonderful food," Faith added.

"Let's retire to the great room. I'll bring the liqueurs. What will it be for you?" looking at each guest. "I have a nice port, cognac, grappa and of course the traditional Italian Limoncello," Stefano offered.

"Tyler, how about you?"

"I think I'll try the grappa."

"Good choice. I make my own invecchiaata, age it in wooden barrels for at least a year. Most of what you taste in bars is just the giovane that comes from the metal casks in only six months."

He handed Tyler the amber liquid and waited for his reaction.

"Whew, that is mighty," Tyler said, his face turning slightly red, suppressing a cough.

Stefano laughed. "One has to develop a taste." He turned to Faith and smiled.

"I think I'll try the Limoncello. It sounds a bit milder, less industrial strength, huh, Tyler?"

Tyler grinned. "What is this, anyway?"

Stefano said, "The grappa was originally made for the workers. After all the grapes are pressed, the remaining pomance is used to make the grappa."

He poured Patrick, Carmella and Sue a small amount of Port as they all sat looking at the fire, digesting the rich food and friendship.

~

"It feels so good to be horizontal. Am I ever tired, but deliciously tired," Faith said as she sank down in the down-filled bed.

Tyler reached to kiss her, "Too tired?"

It had been over a month since Tyler had even made the slightest attempt to be amorous and she didn't know whether it was the wine or the glorious Tuscan air, but it didn't matter as long as he was interested.

"Never too tired for you," she whispered.

They made love in the cushioned luxury of the satin sheets and spoke softly afterwards.

"Tyler, when do you think we can get pregnant?"

"When it's been a year, Hon. It's just a couple of more months, hopefully and I'll get a clean bill of health."

"What if I got pregnant tonight?"

"It would be a miracle. The doctor said it would be highly unlikely that would happen," as he wrapped his arms around her. Soon they fell soundly asleep.

It was almost nine o'clock when Faith awoke. Tyler was sitting in the chair reading a book about Italy.

Faith glanced at the clock in surprise and then at Tyler, flinging the covers back. "How long have you been awake?"

"Not even an hour. I slept like a log. Obviously you did too."

"Yeah," Faith said, still not totally awake it seemed. She fell back onto the sheets. "I'm still sleepy."

"Then go back to sleep. I can read for awhile."

Faith thought about it for a few minutes, her head on her pillow. "No, I'm afraid I'll miss something. Maybe if I took a shower, I'd wake up better. Come take one with me. It's big enough for three people."

"Somebody else you want to ask?" Tyler quizzed with a mischievous grin. He was already taking off the sweats he had pulled on when he got out of bed. They both stood naked, holding each other close, the sun streaming in through one small opening between the drapes.

"Last night was really special again, Faith. I'm sorry I've been so self-centered and crabby lately. I think the closer I get to the year marker, the more frightened I become. I'm so afraid it will come back. It's always in the back of my mind."

"I know, Tyler. I worry too," taking his hand in hers. "You don't have to apologize to me for how you feel. Besides I'm probably pregnant now."

"No way, Baby."

"You don't know. A woman just knows."

"But what makes you think that? We've made love many times since my treatments and you've never mentioned that. And you've never gotten pregnant either."

"Exactly."

They were in the shower now. The warm water peppered their skin. Tyler adjusted the showerhead until the water began to pour out hard against their bodies.

"Ahh, that feels good."

"You mean the water or where I'm touching?"

"Silly man."

"Can you believe they have a marble shower in the bungalow?"

"Nice, huh?"

"You're nice," he said, kissing her under the waterfall.

"If you want to see Italy today, you need to behave yourself, Tyler England."

"Okay, okay." He handed her the lavender scented French-milled soap. "Just wash my back and I'll finish and leave you alone," he said, trying to look pouty.

"I'm going to walk over to your parents while you dress. Is that okay?"

"Sure, I'll be over when I finish."

Patrick and Sue were in the courtyard, drinking espresso when Tyler found them.

"Good morning. You look chipper," Patrick commented.

"Good morning. I feel rested, finally."

"And where is our pretty young daughter?" Sue asked.

Tyler smiled. "She really didn't want to get out of bed. She made herself because she is anxious to see more sights. She's dressing and will be over shortly."

"Are you hungry?"

"A little."

"Sit down and I'll get you something," Sue said, as she stood up.

"No, no, I can get something in a bit," but she was already gone.

Patrick poured Tyler a cup of espresso. "You want it straight or made into a caffé macchiato with a little cream?"

"Cream, please. Espresso I guess is a little like grappa – you have to develop a taste."

Patrick laughed, "The espresso I like, but I haven't quite acquired a taste for the grappa."

Sue came out carrying a bowl full of fruit and a plate of peppery meats and bread.

"This looks good."

"It sure does," Faith said, strolling into the courtyard.

"She knows when there's food every time," Patrick teased.

"I'm a growing girl," she winked at Tyler.

"So what would you two like to see today?"

"We're just along for the ride," Tyler assured them.

"Then I think we'll travel around this area and let you see the olive trees and vineyards and then drive to Cortona for a late lunch. It's an ancient town, set among rich farmland and stunning hills. Today will be rural and easy. Then tomorrow, we'll show you Florence," Patrick said, pleased to be leading the tour.

"Let me grab my purse," Faith said, "and I'll be ready."

~

The next three days were filled with new sights and sounds. Both Tyler and Faith were sad to leave, but excited to board the train for Venice and then on to Rome.

"Don't forget to throw a penny in the Trevi Fountain in Rome," Sue yelled to them as they boarded.

"Why?" Faith shouted over the noise.

"It means you'll be back someday."

"Arrivederci!" Patrick yelled.

They smiled and waved good-bye.

~

Venice was everything the couple had heard it would be, a montage of art, history, architecture and beautiful sites. They found it romantic as they searched the quaint shops filled with linen and beautiful blown glass of amber, hues of blue and bronze. They walked through backstreets and dark, lonely alleys and laughed when they got lost over and over. They rode the gondolas twice in one day, serenaded by weathered Italian men, and despite the stench of the canals and the crumbling walls and dirty sidewalks, they fell in love all over again.

"Nobody but me could get pooped on by a pigeon on the Rialto Bridge," Faith exclaimed as she looked in horror at her streaked skirt.

Tyler was laughing so hard he could hardly speak. "If I didn't know better, I would say you are having a shitty day, My Love."

"Get me something to clean this off with," she shrieked, motioning Patrick to a little café near the bridge.

He walked over to the young woman standing behind the counter full of assortments of bread and cheese, and smiling said, "My wife appears to have attracted a bird. Could I have some napkins, please?"

She smiled, but it was obvious that she did not understand much English so Tyler went over to one of the tables and pulled some from the metal container and looked to her for approval. She nodded, and he left to rescue Faith.

"How long does it take to get napkins, Tyler?" Faith asked, frustrated. "Look at me, I'm ruined."

"You are not ruined. You're just a bit soiled I would say."

"Oh hush, Tyler, you think this is funny."

"And someday you will too, just not today."

Chapter 25

On the airplane going home from Rome, Tyler asked Faith what her favorite memory was about Italy.

"I could never narrow it down to just one. I loved seeing Tuscany and spending time with mother and dad, and of course, meeting Carmella and Stefano, but Venice was extra special, just you and me and that quaint little café on the canal."

"What about Rome?"

"It's hard to believe how old everything is there. Rome to me was interesting, the Vatican, and especially the Colosseum, but Rome is not romantic like Venice and Florence. It's too much a bustling city. I still can't believe my dad was going to be a priest. Seeing all those at the Vatican just made me think about it a lot."

"No, he doesn't fit the stereotype, does he?"

"Not exactly. He really likes his women, wine and song," she snickered, like a young kid.

"So, what was your favorite part, Tyler?"

"Feeding the pigeons." He teased.

She stuck out her tongue and pretended to pout.

"Gosh. I really don't know. I liked everything, even the train ride. Riding the gondolas was fun, but I enjoyed all the history in Rome. I'm glad you convinced me to go," his face was serious when he kissed her gently. "I think our first night in Tuscany was the best."

"You're right," she sighed, remembering how special their lovemaking had been.

But she knew he was worrying about his health again; for some reason he couldn't shake it. Although he tried, he told her he always had a foreboding uneasiness about it.

"I'm glad we have a couple of days to get over our jet-lag," Faith said.

"Me, too, it's harder than I thought it would be. I guess people who travel internationally get better about it, but it does take a day to really not be tired."

"It will be nice to sleep in our own bed. Do you have a big week ahead?"

"Not really. I'm sure my desk will be covered when we get back, but for the first time in awhile I don't even have a case. Or at least, I didn't when I left," Tyler said, sounding relieved.

"I've got that nasty Berkwitz custody case pending. I think the kids should just divorce both their parents. They are so anal. The parents couldn't care less about the kids; they just both want to win over the other one. Of course, if she gets them, then the child support follows. Both of the kids hate her sorry boyfriend. It's a mess. There are no winners."

Tyler agreed, "That's the trouble with domestic cases. You can't help but get a little emotionally involved sometimes. That doesn't generally happen with bankruptcy. What about the Hernandez filing? I'll bet you are interested in how that goes, aren't you?"

"It's in limbo, but it looks as if they may go forward. If so, I guess I'll see if I know enough about immigration to win their case."

He reclined his chair as far back as it would go and Faith put her head on his shoulder.

"We've got three days before we have to worry about anything. Let's just enjoy flying over the deep blue sea and the last of our vacation."

Chapter 26

Shortly after their return from Italy it was Faith's time to feel queasy. She knew she was pregnant, but she wanted to wait until she was positive to surprise Tyler. She ate dry toast for breakfast and made excuses not to go in the kitchen if Tyler was frying bacon and eggs. The thought of a sunny side up egg almost made her throw up and she didn't need much help.

In mid-June Faith scheduled an appointment with her gynecologist who confirmed what she already knew, but she acknowledged that was the extent of her knowledge.

"I know nothing about having a baby, Dr. Sullivan."

"Well, that's why you have me. I know a thing or two," she said as she smiled and patted Faith on the shoulder. "I'll bet I can give you a bit of advice along the way and then I know a few pediatricians I can suggest who will take it from there."

"I told Tyler when we were in Italy…well, the morning after we…" she blushed. "It had been awhile…and I just felt like I had gotten pregnant the night before. So I told him, but he just laughed and brushed it off like I didn't know what I was talking about. Why is it men never believe a woman's intuition? Anyway he said it probably wasn't possible, you know, after his surgery, chemo and everything.

"We thought we would have to do the in vitro and we were going to wait until he was cancer free a year, but I just had this feeling. Does that make sense?"

"Yes, these things happen. And I for one, as a woman doctor, do believe in a woman's intuition. Plus, I've seen too many positive examples to ever question it. If you hadn't cryopreserved the sperm, you would have been taking a chance. His count was probably really low, but you were relaxed, not worrying about it and it just happened. Besides it only takes one little wiggly thing, you know."

Faith giggled. Dr. Sullivan was so poised and professional she wasn't expecting that description coming from her. "This means it's meant to be. He received his one-year report just two weeks ago. Everything was clear so this will be really good news. I'm so happy" Faith said, her face aglow.

"I'm happy for both of you, Faith. I'll see you in a month. You take care of yourself and this little fellow."

"Oh, Dr. Sullivan, do you think it's a boy?"

She laughed, "We'll know in a few months. Right now you can pretend either way," patting her again, turning to leave the room, ready for her next patient.

Faith looked at her watch. It was four o'clock. She wanted to stop at the store to buy a bottle of sparkling white grape juice – no alcohol now for her – a bottle of Champagne and a cigar for Tyler. She hadn't even told him about the appointment so it would be a complete surprise.

The phone was ringing when she walked in. She set the groceries on the counter and answered.

"Hi, I'm going to be a little late, maybe an hour or so. My client is running late. We'll go grab a pizza or something when I get there or I can stop and pick up something."

She tried to hide her disappointment that she would have to wait, but quickly responded. "I just bought a couple of rib-eyes and baked potatoes. I'll fix a salad. How does that sound?"

"Well, great. But what's the occasion? I mean, it's Monday night," he said laughing.

"I just had a little extra time when I left my meeting," she said, stretching the truth.

When she hung up, she didn't know what to do with herself. She was so excited. She wanted to tell someone, especially Alice, the good news, but decided that Tyler should be the first to know so she took the salad fixings out of the refrigerator and placed them on the counter while she hurried to change clothes. Passing the small third bedroom, she stopped and looked in, thinking now they could decorate the nursery.

Back in the kitchen, lost in thought, she chopped onions, carrots, tomatoes, and green peppers with abandonment and then tore a whole head of lettuce. She stopped and laughed. *I think I have enough salad for a small army. Guess I got a little carried away.* She divided the vegetables and put half in a plastic bag and the remainder in a bowl Tyler had bought for her in Florence. It went well with her Italian dishes. Setting the table she placed a new taper in the candelabrum.

Now she was actually glad she had some additional time so she could look for the extra ice bucket to chill the grape juice. With that completed she scrubbed two potatoes and wrapped them in foil. She had been so caught up in her thoughts she had done nothing more than just let Judge and Dusty in the house.

The dog had taken every step with her and now sat beside her feet, but Dusty curled up in the window seat and ignored her. Looking down, Faith said, "Oh, girl, I'm so sorry. I haven't been very attentive."

She reached to pat the collie's head. "I can tell you a secret… now don't tell daddy, okay? We're pregnant. You may not be very happy about this baby at first, but I know you'll love him after you get used to the idea."

Judge tilted her head back and forth as if comprehending completely, her tail wagging as she listened.

"You'll have another playmate. You can chase the ball and follow him everywhere," Faith continued talking to the much loved canine.

She realized that she kept saying "him." In some ways she wanted a little girl, but she knew how much Tyler wanted a boy first, and she was convinced that she was carrying his wish.

When she heard his car in the driveway, she couldn't control herself any longer. She had planned to wait, to bring out the drinks and his cigar, but instead, she ran outside motioning for him to lower the passenger window before he could pull in the garage.

"Tyler, Tyler, we're pregnant!" she yelled in glee.

He turned off the engine and jumped out of the car. "Are you sure?"

"Yes, yes, I went to the doctor today!"

He was grinning broadly and he took her into his arms and brushed back her hair, kissing her over and over.

"But how? I mean, all the odds were against this happening."

"I know. I asked Dr. Sullivan and she said that although your count was low, it can just happen and she reminded me it just takes one."

"After I did the freezing deal and all the chemo I guess Dr. Lawrence never thought I needed another test to see if I were actually producing sperm since I had some banked. This is so much better. Now you don't have to go through all the other…" he stopped. "But does she think the baby will be okay? I mean…"

She put her fingers to his lips. "Tyler, now don't start worrying about that. Nothing seems out of the ordinary and Dr. Sullivan was excited. She would have warned me if there was a potential problem. Now come on in the house and let's celebrate."

He looked at the table setting and the big cigar at his plate and smiled.

"I thought it would be all right if you had a few puffs," Faith explained.

Smiling Tyler said, "Let me change into my jeans and I'll start the grill. What's that?" he asked looking at the grape juice.

"I don't think I should drink alcohol until the baby's born, but I have Champagne for you."

"No, if you can't, I won't," he offered.

"No, I won't have that. It took a long time for you to feel good enough to want a cold beer or glass of wine. So don't even think about not having some. Hurry, so we can sit outside awhile before dinner."

Waiting for the grill to heat up, Tyler looked at Faith. "You know what? I remember your telling me in Tuscany that you thought you were pregnant even though realistically I thought there was no way to know. But you did know, huh?"

Faith grinned. "A woman's intuition, of course, it could have been in Tuscany, Venice or Rome. You were a wild man, Tyler England."

"I think it would be better to say I had romantic leanings on the trip," he corrected her, teasing.

"More like voracious, insatiable desires, but am I glad?"

She poured him a second glass of Champagne. "After dinner, I want to call Mom and then Mother and Dad. Do you want to tell your parents or shall I?"

"Let's get on both phones, but you can start the conversation. They are going to be so excited."

"When can we start painting the nursery?" Faith asked impatiently.

Tyler laughed. "How does Saturday sound?" knowing she was anxious to get started.

"We could go buy paint after your golf game," she said.

"I could just skip golf," he offered.

"No. Besides I want to look in some magazines and catalogues for ideas. I haven't let myself do that before now. Could we do a western, cowboy theme, maybe?"

"What makes you so sure it's going to be a boy?"

"Woman's intuition."

"And if it's not, what do we do with the bunk house?" he asked, sounding amused.

"Hmm, I haven't thought that far ahead, but I'm telling you it's going to be a little Tyler."

"Except no juniors, okay? Everyone should be their own person, with their own name."

"Could Tyler be the middle name?"

"Maybe, but I just don't want him to have the same full name. Besides it's confusing or the kid ends up with a nickname. No Bubbas either, Miss East Texas."

She popped him on the arm "Watch it now! I'm just glad we already have a Dusty."

He chuckled. "Darn," trying to look disappointed.

"Tyler, I can't wait to wear maternity clothes. Do you want to go shopping with me soon?"

He smiled. "If that's what you want me to do, I will, but don't you think you are being a little premature?"

"Well, maybe, but I am so excited."

"I am too, Faith." He kissed her gently. "I am too."

~

The next two weekends they painted the nursery, finally agreeing on a pale shade of yellow just in case Faith's intuitions were slightly off center. Tyler bought fence pickets and cut them to fit on the part of one wall, waiting to paint and attach later. They decided if the baby were a boy they could decorate with lariats and other western accessories, but if it were a girl the room could take on the look of a secret garden with tiny flowers and girly things.

Patrick and Sue brought over a new crib and matching chest and Alice drove up for the day bearing baby blankets and ten newborn outfits all for a boy. "If Faith says it's a boy, then it's a boy." Then she whispered in Tyler's ear, "If not, I've got a lotta taking back to do."

"Okay, Tyler, Mom and I are off to buy maternity clothes."

"Thank you, Mom," Tyler said. "You are a life saver," he whispered in Alice's ear. "I thought I was going to have to tag along and watch."

"Oh Tyler, you don't know nothing about birthing babies," Alice quoted from *Gone With the Wind*. "Tell you the truth, I don't know much either, not personally, but I'll lend my support and tell her she looks beautiful. That's the key. It's a girl thing, but for God's sakes, when she comes in and shows you, tell her the frocks look wonderful and so does she."

~

The summer was the hottest Faith could remember, the stubborn heat draining her energy. In order to sit outside so Tyler could grill, he installed an outdoor ceiling fan on the patio.

"The fan helps, but it is still hot, Tyler."

"I know, Hon, but I think it might be a combination of your being pregnant and the weather. The meteorologist hasn't indicated that this is an unusual heat wave or that the temps are breaking records."

"Well, I don't know about records, but I do know that I am sweating like a pig these days."

Tyler laughed and walked over to give her a kiss on the forehead. "You are also beginning to show a little, and I think you look wonderful."

"Thanks for the compliment; I need to hear that from you. I thought this pregnant thing was going to be a piece of cake, but right now I feel like a toad that needs to jump in a bucket of ice water to cool off. And I look fat, not pregnant, fat all over. I had to lie down on the bed to get my jean shorts on the other day."

"You don't look fat. You look like your belly has a baby growing in it. That's all. I thought you wanted to start showing?"

"I do, oh I'm sorry, Tyler. I'm being a big boob. One minute I'm excited. One minute I'm grumpy."

"I think that comes with the territory. By the way, when do the boobs get bigger? I've always heard they do?"

She picked up a pillow from the outdoor wicker couch and tossed it at him. "You would want to know that!"

He ducked and it hit the floor just as Dusty scampered to chase a butterfly. "Watch the fire; the coals are about ready. I'll be right back."

He was back in a flash, bearing gifts. "I was saving these for a few more weeks, but I think you might be able to use them now." He handed her two boxes, one wrapped in pink and one in blue.

"Why am I getting these? Can I open now?" Faith giggled and reached to pet Judge who had appeared to wake from her quick nap to see if either of the gifts were for her. "Sorry, Girl, these are for mommy." She tore into the pink package and stopped. "Are you hedging your bets, Tyler? I mean you have one wrapped in pink paper and one in blue."

He laughed. "Just open, you'll see."

When she lifted the lid she found a pale yellow, soft cotton top with spaghetti straps, white maternity shorts and yellow sandals. "Oh, Tyler, these are beautiful, plus the fabric is lightweight. I'll go try them on as soon as I open this other package."

"Actually the blue one is…well, you'll see."

This time, she gently removed the blue paper, carefully lifting off the baby rattler and teething rings that were connected to the bow. Inside was a small fuzzy blue Teddy Bear.

"Tyler, he is so cute. I don't think I have ever seen a blue bear, and look that's his name. It's on the collar."

Tyler smiled. "I guess that package is really for the baby, but it is for you too. When he gets fussy, you can put that in the crib with him and that should make him feel safe and loved."

"Oh, no. When he's crying at night and you get up to soothe him, you can put Blue Bear in his crib."

"We'll flip a coin. Heads I win; Tails I win." Tyler said teasingly.

~

The last weekend in August, Tyler's parents came on Friday night. Having learned from Faith of the intended theme, they had framed Tyler's first little western shirt. They gave Faith a wooden box that held the tiny cowboy hat, spurs and size one boots that Tyler had worn as a baby.

"Oh, these will look so cute on the shelf Tyler made. Come look," she said taking her mother-in-law's hand.

"This is so darling, Faith. I sure hope the baby is a boy. Not just because of the room. I know how much Tyler wants a boy, but I know he will never admit it," Joy said.

Faith smiled. "I know that too. He would be fine with a little girl. After all, she would be the apple of his eye, but don't worry. I just know it is a boy. I can just feel it."

Joy reached and patted Faith's tummy. "I understand, and I believe you. I knew when I was pregnant with Tyler that he was going to be a boy, and I just knew Libby was going to be a girl. Now Evan had me confused. I guess I knew Tom wanted a boy on the first, and I wanted a girl for the second, so the third was just a blessing."

"This baby is not just a blessing, he's a miracle."

Chapter 27

Tyler was hesitant for Faith to accompany him to the oncologist, but she insisted. She was concerned about a nasty hacking cough he couldn't seem to shake, but more than anything else she wanted to share this milestone of his being cancer-free a full year.

"I'll wait out here until your tests are complete. Then, come and get me, okay?"

He smiled weakly, not looking forward to another CT scan and chest x-ray along with all the other "poking and prodding," as he described it.

After sitting in the waiting room for more than two hours, unable to concentrate on the work she had brought, Faith began to get fidgety. When the doctor came to the door, looking somber, she knew the news was not good. Jumping to her feet, she frantically asked, "Is everything okay?"

He paused, "No, Faith, I'm afraid it's not. The cancer has recurred in the lungs and it's spread to the liver. Normally I wouldn't get the results of the scan and x-rays back so soon, but I was concerned when I saw Tyler, and especially when I heard his cough, so I called in a favor from the radiologist who is also a racquetball buddy. He called me as soon as he saw the pictures. I wanted to talk to you both. Tyler's in my office."

When she walked in she noticed immediately that Tyler had been crying. He looked up at her not saying anything for a long time.

She hugged him tightly. "Tyler, we'll beat this, we've got to be strong." She had tears in her eyes as she clutched his hand.

"I told you. I just had a strange feeling about all this," he said.

The doctor explained the treatments he proposed. We'll begin immediately with more systemic chemotherapy.

"This time it will be more aggressive, Tyler. You're probably not going to feel as well as before, but we do have some more advanced medicine for your nausea. You may want to cut back on your work schedule for the next month. We need to run an MRI tomorrow and then we'll get started."

Neither asked the prognosis, afraid of what they might hear.

"I'll see you at the hospital at nine in the morning, okay?"

Tyler managed a weak "okay" and stood to shake the doctor's hand.

"We'll give it all we've got, Tyler," Dr. Simmons said, looking him directly in the eye.

A faint smile came to Tyler's face. "I think this is going to be the fight of my life."

And it was. The next three months were filled with chemotherapy and all the negative effects it has on the unlucky ones. Tyler was sick almost immediately and was hospitalized twice. Worse, the tumors were not responding to the drugs and the test results showed the tumors had grown. Slipping into deep depression, he talked very little no matter how much Faith tried to lift his spirits. But when Sid called and asked him to go with him to watch Shea play baseball on Saturday, he agreed. He figured it was the least he could do. After all, he was going to ask Sid to take good care of things Faith might need once he was gone.

Saturday dawned cool and slightly windy, but otherwise it was a beautiful spring day in North Texas. Tyler was up early. He wasn't sleeping well anyway, and he had promised to meet Sid and Shea at the Little League field at 8:45. Faith was still sleeping when he left at 8:00 to run by a mom and pop do-nut shop a couple of miles away. He stopped there often and knew the Asian couple who owned the establishment. They were middle-aged and worked there together, she cooking and he greeting patrons and working the cash register.

The place was packed as it generally was on Saturday mornings, and Tyler got in line to wait his turn. Mr. Wong noticed him and grinned, "Morning Mr. Ty." Tyler smiled and returned the greeting. He had always thought it funny that Mr. Wong had shortened his name, figuring it sounded more Chinese this way.

When it was his turn, they exchanged a few more greetings and Tyler ordered a dozen glazed and two dozen do-nut holes for Shea, his favorite. Looking at his watch, he decided he had time to take some by the house to Faith.

"Make that another dozen do-nuts, chocolate glazed, in a separate box. Have to keep the wife happy. Besides she's eating for two, you know."

Mr. Wong, in his white shirt, pants and apron, turned around, looking surprised. "A baby?"

Tyler forced a grin. "Yes sir, on the way."

"Congratulations, but it looks like you need to eat more of my do-nuts. You are too thin."

"Yeah, I know, just don't have much of any appetite these days."

"You okay?"

"Sure, just working hard, you know."

"Well, if that's the case you need to slow down, enjoy life a little more."

"Yes, I know what you mean—life's short."

When he had his do-nuts he drove quickly home, left the truck running out back and went in the back door quietly, thinking he would leave the breakfast surprise on the kitchen bar.

"Tyler, is that you?" Faith yelled, sounding a little frightened.

"Hi Hon, I didn't think you would be out of bed yet. Brought you some good, greasy, fattening do-nuts"

"Yummy, that sounds wonderful," she said, cupping the coffee mug with both hands.

"I've got to hurry now, but why are you up and dressed?"

"I'm going to clean today, closets and everything."

Tyler looked surprised. "You are going to get rid of something, like throw away?"

"I'm thinking of having a garage sale. What to you think?"

Tyler frowned. "You know I hate that kind of stuff, Faith."

"I was thinking of having Mom come up to help. That's right down her alley."

"That's my girl. You and Alice will be great at that together as long as I don't have to have any part in it. A good rule of thumb is anything you haven't used or worn in a year should go," he yelled as he grabbed a windbreaker he had forgotten earlier and headed for the door. "Be back around noon. Happy cleaning."

Faith was buoyed by his chipper mood. He sounded better than he had in weeks, but she knew he was putting on a good face for her, and trying to be in that upbeat frame of mind with Sid and Shea.

He arrived at Tiger Field right on time and saw Sid waiting. Tyler was so pleased that Shea was with Sid full-time now. He was such a good kid and he needed the stability Sid offered. Sid's ex-wife was on probation for selling stolen goods in Louisiana, and the friends she hung around with were not the kind of people Sid wanted his young son associating with. He hadn't let Shea go back in six months, although he felt bad about the boy not seeing his mother. Truth was Sid needed Shea as well. Sure, he had work and a serious relationship with Sandy, but he needed his son, and he was enjoying every minute of being with him.

"Hey Bro, Over here!" Sid yelled.

"Gotcha in my range, Ole Man." Tyler responded as he moved in Sid's direction. "Where's the Little Man? I brought do-nut holes."

"He's already out on the field, but he'll have them finished in two seconds after the game."

"Sorry I'm late," Tyler said, looking at his watch. "I took some do-nuts to Faith, and she was telling me about her plans for a garage sale."

Sid grinned. "You're not late. You're never late. We got here early and some of Shea's friends yelled for him, and he was gone in a flash. A garage sale? Sounds just like you, Bro."

"Doesn't it? She promised that she would get Alice to come help, and that I don't have to do one thing."

"We'll see, My Man, we'll see," he said, slapping Tyler on the back. "Let's get a seat. Don't want to miss a minute of this thriller. Hand me those do-nuts, man. I'm starving. Where's the coffee?"

Tyler grinned and handed him a thermos. "Don't ever say, I don't think of everything."

As the morning wore on, Tyler wore down.

"You okay, Buddy?"

"Yeah, just a little tired. I feel pretty good when I first get up, but then my energy level wanes."

"Hey, if you need to rest, it's okay if you go. Shea will understand."

"Wouldn't even consider it. I'm okay, really."

They watched the game for a long time without talking. Finally, Tyler said, "Sid, I'm depending on you to do things with my boy. You know, like play ball with him, teach him how to treat girls. Faith will be a wonderful mother, but the guy things well she just won't be able to do those. Hell, take him for his first beer when you think it's time."

"Who says it's a boy, anyway?"

"Didn't Faith tell you? I'm sorry; I thought you knew. We found out last month. Yep, it's for sure," he said, with sadness in his voice.

In a baseball field full of cheering fans, there was silence. Sid didn't know how to respond. He sat looking at his son at first base, and all he could feel was sorrow. Tyler was his best friend. They had a bond. After an interminable time, he said, "I'll do anything you ask me, Bro. But I'm begging you not to give up."

"I don't think it's up to me."

~

A few days later when Faith came home from work late, she found Tyler in the den surrounded by his guitar, a tape recorder, tapes and several legal pads. His eyes were red and puffy.

"Are you working, Hon?" she asked.

"No," he paused. "I thought before I get weaker, especially my voice, I would record a few things for the Little Man. I was waiting because what I have to say or sing would be a little different for a boy, you know…guy things." He smiled for the first time since the outing with Sid.

"But, Tyler, are you just giving up?" She asked, a tinge of anger slipped into the question.

"No, Hon, but I'm being realistic. I'm not getting better. We both know that. I'm afraid I won't be here when he's born." He broke down and began sobbing, followed by long painful gasps for breath, and then Faith began to cry as well.

"Faith, we have to talk about some things as much as we hate to, but first, can we decide on a name for our Little Man? I'd like to write some things to him so he needs a name."

Unprepared for this, she knew he was right, right about needing to talk and right that he wasn't getting better. The cancer was spreading almost faster than the drugs were running through the body.

They sat on the couch for the next four hours, alternately crying and talking, discussing names for the baby boy who was due the first week in January. When they had finished, Faith noticed Tyler seemed stronger and happier. She wondered if it was because he had faced the inevitable and the finality of it had set in, giving him relief. She had read where people who were dying did this and they seemed at peace after that. She hadn't reached that point. She couldn't; she wasn't ready to let the disease win.

~

Now, when he was able, he worked at home, attempting to get his business in order, checking their financial plans and trying to do research for cases Sid was working on. One day in early December when Faith returned from work, her salvation now to keep her mind off Tyler, she found him lying in bed propped up with pillows, obviously feeling better than he had the last several days, though his bilious, pasty appearance had not changed nor had the monster overtaking his body ceased its grip.

"I finished the letters to Jack," his voice steady, but weak and flat.

With a heavy heart, Faith placed a mug of tea by his bed. "You want to read them to me?"

Looking away, he replied, "No Hon. You can do that when I'm gone."

She took his hand, holding it for a long time, just the two of them, her laying on her side next to him, his sheets uncharacteristically rumpled in a rented hospital bed they didn't share. There were too many wires, tubes and gadgets. Tyler looked rested somehow, but Faith found his mood and demeanor unsettling, and she grew fearful that this was a look of utter readiness to give up.

The next day, Faith noticed that Tyler was having trouble concentrating. He complained about an excruciating headache and his blurry vision. A trip to the hospital revealed what he and Faith had feared most; the cancer had spread to his brain.

Three days later the doctor suggested that Faith contact hospice and then he sent Tyler home.

∾

Faith spent their third anniversary at Tyler's bedside. Although she doubted he knew she was there, it felt right. Earlier in the day she had told the hospice nurse to go home for the night because she wanted this time to be for just the two of them. She held Tyler's hand as he slept and though his eyes didn't open the entire night, she never left his side. Appearing in no pain, his breathing was labored.

Faith knew the morphine was making him more comfortable, but she also knew time was running out. In some ways she wished the baby would hurry. Dr. Sullivan said they could induce labor so she could place him for a minute in Tyler's arms, but she declined because she knew Tyler needed her undivided attention. She also knew the time for Tyler and Jack to be together had passed.

In spite of the circumstances, she had purchased a small Christmas tree earlier in the day and decorated it. Tonight, however, she could not bring herself to turn the twinkling lights on, nor could she put a log in the fireplace; it was too painful to be reminded of their Christmases together. The light of her life was fading and no artificial illumination would change that darkness. His struggle to live was becoming more obvious as he gasped for each breath.

"God, please don't let him die tonight."

When he made it through the night, Faith rested a couple of hours. Nothing changed. Christmas came and went. There were no gifts this year, no exchanges of Happy Holidays, but Faith's family and Tyler's gathered together, waiting for what they knew was the inevitable. But when that time came, Faith was alone with him, holding his hand. When she knew it was over, she stayed awhile longer then released her grip on Tyler's lifeless fingers, bent over and kissed him good-bye.

Faith opened her eyes, lying still alone in their bed, wondering for a minute if yesterday had been a bad dream. No, Tyler was gone. She had to face the day. Numbed, she dressed and went downstairs and walked outside. She had sent everyone home before she went to bed. Now she wondered what she had been thinking. She reached down to pet Judge who appeared melancholy, and she wondered if she sensed the vacuum. Dogs usually know when something is wrong, she had always been told. She felt a sudden gust of cold air, realizing she had no idea how long she had been standing outside. Shivering, she turned, letting herself back into the empty house.

Chapter 28

Sitting there in a cold metal chair between Sue and Alice under the tent, Faith looked at the green artificial turf and trembled. She realized she had heard nothing Patrick had said, but was vaguely aware that the rain dripping off the canvas corners was turning to sleet. Paralyzed by the cold and dazed by grief, she saw the casket but refused to think about Tyler's body lying inside. She just wanted this to be over now.

Patrick ended his eulogy with a quote from Albert Schweitzer, "No ray of sunshine is ever lost, but the green, which it awakes into existence, needs time to sprout; and it is not always granted to the sower to see the harvest. All work, which is worth anything, is done in faith."

Faith didn't remember the ride home, but pulling up to the house, she told everyone to come back later. She wanted to go in alone, but Alice insisted in accompanying her.

"I'll hang back, but I'm not letting you do this by yourself again. I'm here if you need me, otherwise, I'll stay out of your way."

Faith took out her key, turned the latch and they went inside, closing the door behind them. Alice stood downstairs watching as Faith climbed the stairs, and walked into the bedroom. It looked the same, but felt different, empty cold. It would never be the same. Trying not to think about her life alone, she changed from her black silk suit into comfortable slacks and a sweater. People would be visiting, she knew, coming to say their condolences. She wasn't sure now that she wanted to be alone, but she didn't think she was up to hearing their sad words of comfort. Although she knew they meant well, she was tired. Straightening her shoulders, she willed herself to be strong, but when the doorbell rang, she thought, *please Mom, talk to whoever it is, give me time to. . .just give me a minute.*

~

The day was a blur. When friends and family had gone home, Alice stayed and put on a pot of coffee.

"I'll sleep down here, Faith. You don't have to talk, you don't even have to acknowledge my presence, but I want to stay."

"I'm glad you're here, Mom. I'm scared. I want to open the box Tyler left, but I don't want to do it alone. I don't think I can," untying the twine that held a bundle of mementoes and letters together.

After listening to the tapes together and reading the letters, she folded the pages and handed them to Alice. She didn't think she had any tears left, but they came, and they wouldn't stop. Alice held her tightly and felt her trembling body. There was nothing else she could do for her, but be there, hold her and let her cry.

November/December, 2002

Faith, My Yellow Rose,

This has taken me awhile to write, partly because I want to find the right words, and a little bit because I continue to hope that I won't need this letter, but instead that I'll wake up tomorrow and it will all be just a bad dream. But, in my gut I know it's not, yet it doesn't keep me from hoping.

I have no regrets when it comes to you, my dear Faith, except that my time with you is being cut short. We had so many plans, so much to share, but time is not something we control. You know I have loved you from the first day I saw you and will until I take my last breath. And beyond if I can. That I can promise. And promises are important, aren't they?

When I am gone, I take nothing with me but I leave memories and promises kept. And don't forget that always, three things remain: Faith, Hope and Love. The first needs no explanation, for you are the embodiment of faith; you are beyond definition, beyond poetry, beyond all the words that try to define this word. You are Faith and all it means.

But hope, now that is different. I've clung to it about as long as I can, but a person has to have it until it finally snuffs itself out. Today, I remain hopeful, not for me, but for you and our beautiful son. So please remember:

> *As long as the stars shine in the sky,*
> *As long as the birds fly,*
> *There is hope.*
> *As long as the sun comes up over the mountains,*

As long as the waters splash in a fountain,
There is hope.
As long as the trees grow,
As long as the winds blow,
There is hope.
As long as there is a part of us left living in some way,
As long as there are lingering thoughts and the memories stay,
There is hope.
As long as there are plans made and promises kept,
As long as there is love at the heart's greatest depth,
There is hope.

But remember, my dearest Faith, as it has been written, the greatest of these is love, always has been, always will be... And there is no shortage of love that I leave with you.

Loving you was magic, my delicate bloom. Go forth and blossom more.

With all mine,
Tyler

~

November 25, 2002

Dear Little Man,

I'm thinking about you a lot today because it appears I may not be around when you're born. It's not what I want, but it's the card that I was dealt. What I hate the most is that I won't be there to watch you grow up, to become a man, and that I won't be there to love you and your Mom.

You'll have to help me out there, Jack. I believe that's what you'll be called. You'll need to take care of your mother. She'll need you. She's strong, but she'll have her days when you'll have to be even stronger than her.

Always stand tall, Little Man, and look people in the eye. Say you're sorry when you've hurt someone's feelings and say you'll help out when you're needed. Listen to you mother. She's the smartest woman I know. And someday if you get another daddy, remember it's okay to love him. Your Mom is too young to live the rest of her life alone. I promise it's okay.

I love you,
Dad

~

December 3, 2002

Dear Jack,

How I wish I could be there to see you when you take your first steps, ride your bicycle without training wheels and catch your first ball. Those will be important times in your life as will your first day of school, your first time to drive and your first date.

I wish I could be there to brush away your tears when you're hurt or help you up when you fall, but at least I can tell you here that both will happen. There will be days when you'll feel like crying so I want you to know that it's okay to shed those tears. It takes a big man to cry so go ahead. You'll feel better. And son, there will be days when you fall flat on your face. Get up and try again. It's okay to stumble, just don't stay down. And just a few more "daddyisms." Be kind to everyone, especially those who have less and to those who are not kind to you. Be honest all the time, even if it means getting in trouble or admitting you're wrong. Love your mother and treat her with respect and someday when you fall in love, treat that special someone like you would want your mother to be treated. And one more thing Jack...dream big, work hard and remember that I love you.

Love, Dad

~

December 14, 2002

Dear Son,

I know I keep telling you what I'm wishing, but wishing is about all I have the strength for these days so bear with me while I repeat myself. How I wish this awful disease was not eating at my body. How I wish I could hold you at least one time before it takes my breath away. You know you are a miracle baby. You weren't even supposed to happen like you did, but I am so glad you did. I guess God knew that your mother would need a Little Man around to help her.

I wasn't going to keep writing you, but I can't help myself. I'm not sure how much longer I can keep it up anyway. My mind sometimes gets fuzzy, but when it's not, I can't help myself from thinking about you, and how much I love you. And you are not even here. Can you imagine how much more love I could give, if

I had a little time? I could teach you so much, things a dad needs to share with his son. If I could only take you on your first deer hunt, or show you how to hold a driver so your golf ball would go soaring toward the green. If only I could show you how to catch a fish, clean it and then cook it over an open campfire. But those are just "if onlys"—nothing more. If only I could live, but I can't. I'm tired now Little Man. Maybe I'll write a little more tomorrow.

Love, Dad

~

Finally, Faith stood and turned on the outside lights. She gazed out the window at the leafless trees, how they shone with the light of the moon and the porch lights. "It's not fair, Mom. These were his trees. This house was a result of his labors. This wasn't supposed to happen. He was supposed to beat this terrible disease. They thought they caught it early. We thought his chances were so good." She couldn't stop herself from asking why. Running over to Alice, she sat down and put her head on her shoulder. "I don't have the energy to cry anymore. I'm angry now. He was so good, so kind. He was everything I ever wanted or needed, and now he's gone. Snuffed out so young with so many plans and dreams."

~

When the clock on the mantle struck midnight, Faith was still awake, pacing, her thoughts on Tyler and life without him. The smell of his Aramis wafted through the room, lingering like a heavy mist. Remembering the first time she saw him, she smiled, thinking about the funny way he blew the hair from his eyes. She thought about his expression each time he said he loved her and how he had so many times quoted the words of his favorite song. He so wanted to make her life sweet with his living and breathing. Now that breath was gone—nothing was sweet. A life was gone, and a lifetime it seemed had vanished; he was not coming back.

She was on her own, and the world they had shared would never be the same. Her back and legs hurt from the extra weight of the baby, but nothing compared to the hurt in her heart. She tried not to think about the life that was growing inside, because death was still so present. She stopped and looked around the room, dark except for a single lamp. With a lump in her throat and hollowness in her heart, she picked up her pillow and slammed it back onto the bed. Bending down as best she could, she hit it dead center with her fist, then harder and harder until she fell on the bed, exhausted not from the released aggression, but from months of worry and finally deep, raw sorrow. Then, in an act of surrender, she reached and pulled Tyler's pillow to her, pressing her face into its softness. For what seemed like hours, she wept until the tears would no long fall. She closed her eyes knowing that morning would come, the days would follow, but tonight she wasn't sure she wanted them to. If only she could exchange tomorrow for just one yesterday.

A week later, in the New Year, Jackson Tyler England was born, a healthy seven pounder with a shock of light brown, curly hair. The waiting room was filled with Faith's family and friends, each individual dealing with his or her emotions for this bitter-sweet event. Tyler's parents were heartsick, fighting against tears of sadness and those of joy, a son lost and a grandson's life just beginning. But their grief was shared in large measure by Patrick and Sue, Ben, Sid, Mr. Jackson, the baby's namesake, and Mrs. Jackson, along with numerous other friends who had gathered in the cramped room to provide support to each other and celebrate what could have been such a different occasion. If only Tyler could have been there to touch and see his Little Man and to be at Faith's side. But instead it was Alice who was with Faith in the delivery room during the whole birthing process, holding her hand, telling her when to push, when to relax. She had been in the room when Faith was born, helping and encouraging Sue. Now, she was there again. And she would be there as long as there was a need, although she knew that Faith would have to go it on her own. That was just the way she was—strong and determined, even in the face of her greatest adversity, even without the love of her life.

"He looks just like Tyler; don't you think?" Faith asked Alice as she gazed down at the baby's dark blue eyes and soft skin.

"He looks like both of you. His daddy would be very proud."

"You know, Mom, when I hold him close, I think I can feel two heartbeats, but I know that's not possible."

"It's very possible, Faith. I believe you'll forever hear and see and feel Tyler in this Little Man."

"I miss him so much. We were so good together. He never let me down once, and in spite of everything that happened to him, all the crummy chemicals that went into his body, all the suffering, he gave me a miracle. He kept every promise he ever made to me, and he left me the best gift anyone could," Faith said, wiping away a tear as she gently kissed the baby's head.

Alice fell silent and gave Faith the time that she needed to absorb the moment, as she reached to place Blue Bear in the bed beside the new mother. Faith clutched the stuffed animal and began to weep softly into it. Within minutes the baby echoed her whimpers and then his cries became louder. Faith turned to Alice with a panicked look, "What's wrong with him?"

Alice chuckled, "I think the boy's hungry and maybe just a little wet. I'll take care of the latter, but you'll have to manage the first." When she handed the newly diapered baby back to his mother, Faith took him to her breast and held him tight while he nursed. When he finished, she smiled for the first time in over an hour. "He's a boob guy, like his daddy."

Alice returned the smile. "There are a lot of people waiting to see this Little Man. Are you up for visitors?"

Other Works by Cindy Bradford

Keeping Faith, 2009, is available on Amazon and select bookstores.

Promises Kept cover graphics by Bill Wilson

Promises Kept is a work of fiction. Names, places, characters, and incidents are either a product of the author's imagination or used fictitiously. Any resemblance to actual persons, living or dead is entirely coincidental.